PANDORA'S TEMPLE

A BLAINE McCRACKEN NOVEL

PANDORA'S TEMPLE

A BLAINE McCRACKEN NOVEL

JON LAND

OPEN ROAD
INTEGRATED MEDIA
NEW YORK

For my readers:
The ride continues

ACKNOWLEDGMENTS

Bet you weren't expecting to hear from me again so soon, within six months of my last book, *Strong Vengeance*, hitting the stands, not to mention with a book that returns our old friend Blaine McCracken to the page! The fact that the page you're reading may be electronic makes it no less entertaining and maybe it's even more so, thanks to the wonderful team at Open Road Media responsible for bringing McCracken back from his extended literary hiatus. That team is headed by the great Jane Friedman who has provided me the opportunity to work with wonderful professionals like Stephanie Gorton, Libby Jordan, Rachel Chou, and Mary Sorrick. I'm especially grateful to my agent Bob Diforio for bringing us together and, even more, to the one holdover from past pages like this, my amazing and brilliant editor Natalia Aponte. Natalia was an invaluable partner in making McCracken and Johnny Wareagle's comeback a successful one; hey, both Blaine and I are getting on a bit these days and you know what they say about old dogs and new tricks.

Speaking of new, I'm eternally grateful to Jeff Ayers for letting me know I was on the right track with *Pandora's Temple* and for pushing me to do this book for maybe a decade now. And if you're wondering how I know so much about deepwater oil rigs, it's because of Brooke Bovo, who was my guide into that world, every step of the way. Also, thanks again to Mireya Starkenberg, who made sure my Spanish was at least passable. This book required a ton of research involving more helping hands than I can count. So know this, my friends: while some of what you're about to read stems purely from a writer's imagination, virtually everything else is the product of fact, not fiction. Even the construction and ultimate fate of Pandora's Temple itself owes more to facts than it does to mythology. But "What if?" is the question that has driven these McCracken books for a generation, and I see no reason to change that now.

And since you surely don't either, settle in and let's get started. "Once upon a time—" Oops! Forgot to tell you to turn the page so Blaine and Johnny can take things from here.

No hero is immortal till he dies.
W. H. Auden

PROLOGUE:
THE ABYSS

The Mediterranean Sea: 2008

"It would help, sir, if I knew what we were looking for," Captain John J. Hightower of the *Aurora* said to the stranger he'd picked up on the island of Crete.

The stranger remained poised by the research ship's deck rail, gazing out into the turbulent seas beyond. His long gray hair, dangling well past his shoulders in tangles and ringlets, was damp with sea spray, left to the whims of the wind.

"Sir?" Hightower prodded again.

The stranger finally turned, chuckling. "You called me sir. That's funny."

"I was told you were a captain," said Hightower.

"In name only, my friend."

"If I'm your friend," Hightower said, "you should be able to tell me what's so important that our current mission was scrapped to pick you up."

Beyond them, the residue of a storm from the previous night kept the seas choppy with occasional frothy swells that rocked the

Aurora even as she battled the stiff winds to keep her speed steady. Gray-black clouds swept across the sky, colored silver at the tips where the sun pushed itself forward enough to break through the thinner patches. Before long, Hightower could tell, those rays would win the battle to leave the day clear and bright with the seas growing calm. But that was hardly the case now.

"I like your name," came the stranger's airy response. Beneath the orange life jacket, he wore a Grateful Dead tie-dyed T-shirt and an old leather vest that was fraying at the edges and missing all three of its buttons. It was so faded that the sun made it look gray in some patches and white in others. The man's eyes, a bit sleepy and almost drunken, had a playful glint about them. "I like anything with the word 'high.' You should rethink your policy about no smoking aboard the ship, if it's for medicinal purposes only."

"I will, if you explain what we're looking for out here."

"Out here" was the Mediterranean Sea where it looped around Greece's ancient, rocky southern coastline. For four straight days now, the *Aurora* had been mapping the seafloor in detailed grids in search of something of unknown size, composition, and origin; or, at least, known only by the man Hightower had mistakenly thought was a captain by rank. Hightower's ship was a hydrographic survey vessel. At nearly thirty meters in length with a top speed of just under twenty-five knots, the *Aurora* had been commissioned just the previous year to fashion nautical charts to ensure safe navigation by military and civilian shipping, tasked with conducting seismic surveys of the seabed and underlying geology. A few times since her commission, the *Aurora* and her eight-person crew had been retasked for other forms of oceanographic research, but her high-tech air cannons, capable of generating high-pressure shock waves to map the strata of the seabed, made her much better suited for more traditional assignments.

"How about I give you a hint?" the stranger said to Hightower. "It's big."

"How about I venture a guess?"

"Take your best shot, dude."

"I know a military mission when I see one. I think you're looking for a weapon."

"Warm."

"Something stuck in a ship or submarine. Maybe even a sunken wreck from years, even centuries ago."

"Cold," the man Hightower knew only as "Captain" told him. "Well, except for the centuries-ago part. That's blazing hot."

Hightower pursed his lips, frustration getting the better of him. "So are we looking for a weapon or not?"

"Another hint, Captain High: only the most powerful ever known to man," the stranger said with a wink. "A game changer of epic proportions for whoever finds it. Gotta make sure the bad guys don't manage that before we do. Hey, did you know marijuana's been approved to treat motion sickness?"

Hightower could only shake his head. "Look, I might not know exactly what you're looking for, but whatever it is, it's not here. You've got us retracing our own steps, running hydrographs in areas we've already covered. Nothing 'big,' as you describe it, is down there."

"I beg to differ, el Capitán."

"Our depth sounders have picked up nothing; the underwater cameras we launched have picked up nothing; the ROVs have picked up nothing."

"It's there," the stranger said with strange assurance, holding his thumb and index finger together against his lips as if smoking an imaginary joint.

"Where?"

"We're missing something, el Capitán. When I figure out what it is, I'll let you know."

Before Hightower could respond, the seas shook violently. On deck it felt as if something had tried to suck the ship underwater, only to spit it up again. The rumbling continued, thrashing the

Aurora from side to side like a toy boat in a bathtub. Hightower finally recovered his breath just as the rumbling ceased, leaving an eerie calm over the sea suddenly devoid of waves and wind for the first time that morning.

"This can't be good," said the stranger, tightening the straps on his life vest.

The ship's pilot, a young, thick-haired Greek named Papadopoulos, looked up from the nest of LED readouts and computer-operated controls on the panel before him, as Hightower entered the bridge.

"Captain," he said wide-eyed, his voice high and almost screeching, "seismic centers in Ankara, Cairo, and Athens are all reporting a subsea earthquake measuring just over six on the scale."

"What's the epi?"

"Forty miles northeast of Crete and thirty from our current position," Papadopoulos said anxiously, a patch of hair dropping over his forehead.

"Jesus Christ," muttered Hightower.

"Tsunami warning is high," Papadopoulos continued, even as Hightower formed the thought himself.

"Whoa, whoa, whoa, we are in for the ride of our lives!" blared the stranger, pulling on the tabs that inflated his life vest with a soft popping sound. "If I sound excited it's 'cause I'm terrified, dudes!"

"Bring us about," the captain ordered. "Hard back to the port of Piraeus at all the speed you can muster."

"Yes, sir!"

Suddenly the bank of screens depicting the seafloor in a quarter-mile radius directly beneath them sprang to life. Readings flew across accompanying monitors, orientations, and graphic depictions of whatever the *Aurora*'s hydrographic equipment and underwater cameras had located appearing in real time before Hightower's already wide eyes.

"What the hell is—"

"Found it!" said the stranger before the ship's captain could finish.

"Found *what*?" followed Hightower immediately. "This is impossible. We've already been over this area. There was *nothing* down there."

"Earthquake must've changed that in a big way, el Capitán. I hope you're recording all this."

"There's nothing to record. It's a blip, an echo, a mistake."

"Or exactly what I came out here to find. Big as life to prove all the doubters wrong."

"Doubters?"

"Of the impossible."

"That's what you brought us out here for, a fool's errand?"

"Not anymore."

The stranger watched as a central screen mounted beneath the others continued to form a shape massive in scale, an animated depiction extrapolated from all the data being processed in real time.

"Wait a minute, is that a . . . It looks like— My God, it's some kind of *structure*!"

"You bet!"

"Intact at that depth? Impossible! No, this is all wrong."

"Hardly, el Capitán."

"Check the readouts, sir. According to the depth gauge, your structure's located five hundred feet beneath the seafloor. Where I come from, they call that impos—"

Hightower's thought ended when the *Aurora* seemed to buckle, as if it had hit a roller-coaster-like dip in the sea. The sensation was eerily akin to floating, the entire ship in the midst of an out-of-body experience, leaving Hightower feeling weightless and light-headed.

"Better fasten your seat belts, dudes," said the stranger, eyes fastened through the bridge windows at something that looked like a waterfall pluming on the ship's aft side.

Hightower had been at sea often and long enough to know this to be a gentle illusion belying something much more vast and terrible: in this case, a giant wave of froth that gained height as it crystallized in shape. It was accompanied by a thrashing sound that shook the *Aurora* as it built in volume and pitch, felt by the bridge's occupants at their very cores like needles digging into their spines.

"Hard about!" Hightower ordered Papadopoulos. "Steer us into it!"

It was, he knew, the ship's only chance for survival, or would have been, had the next moments not shown the great wave turning the world dark as it reared up before them. The *Aurora* suddenly seemed to lift into the air, climbing halfway up the height of the monster wave from a calm sea that had begun to churn mercilessly in an instant. A vast black shadow enveloped the ship in the same moment intense pressure pinned the occupants of the bridge to their chairs or left them feeling as if their feet were glued to the floor. Then there was nothing but an airless abyss dragging darkness behind it.

"Far out, man!" Hightower heard the stranger blare in the last moment before the void claimed him.

PART ONE:
THE DEEPWATER VENTURE

CHAPTER 1

Juárez, Mexico: The present

The black Mercedes SUV slid up to the entrance of the walled compound, chickens skittering from its path in the shimmering heat as it squealed to a halt. Dust hung in the air like a light curtain, adding a dull sheen to everything it touched. A pair of armed guards approached the SUV from either side of the closed gate and tapped on the blacked-out window on both the driver and passenger sides.

"I'm here to see Señor Morales," said the driver, his face cloaked in the darkness of the interior.

"You're early," said the guard, hands closed over the door frame so his fingers were curled inside the cab. A thin layer of dust lifted by the breeze coated both his uniform and face.

"I know."

"By a full day."

The driver feigned surprise. "Really? Guess I messed up with my day planner."

"Then we will see you tomorrow," the guard said, backing away from the SUV as if expecting the driver to take his leave.

"Sorry, I'm not available then. But if Señor Morales would prefer I take my business elsewhere, I'm sure his competition will be most interested in that business when I visit them tomorrow instead."

The lead guard moved up against the door again, two others with almost identical black hair and mustaches inching closer as well. "You will honor the terms of your deal."

"Just what I came here to do, amigo. Now go check with your boss and let's get on with it," said the driver.

He was wearing a cream-colored suit and T-shirt that was only slightly darker. The T-shirt fit him snugly, revealing a taut torso and chest expansive enough to strain the fabric. His face was ruddy, his complexion that of a man who'd spent many hours outside, though not necessarily in the sun. His thin beard was so tightly trimmed to his skin that it could have been confused for a trick of the SUV interior's dark shading. Other than a scar that ran through his right eyebrow and thick black hair sprinkled with a powdering of gray, his only real distinguishing feature was a pair of dark, deep-set eyes that looked like twin black holes spiraling through either side of his face.

"If Señor Morales and I have a deal, then the day shouldn't matter," he told the guard at his window.

"I'll tell him you'll be returning tomorrow."

"In which case, I'll be returning without this," the driver said, turning toward the passenger seat where a smaller man who looked ten years his senior held up a briefcase that was handcuffed to his wrist.

The older man's face was pocked with tiny scars all seeming to point toward a bent and bulbous nose that had been broken on more than one occasion. His eyes didn't seem to blink because when they did the motion was so rapid that it might as well have not happened at all.

"Señor Morales does not like to be threatened," the guard said, taking a step back from the vehicle. "It ruins his day."

"Then it's a good thing I'm not threatening anyone. Now open the gate," the man in the driver's seat said, gazing up at the unmanned watchtowers left over from Spanish colonial times when the compound had been an active fort and these walls had proved to be the staging ground for all manner of attacks launched against native Mexicans.

The guard backed farther away from the vehicle, raising a walkie-talkie to his lips. The window slid back up, quickly vanquishing the heat in favor of the soft cool of the air-conditioning.

"This ain't good, boss," said Sal Belamo from the passenger seat.

"Hope you didn't expect otherwise," Blaine McCracken said to him, smiling ever so slightly as he opened the sunroof, the cabin flooded immediately by light. "Otherwise, somebody else would've taken the job."

With a half-dozen assault rifles trained upon him, McCracken spent the next few moments carefully studying the exterior of the compound belonging to Arturo Nieves Morales, head of the Juárez drug cartel, the largest in a country dominated by them. He could see more guards armed with assault rifles posted strategically atop the walls amid the dust swirl.

"Those college kids Morales is holding should never have been down here in the first place, Sal."

"Spring break, boss. They thought they'd be safe in some resort in Cabo."

McCracken laid his hands on the steering wheel and leaned back. "They got taken outside a nightclub, lured into a van by some girls we now know were Morales's plants. Not exactly what you'd expect from honor students."

"Booze will do that to you."

"I wouldn't know, Sal. These are honor students who seem to lead the world in community service efforts. Their fraternity built a house for those Habitat for Humanity folks—a whole damn house, for God's sake."

"Sounds like you're taking this personal, boss."

"They're good kids who didn't deserve getting snatched in this sinkhole of a country."

"Parents couldn't raise the ransom?"

"What's the difference? You pay Morales, he just asks for more. And if you don't keep paying, you start getting your kid back one piece at a time."

"Uh-oh," from Belamo.

"What?"

"I've heard that tone before."

"Not lately."

"Doesn't matter, boss. You're picking up just where you left off, and only one way this goes, you ask me."

"What's that?"

"With a lot of bodies left behind."

"So long as none of them belong to the hostages, Sal."

CHAPTER 2

Washington: One week earlier

"I thought you were out," Henry Folsom said to Blaine McCracken seven days before.

Folsom had the look of a man born in a button-down shirt. Hair neatly slicked back, horn-rimmed glasses, and youthful features that would make him appear forty forever. There was something in his eyes, though, that unsettled McCracken a bit, a constant shifting of his gaze as if there was something he didn't want McCracken to see lurking there.

"Most people think I'm dead," McCracken said, folding his arms tightly across his chest.

Folsom shifted, as if to widen the space between them at the table. "All the same, I was glad when your name came up in conversation."

"Really? What kind of conversation was that?"

"Independent contractors capable of pulling off the impossible."

"I haven't pulled off anything, impossible or otherwise, for a couple years now."

"Are you saying you're not interested?"

"I'm here, aren't I? But my guess is I wouldn't be, if you hadn't pitched this job elsewhere."

"To more traditional authorities, you mean."

"Younger, anyway," said McCracken.

Folsom seemed to smirk. "The hostages are fraternity brothers from Brown University. One of their parents is a top immigration lawyer. That's why this ended up on my desk."

"You know him?"

"Nope, but I know you," Folsom said, folding his arms tightly and flashing another smirk. "I did my master's thesis on the true birth of covert operations, contrasting the work of the World War II–bred OSS with the Vietnam-era Operation Phoenix where CIA-directed assassins plucked off the North Vietnamese cadre one at a time." Folsom leaned forward, canting his shoulders forward as if he were about to bow. "I've been reading about you for twenty years now."

"There's nothing written about me."

Folsom came up just short of a wink. "I know."

McCracken had met him in the F Street Bistro in the State Plaza Hotel, a pleasant enough venue with cheery light and a slate of windows overlooking the street he instinctively avoided. McCracken had arrived first, as was his custom, and staked out a table in as close to a darkened corner as the place had to offer. He'd used this location in the past because of its status as one of Washington's best-kept secrets. Once he sat down, though, the room began to fill up around him, every table occupied within minutes and an army of waiters scurrying between them. McCracken found all the bustle distinctly unsettling and nursed a ginger ale that was almost all water and ice by the time Folsom arrived.

"You don't drink," Folsom noted.

"Never. So who in the special-ops community did you call first?"

"Maybe I've just always wanted to see your work firsthand."

"That's funny, Hank. A sense of humor makes you a rare commodity these days, what with so many ex-operators running around with their hands out. Guys who could be my kids. I turn sixty in a couple weeks, Hank. That puts me a step beyond even father figure."

"Normal channels had to be bypassed here," Folsom told him. "Can't send the Rangers or SEALs into Mexico with a new trade agreement about to be inked."

"And since you always wanted to work with me . . ."

"I needed someone who could get the job done, McCracken. That immigration lawyer I just mentioned? He does work for us from time to time."

"Who's 'us,' Hank?"

"The State Department, who else?"

McCracken held Folsom's gaze until the younger man broke it. "If you say so, Hank."

"Name your price. It will be considered nonnegotiable."

McCracken chuckled at the promise. "First time for everything, I guess."

"So how much is it going to take to bring you out of retirement?"

"I wasn't aware I'd retired."

"How much, McCracken?"

"Nothing."

"Nothing?"

McCracken sized the man up, from his perfectly tailored suit to professionally styled hair with not a strand out of place. "You been to the Vietnam Memorial lately, Hank?"

"No, I haven't."

"There are some names missing, the names of many of the men I served with in Vietnam who never came back. That's my fee. I pull this off, I want their names up there on the Wall where they belong. I want you to take care of it."

Folsom's eyes moved to McCracken's ring, simple black letters on gold. "D-S. Stands for Dead Simple, right?"

McCracken didn't respond.

"What's it mean?"

"I think you know."

"Because killing came so easy. You still worthy of the nickname 'McCrackenballs'?"

"You want my services or my autograph, Hank?"

Folsom leaned forward. "How many times did they ask you to go after Bin Laden?"

"Not a one."

"That's not what I heard."

"You heard wrong."

Folsom came up just short of a smile. "I heard there was a reason why the SEALs encountered so little resistance. I heard the bodies of eight pretty bad hombres were hauled out after the fact, all dead before the SEALs dropped in. Word is it was you and that big Indian friend of yours."

"His name is Johnny Wareagle."

Folsom said nothing.

"SEALs got Bin Laden, Hank. It's nice to fantasize about things being bigger than they really were, but that raid was big enough all on its own. Weird thing is that when I was in, I never got or wanted credit for anything. Now that I'm out, I get more than I deserve and still don't want any."

"You're not out," Folsom told him.

"Figure of speech. What they say when nobody calls you in anymore."

Across the table, Folsom suddenly looked older and more confident. "I called. And I'll see what I can do about getting those names added to the Wall."

"Is that what you call nonnegotiable?"

"I'll take care of it."

"Better. Now give me your word."

"Why?"

"Because a man's word means something, even in your world where lying rules the day."

"Used to be your world too."

McCracken's black eyes hardened even more. "It was never mine, Hank." He leaned forward, almost face-to-face with Folsom before the man from the State Department could register he'd moved at all. "Now tell me more about the job."

"Mexico," Folsom nodded. He leaned back in his chair to again lengthen the distance between them. "Gun-loving Juárez, specifically. Place is like the Old West. You'll be going up against a hundred guns in a walled fortress."

McCracken rose, jarring the table just enough to send the rest of his watery ginger ale sloshing around amid the melting ice cubes. "Send me the specs and the satellite recon."

"That's it?" Folsom asked.

"Not quite. I don't like working for somebody I can't trust." Folsom opened his mouth to respond, but McCracken rolled right over his words. "You're not from State. State doesn't work with people like me. It's not in their job description. Too busy covering their own asses. Politics, Hank, something you clearly don't give a shit about."

"All right, you got me. I'm Homeland Security," Folsom told him.

"Ah, the new catchall . . ."

"You're right about the tools at State, McCracken. But we, on the other hand, get shit done. Being Homeland gives us a license to do pretty much anything we want."

"Including going outside the system to call in a dinosaur like me?"

Folsom tried to hold McCracken's stare. "Just answer me one question. Your phone doesn't ring until I call, it leaves me wondering."

"That's not a question."

Folsom didn't hesitate. "The question is, do you still have it or not . . . McCrackenballs?"

McCracken smiled tightly. "Let me put it this way, Hank: when this is over, you may want to revise that thesis of yours."

CHAPTER 3

Juárez, Mexico

"What's eating you, boss?" Sal Belamo asked, as McCracken steered the SUV toward the compound's gates after the guards finally waved him through.

"Folsom asked me if I still had it."

"Any doubt in your mind about that?"

"Two years is a long time, Sal."

"You're not saying you're scared."

"Nope, but I was: scared that the call wouldn't come again after the phone stopped ringing two years ago."

Belamo gazed around him. "Well, we can safely say that concern's been put to rest."

The inside of the compound jibed perfectly with the satellite reconnaissance photos Folsom had provided. It reminded McCracken of a typical Spanish mission, not unlike the famed Alamo in San Antonio, with an inner courtyard and a nest of buildings located beyond a walled façade that in olden times would have provided an extra layer of defense from attack. A lavish fountain left over from an earlier era was centered in the courtyard, beautifully restored but no longer functional. The sun burned high in a cloudless sky, flooding the compound with blistering hot light that reflected off the cream-colored array of buildings. The air smelled of scorched dirt mixed with stale perspiration that hung in the air like haze, the combination acrid enough to make McCracken want to hold his breath.

Trays of freshly grilled chicken, fish, and beef smelling of chili powder, pepper, and oregano sharp enough to reach the SUV's now open windows, meanwhile, had been laid out on tables covered by open-sided tent. McCracken could see plates of sliced tomatoes and bowls of freshly made guacamole placed in another section not far from ice chests packed with bottled water. Many of Morales's uniformed guards had lined up to fill their plates. Folsom had told McCracken that many of the men on Morales's payroll were former Zetas, veterans of the Mexican Special Forces originally charged with bringing down the very forces they were now serving.

"Two years, Sal," McCracken repeated, angling the Mercedes toward a parking slot squeezed amid military vehicles that included ancient American-issue Jeeps.

"Took a break that long from the ring once," Belamo related. "Knocked a guy out in the first round when I came back."

"You weren't sixty at the time."

"You're still fifty-nine, boss."

McCracken couldn't judge the prowess of Morales's troops one way or another by what he saw, but their eyes showed no worry or suspicion or wariness of any kind. If they held any expectation of a pending attack, there was no evidence of it. Instead, men clad in sweat-soaked uniforms who'd already gotten their lunches lounged leisurely, their weapons resting nearby but in some cases not even within reach. The bulk of the personnel clung to the cooler shade cast by the walled façade while others, likely those lower on the totem pole, stuck to the thinner patches provided by an old yellow school bus with rust spreading upward from its decaying rocker panels. Morales himself, arguably the world's most infamous drug dealer, held court upon a covered veranda, enclosed by four gunmen and seated in what looked like a rocking chair next to a younger dark-haired beauty who could have been an actress.

McCracken and Sal Belamo climbed out of the SUV into the scorching heat, the sensation worsened by the sudden loss of air-conditioning in favor of stagnant air that was almost too heavy to breathe. The sky above was an endless blue ribbon, fostering an illusion that the sun itself was vibrating madly.

McCracken and Belamo submitted to the thorough, wholly anticipated pat-down, which turned up nothing. Then six more guards escorted them to the veranda and beckoned for them to continue up the three stairs for an audience with the man who many said was the most powerful in Mexico.

"So I understand you want to get our business done early, Mr. Franks," Morales said, rising in the semblance of a greeting.

"I happened to be in the area," McCracken told him, "with time on my hands."

"We had an arrangement."

"We still do. Only the schedule has changed. But if you wish to rethink that arrangement . . ."

Morales sat back down next to the much younger woman who flinched when he settled in alongside her, filling out the entire width of the chair. He was overweight, hardly resembling the most common shots circulated of him from younger days by the US intelligence community. Withdrawing to a life of isolation wrought by his many enemies had clearly left Morales with a taste for too much food and wine to accompany his vast power in the region. Judging by the thick blotches of perspiration dotting the cartel leader's shirt, McCracken doubted any of the buildings here were even equipped with air-conditioning.

Morales's hair was thinning in contrast to the thick mustache drooping over his upper lip. He was dressed casually in linen slacks and a near matching shirt unbuttoned all the way down to the start of the belly that protruded over his belt. A light sheen of perspiration coated his face, and he breathed noisily through his mouth.

He took the dark-haired woman's right hand in his while he stroked her hair with the left. "This is my wife, Elena. But she has borne me no children. Such a disappointment."

With that, he bent one of the woman's fingers back until McCracken heard a snap. He flinched as the woman gasped and bit down the pain, slumping in her chair.

"Everyone is replaceable, eh, Señor Franks?" Morales sneered, seeming to relish the agony he'd caused his wife.

McCracken bit back his anger, keeping his eyes away from the woman who was now choking back sobs. "Men like us aren't, Señor Morales. And I thought coming early was in both our best interests."

"And why is that?" Morales asked him.

"It stopped you from the bother of staging a welcome for me."

"I would have enjoyed making such a gesture, amigo."

"You and I, Señor Morales, we're cautious men pursuing mutual interests. You need my network to provide you with new routes to bring your product into the United States and I need exclusive distribution of that product to eliminate my competition in select markets. I imagine we can agree on that much."

"You wouldn't be here if we didn't already," Morales said, his eyes straying to the briefcase still chained to Belamo's wrist. "You see that school bus over there?"

"You mean the one your soldiers are sleeping against?"

Morales ignored his remark. "I started my career as a runner using that bus to bring drugs into your country. I would recruit local children and pay them a dollar to play students heading to America on field trips. I keep the bus here as a reminder of my humble roots. And even men like us must never lose sight of how hard we worked to get where we are, *si*?"

"For sure," McCracken acknowledged, meaning it this time.

Morales's eyes returned to the briefcase. A woman clad in a tight satin dress laid a heaping plate she had filled from the lunch tables down before him. Another woman who might have been her twin refilled his glass of sangria, making sure just the right amount of floating fruit spilled in. Their moves looked robotic, rehearsed. And the fact that they remained cool amid the scalding heat made them appear like department store mannequins devoid of anything but beauty.

"You have brought your deposit?" Morales asked.

"In exchange for the first shipment to be delivered within the week. That was the deal. A fair exchange."

"Then let me see it," Morales said, again angling his gaze for the briefcase cuffed to Sal Belamo's wrist. "Of course, I could always have one of my men cut your man's hand off."

"But that would leave him with only one," McCracken noted, unruffled. "And then I'd have to take one of yours in return. Also a fair exchange."

Morales grinned broadly, his threat left hanging. "You are good at math, señor."

"Just as you are with women."

The grin vanished.

"Sal," McCracken signaled.

At that, Belamo pried a small key from his shoe and unlocked the handcuffs from both his wrist and the briefcase. Then he handed the case to Morales who laid it in his lap and eagerly flipped the catches, slowly raising the lid. His breathing quieted, his eyes widened.

"Is this some kind of joke?" Morales asked, clearly dismayed as he spun the open briefcase around to reveal nothing inside but two pistols, a sleek semiautomatic and a long-barreled Magnum revolver.

"Those are very valuable guns, señor," McCracken said, as Morales's personal Zeta guards steadied their weapons upon him. "Men have perished under their fire, many with prices on their heads. You're welcome to the rewards in exchange for the hostages."

"Who are you?" Morales asked, tossing the briefcase to the veranda floor as he rose again.

"I'm the man doing you a big favor, Morales. Someday you'll thank me for showing you kidnapping doesn't pay, at least not when you're bringing in as much as you are from your drug business. Here," he said, handing Morales a ruffled piece of paper.

Morales straightened, trying to make sense of the number and letter combinations. "What is this?"

"The latitude and longitude marks denoting the locations of your largest storage facilities. If I don't leave with the hostages, all four go boom."

Morales smiled, chuckled, then outright laughed. "You are threatening *me*? You are really *threatening* me? Here in my *home*, in front of my *men*?" His voice gained volume with each syllable. He seemed to be enjoying himself; the challenge, the threat.

"I'm going to let you keep your drugs, against my better judgment, but the four Americans, the college students, leave with me."

At first it seemed Morales didn't know how to respond. But then he threw his head back and laughed heartily again, both the women and his guards joining in for good measure. Only his wife, Elena, stayed quiet, too busy swiping the tears of pain from her face.

"Just like that?" Morales said, the veranda's other occupants stopping their laughter as soon as he stopped his.

"Yup, just like that."

"And what do I get in return for accepting your gracious offer?"

"You get to stay in business." McCracken tapped his watch for Morales to see. "But the clock's ticking."

"Is it?"

"You have one minute."

Morales started to laugh again but stopped. The two women nuzzled against him on either side in spite of his wife's presence, his private guards slapping each other on the back.

"I have one minute!" he roared, laughing so hard now his face turned scarlet and he wheezed trying to find his breath.

"Forty-five seconds now."

Morales jabbed a finger at the air McCracken's way. "I like you, amigo. You're a real funny guy." He stopped laughing and finally caught his breath. "After you're dead, I think I'll have you stuffed and mounted on the wall so I always have something to make me smile."

"You won't be smiling in thirty seconds time, Morales, unless you agree to give me the Americans. Tick, tick, tick."

Morales reached down toward the briefcase and scooped up the two pistols. "Are these loaded?"

"They are."

"So I could kill you with them now."

"You could."

"Let me see," Morales said dramatically, looking from one pistol to the other, "which one should I use. . . ." A broad smile crossed his lips. "Eeney, meeney, miney . . ."

And in that moment a portion of the compound's façade around the gated entrance exploded in a fountain of rubble and dust. The remainder of the first wave of missiles that followed in the next instant obliterated the unmanned watchtowers and took out the compound's armory in a sizzling display of light and ear-ringing blasts that grew like a fireworks display.

"Mo," said McCracken.

CHAPTER 4

Juárez, Mexico

The missiles were Hellfires, fired from a pair of Hank Folsom's drones that had been stationed over the compound. The countdown to fire had been triggered by Sal Belamo twisting the key into the handcuffs latching him to the briefcase, a signal sent to an operative at a base in Nevada whose hand was already poised on the button.

For McCracken, the deafening blasts of the missile strikes slowed time to a crawl. He saw the series of blasts hurl any number of Morales's men through the air to land in bloody clumps. He saw showers of vegetables, sliced meat, chicken, fish, and what looked like sangria kicked up from the luncheon tables behind the shock wave from a nearby strike. He saw the soldiers who'd been spared by the initial explosions springing desperately for their weapons, even as their eyes turned toward the sky in fear of falling to the next round of blasts. He saw the pistols Morales had been holding rattle to the veranda floor, and he ducked to retrieve the SIG Sauer in the same moment Sal Belamo grabbed hold of the .44 Magnum, the scorched air smelling like it was on fire now.

In that moment the last two years vanished behind the haze of battle McCracken knew so well. Age lost all meaning, time measured in the breaths and moments between explosions, gunshots, and screams.

Do I still have it?

As if to answer that, McCracken and Belamo shot all six of Morales's private guards, neither sure of whose bullets had felled which men. McCracken recorded the bodies tumbling in the same splotchy glimpses he caught of the barrel's muzzle flash and smelled the smoke wafting upward before being swallowed by the air and breeze. The most powerful man in Mexico was left cowering on the floor using his wife with a now broken finger as a shield. By then, though, his soldiers who'd recovered their weapons in the courtyard just below also recovered enough of their senses to launch an all-out charge for the veranda.

A few had actually opened fire wildly on McCracken and Belamo, when a huge figure burst up through the Mercedes SUV's open sunroof. Johnny Wareagle, all seven feet of him, held M1A4 modified M-16s in either hand, clacking rounds off in two directions at once as if capable of focusing his eyes separately. Those eyes were deep-set and ice blue, his mostly jet-black ponytail whipping from side to side with each twist of his head.

More missiles rained down, kicking up so much ground dirt and debris that Wareagle and the entire SUV vanished in the resulting cloud. The soldiers his bullets had spared opened up into that cloud with an unrelenting and deafening barrage. Spent shells clanged against each other on the ground in soft counterpoint to the shrill sound of the steel of the Mercedes being punctured, its windows shattered, and tires popped.

Several of Morales's soldiers were still firing when the dust cloud cleared enough to reveal Wareagle now standing behind them, opening up with fresh magazines at his targets caught totally by surprise.

"Who *are* you?" Morales asked again, fearfully this time as

McCracken jerked him to his feet with the SIG pressed against his skull.

"Wanna try breaking my finger, amigo? Now let's go get those kids."

He steered Morales through the courtyard, Belamo covering his rear flank with quick three-shot bursts from a salvaged assault rifle: an M-16, procured by Morales from his American contacts no doubt. Half-dressed reinforcements were spilling out of what must have been the barracks among the nest of interconnected buildings beyond, struggling to right their weapons once they recorded the sight before them.

"Tell them not to shoot," McCracken said into Morales's ear.

"*No mi fuego, no mi fuego!*" Morales screamed, as more of the drone-fired Hellfires erupted all around them.

"Now, tell them to bring the Americans here. Tell them to bring those kids to me *now*!"

Morales spouted out more Spanish, shouting to be heard over a fresh wave of explosions.

McCracken remained in the open, continuing to hold Morales before him, the man's bulk more than enough to keep him shielded and prevent any of the drug lord's soldiers from risking an almost impossible shot much more likely to take their leader. Still, the moments lengthened, twenty seconds feeling like twice that, stretching into thirty and then forty.

That's when two bearded soldiers wearing only their boxer shorts and wife-beater T-shirts emerged from another of the buildings, each dragging two of the missing Americans forward. The boys, filthy, weak, and emaciated, had all they could do to stay on their feet.

The staccato bursts of gunfire, meanwhile, had lessened in intensity, dominated now by the distinctive clacking of Johnny Wareagle's twin assault rifles. McCracken felt motion behind him, sensing the seven-foot Native American alongside whom he'd been fighting for over forty years taking up position on his rear flank to make sure no surprises awaited in the course of their escape.

McCracken backpedaled, dragging Morales with him by the collar, his hand slippery with the oily paste the drug lord used on his thinning hair. Belamo hovered just to his side and herded the college kids together behind him.

"Nice work, Indian," McCracken said drawing even with Wareagle.

"Problems, Blainey," was all he said, continuing to clack off rounds in three-shot bursts.

Pistol still pressed against Morales's skull, McCracken followed Johnny's gaze to their Mercedes SUV, or what was left of it.

"Guess we better call a taxi," he said.

"How about that?" suggested Sal Belamo, his gaze tilting toward the yellow school bus.

CHAPTER 5

Juárez, Mexico

McCracken could only hope the monument-like memorial to Morales's past would still work. "Hope you don't mind us borrowing your bus, amigo," he said, dragging Morales on again.

He felt the drug lord stiffen even more under his grasp. "You're *loco*!"

"For a long time now. Explains why you should have listened to me in the first place. When something works for me, I stick with it."

McCracken reached the door just before Wareagle, who was concentrating his fire upward now, toward Morales's soldiers crawling across the walls in search of better vantage points. Belamo got to the bus last and shouldered the door open, shoving the college students up the stairs under Wareagle's protective cover.

"Down!" Belamo yelled in after them. "I want you lying in the aisles!"

"Get her moving, Sal," McCracken ordered.

"This thing's a hundred years old, boss."

"Just like us. Vintage."

"You'll die for this," Morales rasped, canting his head to try to look back at McCracken.

McCracken jerked him back into place. "Not today."

The engine fought Sal Belamo, refusing to catch. Hotwiring the bus had been a snap since the ignition was already long gone and the remaining wires hung in place, ready to be twisted. But the tires were low on air and badly warped as well as laden with bumps from having sat for so long in the same place. The one saving grace was that the engine was diesel and diesel fuel was much less likely to evaporate over time, and sure enough the engine rumbled to life after the initial sputter. Belamo started the vehicle backward toward what was left of the gate, doing his best to ignore its bouncing shimmy.

Wareagle moved on foot with the bus and hurled smoke grenades from his weapons vest in all directions. The thick gray smoke blew outward, combining with the black smoke and flames climbing from the impact points of the Hellfires, to create the cover they needed. Belamo felt the bus crunch over the various debris strewn behind it. And then a charred vehicle frame snared on its underside and the bus dragged it all the way to the remnants of the main gate, shedding the frame as soon as Belamo shifted into gear. The transmission ground and bucked before it finally churned through what was left of the gate.

Wareagle chose that moment to slip past McCracken up the stairs and onto the bus. He'd shouldered another half-dozen assault rifles and two rocket launchers salvaged off Morales's dead soldiers to add firepower to their escape. McCracken remained in the open doorway, holding Morales on the lowermost step with the SIG Sauer pistol still trained on his skull until the school bus started putting distance between itself and the smoldering compound that belched smoke into the air. Then he dragged Morales all the way inside and flung him hard to the bus floor. The man turned onto his back and lay still, his hate-filled eyes finding McCracken's.

"I'm going to kill you myself," he rasped.

"Move from that spot before we reach the border and you'll never get the chance."

The bus backfired as it climbed onto the road at a jogger's pace, slowly gathering speed.

"Come on, come on!" Belamo urged from behind the wheel. "Hey, you think you can find me something slower next time?"

"The space shuttle wasn't available, Sal."

Morales started crawling forward and McCracken kicked him in the head. "I told you not to move." McCracken kicked him a second time in the ribs. "And that was for what you did to your wife's finger."

"One more thing, boss."

"What, Sal?"

"Welcome back." Belamo smiled.

McCracken turned his attention to the fraternity brothers they'd just rescued, the boys looking thin, filthy, and wide-eyed with terror from their positions on the floor. "Under the seats! Now!"

They moved tentatively, slowed and weakened by their ordeal. McCracken crouched to help them as gently as he could, feeling them stiffen and wince from the sudden motions racking their bruised and battered frames. He glared at the sprawled form of Morales, dazed and still grimacing from the pain in his ribs and head.

Johnny Wareagle, meanwhile, had poised himself by the emergency exit door, watching when a thin convoy of still functional vehicles poured out of Morales's compound to give chase.

"Company!" McCracken yelled up to the front.

"Give me till tomorrow and I'll have this thing up to fifty," Belamo called back to him.

"Five miles to the border, Sal."

"How far you figure to those police cars coming our way?"

McCracken swung from the bus's rear, away from three of Morales's Jeeps and two open troop carriers coming on fast in their wake, toward the front. There, on the opposite side of the road, a parade of police cars tore across the median and twisted into screeching halts on the bus's side of the freeway that left the cars sideways across the road, blocking their escape route.

"This oughtta be fun," Belamo said softly to himself.

CHAPTER 6

Juárez, Mexico

Belamo jammed the transmission up one gear and then another. The bus jolted forward, shook, then began gathering speed as it barreled straight for the *federales* who were still lurching from their cars and racing to steady weapons atop roofs or hoods.

"Hey, boss, you know that movie about the bus that'll blow up if it goes over fifty?"

"It was under fifty, Sal."

"Doesn't matter since we're gonna get that high. Now, hang on!" Belamo shouted.

The bus crashed through the makeshift barricade, its windshield obliterated by bullets as it surged on down the road. From the rear, McCracken watched the *federales* leaping into the police cars left reasonably whole and functional. They tore off just as Morales's convoy drew even with them, led by a Jeep with an M-60 machine gun mounted on a tripod in its open rear.

Its first burst of fire cut through the bus's steel and glass, forcing McCracken and Wareagle to the rusted-out floor.

"No time to get fancy, Indian."

"Couldn't agree more, Blainey," Wareagle said back to him, already reaching for a rocket launcher.

"Where are those spirits of yours when we need them?"

"Just arriving."

Johnny moved to a squatting position with the launcher perched effortlessly upon his shoulder, exhaust tube even with where the windshield had been thirty feet away.

McCracken got ready at the emergency exit door. "Tell me when."

"Now, Blainey."

"Hey, Sal!"

"I'm a little busy here, boss!"

"Duck!"

And with that McCracken jerked the latch downward and shoved the door open. In crazed counterpoint, a buzzing emergency alarm began to wail just before Wareagle pressed the trigger. The rocket burst outward on direct line with the onrushing Jeep still firing off shells that continued to pulverize the bus's frame. Smoke and flames from the exhaust tube, meanwhile, shot out in a neat arc toward the front of the bus, blowing out the remnants of the windshield and singeing the cracked, faded upholstery on the seats. Smoke rose from it, smelling like burning plastic as the bus surged on.

Police vehicles and Morales's other Jeeps drew even with the bus on either side, pouring an endless stream of fire inside that was returned by McCracken to one flank and Wareagle to the other.

"Fuck this," Belamo said under his breath and proceeded to whipsaw the bus from side to side, playing demolition derby with the cars alongside it until he forced them both all the way off the road. "And fuck you too!" he screamed out his window.

"Four miles, Sal!" McCracken yelled up toward the front.

"We'll never make it on this road!" And then Belamo spotted a turnoff just up ahead. "Like I was saying . . ."

Belamo jerked the wheel hard to the left, sending McCracken

and Wareagle banging against that side. The bus wobbled, seemed on the verge of tipping over on its underinflated tires when it found purchase on flattened gravel lining the outskirts of Juárez's slum-dominated residential zone. Both the old and new sections of the cities appeared in the narrowing distance as animals and pedestrians alike scattered from the path of the onrushing school bus that coughed more glass with each thump and rattle.

The chase vehicles tore after it, able to follow only in single file through the narrow winding streets, allowing McCracken and Wareagle to more easily match their firepower. Their bullets took out another Jeep, then two more *federale* police cars, losing a single back tire in the process and leaving the bus to thump and buck along the narrow roads. Its rear end dragged along the higher points, spitting ravaged rubber, the stench of which flooded the interior like burning sulfur as sparks flew backward.

Sal Belamo took out several clotheslines, a picnic table, three food pushcarts, and a skate wheel platform on which a boy had balanced four jugs of water, the impact sending liquid splashing up and over the bus's frame. McCracken and Wareagle exchanged two more empty rifles for fresh ones and opened up anew on their pursuers. Through it all, the smell of raw sewage rising from the cluttered slums that still lacked running water dominated the air, the bus drifting in and out of pockets of the stench.

"You gotta be fucking kidding me. . . ."

McCracken swung back toward the bus's front to see the pair of motorcycles that had spooked Sal Belamo pulling ahead of the trailing convoy and risking fire to charge forward in line with the bus. Wareagle shot one of the drivers and then the second, but not before that second managed to fire a series of rounds at the bus's gas tank, puncturing it and sending a flood of diesel fuel spreading backward in the bus's wake.

"You thinking what I'm thinking, Indian?" McCracken raised, returning the fire of the lead-most chase vehicles.

Wareagle had grabbed the second rocket launcher, the old city's once-thriving commercial district fast approaching. They had just surged into the clutter of shops, stores, kiosks, and pushcarts when he fired—not for any vehicle, but downward for the road. The rocket skimmed the surface, shredding itself apart. The resulting friction created sufficient sparks to ignite the fuel left in the bus's wake. Then the rocket exploded, the force of the heat wave blowing a long line of flames down the road as far as McCracken could see and consuming every vehicle in its fiery path. A final Jeep and police car emerged from the glow, their undersides aflame.

But the flames didn't stop there. They continued chasing the bus, igniting spilled diesel and drawing dangerously close to its ruptured tank.

"Step on it, Sal!"

"What the hell you think I've been doing?"

Giving the bus more gas caused it to shed its ruined tire altogether, just a heavy steel rim dragging across the gravel now before Belamo felt smooth pavement beneath him. The flames were catching on the frame's underside, when he tore across the parking lot of a car wash, scattering workers in all directions. Belamo drove into one of the bays, slamming into a car currently being bathed in jet spray water and shoving it forward as the water doused the flames in a cloud of hissing steam.

The bus pushed the car the rest of the way from the bay, then aside, and struggled on, sputtering, the sound of the wheel dragging across pavement like fingernails down a chalkboard.

"Next time, don't forget the wax, Sal," McCracken said.

CHAPTER 7

Juárez, Mexico

"Bridge is dead ahead, boss!"

Belamo never slowed, giving the old bus every bit of gas it had left. It sputtered and coughed across the last stretch of the Bridge of the Americas before grinding to a final halt with its frame straddling the US and Mexican sides of the border. Through the empty hole where the windshield had been, McCracken spotted armed United States Border Patrol agents approaching tentatively with their weapons raised. Then a roar from the Mexican side of the border made him swing round toward the bus's rear to the sight of an angry mob brandishing all manner of weapons from rakes and baseball bats to pistols and knives, streaming toward the bridge.

"Indian!" McCracken shouted to Wareagle, who was already easing the rescued hostages from beneath the bus's faded and cracked seats.

The door had jammed, so Belamo kicked it open. Wareagle helped two of the boys out and McCracken the other two, Belamo hanging back now with a pistol in one hand and a barely conscious Arturo Morales grasped by the hair with the other. At the bottom of the stairs, one of kids McCracken was hoisting collapsed, a dark swatch of red spreading along his rib cage from what looked like a bullet wound.

"Oh, shit . . ."

Behind them the Mexican mob had reached the far end of the Bridge of the Americas, random gunfire starting to split the air, while the armed border agents froze with no idea how to respond, protocol having been thrown out the window.

That changed when they saw Johnny Wareagle in the lead with a boy slung over each shoulder, McCracken lagging a bit with the bleeding boy feeling heavy in his arms, and the fourth limping alongside him. Sal Belamo continued to hold tight to Morales by the hair, while clacking off rounds from his pistol back toward the surging mob. The border agents met them a dozen yards from the American side of the bridge, rifles fired into the air in the hope that would be enough to turn the mob around. Instead it only incensed them more, McCracken swinging toward Wareagle as they reached the far side of the bridge.

"Let's finish this, Indian."

"On it, Blainey."

In one swift, sure motion Wareagle lowered both boys to the road and stripped a hand grenade from his ammo vest. He hurled the grenade forward, arching it through the air. It hit the concrete and skittered beneath the mangled bus just as the leading edge of the mob drew almost even with the now blackened frame.

BOOM!

No matter how often McCracken heard that sound and the screeching twist of metal that followed, he'd never get used to it. The grenade exploded directly beneath the bus's engine block, igniting the last of the diesel fuel clinging to the line and sending a curtain of flames and steel spreading up and out. The wall of flames and crackle of roasting metal proved enough to turn the angry mob around and send it scurrying back across the Bridge of the Americas toward the Mexican side of the border.

"Need a medic here!" McCracken yelled out, rising from his guarded position over the bleeding boy and vaguely conscious of Sal Belamo dropping Arturo Morales at the feet of two Border Control agents.

He saw the kid's lids were fluttering over dimming eyes, heard him gasping for breath.

"Goddamn it!" He tore the boy's shirt back to expose the entry wound. "I need some help here!" he yelled out, easing his finger over the wound to stanch the steady seepage.

But McCracken knew the real damage was likely internal, even as the kid began to thrash and writhe. His eyes suddenly bulged, terrified, his hand grasping hold of McCracken's shirt an instant before his gaze locked sightlessly.

"I need a medic! I need a medic!" McCracken kept repeating, holding the boy tighter in a futile attempt to comfort him.

Welcome back, Sal Belamo had said just minutes before.

Shadows danced around him. Hands lowered and someone began CPR. It was the jungle all over again, the Hellfire as Johnny called it, something McCracken hardly thought of anymore while he never really stopped thinking about it. The dichotomy played itself out before him as Wareagle eased him aside, the coppery stench of blood everywhere by the time the first sirens began to wail.

He was back, all right.

CHAPTER 8

Deepwater Venture, Gulf of Mexico: One week later

"Attention!" a voice boomed over the public address system. "We are three hundred feet from history."

Then why am I so goddamn scared? Paul Basmajian asked himself.

Basmajian, the assistant operations manager of the *Deepwater Venture* offshore oil rig, watched a deckhand lift the last bottle of alcohol-free champagne from one case and immediately dipped his hand into the next. It had been on ice until only minutes ago, but the blast-oven effects of the rig's steel multilevel superstructure had already bled the cool from the bottles. Baffles and mounts rose from the main deck surface everywhere, fighting for space amid what looked to be a random assortment of stacked clutter when men like Basmajian knew quite the opposite was true. He smelled grease and paint where the deck rails had been given a fresh coat. The pungent odor of a strong industrial solvent laced the air as well, evidence of the decks being recently swabbed down. He caught the sour stench of drilling mud that was actually produced in another area of the rig to be stored in fifty-five-gallon black drums stacked on shelves reachable only by cranes that hovered over the *Venture* like silent sentinels. The platform was rectangular with several abutments jutting outward over the sea. One held a helipad that was currently empty, twin towering drilling derricks resting atop two more.

"Have at it, boys," the deckhand said, passing out the final bottles, "but no celebrating until we get to where no rig worker has ever gone before."

We shouldn't be celebrating, thought Paul Basmajian, the strange sixth sense he'd experienced for the first time in Vietnam alerting him to something amiss. It felt like a cat scratching at the back of his neck and left him patting the area with his fingers as if expecting to come away with blood on the tips. He wanted, *needed*, this to go smoothly since he planned to take some off-rig time today to meet up with two old friends he hadn't seen in much too long. There wasn't much that could distract Basmajian from his work at sea, but a reunion like this has been too much to pass up.

In a matter of minutes the *Deepwater Venture*'s main drill was going to reach the lowest depth ever achieved in these or any waters: just past 32,000 feet, 4,000 through water, and another 28,000 through shale and sediment. The *Venture* was among the largest offshore rigs ever constructed, essentially a floating, self-contained community with its own water, electricity, and sanitary systems. The first time Basmajian's grandsons had visited the *Venture* they had eyed it from the sea with wide-eyed amazement, convinced it was some kind of robotic creature lifted from a video game with cranes for arms, a hydraulic drill for its head, and a pair of two-hundred-foot derricks for a body.

To Basmajian, their critique pretty much summed it up; impressive technical specifications aside, the *Venture* really was a massive technological toy. In truth it was part of the deepwater subsea class of drilling rigs and the most advanced by a generation, supported by TLP. The tension leg platform was a floating production system. Tension leg platforms were buoyant production facilities vertically moored to the seafloor four thousand feet down by tendons. The buoyancy of the hull offset the weight of the platform, requiring clusters of tension legs to secure the structure to the foundation on the seabed. The foundation itself was kept stationary by piles driven into the very bottom, built that way for the TLP mooring system to allow for horizontal movement with wave disturbances, while eliminating all vertical or bobbing motions.

That explained why TLPs were the rig of choice in the hurricane-prone Gulf of Mexico. The four yellow support columns were air filled and formed a square, both supported and connected by pontoons. Those columns formed the top, visible part of the TLP system that kept a deepwater subsea rig like the *Venture* stationary and stable. Strung beneath them were multicolored, spaghetti-like strands of piping connected to the different pumps on the ocean floor.

Today, the rig was about to make history under the stewardship of a first-generation Armenian American who'd long lost the battle to stop his belly from protruding over his belt. Basmajian had grown up in this business upon returning from a long stint in the army before anyone knew what SPF stood for, leaving his skin a leathery, spotted patchwork of sections that looked stitched together. He figured a pair of tours in Vietnam had probably ruined his complexion forever, so why bother anyway?

"Attention! We are now two hundred feet from history!"

But what history was that? Basmajian was well aware the coordinates of this particular location in the Gulf made no sense, because all the seismic studies, analysis, and imagery indicated there were far richer potential oil strikes elsewhere in the endless square miles of water around them. Being capable of drilling down thirty thousand feet–plus opened up a new world of options so vast that anchoring here where all research indicated a dry earth bed below continued to plague him, even with history in the offing.

Basmajian hadn't been involved in the scouting process aimed at building a cartoonlike animation of the seafloor to home in on the most promising potential reservoir of oils. To create this Disney-like rendering, Ocean Bore Technologies, the rig's operator, had first deployed ships that cruised through the Gulf popping off air guns, essentially underwater cannons that bounced sound waves off subsurface rock formations. Hydrophones, sophisticated aquatic microphones really, tethered to the vessels taped the response, taking in hundreds of thousands of recordings simultaneously. These allowed the company to determine the composition and shape of the rocks below. Ocean Bore needed to use huge numbers of microphones to compensate for the distortions caused by a layer of salt as jagged as the Swiss Alps beneath the seafloor in the ultradeep regions of the Gulf.

Once the map was assembled, Ocean Bore should have pored over the data in search of sandy layers of sediment under domelike caps of shale. These normally signified the location of a potential reservoir since oil rises through permeable sediment to the highest point it can go, collecting under unyielding shale mounds. And that's what was bothering Basmajian here. As far as he could tell, millions of dollars spent to create a cartoon rendering that would make Walt Disney himself proud had yielded little or no evidence of those telltale sandy sediment layers.

As assistant operations manager, Basmajian almost never left the rig in its long duration at sea, and he wasn't ordinarily expected to be able to comprehend such sophisticated technology. But he was also no ordinary industry executive, having learned every phase of the business from the ground up, just as he'd insisted in the military on learning all facets required of the Special Forces team he was a part of. He had never expected to put all that knowledge to use, but it certainly helped him better understand the challenges the other members of his team faced. His problem was that his job as assistant operations manager left him no real recourse, no magic 800 number he could dial to get his questions answered at Ocean Bore headquarters in Houston. The only people he could talk to were those who'd commissioned the studies and planted the *Deepwater Venture* here in the first place.

But if Ocean Bore wasn't looking for oil in the deepest well ever drilled, what exactly did the company expect to find once their platinum-tipped rotary drill with fluid desanders, shale shakers, and desilters broke through the earth's crust?

That question wasn't just unsettling Basmajian any longer, it was scaring him in a way he never thought he'd feel again after boarding a helicopter for the last time in Vietnam.

The *Deepwater Venture* was a sixth-generation rig, nearly four hundred feet in length and two hundred and fifty in width. It could operate in depths up to seventy-five hundred feet and in sustained winds of seventy knots accompanied by a ten-second wave period. But field tests had shown the rig capable of also operating in hundred-knot storm winds that brought twelve-second wave periods with them—unheard of even by the most ambitious of modern standards, again thanks to its TLP system. The rig's quarters, located on the shaded levels below the main deck, housed a hundred and fifty workers, staff, and support personnel in closet-sized spaces with fold-down cots that would've been nearly impossible to sleep upon had the workers not been so beat at the end of their fourteen-hour shifts. They were normally too exhausted to take advantage of the *Venture*'s fully equipped gym, game room, or media center.

Those stepping off the telescopic gangway that linked the rig to barges and supply ships for the first time were immediately struck by the lack of open space on deck. Every square inch on all five levels, with the power module alone taking up a large portion of the lowermost one, was accounted for, space at such a premium that none could be wasted. That's what amazed Basmajian about the celebration about to commence. Many of the men were separated from the next closest by distances of up to six feet and often hidden from sight by some piece of equipment or the superstructure itself.

In the event a rapid evacuation or quick insertion was required, the rig was outfitted for not one, but two helipads perched on raised platforms that looked like trampolines from the sky. Though affixed to the superstructure, the platforms actually extended out over the water on the north and south ends, watched over by the twin massive cranes bracketing the derricks. Add to that the most sophisticated emergency escape system known to the industry, and Basmajian often mused that this was the safest place to be on the planet.

So why didn't he feel that way right now, with history on the verge of being made? Maybe it had something to do with the female crewmember, administrative assistant to the mostly absent operations manager, who had slipped off the rig on the same supply ship that had brought the nonalcoholic champagne earlier that morning. Security personnel confirmed she boarded the supply ship, but that carrier claimed to have no knowledge of her either being on board or exiting when they returned to port in New Orleans. Port security had proven similarly clueless.

"Attention! We are now one hundred feet from history!"

Amid the hoots and hollers around him, Paul Basmajian leaned against a deck rail to steady himself, certain somehow that they were a hundred feet from something else as well.

CHAPTER 9

Deepwater Venture, Gulf of Mexico

Basmajian noticed his chief engineer, George Arnold, standing off by himself on the main deck, no bottle of champagne in hand with which to celebrate, looking detached and disinterested.

"Do I look as bad as you?" Basmajian asked him.

"Worse."

"Something feels wrong about this, Arnie."

"Nickel for your thoughts."

"What happened to a penny?"

"Have you seen the price of oil lately, Bas?"

Arnold was frightfully thin, his face growing more skeletal by the day when he was crewing a long rotation like this one. All in all, an odd match for the bearlike Basmajian. But that hadn't stopped them from working together steadily for going on twenty years, watching the industry blossom from jack-up and gorilla rigs to this floating city on the sea.

"Female crewmember fled the rig this morning," Basmajian told George Arnold. "I'll be damned if I can figure that one out."

"But that's not what's bothering you."

"No, that's not what's bothering me at all."

"I want to shut down the drill," Arnold told him.

"So do I, but we can't, not mere yards from the record. Company would hang us by our asses from a drilling derrick."

"Let them. There's something those fuckers aren't telling us and you know it."

"Attention! We are now fifty feet from history!"

"Let me shut down the drill, Bas," Arnold continued, his voice starting to crack and eyes widening in what was as close to panic as Basmajian had ever seen in him. He kept tugging at his shirt, as if to peel it from the sweat gluing the fabric to his skin.

Basmajian drummed his ring on the deck rail, Arnold left to focus on the two scratched-up letters rising from its center.

"D-S," he said, as much to distract himself as anything. "All these years you never told me what that means."

"Yes, I did, maybe a hundred times. 'Dead Simple.'"

"Not what they stand for, what they mean."

"George . . ."

"No, I get it. It's all about the war and you hate talking about the war. What I'm telling you now is I believe you're gonna have something else you don't want to talk about if you don't give the order to shut down that drill."

"*Twenty-five . . .*"

"*Now*, Bas, before it's too late."

Basmajian looked into Arnold's eyes and imagined his own being just as full of fear.

"*Ten, nine, eight . . .*"

Basmajian grabbed the walkie-talkie clipped to his belt. "Engine room, hold the drill! Repeat, cease operations!"

"*Five, four, three*," the crew recited in cadence, bottles thrust for the sky.

"Engine room, do you copy? Engine room, come in!"

"Two, one!"

"Engine room!" Basmajian blared again, as the drill continued to churn thirty-two-thousand-plus feet below the surface, breaking the *Venture*'s just established record with each spin as the crewmembers dotting the main deck continued to hoot, holler, and dance about the clutter with history tucked in their pockets. "Engine room, do you—"

Basmajian stopped when the alarm bell began to sound. The celebratory crew fell silent in the next moment, Basmajian and Arnold dodging through them for the elevated bridge. The crew's reaction might have been momentarily delayed, but they were an experienced lot to a man, each of whom knew his place in an emergency. They scattered in every direction like ants from a fallen rock.

Basmajian and Arnold reached the bridge to find monitor readings dancing in the red and off the charts, and engineering personnel struggling to make sense of them.

"What's happening?" Basmajian demanded. "Talk to me!"

"We're losing structural integrity on the line!" George Arnold replied, his eyes sweeping over the readouts and computer monitors. "It's breaking apart from the bottom!"

"Trigger the blow-out preventer!"

A technician did just that with a hardly dramatic click of the mouse. Basmajian watched him click the mouse again.

"Nothing, sir," he reported fearfully. "It's, it's . . .

"It's *what*?"

The technician swung his chair toward Basmajian. "Gone, sir."

"What do you mean *gone*?"

The technician could only shrug, Basmajian's attention turning to the four closed-circuit monitors providing varying viewpoints of the seafloor and drilling apparatus from four robotic submersibles, known as ROVs, that could also perform emergency repairs.

All four screens were dark.

"Why are the ROVERs off-line?"

"We lost the signals," said a marine geologist responsible for analyzing and processing the constant stream of data transferred from the submersibles.

"No," said a stone-faced Arnold. "If it were a signal issue, we'd have snow. Since the screens have gone dark, something must have taken the ROVERs out altogether."

Basmajian felt something sink in the pit of his stomach. There was a dreamlike quality to what was transpiring, the impossible unfolding before his eyes. He actually wondered if he was about to wake up from an experience soon to be lost from memory.

A fresh alarm began to wail.

No such luck.

"Something's coming up, sir!" a new voice on the bridge blared. "Something in the line!"

"Shut it down! You hear me? Shut the line down!"

More clicks on a different mouse. "System's not responding, sir! System's not responding!"

"Go to Failsafe!" Basmajian ordered without hesitation.

The eyes of the half-dozen men in the control room swung toward him, aware that triggering that system would destroy everything they'd laid below the surface, turning $10,000,000 worth of equipment into undersea garbage. Only George Arnold responded by slicing his way to the manual Failsafe trigger switch, yanking open the glass seal and pulling down on a handle.

In that moment, the control room crew thought the subsurface rumble was the result of the Failsafe explosives triggering. In that moment, they felt the drill and all beneath it had been killed, that whatever had penetrated the line on a rapid rise to the surface was gone.

But in the next moment the drill housing exploded in a curtain of white flame, more of a flash that crumpled the nearest derrick and tipped it over toward the main deck. Screams penetrated the bridge with a fury that stole Paul Basmajian's breath.

Literally.

Basmajian's last conscious thought was that he couldn't breathe, as if the oxygen had been sucked out of the air—no, it was the air itself. The air was . . . gone.

And then the rest of the world around the *Deepwater Venture* followed it into oblivion.

When the *Venture* failed to respond to radio calls in response to its MAYDAY signal, a pair of F-16s were scrambled out of Barksdale Air Force Base for a flyover. Both pilots had been trained in all areas of emergency response, and their jets were outfitted with the latest generation of rotating cameras to capture both motion and still shots and then transmit them in real time to the Pentagon, NORAD, and Washington headquarters of Homeland Security. The pilots could see exactly what they were transmitting on a console-mounted screen in order to provide a verbal report as well.

The F-16s had been ordered to do a series of crisscrossing flyovers, maintaining a safe distance from each other to assure that both of them could not be knocked out from below by a single attack.

"Base, this is Alpha One," the pilot of the lead jet reported after only a single pass.

"Go ahead, Alpha One."

"Base, we have confirmation of a Level Six event. Repeat, a Level Six event."

A pause followed.

"Alpha One, did you say *Level Six*?"

"That's an affirmative," the pilot replied, keenly aware that the phrase had never before been uttered in anything but drills.

"Alpha One, stand by for further orders and routing instructions and continue transmission."

"Roger that, Base. Standing by and continuing transmission."

"Go with God, Alpha One."

"Looks like He's sitting this one out, Base."

CHAPTER 10

New Orleans

"Something wrong, my friend?"

Roused from his daze, McCracken gazed up at the stout man standing behind the shop's counter. "Just the usual," he lied.

"Because today is your birthday, reason for celebration, not melancholy in spite of the milestone."

"I guess the alternative is worse," McCracken said, trying to smile.

A week had passed since Arturo Morales had been handed over to American authorities and three college students returned to their parents, while a fourth had been lain to rest two days ago.

"Feast your eyes," the man behind the counter was saying. "Have you ever seen anything more beautiful in your life?"

The truth was that McCracken hadn't, glad for the distraction no matter how fleeting. The samurai sword had been polished to such a shine that he could actually see a blur of his distorted reflection. The sword was a true beauty, expertly restored to its original condition from feudal Japan and presented in *shirasaya* without any ornamental trappings. Just a blade that had almost certainly taken its share of lives at the hands of its original owner.

"It dates back to the time of the great Masamune," shop proprietor Levander Levy continued, "and it's signed by a sword maker my historical records indicate was one of the master's actual disciples."

McCracken held the sword by its plain wooden handle that someday would be replaced by one fashioned of ivory and shark skin perfectly sized and fitted to its new owner's hands. Twenty-eight deadly inches and yet it felt feather light in his grasp. Its balance was exquisite, indicative of a truly master sword maker indeed.

"What do you think it's worth?" McCracken asked.

At just over six feet tall, he towered over the diminutive Levy who bore a passing and unfortunate resemblance to the classic actor Peter Lorre. The shop, more of a museum-quality resale store, was located in the Garden District of New Orleans just off the main drag on a side street that sloped slightly upward. McCracken had known "Sir" Levander for any number of years and had serious doubts that he was a "sir" at all, or even a Brit for that matter. That, though, hardly detracted from the quality of the merchandise he'd obtained over the years to add to McCracken's impressive collection of weapons always restored to full working order.

"Worth?" the portly, flabby-cheeked Levy asked, smoothing some stray hair that looked painted onto his scalp back into place. "Impossible to say. I can't even estimate it."

"If you're trying to drive the price up, Lee, you've done it."

Levy looked honestly hurt. "This is my gift to you, my friend, on the occasion of such a momentous birthday."

McCracken wished he could feel happier about that, but even holding such a wondrous gift did little to brighten his mood. The shelves around him were lined with all sorts of historical artifacts, each and every one genuine. Levy seemed to specialize in the eighteenth and nineteenth centuries, and his tastes as well as his inventory ran the gamut from women's jewelry to first-edition novels by the likes of

Thackeray and Eliot, to collectible pieces produced by the finest craftsmen of their time. It left McCracken wondering how Levy's small shop managed to thrive among tourists and revelers who came to New Orleans for different reasons entirely. But he guessed it was supported almost exclusively by private collectors like himself who dabbled in antiquities and maintained an appreciation for historical beauty.

"It's too much," he said, returning the blade to its rectangular wooden saya fitted to its precise specification and handed it back across the counter. "I can't accept it."

Levy took the sword reluctantly, looking even more hurt. "After all you've done for me . . ."

"That was a long time ago, Lee."

"You saved my life. A man tends not to forget such things. You want to speak of gifts? Put a price tag on that one."

"It's what I do, Lee. I never expected anything in return."

"Nor did you ask for it. Yet I have waited all these years for just a occasion like this to repay at least a measure of my debt to you." With that he extended the sword back across the counter. "Please, my friend, I beg you."

"Well, since you put it that way."

Ever since McCracken had saved Levy from modern-day Turkish pirates who promised to kill him if he did not begin moving merchandise on their behalf, the trusty Brit had served as a wonderful source for all things pertaining to weaponry. And not just from a historical perspective either; Levander Levy was also a creative and masterful craftsman in his own right, capable of devising virtually anything McCracken requested made to his precise specifications. That relationship had led Levy to seek McCracken's help after the Turks threatened Levy's family as well, promising to kill his relatives in chronological order starting with the youngest. In response, McCracken and Johnny Wareagle had blown up four of the pirates' boats and left a note on the fifth that blood would follow the flames if Levander Levy wasn't left alone. The pirates never bothered him again.

The little man was smiling behind the counter. “So glad you’ve come to your senses, my friend.”

“I’m gaining a new appreciation for relics,” McCracken told him. “You know, things that are better fit for the past.”

Levy glanced at the samurai sword in McCracken’s grasp. “My good friend, just because something’s old doesn’t mean it can’t still be functional, especially when meticulously restored to its original condition.”

McCracken held his stare on his old friend. “On the surface, you mean.”

“On the contrary, this sword is as sharp and sure as the first time it was wielded.”

“If only the same could be said for flesh and blood, Lee.”

CHAPTER 11

New Orleans

Katie DeMarco had clung to cover provided by the cargo pods, ships, and storage hangars at the Port of New Orleans until there was no sign of the men who'd been waiting when the supply ship returned from the *Deepwater Venture* that morning. She evaded them initially by exiting the ship behind a rolling pallet packed with shipping crates. She took solace only in the fact that at such an early hour it was doubtful her absence from the rig had been noted yet, meaning these were strictly precautionary steps. Men lying in wait for her expected flight, now that the ruse was up. A two-mile-long quay squeezed between Henry Clay Avenue and the Milan Street terminals offered plenty of concealment from the building heat as well, but fleeing the area before her absence from the *Venture* was noted remained her primary goal. Her jeans felt damp and sticky, and perspiration born of the unusual spring humidity glued her T-shirt to her back, while droplets soaked through the front in now widening splotches.

Katie had been aboard the rig for three weeks in the carefully scripted guise of administrative assistant to the operations manager. Yesterday, she'd intercepted a confidential e-mail to his second in command, the rawboned Paul Basmajian, with instructions to detain her; further information to be forthcoming.

Further information . . .

Such information, no doubt, would include a security team dispatched by Ocean Bore to take her into custody. She didn't expect the company to involve the traditional authorities, at least not until ascertaining exactly what she knew about the *Venture*'s strange, if not inexplicable, mission in the Gulf.

Katie had seen the correspondence from Basmajian to Operations requesting clarification about the results of a series of geophysical surveys. If Basmajian's e-mails were to be believed, there was little or no chance of striking oil where the *Venture* had been ordered to drill. Which made no sense and left her wondering if she'd stumbled upon something entirely different from what she'd been expecting upon infiltrating the rig.

Katie was part of the environmental activist group WorldSafe, the group's specialty being to plant environmentalists like her in settings where they could get a firsthand look at how business was conducted in ways that continued to ravage the environment. Her assignment on board the *Deepwater Venture* had started out as routine, but that had changed the moment she'd read Basmajian's series of e-mails demanding an explanation from Ocean Bore headquarters that never came. Cell phones had been strictly prohibited on board the *Venture*, leaving her with no way right now to contact WorldSafe's leader, Todd Lipton, at the group's remote location in Greenland.

Katie DeMarco wasn't her real name, of course, and she couldn't remember now exactly why she'd chosen it. She'd thought about Katie "Black," because of the color of the hair that tumbled past her shoulders. Or Katie "Gray," because of the unusual shade of her eyes. "DeMarco," though, had seemed both generic and somehow romantic at the same time, so she'd gone with that.

Among other attributes, the Port of New Orleans was the nation's premier coffee-handling port with fourteen warehouses and more than five and a half million square feet of storage space. Katie was making her way to that area when she noticed additional teams of uniformed harbor police scouring the docks and pier. Reinforcements, apparently, that could waylay her plans for flight for good.

"Over there!" she heard a voice cry out, followed by the blare of static over a walkie-talkie.

Katie took off, immediately conscious of footsteps pounding in her wake. Quick glimpses to the sides revealed harbor police converging on her from seemingly all angles until she darted into the labyrinthine array of pallets and storage containers packed with coffee and waiting for transport. She dipped one way, then the other, the police concentrated behind her when she spotted the open cargo hold of an eighteen-wheeler, packed with just-delivered bags of freshly harvested coffee beans. The truck was likely bound for New Orleans's Dupuy Storage and Forwarding, home to one of the country's largest bulk-processing operations.

Katie didn't hesitate, launching herself into a mad dash that ended with a leap into the eighteen-wheeler's hold. She stumbled upon landing, turning her ankle but still managing to squeeze herself between a pair of pallets packed to the brim with khaki-colored canvas bags of whole beans. The aroma was richer and stronger than any Starbucks brew she'd ever drunk. Stronger still once the hold door was yanked downward and sealed, plunging Katie into darkness.

She felt the rumble of the engine starting and a jolt as the truck pulled out of the loading line, heading toward the access road. Katie longed for a cell phone, a computer, anything she could use to contact Todd Lipton in Greenland.

Because if Ocean Bore had found her, it could well be they'd found WorldSafe's base as well.

Katie needed to report what she knew to him, some secret mission the *Deepwater Venture* had been on in search of something other than oil.

But what?

CHAPTER 12

New Orleans

Johnny Wareagle was waiting at a table well past the bar inside K-Paul's Louisiana Kitchen on Chartres Street in the French Quarter when McCracken entered. Wareagle rose when he saw him approaching, his knees banging the underside of the table and nearly upending it. He looked distinctly uncomfortable so far from his wooded retreat in Maine, or more recent temporary home in South Dakota, but forced a smile nonetheless.

"Little late for Mardi Gras, aren't you, Indian?" McCracken greeted, unable to disguise how happy he was to see the man he'd known for forty-plus years now. Their friendship dated back to serving in the same Special Forces unit in Vietnam, a covert-ops team specializing in behind-enemy-lines infiltration missions as part of Operation Phoenix. Phoenix had been the CIA and army's dedicated attempt to lift the failing war from the ashes and, from an operational standpoint, it succeeded, though too late to have a measurable effect on the eventual outcome.

The thing that was an endless source of great pride to men like

McCracken and Wareagle, though, was how much the current special-operations community owed to the lessons learned from their work in Operation Phoenix. Vietnam was justly credited with creating the entire concept of Special Forces "A" teams, small groups of professional specialist soldiers who were as attuned to training a local resistance or guerrilla force as they were mixing it up themselves. McCracken and Wareagle were hardly alone among other Vietnam-era SF veterans in marveling at the efforts of their descendants in equally hellish places like Somalia, Iraq, and Afghanistan. Now, like then, most of their work, with the exception of the celebrated SEAL Team 6, went unknown and unnoticed. Covert ops were called that for a reason, after all, and McCracken knew the operators of today willingly shunned the spotlight just as much as he and Wareagle had.

And still did, for that matter.

"But right on time to help celebrate your birthday, Blainey."

McCracken laid the soft case containing the restored samurai sword down across an empty chair. "How'd you know I'd be here?"

"You come to K-Paul's every year on your birthday," Wareagle said, grateful to sit back down so the stares of the crowded restaurant's occupants were no longer drawn to his seven-foot frame.

"Yet you never felt the urge to help me celebrate before."

"This is a special year."

"That because I'm turning sixty or since we lost a hostage last week?"

"We've lost hostages before, Blainey."

McCracken clenched his fists and tapped his knuckles together. "Not with me on the verge of such a momentous occasion we haven't. Not after two years of being away from the game." He picked up his chair to move it farther under the table, then just set it back down again.

"Just what I thought," Wareagle said, nodding.

"What's that?"

"You're still blaming yourself, still failing to consider the three hostages we saved and the fact that all four would've died if we hadn't intervened."

McCracken crossed his arms and gazed across the table at Wareagle who was struggling to find comfort in a chair that wasn't built to accommodate his vast size. "So where's my present?"

"Coming."

"Dancing girl?"

"Better."

"What?"

"The third of us left from the original group." Wareagle hesitated for effect. "Paul Basmajian."

CHAPTER 13

Crazy Horse, South Dakota: One month earlier

Immediately after his initial meeting with Hank Folsom about the hostage college students, McCracken made the trek to Crazy Horse, South Dakota, where Johnny Wareagle had been holed up for months on his latest mission. Not reconnaissance, rescue, or extraction, but the completion of a monument to the greatest Sioux warrior of all time, Chief Crazy Horse.

Once completed it would be the largest sculpture in the world: a granite portrait of the famed warrior on horseback carved, blown, and whittled out of the imposing Black Hills. In scale as well as complexity, the final product would dwarf even the collection of presidential profiles on nearby Mount Rushmore, the portrait's nose alone stretching to twenty-seven feet. Construction had actually started way back in 1948, subjected over the years to endless financial and political setbacks before suffering further stagnation in recent years despite eighty-five full-time staff members dedicated to its construction.

Wareagle's involvement originated in the lack of an accurate rendering of what Crazy Horse actually looked like. Descended from a long line of Sioux warriors, Johnny had been the beneficiary of old drawings picturing subjects from his own warrior lineage standing with the legend himself: his great-grandfather and great-great-grandfather if memory served McCracken correctly. These were deemed the most accurate of any Crazy Horse portraits, with the added benefit of picturing him as both an old and young man, though he looked remarkably similar in both. But the level of Wareagle's contribution changed as soon as he visited the site and proclaimed he could not, would not leave until he saw the portrait out of granite completed.

McCracken had found Wareagle hard at work with hammer and chisel in hand amid the harsh winds and biting temperatures of late winter in South Dakota. He worked without a safety harness or belay on a narrow ledge barely wide enough to accommodate his feet, making McCracken feel almost guilty for hammering a restraining bolt into the face alongside his oldest friend and tying himself down.

"Nice work, Indian."

"It's good to see you too, Blainey."

McCracken felt the cold breeze blow some of Wareagle's etchings into his face. "This your version of retirement?"

"Anything but," Wareagle said, barely looking up from his labor. "Honoring the greatest Sioux of all time reminds me of a legacy I can never totally live up to." He met McCracken's gaze and held it this time. "Crazy Horse was a warrior until his very last day on Earth and I will be too."

"That's good, because we've got a job."

Wareagle glanced at him, but only briefly. "As I figured."

"'Cause why else would I be here."

"It was only a matter of time, Blainey, but this job will still have to wait until I'm finished."

McCracken looked up and around to regard their place amid the massive carving. "I don't think the college students held hostage by a drug cartel in Mexico can wait that long."

Wareagle tensed visibly, then did his best to reposition the chisel before lowering it to face McCracken again. "So you came here to rescue me first."

"An assault rifle or an MK-2 knife would look a lot better in your hand than a hammer."

"Different weapons, different tasks."

"Statues don't bleed, Indian, and granite is plenty harder than flesh and bone."

"You know why I came here?"

"Not really, no."

"To find out if I could stay, to find out how long I could live without that part of me birthed by the Hellfire."

"End result?"

"I knew you'd be coming and in my mind's eye did not welcome your presence. I saw myself turning you away, refusing a return to the world we have so long known."

McCracken shifted on the thin ledge slightly to better face Wareagle. "So here I am."

"And when I got your message, the vision from my mind's eye proved wrong. I felt something stir in the pit of my stomach, a familiar feeling I could not ignore or deny, confronting my true nature."

McCracken again regarded the product of Johnny's labor. "As a warrior instead of an artist, you mean."

"Like the tale of the scorpion and the frog."

"I figured I owed you, Indian."

"Blainey?"

"How many times have you lifted me from a funk with words I didn't fully understand but somehow made things feel right? How many times have you made sense of what we were facing, put it in perspective? So that's what I'm doing, returning the favor."

"Because you feel I've strayed from the path."

"Not in so many words, but that's the general idea. You and I were bred for one thing, Indian—wet work, not art work. Here you are turning the legend of your people into the face of a memorial when the real memorial is how many lives we've saved over the years."

Wareagle smiled thinly. "How many lives this time, Blainey?"

"Four."

"And how many captors?"

"A hundred, maybe more."

And then, undramatically, Wareagle returned the hammer and chisel to his work belt. "The Hellfire all over again."

"Wouldn't have it any other way, would you?"

CHAPTER 14

New Orleans

"Baz?" McCracken asked now. "Is he still working the Gulf? I thought he retired."

"Twice," Johnny Wareagle told him. "But he can't manage the task any more than we can."

"Except he's got the good sense to stay away from guns, drug dealers, hostage rescues, rocket-propelled grenades, Hellfire missiles—should I go on?"

Wareagle seemed unmoved. "It's worked for us for forty years, Blainey."

"Minus the last two." McCracken shook his head. "Why the hell are we still alive? I mean, we've both known soldiers, operatives, operators—whatever you want to call them—who didn't make it through their first field op. We've survived what feels like a thousand of them."

Wareagle settled back in his chair at the K-Paul's table, suddenly pensive. "There is a legend among my people called the Rabbit and the Elk. The rabbit lived with his old grandmother, who needed a new dress. 'I will go out and trap a deer or an elk for you,' he said. 'Then you shall have a new dress.' When he went out hunting, he laid down his bow in the path while he looked at his snares. An elk coming by saw the bow. 'I will play a joke on the rabbit,' said the elk to himself. 'I will make him think I have been caught in his bow string.' He then put one foot on the string and lay down as if dead. By and by the rabbit returned. When he saw the elk, he was filled with joy and ran home crying: 'Grandmother, I have trapped a fine elk. You shall have a new dress from his skin. Throw the old one in the fire!' This the old grandmother did. But when he returned to the snare, the elk sprang to his feet laughing. 'Ho, friend rabbit,' he called, 'You thought to trap me; now I have mocked you.' And he ran away into the thicket. The rabbit who had come back to skin the elk now ran home again. 'Grandmother, don't throw your dress in the fire,' he cried. But it was too late. The old dress was burned."

"Okay," McCracken said, after Wareagle had finished, "I'm waiting."

"For what?"

"The point."

"Among young Sioux, the point of the legend has always been the folly of assumption, of fooling oneself into believing something is what it isn't. We—you, me, Bas—have never suffered from that. We live today because we see the world for what it is and accept our place in it."

McCracken looked at Wareagle across the table, grinning. "Good. Because I was having trouble picturing you in a dress."

Wareagle looked down at the hand that had just set the water glass down on the table. "You're not wearing your ring, Blainey."

"Neither are you."

"The difference being I never do."

"Maybe I don't feel especially worthy of it right now."

Wareagle turned his gaze toward the soft case lying across the extra chair. "How old is the sword?"

"Five hundred years, give or take a decade."

"How old was it yesterday?"

"About the same."

Wareagle leaned back just enough to make his chair creak. "My point exactly."

"What about last week? Believe I was considerably younger before Juárez."

"Why us after so long, Blainey?"

"Suit who came calling said he came to us because we were the only ones who could get it done."

"But you don't believe him."

"I think he came to us because no one else would take the job. Suicide mission."

"Anything but, as it turned out."

"I don't know what's worse, Indian. The feeling we were done or the feeling maybe we should be."

Wareagle leaned forward, so fluidly that his chair didn't make a sound this time. "There's another story my people tell of a Sioux warrior who once defended his tribe single-handedly against a Cherokee raiding party. It was winter and the Cherokees were foraging for food when they came upon the village. But in snow and cold, the Sioux warrior struck them all down. The legend says he covered himself in ice and snow so the Cherokee looked past him into the air. And when it was over, instead of celebrating, he wept. Not out of guilt or remorse, but because there was no one left to kill."

"Did he live to fight another day?"

"The legend doesn't say, Blainey."

"Neither does ours."

CHAPTER 15

New Orleans

Katie DeMarco moved quickly down the sidewalk, cell phone glued to her ear, willing the connection to come through. She knew they'd found her again; spotting jacket-clad men on this blistering hot New Orleans day baking the asphalt beneath a sun-drenched sky was a dead giveaway there, even before she glimpsed them talking into their wrist-mounted microphones when she passed by.

She'd ridden the eighteen-wheeler all the way to the Dupuy Storage and Forwarding facility, climbing down once the cargo door was raised open to the shocked stares of the workers. Katie paid them no heed, just hurried off before they could gather their thoughts.

"Hey! . . . *Hey!*"

She never acknowledged the calls shouted her way, walking until she found a bus stop and climbed onto a bus bound for the nearby downtown district. She stank of coffee, the pungent aroma so imbedded in her nostrils that she couldn't shake it.

Upon reaching the French Quarter, Katie had purchased a throwaway cell phone in a drugstore, stepping outside to find more jacketed figures seemingly talking into their hands directly across the street from her. There was no choice now; she had to risk making the call while she still had the chance, convinced those at the other end were in at least as much danger as she.

Katie dialed Todd Lipton's satellite number, her pace kicked up to a fast walk just short of a jog. She heard a click, followed by a harsh buzzing sound that indicated his phone was ringing in Greenland.

"Hello," Lipton answered finally, through the static bursts clogging the line.

"Todd, it's me."

"Is that you—"

"Don't use my name. It's not safe. None of us are safe."

"You're breaking up. I can hardly hear you. Could you say that again?"

Katie DeMarco moved the phone closer to her mouth, continuing to weave through pedestrian traffic on the sidewalk. "I said you're not *safe*. I think Ocean Bore is on to us."

"I heard 'on to us.' Did you say on to us?"

"Yes, Todd. You need to take—"

"I can't hear you . . ."

"—precautions."

"Precautions? What precautions?"

"I stepped in a load of shit here in the Gulf. I don't know what Ocean Bore is after, but it's big and it's not oil. Repeat, not oil."

"What about oil?"

"Did you hear what I just said? Can you hear me now?"

No response amid the static.

Katie swallowed hard, as she composed her next words. "Listen to me, Todd. They're after me. They know I was on board the *Venture*." Katie waited for him to respond. "Todd, are you there? Can you hear me?"

Silence followed, interminable and empty, that left Katie's mind racing.

"Todd?" she posed, hoping he was still there, the connection intact.

"I heard you say they were after you," his voice returned finally.

"I've got to move. Don't try calling me. I'll call you again as soon as I'm safe."

"Did you say *safe*? Are you in danger? What's going on?"

"Todd, please, there's no time. Just listen!"

"You need to contact Twist," he said instead.

"Todd—"

"He's your backup in New Orleans. He'll help you, he'll . . . "

"Todd, you've got to listen to—"

" . . . get you out of this."

Katie squeezed the phone tighter. "Todd, can you hear me?"

"I can hear you."

"Hide if you can. Flee the village. You're in danger."

Silence again.

"Todd? . . . Todd?"

"Call Twist, call—"

Click.

That was it; the line had gone dead. And the men were closing from both sides and across the street, the phone call having branded her an easy target. She couldn't go back, couldn't continue forward. All she could do was veer suddenly toward a restaurant called K-Paul's on Chartres Street.

CHAPTER 16

New Orleans

McCracken and Wareagle both ordered the blackened Louisiana drum, fish caught just miles away.

"I feel better already," McCracken said, taking a bite of his.

"Have you spoken with the family of the student who died?"

"Now why would I do something like that?"

"Because you'd want them to hear what happened from you, Blainey. You'd want to put a face to the grief to better deal with your own."

"Not yet, no," McCracken said, almost shyly. "But I've got their contact info. Not sure if just showing up on their doorstep is in anyone's best interest. Folsom said he'd handle it, which means it won't happen or be a waste of time. . . . What?" McCracken asked, when Wareagle continue to stare at him in silence.

"It's refreshing."

"What?"

"How you've always valued one life as much as a hundred. In the Hellfire and after."

"Well, Indian, I'm too old to change now." The entry door being thrust open ahead of a young woman bursting through drew his attention immediately that way. "Like I was saying."

She had wavy black hair and eyes that seemed to shine in the restaurant's light. She swung toward the door again as she backed away, as if expecting someone to barge in after her. Keeping her eyes peeled in that direction, she angled for the bar while scanning the room, in search perhaps of an alternative exit.

Just like McCracken would have done if he were being chased.

"You thinking what I'm thinking, Indian?" he asked, aware Wareagle's gaze had been drawn to her as well.

In that moment, a pair of big-shouldered men burst through the restaurant entrance.

"Not our problem, Blainey."

But then pistols flashed in the big-shouldered men's hands.

"It is now," McCracken told him, reaching for the chair across which he'd laid his samurai sword.

Katie DeMarco veered away from the bar when she saw the men coming, steering toward an exit sign posted near the south side of K-Paul's rear just past a similar sign for the restrooms. Coming that way straight toward her, though, were another pair of men who might have been twins of the first pair. Dressed almost identically, their hands were starting to emerge from beneath their jackets.

Katie thought of crying out, screaming, anything to draw attention to herself and stop the coming attack. But the resolve she glimpsed in the men's eyes told her no response that feeble could forestall their intentions. So she turned again, intending to cut through the center of the restaurant, when a man at a table just past the bar whipped out a sword from inside a wooden scabbard, its mirrorlike steel glinting in the naked light of the restaurant.

At that point, McCracken was utterly unsure of his own intentions. He'd always described moments like this as swimming with the currents, letting the flow dictate his actions based on what unfolded before him.

He had just brought the katana overhead when the two men angling for the woman from the bar area halted and steadied their pistols on her.

They're going to fire.

McCracken didn't think, didn't hesitate. Holding fast to the simple wooden handle, he brought the back edge of the blade down hard on both men's wrists at once, catching them totally by surprise. The force of the blow stripped the pistols from their grasps and sent them clanging to the floor, one coughing a bullet through the crowded restaurant on impact.

That was more than enough to send patrons ducking, diving, or scurrying for cover, as McCracken rammed the hilt of the sword's wooden handle hard into the nearer man's forehead. He seemed to fly backward through the air on impact, feet torn from under him until a plate-laden table broke his fall and collapsed beneath him. The second man spun and had the presence of mind to go for a second pistol holstered back on his hip, steel starting to show when McCracken whipped the blade edge outward and caught enough of the man's wrist to open up a deep, nasty gash that left the hand on that side useless.

McCracken couldn't believe the sword's power, as elegant in motion as it was deadly. It felt as though he were wielding air, effortlessly able to slice though bone and flesh and almost difficult to measure his blows enough to avoid severing a limb. And, with the second man's focus rooted on the sword now, McCracken looped in with an elbow that mashed jaw and nose under its force on impact. The man's head whiplashed backward, and he dropped to the floor like a felled tree.

McCracken swung, sword angled anew when screams rang out, and he spotted one of the attackers on Johnny Wareagle's side wheeling about the tables with a huge knife sticking out of his arm.

~

Wareagle had seen the pistol coming up on the raven-haired woman. Knew there was nothing he could do from this distance, other than hurl the blade now grasped in his hand. It twirled through the air in a blur, ultimately piercing the gunman's forearm.

The gunman's pistol fired wildly, severed nerves forcing his hand to lock in place without being able to fire it again since he couldn't make his finger curl back over the trigger. But now the second man on Johnny's side was angling his pistol on the young woman rushing toward an emergency exit in the restaurant's rear, no thought given to the frenzied crowd or the very real possibility that a bullet could just as easily find a bystander. The man simply opened fire, bullets tracing the young woman's path toward the back exit, panicked patrons now blocking Johnny's path to reach the man. Options reduced to one, Wareagle leaped atop one of K-Paul's tables and hopped across others en route to the final gunman who was jamming a fresh magazine home.

From the table nearest him, Wareagle lashed out with a kick that impacted just under his chin, literally lifting the gunman off his feet. He looked as if he were trying to perform a somersault, then hit the floor with his skull breaking his fall.

McCracken watched the final gunman go down, just as a shaft of light shined inside from the open emergency exit through which the raven-haired young woman had disappeared. Before he could even think about pursuing her, a pair of uniformed New Orleans cops burst through the front door with pistols drawn.

"Police!" the older of the two officers screamed, gaze darting between him and Johnny with eyes bulging at the sight of the samurai sword in McCracken's grasp. "Drop to the floor! You hear me, *down on the floor, both of you*!"

McCracken and Wareagle had no choice but to oblige, as sirens wailed in the narrowing distance.

CHAPTER 17

Greenland

"Is there something wrong, Mr. Lipton?"

Todd Lipton looked up from his satellite phone back at the reporter. "Friend of mine's gotten herself in a bit of trouble," he said.

"WorldSafe trouble?" she asked him.

"I came out here to escape these things," Lipton told her, clipping the satellite phone back on his belt.

"I'll take that as a yes," said Beth Douglas, the reporter doing the story on WorldSafe from "an undisclosed location," as she scribbled something down on her notepad. "Can we continue?"

"Please."

"So what are you, Mr. Lipton, the rugged protector of the world's natural resources or an environmental terrorist?"

Lipton ran a hand through his nest of thick black hair, which was a perfect match for his long beard. "That's a rather extreme distinction."

"Then let me rephrase the question," Douglas offered. "Is World-Safe's reputation deserved or are you denying responsibility for the attacks on several alleged polluters?"

"I categorically deny being involved in any crime. How's that?"

Beth Douglas scribbled some more, didn't respond. Lipton watched, trying to read what she was writing and starting to question the strategy of consenting to this interview. But money was low and the article was certain to aid the new fund-raising efforts currently under way for the group.

Right now he found himself more concerned about Katie DeMarco and would have to overcome the distraction, as well as resist the temptation to call her back as many times as it took to get a clear line. She had used the word *danger*, warned him to flee and hide. No easy task since the team had based itself in the obscure fishing village of Qepertarsuag in Greenland amid rolling hills, crystal water, and lush greenery. It was a place time itself had forgotten. But none of the natives seemed to mind, and certainly Lipton and his people didn't either. Going back to living off the unspoiled land was exactly what they were about. The locals were friendly and welcoming and refused to take a single cent to allow WorldSafe to base their camp within a grove of trees in view of the water's edge between the village's rustic royal blue church and the start of the sloping hillside that held many of the homes of its residents.

"Mr. Lipton?"

"What? Er, sorry. You were saying . . ."

"I was asking if you consider yourself part of Greenpeace."

"No. We broke away years ago when the politics got to be a bit much. And too high an amount of the funds Greenpeace raised went to administrative costs—salaries, in other words. As you can see, Ms. Douglas," Lipton continued, pointing at the modest camp around them, "we spend our money to support our cause, not fatten our wallets."

Douglas seemed to like that quote, underlining it after she'd jotted it down, while Lipton scratched at his beard.

"How would you describe the differences with which you operate?" she asked him.

"Well, while our goals are similar to Greenpeace's, WorldSafe's methods are neither as confrontational nor as militant. Instead our organization has come to rely on infiltration and embedment to uncover truths that simple sign wagging and protests could never reveal. Information makes for a much better weapon than sabotage and, thanks to the web, the revelations we uncover are able to reach the widest possible audience."

"So you deny involvement in any of the violent actions that have been taken against your targets?"

"Categorically, Ms. Douglas. And we don't 'target' anyone; we merely expose the truth."

"People died in those attacks, Mr. Lipton, a number of them. Over twenty."

"Maybe you should ask Greenpeace about their involvement. The closest we've ever come to aggression is launching a computer virus or two," he said, trying for a smile but failing to muster one.

"And yet," Beth Douglas continued, "the nearest Internet access is a ninety-minute drive from here."

"We also have no electricity, plumbing, or running water. Our members here live in two-hundred-square-foot eco-shacks formed of thinly insulated corrugated metal that take about a half day to assemble. Not a lot of room for anything except a pair of fold-down bunks, but the simple lifestyle we prefer doesn't call for much at all."

"Are you worried about your enemies finding you here?"

"We don't have enemies, Ms. Douglas, only corporations that don't like the truth exposed."

"And if they decided to retaliate?"

"I fully expect they'd do so in a court of law."

"Difficult to adjudicate your actions in an American court with you based in Greenland now."

"That thought had crossed my mind," Lipton said with a wink, at his most gracious and charming, even though he couldn't get his mind off whatever had befallen Katie. "What do you say we continue our tour of the site?"

"I need to send a text first," Beth Douglas told him, Android phone already in hand.

Lipton turned away, thinking of Katie DeMarco again as the reporter typed a simple message:

IT'S A GO. SEND THEM IN.

CHAPTER 18

New Orleans

McCracken used his one phone call at the police precinct to which he and Johnny Wareagle had been taken to dial Hank Folsom's number at Homeland Security in Washington.

"Guess who?" he greeted, after Folsom answered his emergency private line.

"McCracken?"

"Time to return that favor you owe me, Washington."

"That's not my name."

"No, just your city and you're all the same to me."

"And you want a favor?"

"Little entanglement down here in New Orleans I need you to extricate me from."

"So you've heard . . ."

McCracken caught the edge in Folsom's voice. "Heard what?"

The man from Homeland cleared his throat, clearly caught having said too much. "This isn't a secure line. That's as far as this goes."

"As far as *what* goes?"

"Just tell me where you are, McCracken. Homeland's been looking for you."

Folsom wouldn't say what for, asking instead for the details on what exactly McCracken and Wareagle had gotten themselves embroiled in.

"You're not making any of this up?" he asked at the end.

"Nope."

"Even the part about the samurai sword? No, never mind. I think I get it now."

"Get what, D.C.?"

"How you came by that famous nickname of yours—McCrackenballs. You still know how to crack them, don't you?"

"In this case I could have sliced a few off, but chose not to. I'm getting discreet in my old age."

"Tell that to the Mexican authorities. Your actions down there caused a diplomatic nightmare."

"Department of State's problem, not Homeland's."

"Get back to this woman in the restaurant," said Folsom. "What else can you tell me about her?"

"I've told you everything already. Never saw her before in my life. She runs into K-Paul's chased by four thugs determined to kill her."

A pause followed during which McCracken could hear Folsom breathing. "You're certain about that?"

"Shots were fired, Capitol."

"Can you just call me by my name?"

"Sure, Hank, or would you prefer junior? Your father was in I-Corps back in the day before he landed that cushy diplomatic gig. Following in his footsteps, are you?"

"Touché."

"You really think I'd work for a man without checking him out?"

"You weren't working for me."

"Sure, Hank, whatever you say."

"Tell me more about these four men."

"All currently hospitalized and sure to be out of custody before you file your next memo."

"And how's that exactly?"

"Someone's pulling strings, someone who knows how to make problems go away in a hurry."

"That's a pretty big assumption, McCracken."

"Is it, Hank? How about I bet you your pension that they're free by the time the hospital finishes stitching them back together?"

"You're making this into something bigger than it is."

"Right, my lousy judgment's why you came to me in the first place to rescue those frat boys."

"I came to you because I knew you were the only one who could get it done and I was right."

"Now tell me why Homeland's looking for me again."

Folsom hesitated for a moment before responding. "Because of a friend of yours named Paul Basmajian."

McCracken felt himself stiffen, Wareagle sensing the change immediately in his demeanor. "He's a lot more than a friend, Hank."

"So I gathered." Folsom hesitated, the sound of his breathing filling the line. "He's missing, along with an entire hundred-man crew from an offshore oil rig called the *Venture*."

McCracken felt like someone had struck him hard everywhere at once. For a moment the words didn't come and, when they finally did, it felt as if someone else was speaking them.

"If they were just missing, Hank, if there'd been an accident or an attack, Homeland wouldn't need Johnny and me. That means there's got to be more."

"Oh, there is," Folsom told him, "a lot more. You know what a Level Six event is?"

"No. Must be a term that came up since I went on hiatus. Enlighten me."

"Let me put it this way. Level Five is a nuclear attack. Does that give you a clear enough idea?"

McCracken felt his pulse rate increasing. "You're talking a potential threat to the entire country."

"Not quite, McCracken. Try the world."

CHAPTER 19

Greenland

Lipton was glad when Beth Douglas finally left, allowing him to turn all his attention back to Katie DeMarco, but finding himself increasingly unnerved when he remained unable to get through.

What if someone had jammed her phone . . . or his?

Katie's message, rendered cryptic by the terrible signal, had left Lipton's neck hairs standing on end. With night having fallen now, and WorldSafe hardly seeing the need to assign a security guard to watch over the camp, Lipton decided to check the grounds for possible trouble himself.

"I said you're not safe. I think Ocean Bore is on to us."

Katie DeMarco's words continued to unnerve him as he stepped out of his eco-shack into the crystal clear night air. Amazing what real air smelled and looked like, Lipton thought. People often laughed at him when he insisted air could look like anything. They just didn't understand how much ugly light shed by cities and towns did to detract from what the unspoiled world should be. Entertainment here came instead from the majestic brilliance of a star-filled sky, never looking the same from one night to the next. And had WorldSafe based their camp farther to the north of the world's largest island, they would have found themselves in the land of the Midnight Sun, capable of enjoying daylight all day long during the summer months.

Lipton had started his check of the encampment's perimeter, the eco-shacks placed where flat land allowed, when he spotted something out of place by the water's edge. Out of place because he didn't recall it being there earlier when the sun had still been up. Traipsing through the brush toward the shoreline, he figured it was likely a fisherman's dinghy, beached with the man's own camp likely not too far from WorldSafe's.

Drawing closer to the currents gently lapping up onshore, though, Lipton saw it wasn't a dinghy at all, but some kind of sleek black craft left in the camouflage of darkness only to be betrayed by a sliver of moonlight. A Zodiac, an inflatable model stretching nearly eighteen feet in length, outfitted with an aluminum floor, Decitex speed tubes, and a sleek outboard motor.

Lipton felt himself shiver, even though the night wasn't cold at all. This was Zodiac's assault model, a favorite of the Special Forces.

His senses sharpened, hearing and sight suddenly more attuned. He could only hope the group that had come on the Zodiac had reconnoitered somewhere else, giving Lipton enough time to get his people to safety. He touched the engine, finding some solace in the fact that it was still warm, indicating they hadn't been onshore for long.

"Hide if you can. Flee the village. You're in danger."

Fighting against panic, he reminded himself to stick to darkness and brush cover in taking a circuitous path back to the WorldSafe camp. His plan was to sneak into the outlying eco-shacks and rouse their occupants first to enlist them to help in the process down the line. With luck, any luck, they'd be able to evacuate the camp before whoever had come in the Zodiac stormed the camp.

You're in danger.

Lipton could only pray Katie DeMarco's warning hadn't come too late. He reached the first eco-shack, fortunately occupied by an ex-marine named Ben Holcomb. Lipton slipped through the open door and slid toward Ben's cot in the darkness.

"Ben," he said softly before he got there. "Ben, it's me, Todd." Lipton leaned over to gently rouse the ex-marine with a shake of his shoulder. Then a bit less gently when this failed to do the trick. "We've got prob—"

Lipton's words lodged in his throat when Holcomb's neatly severed head rolled off the cot and plopped to the floor. The air was thick with the coppery scent of blood, and Lipton had no idea why he hadn't noticed it until now. He stifled a scream, stuck part of his hand in his mouth, and started to backpedal from the murdered man's shack.

Pffft . . . pffft . . . pffft . . .

Lipton had heard suppressed gunfire before only in movies and that's exactly what it sounded like here in the camp now. The discomforting sound jostled his senses enough to make him twist from Holcomb's shack with a start, the night suddenly alive with orange muzzle flashes fired by black shapes standing in the doorways of six more of the eco-shacks. The screams that followed seemed to have a delayed reaction, as if the members of WorldSafe had to wake up before realizing they were being killed. More dark shapes slithered about the trees and brush, one with the night.

Todd Lipton was no hero, not even close, and even if he had been, there was no weapon on God's green earth that could be an equalizer against such a force. A hero, no, but a thinker always, and now his thoughts propelled him back into the night toward the shoreline and his only chance:

The Zodiac.

It didn't occur to him that he was abandoning his people in cowardly fashion, because he could do nothing for them now other than help avenge their deaths and likely Katie DeMarco's too. The Zodiac not only provided his means of flight, but it would also deny the killers the means to pursue him.

Lipton broke into a sprint as soon as the relatively flat ridge dropped into a slope that would hide him from sight. The Zodiac was in plain view when an exposed tree branch tripped him up and sent pain shooting through his right ankle. He hit the ground hard, landing on his chin with enough force to rattle his teeth and jaws. Lipton crawled through the saw grass toward the shore, chewing down the pain, feeling the sand finally under the pads of his fingers and then palms.

Then he saw the black, tightly laced boots directly before him.

Lipton didn't look up, not wanting to see the man attached to them. Just closed his eyes and pressed his face into the ground, hoping it wouldn't hurt.

CHAPTER 20

New Orleans

"Gentlemen," Coast Guard Captain Merch began in a deep southern drawl, greeting McCracken and Wareagle in the ready room after Hank Folsom had arranged passage for them to the cutter *Nero* at the Port of New Orleans from police custody, "I don't know who you are or what the hell your stake is in a Level Six. But all this makes about as much sense as a dog driving through a traffic light."

"Why don't you start with anything you can tell us about the *Venture*'s crew," McCracken said, thinking of Paul Basmajian.

"I'm sorry, sir, I can't. Not because I don't want to, but because I don't know, not a damn thing."

"Then tell us what you do know."

"F-16s out of Barksdale made the call and rightly so five hours ago. Homeland Security assumed jurisdiction and next thing I know the Coast Guard's local command center is overrun with plain-faced men who don't bother with introductions or anything traditional like showing an ID. I guess that means this is now all yours. We've been relegated to the sidelines to follow your lead, which suits me just fine 'cause whatever's going on here is way out of my league, *anybody's* league. Explains why they called you, I guess."

"They called us because we've got a friend on board."

"Had."

"Talk to me in English, Captain."

"So what exactly did the button-downs from Homeland tell you?"

"Nothing," McCracken told him, as Johnny Wareagle looked on in silence.

"Sounds like they treat all their people with the same consideration they give grunts like me."

"We're not their people, Captain."

"You always get the call when so much shit hits the fan the blades jam up?"

"Used to. We're kind of retired now. Isn't that right, Indian?"

"Not so much anymore it would seem, Blainey."

"What the big fella means," McCracken picked up, "is that we're here because we were told a friend of ours running a deepwater oil rig is missing along with his entire crew. If you've got more to say on the subject, let's hear it."

At that point, Merch switched on a wide-screen television monitor and started working the keys of a wireless laptop computer. "Here's satellite imagery taken of the *Deepwater Venture* this morning at ten hundred hours when it was about to break the record for a deepwater drilling rig."

A number of images rotated across the screen, each picturing scenes typical to someone who understood the workings on board an oil rig.

"And here's satellite imagery starting seventeen minutes later," Merch continued, working fresh keys on his laptop.

This satellite image pictured the *Venture*'s entire structure immersed in a white cloud like nothing either McCracken or Wareagle had ever seen before. Almost like the white squalls of legend known to spring up out of nowhere and disappear just as fast. The next image showed an eruption of light like that of a giant flashbulb.

The third showed a burst of what looked like white-hot flames that had burned out by the fourth image.

"What's the time lapse between shots?" McCracken asked.

"Just over six seconds."

McCracken exchanged a glance with Wareagle, both of them awaiting Merch's next words.

"Either of you boys care to tell me what kind of fire burns out in six seconds?"

"This wasn't a fire," McCracken told him.

"Come again?"

"You heard me, Captain."

"But you haven't heard the bridge tapes yet. Soon as they triggered the blowout preventer, automated audio transmission began via an emergency channel. Unfortunately, it makes no more sense than anything else we've got here."

"Give us the short version."

"Okay: they were dealing with something they couldn't make any more sense out of then than we can now."

Merch put on a pair of reading glasses to consult the transcript on his laptop, highlighting the portion he wanted to play before hitting the Enter key. With that, a series of scratchy unidentified voices rose through the laptop's tiny speakers.

"Something's coming up, sir! Something in the line!"

"Shut it down! You hear me? Shut it down!" Paul Basmajian's voice, provoking an eerie chilled feeling in McCracken.

"System's not responding, sir! System's not responding!"

"Go to Failsafe!"

The highlighted portion completed, Merch said, "Apparently Failsafe didn't work either."

"Play the recording again, Captain," McCracken requested.

And this time he reached over and stopped it after *"Something's coming up, sir! Something in the line!"*

"I'm open to ideas, gentlemen," said Merch.

"How deep were they?" Wareagle asked.

"Just past thirty-two thousand feet. New record, like I said."

"A whole other world," Wareagle followed, words aimed more at McCracken. "The Sioux always looked to the sky for their legends and mysteries in times past. They could just as easily have been looking toward the seas."

"In other words, Captain," McCracken said, "right now your guess is as good as ours. Have any of your people gotten up close and personal with what's left of the rig?"

Merch shook his head. "No, sir, just reconnaissance from afar. Those were our orders. I can tell you the air checks out fine. I can tell you there are no contaminants or toxins whatsoever. But I can also tell you there's no one on board left alive, no trace anyone was ever there at all. It's like the whole crew just vanished." Merch scratched at the bridge of his nose, leaving a blotchy red mark behind. "What I can't tell you is what happened to them or how a fire, or whatever the hell it was, leaves no sign of burning or charring. Just . . ."

"What?"

"Better you see for yourself, sir."

"Fine. When do we leave for the rig?"

Merch hesitated before answering. "There's something else you need to consider first."

"What's that, Captain?"

"A Level Six runs the gamut anywhere between extinction event to alien invasion. In other words, a threat like nothing else we've ever faced before."

"Also nothing new for Johnny and me."

"Then consider this: maybe whatever did this to your friend and the others is still on that rig."

CHAPTER 21

Northern Gulf Stream

The Bell 430 helicopter sliced through the sky over the neat blue ribbon of the Gulf below. Storm clouds gathering to the south and east, meanwhile, darkened the horizon ominously and similarly darkened McCracken's mood once more.

They soared over the perimeter the Coast Guard had set up a mile around the *Deepwater Venture* with cutters, crash ships, and patrolling helicopters. Drawing closer, McCracken and Wareagle could see that the rig's tension leg platform, superstructure, and massive support columns were still intact, the *Venture* left stable by whatever had befallen it. Her main deck was something else again. McCracken felt his breathing go thick and labored, slogging up his throat as the first of the carnage left behind by whatever had destroyed the rig came into clear view.

The deck looked to be a molten mass of bubbled steel, with no evidence of char or any residue typical of a massive blaze.

"You said you checked for airborne contaminants and toxins?" McCracken raised.

"Yes, sir, we did and found no trace whatsoever," Merch told him. "But I've been advised you need to wear hazmat suits, masks, and breathing apparatus."

"What about something organic?"

"Wait a minute," Merch said, adjusting his headphones in the Bell 430, "you suggesting something *alive* was responsible for this?"

McCracken and Wareagle exchanged a glance, both of them thinking the same thing.

"Something's coming up, sir! Something in the line!"

"I'm not saying anything. I'm only asking."

"Then let me answer you. No, nothing on this earth could've done what we're looking at down there."

"You mean nothing we know of."

The helicopter settled a safe distance over the deck well away from either of the *Venture*'s two vacant helipads.

"No way to be sure they're stable enough to handle the weight," Merch told them. "We're going to have to winch you down, as long as you don't have a problem with that."

McCracken exchanged a glance with a grinning Wareagle. "Captain, the Indian and I have spent most of our adult lives being dropped into hot LZs by helicopter, so I don't think we have any problem with a nice comfortable ride downward. What about that tech expert I requested?"

"En route now, sir. Turned out he was close by in the Florida panhandle collecting jellyfish. Any idea why?"

"My guess is because panhandle jellyfish are incredibly toxic. The captain is a specialist in weapons development."

"Jellyfish?"

"*Nontraditional* weapons development," McCracken told Merch.

"Look, sir, I'm told Homeland has its own experts on pretty much everything scientific standing by."

"My man has a reputation for solving the unsolvable, and he's no stranger to the bizarre or the danger that comes with it."

"Vietnam?"

"And every war since."

Merch consulted his clipboard. "I think we may have written his name down wrong."

"What have you got?"

"Seven. No first name. Just Captain Seven."

McCracken couldn't help but smile at the thought of the captain's imminent arrival. "Right as rain." His eyes focused on the shape of the *Deepwater Venture*, growing as they neared it. "You ever play with Erector sets when you were a kid?" he asked Wareagle.

"Only if I could make them out of what the reservation had to offer."

"I did. Imagined myself building superstructures of steel. Problem was I didn't like following directions, preferring instead to either re-create intricate real-life structures from pictures or conjure up something totally on my own. Except there were never enough parts to finish what I started. I threw a tantrum once and stomped my erected concoction into the floor, pounded the pieces with my shoe until I couldn't recognize them anymore."

"Nice childhood memory," Merch quipped.

"Comes to mind because that's what the deck of the *Venture* reminds me of. Like some giant crushed the hell out of it."

"Then what did he do with the people, Blainey?" Wareagle asked him.

"Guess we'll find out soon enough."

The bulky hazmat suit made it a chore for McCracken to belt himself into the harness even before he felt the stiff Gulf winds pushing up against the chopper, forcing it into a wobble.

"Just got word that storm we've been tracking has picked up speed, Mr. McCracken," Captain Merch reported. "So whatever you boys are gonna do down there, you better do it fast."

McCracken clipped the harness cable to the winch line and positioned himself at the now open hatch door.

"A microphone's built into your helmets. You need to stay in touch. Regularly. I can't stress that enough."

As if to punctuate Merch's instruction, McCracken noticed a pair of F-16s overhead, mere specks thousands of feet up but in a circling pattern he knew all too well.

"They've got their orders too, sir," Merch said, noting his gaze. "And if anything happens to you down there, those fighters are gonna splash the whole damn rig."

CHAPTER 22

Pyrenees Mountains, Spain

"I trust you had a pleasant flight, Mr. Landsdale," the man named Pierce said, leading Thomas Landsdale toward the entrance to the vast compound that was virtually invisible even from directly above.

It had been built to conform perfectly to the landscape and flora around it. Impressive in all respects, its sprawl was difficult to estimate in terms of square footage, but it was an architectural marvel in any event. Landsdale couldn't take his eyes off the way stilts formed of woods native to these mountains supported those portions that hung out over a bottomless void, defying gravity and nature.

The helicopter had repeatedly battled the blistering crosswinds that were a fixture this high in the Pyrenees Mountains, before finally lurching to a landing that left one of its pods dangerously close to the edge of the helipad. Landsdale felt the queasiness in his stomach begin to abate almost immediately and couldn't help but marvel at how even a man as wealthy as Sebastian Roy could have managed such an effort with no accessible roads anywhere nearby.

But Landsdale quickly remembered the purpose of his being summoned here and steeled himself again to the task before him.

The main crest of the Pyrenees where Roy had constructed his compound straddled the border between France and Spain in what was actually the tiny country of Andorra. As a naturalist, Landsdale appreciated that the Pyrenees were older than the Alps, their sediments first deposited in coastal basins during the Paleozoic and Mesozoic eras. The massive and unworn character of the chain came from its abundance of granite, which was particularly resistant to erosion, as well as weak glacial development. And somehow, in a way unknown to any but the most expert eye, Sebastian Roy had managed to erect a structure that looked formed out of that rock itself. One with nature, making for an absurd irony given his penchant for destroying it.

The man named Pierce led Landsdale past a bevy of strategically posted armed guards and into the fortresslike compound. Pierce was a stout, slightly portly man with thinning hair in stark contrast to the tall, lanky, and athletically obsessed Landsdale, whose weight and waist hadn't changed since high school. A pair of guards armed with assault rifles trailed them at a discreet distance as they climbed a pair of ornate staircases to the top floor where two more guards were posted.

"How much do you know about Mr. Roy, Mr. Landsdale?" Pierce asked him.

"I know I'm not selling him my company, no matter the price."

"I was speaking of a personal nature."

"Rumors or truth?"

"Take your pick."

"I'm only familiar with the rumors. That he went mad, or died, or had himself cytogenetically frozen but his brain is still functional."

"Rumors."

"That he hasn't spoken to the media in decades, that Roy Industries is one of the ten most profitable companies in the world thanks to its energy holdings, and Sebastian Roy himself is one of the five richest men."

"Truth," said Pierce.

"And that he's made his fortune with no regard for the environment. That he's destroyed millions of acres of forestland the world over, polluted huge portions of the oceans, ravaged the ecosystem, and weakened or eradicated the food chains of thousands of species and subspecies vital to the intrinsic survival of our planet."

"Absurdities," noted Pierce, unmoved by Landsdale's litany of allegations. "What you really need to know is this. Several years ago, there was a fire in a Roy Industries plant reserved for fossil fuel enhancement in Stuttgart, Germany."

"I think I participated in the protest held outside it," Landsdale recalled, coming up just short of a grin.

If the lame attempt at humor affected Pierce, he didn't show it. "The fire was the result of sabotage, terrorism. This is no laughing matter."

"My apologies," Landsdale stammered.

"Mr. Roy's wife, daughter, and son were killed. Mr. Roy was badly burned after rushing back into the blaze to save them. Are you familiar with chronic venous insufficiency, or CVI?"

"A condition that impedes wound healing, I believe."

"Infection caused it in Mr. Roy's case. There is treatment, but no cure, treatment Mr. Roy has been forced to make allowances for."

"I don't think I understand what—"

"You will," Pierce said, as they reached the third floor.

CHAPTER 23

Pyrenees Mountains, Spain

Landsdale felt cold as they moved down a hall on the compound's top floor toward a door that looked more like a bank vault. He wasn't sure if the sudden chill was the result of the lingering effects of the misty mountain air, his trepidation over his coming audience before Sebastian Roy, or something else entirely. It was the latter Landsdale opted for when they reached the vaultlike door, certain the temperature had dropped appreciably in air totally devoid of humidity.

"This is a hyperbaric chamber," Pierce explained. "Mr. Roy's condition requires that he venture beyond it only for the briefest intervals possible to forestall any further spread of infection from his wounds." With that he reached up to the wall and plucked a surgical gown encased in a plastic sleeve. "If you don't mind, Mr. Landsdale."

Landsdale tore open the plastic and pulled the gown over his clothes, tightening the sash in the back before fitting gloves upon his hands and then a surgical mask over his mouth.

Pierce watched, satisfied, then punched in the proper code. Landsdale heard a loud click as the heavy door eased mechanically open. Pierce bid him to enter and Landsdale was struck instantly by the intensity of the chill, like that of a room with the air-conditioning turned up too high.

The chamber wasn't really a chamber at all, so much as an elegant suite of rooms dominated by a large window overlooking the mountain range beyond, which stretched to the horizon. The room was decorated much like the library of an English manor house, rich in wood and leather, with faux flames burning in an ornamental fireplace, ornamental because Landsdale was certain the fire gave off no heat.

An alcove lay on the far side of the hearth, lit by recessed ceiling-mounted floods. Landsdale found himself drawn by the soft lighting and entered the alcove to find himself surrounded by a magnificent floor-to-ceiling collection of artifacts dominated by jars, urns, and vases that looked, even to his novice eyes, like the products of ancient Greece. Several commanded his eye, especially one brilliantly colored in red and adorned with lavish golden designs.

"Impressive, isn't it?"

The voice took him aback and Landsdale swung to find Sebastian Roy standing at the entrance to the alcove suspended, it seemed, between darkness and light.

"That's called the Euphronios krater. Such a krater, or vase or bowl as we'd call it, was used in ancient Greece for mixing wine and water. This one was fashioned by Euphronios himself, a legendary artist of the sixth century B.C. who signed the vessel as did the potter who fashioned it." Roy stepped farther inside the alcove, denying Landsdale a clear look at him in the subtle half-light. "One side depicts Hermes directing Sleep and Death as they transport Sarpedon, a son of Zeus, to Lycia for burial; the other side shows young warriors arming for battle."

Even in the dim lighting, Landsdale could see Roy smile tightly. "Is the latter destined to be a metaphor for our meeting today?"

"I wouldn't be here if I believed that, Mr. Roy."

"Nor would I have summoned you here, if I wasn't convinced an accommodation couldn't be struck."

"How gratifying," Landsdale said, even more uncomfortable than he had been before.

Roy came up alongside him in front of the Euphronios krater, a smell of something sharp, antiseptic, and vaguely spoiled wafting through the air now. "You see before you, Mr. Landsdale, the greatest individual collection of Greek artifacts, specifically urns and jars, in the world. Many have been acquired through exhaustive efforts with archaeological brokers normally used to dealing with museums. Others, the bulk in fact, came to me in the wake of a suspicious fire at the Archaeological Museum at Agrigento, Italy, and a flood at a comparable facility outside of Athens."

Sebastian Roy let that final comment hang in the air between them, his eyes tightening in intensity before relaxing again.

"Do you have a favorite, Mr. Landsdale?"

"All of them, really."

"Pick one."

Landsdale pointed to the next artifact to which his eyes were drawn, a deceptively simple jar stitched with strange symbols that seemed woven into the fired clay. Easily the largest by far in Roy's exquisite collection, the jar stood almost four feet in height. As far as Landsdale could tell in the meager spill of light, the jar's shape ended where its lid should have been.

"This," he said.

"Interesting choice. A mystery, a puzzle, dating back to a thousand B.C. or even before. The symbols are believed to be a lost language of the early Minoans no one's ever been able to translate. Did you notice it has no lid, no top to remove? Quite unprecedented, perhaps best explained by the simple fact that the man who forged it made a mistake. Save for that, I'd venture to say it's one of my collection's simplest pieces. Is that why you chose it, Mr. Landsdale?"

"I chose it because it caught my eye."

"Then perhaps you're attracted by simplicity in general, that which can be easily explained and isn't too challenging. Look around you. Virtually all the other items in my collection, and others that fill museums and art galleries all over the world, are prized not for their historical importance but for the scene they depict. Ancient Greek craftsmen used urns to depict narratives of gods and goddesses, along with wars and other significant events. Turning an urn or jar to read its story is akin to unrolling a scroll and seeing the narrative unfold. And yet this jar that has caught your eye tells no story at all, a blank slate. Like you perhaps."

Landsdale looked away from Sebastian Roy, his gaze drawn back to the jar.

"Come, sir," Roy said, leading the way from the alcove back into the spacious great room.

Once the brighter light struck Roy, Landsdale spotted the gauze wrapping peeking out from the arms of his perfectly tailored, truly exquisite suit. His motions looked labored, pained, Landsdale's imagination left to concoct what awful unhealed wounds may have lain beneath the tropical wool. Roy's face was remarkably untouched, his sallow skin tone glowing with a sheen of moisturizer he used to combat the chamber's oxygen-rich dry air.

"For the reasons Mr. Pierce explained to you," Roy resumed, "I must keep my time outside this chamber to a bare minimum. So, in large part to compensate, I've surrounded myself with treasures that remind me of the beauty in the world I can never see firsthand again. Strange, isn't it, how much you learn to live without when you are given no choice?"

Landsdale caught that dark glint in Roy's gaze again, chose to remain silent.

"You should feel honored," Roy said to him, his tone the same and yet more conciliatory at the same time. "For obvious reasons I have very few guests. But we've never met and I felt this was the opportune time."

"I appreciate the courtesy, but—"

"You say 'but' with no knowledge of what I intend to say."

"My companies are not for sale, Mr. Roy," Landsdale said, feeling his spine stiffen.

He was shivering slightly from both the temperature in the room and the fact that he'd come to realize that Sebastian Roy looked above all else like a perfectly preserved corpse. His skin was pale, his cheeks sunken. Beyond that, he appeared not to have aged a day since pictures taken of him from before the explosion and fire that had killed his family seven years before, his face the spitting image of the visage that had once graced the covers of *Time*, *Fortune*, and *Money* within a two-month span. To Landsdale's knowledge, Roy had given only a single interview since then, to an antiquities and architectural magazine of all things, choosing a life apart from humanity in this mountain fortress he'd had constructed at incredible expense.

"Everything's for sale," Roy said, smiling so tightly the expression looked more like a sneer, before the smile vanished as quickly as it had appeared. "And everything has a price."

CHAPTER 24

Pyrenees Mountains, Spain

"What do you know about my company, Mr. Landsdale?" Roy continued.

"I know all its various subsidiaries champion the very sources of energy I've been waging war on all my career. I know you have no problem destroying the environment to fuel, no pun intended, your profit motive."

Roy clapped his hands dramatically.

"Nice speech. But I notice you left out the fact that the need for energy is growing at an exponential rate in direct contrast to the drain on available supply. You talk a good game, Mr. Landsdale, but I wonder if you'll still talk that way when the lights won't turn on and there's nothing to heat your home with."

"Oh, there will be such times," Landsdale said. "On that much we agree. The source is where we differ and I don't see much middle ground there."

"Of course you don't—I never expected you to. After all, you are the foremost party involved in green and renewable energy. You've been investing in it for decades, way ahead of the curve, starting literally with the first paycheck you ever received. So many of your contemporaries laughed at your obsession and excess."

"But they're not laughing now," Landsdale reminded.

"Indeed," Roy agreed. "When the world finally smartened up, you were positioned to reap the lion's share of the rewards. Your companies run the gamut of solar, wind, and water power. One of your companies just won an exclusive contract to manufacture the batteries that power every electric or hybrid car manufactured inside the United States. And you control no less than two hundred patents on emerging technology you believe will form the next generation of alternatives to the fossil fuels that, let me see if I can quote you properly here, 'had raped the environment and threatened to destroy the planet as Roy Industries seems inclined to do.' How's that?"

"Close enough."

"You have my admiration and respect, and I don't believe our aims or our methods are as disparate as you think." Roy hesitated long enough to hold Landsdale's gaze. "I'm prepared to prove that to you in a tangible way by offering you a hundred and fifty percent of the market value of your companies in an amicable merger that will leave you as president with a seat on the board."

"I'm not interested."

"Maybe you don't fully understand the terms."

"I understand them perfectly. I didn't come here to sell or negotiate."

"I have no interest in negotiations either," Roy told him. "What's the point if the original offer is as fair as mine is? Life is too short to mince words or play games. It's like that Minoan jar that so caught your attention. It has survived more than three thousand years, but if I were to drop the jar, it would shatter into a hundred unrecognizable pieces." Roy hesitated to better make his point. "Life is just as fragile, Mr. Landsdale. I believe we've both learned that the hard way. You've experienced your own share of hardship, haven't you? That daughter recently diagnosed with Huntington's disease, for example."

Landsdale's mouth dropped above his lowered surgical mask. "How could you know that?"

"You mean because you only found out recently yourself? You mean because the only way I could know was if I had access to your daughter's private medical records which, of course, should be impossible? Anyway, I'm sorry too. So we have that much in common. I was hoping we could find more."

"What makes you think there's any chance of that?"

"Because in spite of our differences, Mr. Landsdale, we want the same thing: energy for all at the lowest price possible."

"And in your mind at the expense of the environment."

"I didn't invite you here to rehash old arguments."

"No? Did you think I'd have a sudden change of heart? Did you think your knowledge of my daughter's illness would intimidate me somehow?"

"What if there was a cure?"

Landsdale found himself speechless again, wondering if there was a message behind Roy's question. He had vast holdings in the medical and pharmaceutical industries as well, after all. Maybe, just maybe . . .

"There isn't, of course," Roy said, deflating Landsdale's hopes as quickly as he had raised them. "But I imagine you would've signed over all your companies to me if I could have provided you one. How did it feel, that slight glimmer of hope?"

"Bastard," Landsdale muttered under his breath.

"Am I?" Roy asked, stepping farther into the spray of the lamps, his face shining in the light. "For giving you something I have lost in entirety myself? There's no *hope* for my family, Mr. Landsdale. Everyone I ever loved is gone. All I have left to live for is the world beyond these walls, a world I can never live within again. What I have left, Mr. Landsdale, are my dreams of a country and a world no longer dependent on oil alone to sustain itself."

"That should make you my ally, Mr. Roy, not my rival."

"Rival? You aren't my rival. You're an inconvenience, a joke filling the minds of the miseducated with distractions collected under the phrase 'green energy.' Green for money, since that's what all your efforts are a waste of. You distract people from the truth of their plight and fill them with the illusion you hold the answers for providing them with a safe and secure future. And these efforts of yours, which have forced up the prices of *real* energy under the mistaken assumption that taxing it and eliminating my tax incentives in favor of your own would improve costs, have led to you progressing from minor inconvenience to major impediment to my far-reaching goals."

Landsdale felt cold, dank sweat starting to soak through his shirt, sticking the fabric to his surgical gown. "You brought me four thousand miles to lecture me?"

"I'm aware that you and the truth are not well acquainted, Mr. Landsdale. Unlike me, you live with windows that open, but you're not really seeing the truth of what lies beyond them."

"My companies are not for sale," Landsdale repeated.

"Do you recall what I just said about how much you learn to live without when you are given no choice?"

"What's the difference?"

"The difference lies in the fact that your companies no longer hold very much value at all."

As cold as Landsdale felt before, he now felt chilled to the bone, Sebastian Roy's words more icily potent than any thermostat.

"While you were in transit, I purchased four of your five leading suppliers. A terrible investment financially, given the fact I'm about to issue stop orders from their leading buyer, but you forced my hand."

The breath caught in Landsdale's throat. He'd taken every possible precaution, thought he had insulated himself from anything Roy, even with all his power, could do. But he had never considered his archenemy would squander a billion dollars in an effort to destroy him.

"My offer is still on the table. We can still fight this battle together, though on my terms. Yes or no?"

"No," Landsdale managed.

"Then I reduce my level on the order of half, to seventy-five percent of your companies' market value. Refuse again and the offer drops to fifty percent." He shook his head, looking almost amused. "People like you never surprise me; you're all so predictable. I brought you here because I wanted to see the look on your face in person. Since I've lost so much myself, I take great pleasure in having others join me in that particular agony. I have more money than I'll ever have cause to spend now. But before I die I will control all the energy on this planet. Every drop of oil, every ion of natural gas. The nuclear plants, the coal refineries—everything. You know my company's motto."

Landsdale did but was of no mind to repeat it.

"'Energy Is Power.' Perfectly fitting, don't you think? And your green energy is now part of my power. Seventy-five percent of current market value. Yes or no?"

Landsdale started to nod, but stopped.

"I'll take that as a yes. Mr. Pierce is waiting with the paperwork for you to sign. Leave here without final execution and I'll bankrupt you instead. Your choice."

There was a buzz, and Roy moved to an intercom built into a wall of the lavish chamber.

"I told you not to interrupt me," he said.

"We have the latest report from the Gulf, Mr. Roy," Pierce reported. "You need to hear it. Immediately."

Roy detected the undercurrent of excitement in Pierce's voice, restrained but undeniable. "Fine. Mr. Landsdale and I were just finishing up, weren't we, Mr. Landsdale?"

Landsdale just stood there, watching Roy from across the room.

"Weren't we, Mr. Landsdale?" Roy repeated. "Why don't I give you that Minoan jar you found so captivating as a token of our mutually beneficial dealings? The simplest item in my collection to remind you of how simple life is when it's reduced to a single choice."

Landsdale stiffened. "I don't want anything from you."

"How about a pen to sign the paperwork? It shouldn't take too long and then you can be on your way back to your simple, pedestrian life. When you die, no one will even remember your name while mine will be part of everyone's life when they flip a switch, turn on a burner, or fire up the furnace." Roy steadied himself with a deep breath, that sound wet and labored. "Leave me now. Our business is done. Mr. Pierce is waiting."

Landsdale started for the door.

"Pierce," Roy said toward the speakerphone, "Mr. Landsdale is ready to sign the paperwork. Please make sure it's ready for him. Then come in here and tell me what happened in the Gulf."

PART TWO:
THE STORM

CHAPTER 25

Deepwater Venture

The last few yards were the worst, McCracken stiffening at the uncertainty of exactly what his feet were going to touch down upon. He could feel the increasing winds buffeting him and billowing his hazmat suit. He'd expected his descent to be greeted by any number of noxious odors, from the residue of whatever had transpired here if nothing else. But McCracken smelled nothing through his soft helmet's respirator, and that was strange indeed, because there should have been *something*.

The main deck of the *Deepwater Venture* looked like a football-field-sized platform riddled with debris. McCracken thought again of his boyhood Erector set rendered unrecognizable. Nothing was left standing, from the derricks that had once spiraled toward the sky, to the bridge and command center, cranes, and storage tanks that had housed water and propane. An offshore oil rig was like a submarine in that space was at a premium, none to be wasted. The clutter that defined the deck in normal circumstances had turned into a serpentine junk pile of unrecognizable elements, as if the component pieces of the *Venture* had been dumped into a blender on high and then poured back out. The only objects to survive whole—a helicopter, some emergency evacuation rafts and life pods, and a forklift—were floating in the waters around the rig itself. McCracken had yet to view the damage on the sublevels, identical in design to the main deck but each constructed with a different set of tasks in mind, including storage and housing for the crew. Ultimately, the efforts of more than a hundred crewmembers spread among all levels combined on massive subsea deepwater rigs like the *Venture* to create a constant din of energy and activity.

But not today.

The latest generation of subsea rigs like the *Venture* boasted four massive floating leglike support columns. From a distance the columns looked more like monstrous pillars rising out of the water. Segments of multicolored piping descended from the support legs, all still intact according to the Coast Guard's report.

McCracken had been around danger more than enough times to know it carried its own signature, something that alerted the most primordial segments of the brain to a threat so instinct could lay in the proper defensive measures. But no such signature seemed in evidence here, as if that had been sucked out of the very air along with any scents. He felt a profound eeriness intensified by the fact that at the very least there should be bodies in evidence. Yet there were none, the crew having vanished into some unknown ether.

Thunk.

McCracken's pliable hazmat boots touched down as his eyes were still sweeping the deck, trying to make sense of the sights that up close defied it even more. He unbuckled the harness and watched the winch hoist it back up, then flexed his knees as if to make sure the world was solid beneath him. He'd wait for Johnny Wareagle to be winched down before making any other additional survey. His thoughts turned to Paul Basmajian being among the victims of whatever had happened here and the heightened edge he felt vanished, replaced by the grim awareness of loss and somber realization that someone would have to pay.

Because in McCracken's experience, nothing ever just happened.

A heavy gust of wind shook the platform, storm clouds now growing thicker to the south and east, as McCracken reached up to steady Wareagle's legs for the last of his descent.

"Welcome to the party, Indian," he said after Wareagle had touched down, his words echoing inside his helmet.

Captain Merch tossed them a wave from the Bell 430, which then banked in the air and soared away toward the Coast Guard cutter *Nero* that was now cruising the perimeter where it would wait until the time came to extract them.

"Something here you need to see, Blainey," Wareagle was saying.

He knelt down and ran a gloved hand about the steel surface of the deck. McCracken mimicked his motions, his hand feeling uneven patches along the steel that felt flat underfoot.

"You gonna tell me evil spirits did this, I'm ready to listen."

"Not quite. But the steel's ridged, not bubbled," Wareagle reported.

"Explain."

"Bubbling steel would require temperatures of, oh, say a thousand degrees or so. These ridges tell me it actually melted and re-formed. That would take temperatures of several thousand."

McCracken looked at his friend skeptically. "You saw the satellite imagery. No melting we could detect and the only time the rig wasn't visible was in that mist cloud, or whatever it was."

"You're missing the point, Blainey. Steel would take much longer than that to re-form and harden anyway."

"I'm not missing it, I just didn't consider it. There was no reason to, since the satellite images were mere seconds apart."

"How many seconds was it again?"

"Six, I think."

Wareagle just looked at him.

"You're suggesting the steel melted and re-formed in *six seconds*?"

"Or less."

McCracken studied Wareagle's expression, trying to see on it what he wasn't saying out loud. "What is it, Johnny? What do you feel?"

Wareagle seemed to be sniffing the air, watching everything around him at the same time. "We're not alone, Blainey."

"Indian?"

"There's something still alive here."

"Not that I can see."

Wareagle rotated his eyes around the deck, the foreboding and concern on his expression visible even through his faceplate. "That's the problem."

CHAPTER 26

Deepwater Venture

McCracken felt another gust of wind slam into him and looked toward the southeast and the approaching storm.

"That storm hits with the kind of wallop it looks like . . ."

"We lose the evidence we need to figure out the truth," Wareagle completed for him.

"Means we're on the clock here, Johnny. What do you think we're talking about for temperatures at the thirty-two-thousand-foot depth their drill had reached?"

"At the earth's core itself, eighteen hundred miles down, temperatures can reach ten thousand degrees—as hot as the surface of the sun. That level of heat holds fifty thousand times more energy than all global oil and natural gas on the planet. Untapped geothermal energy contained beneath miles of prehistoric rock that runs straight to the earth's core."

McCracken scratched at his scalp through his soft helmet. "You suggesting that's what killed Paul Basmajian?"

"No," Wareagle told him, "because the effects and force of that kind of geothermal burst, even if the *Venture*'s line had been able to contain it, would look nothing like what we've got here. First off, you'd have remains in some form, except for the fact that the integrity of the entire structure would have been compromised to the point of collapsing into the sea."

"So this wasn't temperature."

"Not temperature alone, Blainey."

McCracken joined Wareagle in gazing about the deck. The remains of the two-hundred-foot-high derrick, the bottom half, had toppled over. The bases of the lifting cranes bracketing it on either side were visible, but the orange extensions were gone, as if shorn off and dumped into the sea, absent of a cut, sheer or otherwise. The other structures on the main deck had collapsed, though not in a pile of refuse-strewn rubble. Just flattened, as if crushed by something bearing incredible weight. In the satellite photo arrays and real-time motion shots, they'd been intact in the moments before the white cloud enveloped the *Deepwater Venture*, then essentially gone afterward.

Even through his faceplate, Wareagle looked suddenly and atypically hesitant.

"What's on your mind, Indian?"

"I'm wondering if there's a weapon capable of doing something like what we see before us."

"Realistically or theoretically?"

"In our experience they're usually the same."

"The answer's no, in either case."

Wareagle started to shake his head, then stopped. "Thirty-two thousand feet below the surface. . . . Baz and his crew sucked something up never seen in this world before."

A rumbling sound broke into their analyzing, and both men looked up to see another chopper, a Sikorsky, hovering overhead. A man wearing a tattered leather vest and Grateful Dead T-shirt over his hazmat suit emerged from inside clinging to the sides of a rescue basket.

"Maybe he can tell us what," said McCracken.

Captain Seven had arrived.

CHAPTER 27

Deepwater Venture

McCracken had no idea what Captain Seven's real name was, only that he had gotten this one thanks to behavior, eccentricities, and intelligence that had led one military commander to call the tech whiz a visitor from the seventh planet from a distant galaxy. "Captain," accordingly, wasn't a real military rank. Even though he'd never spent a day in boot camp or wearing a uniform, his efforts along with his scientific knowledge and creativity had saved countless lives. Captain Seven had been one of those on the forefront of using technology as a prime weapon against opponents of all levels. Though he'd pioneered work with aerial surveillance and mapping, his true strengths lay in weapons analysis and development, both of which might well be required here after his trip to the Florida panhandle in search of jellyfish toxin was cut short.

Captain Seven's respect for the mysteries filling the world around him came with one special caveat: understanding was the greatest weapon against the unknown. But it had to be an understanding based on that very unknown's terms, not currently applied ones.

That's where the fluidity in his approach came in, along with the need to write new rules to come to grips with new challenges.

"Dude," Captain Seven said, as soon as McCracken helped him from the basket, "how am I supposed to toke up through this helmet?"

"Don't tell me you brought . . ."

Captain Seven winked, his shock of matted-down wild gray hair visible through his faceplate. "How you expect me to get through the day without a little ganja to stimulate my creative juices?"

"And you're how old now, Captain?"

"A day older than yesterday, a day younger than tomorrow. Beyond that, I don't think much about it."

If the eerie surroundings or bizarre circumstances bothered him at all, he didn't show it. Then again, Captain Seven had been solving impossible technological riddles dating all the way back to Vietnam, though his work since had linked him more with a man McCracken judged to be pretty much a younger version of himself.

"How's Kimberlain, Captain?"

"The Ferryman's never been better or busier. No shortage of monsters to take to their deaths these days."

"Nice T-shirt, by the way," McCracken said, smiling through his mask at the design featuring a peace sign with MAKE LOVE above it and NOT WAR below. "Especially since war's what you've helped the Indian and me make a whole bunch of times."

"Yeah, I'm a portrait in irony. Thing is, life hasn't been nearly as good since Jerry Garcia finally bought the farm. Hey, I know it was a long time coming, but my world just isn't the same. But when we crack this case, I'll smoke you boys up with high-end homegrown. What you say to that, big fella?" Captain Seven asked Wareagle. "I hear Indians are veritable master growers born with an herbal thumb."

"You mind if we get started, Captain?" McCracken prodded. He knew Captain Seven was a long way from home in the form of a pair of linked train cars parked in Sunnyside Yard in Queens, not far from New York's Penn Station, leaving him to wonder how the captain could grow anything at all. "There's a storm brewing."

"In more ways than one, MacNuts," Captain Seven said, using a nickname reserved only for him.

"What's that mean?"

"Not sure yet. But if I'm right," the captain continued, touching an unrecognizable hunk of debris formed of fused-together portions of the rig, "we might not make it until the storm."

Captain Seven had an overstuffed backpack strapped to his shoulders, containing the various technological tools of his trade that would help decipher whatever had happened to the *Deepwater Venture.* Since none of the machines or technology aboard the rig were likely to be functional anymore, they could only rely on what they could carry, which for the captain was considerable.

"How much do you know?" McCracken asked him, his faceplate starting to mist up ever so slightly.

"I could write books about what I know."

"I'm talking about what happened on this rig."

Captain Seven looked about, as if realizing where he was for the first time. "I'm guessing pretty much the same as you. They hit something thirty thousand–plus feet down that apparently took things personally. And the only thing left alive on this thing, apparently, is us. Speaking of which, any of your friends in uniform do thermal-imaging scans?"

"Several. Flatlines on the readouts."

"Like I was saying."

With that, Captain Seven began unpacking the contents of his backpack, starting with a small satellite dish.

"Need a wireless relay to connect up with the mainframes at NSA," he explained.

"Didn't know you'd been granted access," McCracken noted.

Which drew a wink from the captain. "Who said I was granted access? I've been making their system my own since the IBM 360

Model 90 was state of the art. Anything we need to help us solve this mystery will soon be a click away."

Once the satellite array, looking like a high-tech version of an old-fashioned rabbit ears antenna, was set up, McCracken and Wareagle helped Captain Seven lay out a varied group of sensors and analytical tools that would help them determine what had transpired here and what exactly had befallen the missing crew. The first device he assembled looked like the kind of metal detector wielded at beaches in search of lost change and jewelry.

"Seems a bit low tech by your standards, Captain," McCracken noted.

"I made all these myself, so appearances can be deceiving. Know what this one is?" the captain asked him, holding the waist-high wand that looked like a metal detector.

"Nope," McCracken told him.

"Basically, it's an organic materials sensor capable of homing in on organic matter, like hair, blood, as well as flesh and bone residue, in the hopes of uncovering the remains of the crew. Even a blast hot enough to melt and re-form steel would leave some of that organic residue behind, and following the trail of it should allow me to trace the final moments of the *Deepwater Venture*'s missing crewmembers." Captain Seven hesitated long enough to meet McCracken's gaze through his faceplate. "One of them was a friend of yours."

"Somebody tell you that?"

"Nobody had to."

McCracken took a deeper breath, letting it out slowly. "Indian thinks we might not be alone up here."

Captain Seven stiffened briefly, then relaxed again. "We'll know soon enough," he said with uncharacteristic evasiveness.

"What is it you're not saying, Captain?"

"I'm not saying."

Next McCracken and Wareagle watched Captain Seven assemble a similar-looking device with a smaller, flatter head.

"'Nother one of my techno concoctions. A minerals and elements analyzer to better help figure out what got done to the rig in those missing six seconds."

"We've got confirmation that whatever did this is localized to the rig," McCracken said, as the captain tested the assembled devices to make sure they were fully operational. "No evidence of any similar phenomenon anywhere in the Gulf, surrounding barrier islands, or land. No reports from any other ships or rigs. But there is a vague report of an undersea seismic disturbance below us right around the same time."

"Seismic disturbance?" Captain Seven echoed, as if it bore some special significance to him.

"That mean something?"

"Been there, done that is all," Captain Seven said, his eyes even more glassy than usual.

"It's all we know for now."

"We'll know a hell of a lot more than that soon," Captain Seven assured him. "Hey, do either of you have a joint?"

The sky directly overhead had storm darkened considerably more by the time the captain was ready to survey the ship with his two separate sensing devices, as well as a digital camera and something that looked like a Geiger counter hanging from his shoulder. The wind had shifted, and McCracken could feel the first taste of rain on the air. No light or sound emanated from Captain Seven's high-tech instruments, looking more like toys assembled without benefit of batteries. But McCracken knew all the data was being recorded by the machines' miniature hard drives to be linked with NSA's pilfered mainframe once their sweep of the rig was complete.

McCracken and Wareagle walked the *Venture* with him, starting with the unrecognizable remnants of the rig's debris-strewn main deck. They moved stiffly, suddenly missing the weapons they'd originally seen no reason to bring. But now, as darkness descended, the hulking shapes of what had been fully functional equipment seemed ready to burst upon them at any moment in some concerted attack. Each gust of wind created a creaking shift of movement somewhere nearby that could just as easily have been the stealthy approach of their unseen enemy.

"There's something still alive here."

Johnny's words now seemed more like a warning.

McCracken tried to shake the stiffness from his frame, but failed. The *Venture*'s five decks, the main with four below, had remained structurally intact and sound underfoot, although he thought he could feel heat radiating up through his feet. The sensation was strange, almost soothing, and he wasn't sure if the rig was the actual source or if the tight-fitting hazmat boots were to blame instead.

"I feel it too, Blainey," Wareagle said on the rig's second level, seeing the discomfort in his steps. "But there's no blast residue," he noted, as they continued along the rig's second level, "no heat signature whatsoever."

"Any explanation for that come to mind, Captain?" McCracken wondered.

Captain Seven replied without looking up from the LED readouts on the sensors he held in either hand like walking canes. "Well, I've seen the results of underwater volcanic eruptions that reach the surface, but neither that nor anything else is really comparable to what we're facing here. Yo, boys, has anybody raised the possibility that this wasn't an accident?"

"Meaning?"

"Meaning what I just said."

"There's no weapon on the planet that can do what was done to this rig."

"You mean, there didn't used to be," the captain reminded him.

"The real question being," McCracken followed, "if you're right, who was wielding it?"

CHAPTER 28

Deepwater Venture

His scan of all five levels complete, back on the main deck Captain Seven started to assemble a makeshift technological and communications center beneath a thin reinforced tarpaulin suspended over poles magnetically affixed to the deck. McCracken and Wareagle helped him ease the poles into place at the proper intervals, befuddled when they refused to stick.

"Please tell me there's something wrong with the magnets," said McCracken.

"Oh, there's something wrong all right, but not with them." The captain struggled to readjust his leather vest with his hazmat gloves. "The steel forming the deck's been demagnetized."

"That doesn't sound good."

"Fucking fantastic is what it is. Maybe what we got here is a genuine close encounter of the whatever kind. What was the number again?"

"Third," McCracken told him.

"Yeah, Richard Dreyfuss building a mountain out of mashed potatoes in the movie. And people think *I'm* crazy."

"You are, Captain."

"Then I fit in just fine here, because we've just entered the realm of the impossible."

McCracken moved away when Captain Merch hailed him over the communicator built into his helmet.

"Get your people ready to move in twenty, sir. That's an order."

"Say again."

"We're evacuating the area. Got a tropical depression crawling straight up our ass, in case you didn't notice."

McCracken looked back toward Wareagle and Captain Seven. "I'll get back to you on that."

"You hear me say it was an order?"

"I heard you."

The silence lingered long enough for McCracken to wonder if he'd lost the connection.

"They warned me this might happen," Merch said finally.

"Warned you *what* might happen?"

"You going rogue, forgetting the mission parameters."

"Mission parameters," McCracken repeated. "Ever been in a firefight, Merch?"

"What's that have to do with anything?"

"Paul Basmajian and I were in a whole bunch of them, often side by side with the Indian here. And anyone who thought I was going to leave this rig until I found out what happened to him, and who was responsible, was wrong in a big way."

"These are my waters, sir, and what happened on that rig is tragedy enough for one day."

"Your waters, Captain, but it's my rig now. That makes it my call."

"Twenty minutes, McCracken. That's as much as I can give you. After that it won't matter whose call it is."

"This is great!" Captain Seven proclaimed exactly sixteen minutes later under light shed by small portable floods he'd brought with him as well, the initial analysis NSA's mainframe had made of the data he'd collected displayed on the screens of his dual laptops. "No, better than great—fantastic! Christmas morning come early! Did you know I believed in Santa Claus until I was eleven?"

McCracken crouched to better see the captain's laptops poised atop waist-high portable tables. Both were military grade, reinforced with hard rubber and a special polymer to cushion falls and remain functional even when doused in water or damaged by explosives or a bullet. "What am I looking at?"

"The screen on the right shows the chemical and molecular structure of plate steel."

"So?"

"So the screen on the left shows the chemical and molecular structure of the *Venture*'s deck from the readings we just took," Captain Seven continued.

"They're different," noted Wareagle, as the wind howled around them and nearly tore the thin tarp from the now jerry-rigged poles supporting it. "Not entirely, but enough to stand out."

"Right you are, kemosabe. Because what we're standing on is no longer steel, not steel as we know it anyway."

"Explain," said McCracken.

"You got that joint?"

"Not on me."

"Then I can't. And neither can NSA's mainframe."

"You need a joint to take a guess?"

"An educated one, yeah," Captain Seven quipped. "In the meantime, you'll have to settle for molecular reorganization."

"Come again?" said McCracken.

"Molecular reorganization," he repeated. "Goes to your observation about ripples in the steel, about something melting and then re-forming it. Only when it re-formed, it had a different molecular composition. Be a few more hours before we see the next set of data from NSA but we're talking about something that until now has only existed in theory."

McCracken and Wareagle glanced at each other, then back at Captain Seven.

"Gentlemen," he proclaimed, "we are looking at the ultimate proof of Einstein's unified field and conservation of matter theories. I can't tell you how yet, although I expect that to change once we get a more detailed analysis of the rig's components. But I can tell you something else that is absolutely freaking fascinating. I mean, if I still remembered what sex felt like, I'd tell you this was better."

With that, Captain Seven worked one of the laptops until the screen shifted to an entirely new data analysis courtesy of the other sensor device, picturing a twisting funnel shape eminently familiar to both Wareagle and McCracken.

"DNA," Wareagle noted, his shoulders stiffening.

"You bet," the captain told him. "Not human exactly, but something organic for sure."

McCracken tried to make sense of what he was hearing. "Looks like we found what you got a sense of before, Indian."

"Yes . . . and no."

"How's that, Captain?"

"Organic as in functional cellular activity, MacNuts, but that's about the only thing whatever you're looking at has in common with life as we know it. As in an entirely new life-form. As in something that may really not want us here, if it finds the ability to think."

"Now or never." Captain Merch's voice blared through McCracken's helmet, loud enough for the others to hear.

McCracken gazed up at the sky that had turned utterly black. Thick raindrops that felt like needles began to stab at him through his hazmat suit, the wind that threatened to ravage whatever evidence remained on the *Venture* picking up to a steady gust.

He looked around him at the vast assemblages of re-formed and remolded steel, picturing them coming to life as Captain Seven suggested they might to wage war on those deemed to be interlopers in this new world.

"We're staying," McCracken said into his hidden microphone.

CHAPTER 29

New Orleans

Katie DeMarco sat in the dim murkiness of the Canal Place Theater, watching an independent, subtitled film for the third time through and paying no attention to the screen whatsoever. Her feet stuck to a dried pool of spilled soda, and the stench of body odor drifted faintly on the air.

After fleeing K-Paul's, she had opted to remain in the city for fear the same men sent to kill or capture her would be watching the airport as well as train and bus stations and rent-a-car centers. They clearly knew who she was and any car she rented or ticket she purchased would be immediately traceable, and she had neither the time nor funds required to build a false identification.

Another false identification, that is. There'd been several of them these past few years, one for each of her infiltrations. That made it hard sometimes to recall her actual identity and background, in large part since she'd done her best to erase it from memory as well. "Katie DeMarco" was only the most recent she'd concocted with WorldSafe's help and expertise.

She'd been trying to reach Todd Lipton again for hours now without success. Something had clearly changed since she fled the *Deepwater Venture*, the stakes raised considerably. Pursuit alone had not surprised her; pursuit by men determined to kill her—that was something else again. She had no idea who her two saviors had been in K-Paul's. Coincidence, of course, but she'd glimpsed enough of their actions before resuming her flight to know they were no ordinary good Samaritans, at least as polished as her deadly pursuers.

Katie checked her watch. If the person she was expecting, a WorldSafe connection based here in New Orleans who called himself Twist, didn't show up by the end of this film, she'd have to find an alternative route out of the city as well as another means of finding the information she needed. And that's when she felt someone settle into the seat next to her.

"Kiss me," the young man said, smelling of McDonald's fast food.

Katie pulled away reflexively, taken aback.

"I'm Twist," he continued, using a name that was no more real than hers. "Now kiss me so it seems like we know each other."

Katie finally did, his mouth tasting of onions and heavily salted french fries. His hair had the texture and shape of a bird's nest.

Twist eased his arm over her shoulder and drew her in against him.

"It's about time," Katie whispered.

"I've been here since the flower scene. Had to make sure no one else was watching you. Could you have chosen a more boring movie?"

"I haven't been able to reach Todd."

She felt Twist stiffen. "He's gone, they're all gone."

"What?"

"A raid on the camp in Greenland. Very professional and with good reason, the same reason why they came after you."

"What reason? What are you talking about?"

"Something happened on that rig, Katie."

"I only left today, this morning."

"And if you'd stayed, you'd be dead along with everyone else on board."

"Dead? Jesus Christ . . . It wasn't, I don't . . ." Katie couldn't finish a sentence or a thought, could only wait for Twist to say more.

Twist looked away, uncharacteristically evasive. He'd been the one who arranged her placement on the *Deepwater Venture*, including altering her résumé to include the proper qualifications and credentials. It had proven to be a long, laborious process with Katie ultimately gaining access to the rig months after it began. Twist strongly suggested she "apply" for pretty much the same job with additional rig operators, but Katie insisted on an Ocean Bore–owned facility.

For her own reasons.

Twist swung back toward her suddenly. Even in the darkness of the theater, she could see the fear glowing on his face like a light sheen.

"For God's sake, Katie, what did you do?"

"I don't know what you're—"

"You think you could get away with something like this?"

Now Katie DeMarco's fear was beginning to mirror Twist's. "Something like *what*?"

Something changed on Twist's expression, the fear giving way to utter befuddlement. "You really don't know, do you?"

She continued to regard him. "Tell me, for God's sake!" she blared, loud enough for those nearest her in the theater to swing her way.

"Original reports from the scene were panicked, sketchy. Then nothing at all. But it's big, Katie, really big. And bad."

She swallowed hard. "They tried to kill me in the city. I called you after I couldn't raise Todd again."

"That's because he's dead, they're all dead."

"Oh my God . . ."

"It's the rig; it all comes back to the rig."

Katie steadied herself. "I'm going to get up and leave now. Wait five minutes and then meet me outside, in case they're waiting for us. I'll be at the bus stop on the corner."

She started to stand up, felt Twist's hand latch on to her wrist, holding her in place.

"What they're saying about that rig . . ."

Katie looked down, waiting for him to continue.

"The logs will list you as fleeing the *Venture* in the hours before whatever it was happened. That means you're going to be a suspect. That means there's nowhere you can hide. There'll be pictures from the rig's security cameras. Your face is all they'll need."

"Meet me outside, Twist. We've got to figure out something, maybe how what I filed in my reports fits in to all this."

Twist managed a nod. "To the effect of you didn't believe the *Venture* wasn't just drilling for oil. That somebody had placed it there to look for something else as well. So?"

"So," Katie told him, "maybe they found it."

CHAPTER 30

New Orleans

Katie slid out of the theater, pausing briefly near the refreshment stand to check for lingering stares or men loitering about who looked similar to the ones who'd trailed her into K-Paul's. When neither of these alerted her senses, she emerged into the night on Canal Street and walked as leisurely as she could manage to a covered bus stop at the corner. It had started to drizzle, flashes of heat lightning in the distance and the smell of ozone in the air telling her a storm was coming.

If it hadn't struck already, that is.

The *Venture* never should have been out there in the first place drilling so deep. In the wake of the Gulf oil disaster on board the *Deepwater Horizon* at the hands of BP, the world should have shunned such operations until they could be made safe for the environment. Instead, in the face of rising gas prices, the world had only embraced them more. WorldSafe's reason for planting Katie on the *Venture* was for her to provide a chronicle of the truth, ultimate proof that the industry had learned nothing from its mistakes and overreaches. To think even now drilling in the Arctic and another dozen sites unspoiled by industry and business was about to commence was repugnant. What would it take to make normal people pay attention?

Katie checked her watch. Twist should have joined her by now.

But he hadn't.

She realized she was trembling, fear the only thing that was suppressing the vast shock over the deaths of Todd Lipton and the other WorldSafe members housed at base camp in Greenland. She gazed back up the street to find the crowd spilling out the theater's front doors, Twist sure to be among them. He had contacts, both in the media and the little known world of environmental law. In the wake of what he insisted had transpired at base camp, these were the kind of forces he could bring to bear, new fronts opened in an old war.

But there was still no sign of him. Then police sirens blared, a pair of squad cars streaming past her covered bench with lights flashing in eerie synchronicity with the heat lightning that flashed ever closer. Two more squad cars raced from the head of the street, the four of them converging on the theater façade where a manager in a red jacket rushed out to greet their arrival.

Katie felt a surge of cold through the fetid heat of the night. Something must have happened to Twist, and that could only mean Todd Lipton's killers and her pursuers had tracked him to the theater. Or perhaps happened upon him while looking for her. Either way, they'd know she was nearby; they could be closing in even now. Katie longed for a bus, a cab, anything to help spirit her from the area.

A black woman wearing a coat too big and bulky for the spring heat wave took a seat on the opposite end of the bench, started to reach inside her handbag. Katie froze, perhaps about to cry out to draw attention from anyone within earshot when the woman emerged with an old cell phone held together by duct tape. Katie breathed easier, even as the four police officers disappeared inside the theater an instant before a rescue wagon joined the four squad cars on the street. She watched a pair of paramedics charge through the doors lugging a gurney in the officers' wake.

A bus snailed past the collection of flashing lights and cruised toward the covered bench. The black woman gave up trying to work her cell phone and dropped it back into her handbag with a clunking sound.

"Right on time," she said to Katie. "Ten minutes late."

The bus ground to a halt, its doors hissing open. The black woman lumbered up the stairs, bus card already in view. But something stopped Katie from following; maybe the way the driver eyed her with what looked like a flash of recognition, or maybe just the fact that she'd feel powerless once on board.

So she started walking, using the bus as cover to hopefully disappear into the night. The bus's windshield wipers were sweeping back and forth, and she felt the heavier drops of intermittent rain in advance of the storm's coming deluge. Torrents began to spill from the sky as soon as she was clear of the bus and it rumbled past her, drenching Katie and every other pedestrian on the street. People dashed, people darted, clutching newspapers or jackets over their heads.

More cover for her. A blessing, Katie thought, as she approached the head of an alley, intending to veer down it.

Hands that stank of grime and sweat flailed out for her before Katie got there. One of them closed over her mouth, nearly making her gag from the stench. Her eyes bulged, recording only flicks of motion in the darkness lit regularly now by lightning flashes. She tried to bite the hand covering her mouth and retched from the stench again. She was dragged on toward a car being hammered by heavy raindrops that suddenly claimed the air.

Katie felt them too, colorless faces flitting in the flashes of lightning, before darkness consumed her.

CHAPTER 31

Deepwater Venture

The rain had just started to pelt the deck when Captain Seven looked up from the shroudlike tent keeping his laptops dry in the storm.

"Now this is really fucked up."

"Make it good, Captain," McCracken told him. "And fast."

"I think I found the crew."

McCracken let himself hope Paul Basmajian was somehow still alive, still within the ability of him and Johnny Wareagle to save.

"Where? Talk to us, Captain."

"Here. Right under our very noses . . . and feet. Literally."

McCracken looked up at Wareagle, both of them soaked by the rain that at least gave life to the dead air that had enveloped the *Venture*.

"You're standing on them," Captain Seven elaborated.

The storm's wind and rain had tossed the captain's long gray hair into a mass of soaked tangles that resembled strands of string twisted together. His eyes looked overly bright in the spill of the portable, battery-operated floods they'd rigged to nearby clumped assemblages of steel that seemed sturdy enough to accommodate them. They'd all removed their helmets, now secure in the notion that nothing toxic had been released into the air and tired of having their faceplates mist up on them because of the humidity.

"Indian?" Blaine said, wanting Johnny's response to Captain Seven's latest revelation.

"Makes sense. Enough for me to detect that sense of life when I first reached the rig."

"Your spirits have anything to say on the subject?"

"This is all new to them too, Blainey."

"We don't need spirits when we've got these DNA readings here," the captain resumed. "It's just like I figured."

"Figured what?"

Captain Seven began humming the theme music from *The Twilight Zone*. "We're traveling through another dimension. Forget the next stop being the Twilight Zone; we're already there."

"Those missing six seconds . . ."

"You're getting good at this."

"The Indian and I have had lots of experience, haven't we, Johnny?"

"Too much, Blainey."

"Not with what I believe we're facing here, you haven't," the captain told him. "Good thing is I have. Going back five years in the Mediterranean Sea."

"Keep talking."

Captain Seven shook his head. "Uh-uh, not ready to yet. Not until I'm sure this is all about the same thing that got me smacked by a tsunami off Greece. Gives a whole new meaning to the phrase hang ten, I shit you not. Anyway, MacNuts, add up everything you've faced before and it still wouldn't equal what we may be facing here, not even close."

"And what *are* we facing here exactly, Captain?"

He stepped out from beneath the slim confines of the makeshift tent and joined them in the storm. "Whatever picked this rig up and dumped it into some kind of cosmic mixing bowl must have dropped the crew in too for good measure; that's what those DNA readings meant."

"You said they weren't human."

"Because they're not. Not anymore, anyway."

"So what then? Mixed in with the steel and everything else?"

"Ever see the movie *The Fly*?"

"No."

"Neither one, not even the original?"

"No to both."

"The scientific principle in both was molecular transference. Problem was in both movies the scientist had the misfortune of a fly entering the mix. So when he emerged from the pod, the fly's DNA was fused to his."

"You saying that's what happened here?" McCracken asked, as lightning flashed closer, accompanied almost immediately by a deafening blast of thunder.

"Not exactly. The poor scientist in *The Fly*, both the original and the remake, was turned into a hybrid, not entirely insect and not entirely human, but some crossbred combination of the two. That's what happened here. We're not standing on steel or flesh and blood. We're standing on something entirely new and unknown, something remade from scratch in those six seconds. We're talking Day One here. We're talking those six seconds being like the six days it took God himself to create the world before resting on the seventh."

"Sounds like you're describing the big bang theory, Captain. How the universe itself was created."

"That'll do for starters, only in reverse. The world *de*constructed instead of constructed."

The wind picked up to near gale force. The rig creaked and groaned around them. A vibration, almost like a quivering, turned the deck wobbly beneath their feet. McCracken and Wareagle noticed the pooling water running suddenly southward, then back to the north in rhythm with the suddenly shifting platform.

"Remember when I said we might not make it until the storm," said Captain Seven.

McCracken and Wareagle both looked at him.

"Looks like I was close."

CHAPTER 32

Deepwater Venture

"Evac by helicopter's out, Indian," McCracken told Wareagle.

"No crane to use to lower us off in a basket, even if a ship could get close enough, Blainey. And the extendable gangway's long gone."

"And me without a joint," Captain Seven commented, shaking his head.

"You were talking big bang theory, Captain, in reverse."

"Rather put my mind toward coming up with a way to get us off this hunk of steel."

"But that's not really what it is anymore, is it?"

"Nope, not exactly."

The rig creaked louder and then shifted mightily enough in the wind to jostle its three occupants.

"Seems like we should be focusing our attention elsewhere."

"Do you know what killed Paul Basmajian or not?"

"Yes and no."

"Which?"

"No, I don't know and, yes, I may."

"You sure you're not stoned?"

Captain Seven shook his head again, this time tossing water sprayed from his wet tangle of hair in all directions. "Wish I was. I've been dealing with the impossible for what seems like my whole life. What we've got here is just a little more impossible than usual."

The whole of the *Venture* seemed to list leeward in the wind, the deck ending up canted at a deepening angle ever closer to toppling over altogether and plunging its occupants into the swollen seas below.

"But maybe no more impossible than getting off this rig," Captain Seven continued.

"Johnny?" McCracken prodded.

"That stray life pod we glimpsed when we arrived is still wedged against one of the support columns below."

"A hundred and forty feet down in not the friendliest of seas, Indian."

"I've got an idea, Blainey."

The rig continued to shake and wobble, growing increasingly unsteady by the moment. Captain Seven worked feverishly, a hand darting back and forth between the keyboards beneath the canvas he now manually held over them to keep the computers dry long enough for him to complete his work and transmit all his findings to the central server at NSA.

"Anything on board you need to take with you, Captain?" McCracken asked him.

"Already stuck some samples in my backpack. Laptops are trashed, but we shouldn't lose any of the data, any of the proof."

"Proof of what?"

"Don't know since I haven't exactly proved it yet. I'll let you know soon as I do."

"How about a hint?"

"It's impossible."

"You said that already."

"Still the case."

"This coming from someone who specializes in the impossible."

"Everything's relative," Captain Seven told him.

A grinding sound of metal scraping against metal left McCracken's breath bottlenecked in his throat until a twist to his right found Johnny Wareagle lugging a huge flattened chunk of steel.

Wareagle laid the husk of what once had been steel at their feet.

"Looks like a derrick arm," McCracken noted.

"Used to be anyway, Blainey. It was hanging off the starboard side. Just needed a little coaxing to come free."

McCracken tried to estimate the arm's weight, amazed as always by Johnny Wareagle's incredible strength. "Those spirits of yours help you with this, Indian?"

"They warn of an all-powerful force being unleashed here, capable of far more destruction than what we've ever witnessed before."

"They offer any specifics?"

"The whole of the world hangs in the balance, Blainey."

Level Six, thought McCracken. "So what else is new?"

The remnants of the derrick arm, nearly thirty feet in length, were smooth and flat, its contours hardly ideal for its intended purpose, but still offering the best hope they had to get off the rig and reach the life pod moored against the support column below.

The *Venture* continued to cant heavily leeward, its downward angle growing steeper and steeper by the moment as it shook and rattled around them. A square tool chest of some kind, melted only to be re-formed as a semblance of its original shape, slid across the deck and slammed into Captain Seven's computer assemblage, driving it forward for the sea. Hunks of the misshapen and hulking appendages of remolded iron and steel began to break off, as if shed, the smaller shards turned into deadly projectiles with each gust of wind. As that wind grew more intense, heavier chunks churned through the air like birds of prey, seeming to swoop down on the rig's final occupants, crashing back to the deck with heavy thuds that rose over the swirling wind, rain, and thunder.

Wareagle had located long bands that had once been rubber cables and remained pliable enough to fasten the derrick arm to the sturdiest deck rails he could find on the aft side. Fortune's one gift to them had been to angle the *Venture*'s collapse toward the side of the rig where the life pod bobbed amid the waves churned madly by the force of the storm. Lack of visibility became as much a problem here as any, the torrents of windswept rain rendering the view of anything beyond a few feet impossible.

Wareagle lowered the derrick arm, angled like a playground slide, for the waters below. While he held it in place, McCracken used the long bands of rubber cabling to lash it tighter into place against the deck rail. He was just starting to feel the odds had swung in their favor when the support column to their right broke away, pitching the rig into a severe downward list.

McCracken grabbed hold of the deck rail to which he had just fastened the derrick arm, fearing it would give way from the strain. But it held and he glimpsed Wareagle clinging in similar fashion to the arm itself, seemingly suspended between the rig and the storm-ravaged night. Then Captain Seven came sliding his way across the deck, clutching fast to the backpack containing the last of the samples he had moved off to collect. McCracken swept a hand downward and caught the captain by his silvery mane of tangled hair just before he went over the side.

"What a rush!" Captain Seven cried out, pulling himself back in wobbly fashion to his feet. "Better than drugs, man, better than drugs!"

"If you liked that, you're going to love this," McCracken told him as the rig continued to collapse around them.

CHAPTER 33

Deepwater Venture

The platform was shaking and quaking, seeming to sway back and forth on an increasingly unsteady base beneath it.

"You're first to take the ride, Captain," McCracken said, as the rig listed farther over to the side off which the former derrick arm was placed.

"You would've thought I'd learned my lesson five years ago in the Med. I hate the fucking water."

"You like living?"

In that moment, McCracken could only count his blessings that Captain Merch had insisted that they bring lightweight, inflatable life jackets with them from the chopper that had ferried them to the *Venture* from the Coast Guard cutter. But he was also under no illusion that the vests could prolong life all that long in these seas. Waves this powerful could take a man under and fill his lungs with water no matter how good a swimmer he was or how well his vest performed. The best McCracken could hope for now, for starters, was that their plunges into the raging waters below would leave them close enough to find one another and plan from there. Perhaps locate some debris to cling to or, even better, use to fashion some form of craft to ride the waves well enough to survive the storm. With the life pod likely gone, it was the best they could hope for.

If falling hunks and jagged fragments of twisted steel from the collapsing rig didn't kill them first, that is.

For now there was only the darkness, the raging waters below, and the storm itself. McCracken could feel its force buckling his knees, as he and Wareagle hoisted Captain Seven atop the makeshift slide, holding their collective breath when they shoved him forward to whisk him on his way.

They could hear Captain Seven wailing, riding the slide the way Slim Pickens rode an atomic bomb in the final scene of *Dr. Strange-love.* He disappeared from view, swallowed by the night, the storm giving up no trace of him again.

"You're next, Blainey," Wareagle said over the howling winds and pelting rain.

"Since when?"

"Since my weight could be too much for the arm to handle and one of us has to get our findings back to shore."

"For Baz, then," McCracken conceded, easing himself up onto the slide.

"For Baz," Wareagle acknowledged.

And then McCracken pushed himself into motion.

The plummet was like nothing he'd ever experienced before. Not the high-altitude, low-opening parachute drops from five miles up. Not drops into the ocean in full battle gear. Not even the feeling of the g-forces of a space shuttle launch a generation before upon his return, at least unofficially, to government service.

The makeshift slide's drop approached forty-five degrees. But gravity kept McCracken braced to the steel, arms tucked by his sides to avoid slipping off and eyes squeezed open to the storm to steady his plunge into the water once the end of the slide came up.

Ultimately, it came much quicker than he'd expected, no more than the length of one desperately held breath. He had barely registered he was coming upon the end of his ride when the blackness of the night welcomed him, followed almost immediately by the crashing waves of the sea. He felt himself plunging beneath frigid waters and then clawed back to the surface only to be smacked by a swell. Salt water flooded his lungs and he hacked it out with the taste of fuel oil lingering in his mouth. The surface was thick with dark drilling mud that smelled sour and spoiled. McCracken finally found his breath just as the storm-fueled currents slammed into him again. A sweep of his gaze found nothing until he glimpsed Johnny Wareagle fighting the waves toward him.

"Captain!" McCracken yelled out, the storm swallowing his cry. "Captain!" he wailed again anyway.

Wareagle somehow managed to reach him just as a grinding screech found both their ears. They looked up to see the last of the *Deepwater Venture* toppling over above them, its steel carcass seeming to tilt straight in their direction as its remaining three columns collapsed into the sea. They dove into the pounding swells instinctively, both feeling the vibration of thousands of tons of steel smacking the wave-ravaged surface, the sensation grinding their teeth together even with their breaths held.

McCracken had seldom known fear like he felt in that moment, the very real fear that reaching the surface again would be impossible. That whatever terrible secrets this rig had held would remain just that and the death of Paul Basmajian would never be avenged. Recharged by that resolve, McCracken drove himself toward the surface, coming up in a valley between two mountainous waves to find Wareagle close enough to reach out for. He grabbed Johnny's life vest at the epaulet just before the heavy seas splashed more of the refuse from the drilling mud into his face, making it feel as if it was raining gravel.

"Any sign of the captain?" McCracken shouted over the storm.

Wareagle shook his head, his long black hair freed of its ponytail and pasted across his face. The *Venture* had seemingly broken apart on impact with the sea, the scattered pieces of it turned into potential weapons set in motion by the waves. Even if they managed to avoid that threat, the churning seas seemed destined to take them well before the Coast Guard could mount any rescue operation.

Wareagle had grabbed a twisted, mangled husk of steel and drawn it between them to better support their weight and ride the waves as best they could. Then McCracken spotted something that looked like a glowing orb slicing through the waves and driving rain, coming straight for them.

CHAPTER 34

New Orleans

Katie DeMarco awoke to the pungent sour scents of must and mold, aware almost immediately her captors had brought her to a basement. She snapped all the way upright, nearly falling off the stiff wooden chair on which she'd been placed, her arms and legs both unbound. Her clothes, wet with both rain and perspiration, stuck to the chair, and the basement air felt too thick and steamy to breathe.

How much time did that mean had passed? Not enough for her clothes to dry was the only conclusion Katie could draw. Her head was cloudy, her vision slowly sharpening as the grogginess receded to the sight of several figures shrouded by the murky light before her. There was no pain until she moved her eyes, at which point the mere motion sent a cascade of light flashing before her to mirror the sudden burst of agony. Her head felt heavy, a bowling ball atop her neck, and the residue of whatever drug her captors had used to knock her out had left her mouth so bone dry, her tongue felt pasted to its roof.

A single bulb dangled almost directly overhead, the only one she spotted in the dingy confines. None of the men around her moved, none spoke.

"Who are you? Where am I?"

Katie's words echoed in her own ears, sounding as lame to her as they must have to her captors, when a smaller figure appeared amid the others, gliding through the shadows as if comfortable in their midst and stopping close enough to Katie's chair for her to realize he was Japanese. His skin was porcelain smooth, seeming to shine even in the faint light. He smelled of musky talcum powder or, perhaps, lightly scented cologne. He looked at her, not seeming to blink, his eyes as detached and focused as a camera's lens.

"Katie DeMarco," he said in thinly accented English. "What is your real name?"

Katie remained silent.

"There is no such person as Katie DeMarco. You are fortunate the company responsible for the *Deepwater Venture* did not check your credentials as closely as we did."

"Who's *we*?" Katie heard herself ask.

She thought she saw the Japanese man smile. "What do you know of the *Venture*'s true purpose, *Katie DeMarco*?" he asked, her name spoken in a lower tone with an edge of contempt.

"It's an oil rig. What do you think its purpose was?" she shot back, forcing contempt into her own voice as if that might have made her sound braver.

"*Was* an oil rig. Now . . ." The Japanese man finished his comment with a shrug. "Tell me what you know, Katie DeMarco, the truth."

"I don't know anything for sure."

The Japanese seemed to perk up a bit at that. "But you know *something*, don't you?"

"I know the crew was killed. I know the rig was destroyed," she said, trying to figure out the Japanese man's part in all this. He wasn't part of Ocean Bore, meaning he had nothing to do with the men who'd pursued her through New Orleans, those who were behind

Twist's death or the murder of the WorldSafe team in Greenland. So who was he and what did he want exactly?

"The crew was killed? You think that's all that happened?" he snapped at her.

"It's enough," Katie said, her mind still not totally clear.

"If you have no answers for me, Katie DeMarco, you serve no purpose. Oil rigs drill for oil. There was no oil where the *Venture* was drilling. Ocean Bore was in search of something else entirely. I know this because I am in search of the very same thing, and I believe you know what it is and where the *Venture* found it."

"I have no idea what you're talking about."

"And yet you fled the rig at the most opportune time. You would expect me to believe that was just coincidence, that you didn't have some idea of what was to come?"

"I didn't. That's the truth."

"No. Since you fled the rig just before disaster struck," the Japanese man continued, "I must assume you suspected what was about to happen. That means you know more about what I seek than you are saying."

"I've told you everything I know."

"You think me a fool, Katie DeMarco?" the Japanese man asked. "You think I don't realize you infiltrated that rig for your own purpose? You think I don't know you must have caught on to what the *Venture* was really up to?" He took another slight step forward. "And now you will tell me what you know about the *Venture*'s true mission."

"I don't know how many different ways I can say it: I don't have any idea what you're talking about."

At that, the Japanese man edged yet closer to her, moving into the reach of the single dangling bulb. Even the dim light seemed to bother his eyes, making them narrow. He dabbed at them with a handkerchief as if they were watering, and Katie noticed his left hand was clothed in some kind of thin, black mitten.

"My name is Shinzo Asahara, Katie DeMarco."

Katie tensed, her empty stomach quivering.

"I see that name is familiar to you."

"Your father was Shoho Asahara, leader of the Aum Shinrikyo."

Asahara studied her briefly. "You know of him."

"I know he was a murderer, leader of fanatics."

Asahara stiffened. "You would be wise not to mock me."

"I've done nothing to you!"

He grinned. "That's better."

Katie eyed him questioningly.

"There is fear in your voice now. That tells me you understand the depths of your plight. 'Shinrikyo' means 'supreme truth,' Katie DeMarco. And right now the only truth that matters is what the *Venture* uncovered holds the means for Aum Shinrikyo to fulfill its destiny."

"The end of the world," Katie said as much to herself as Asahara.

Aum Shinrikyo was a doomsday cult centered in Japan and founded in 1987 by Shinzo's father, Shoho, the partially blind son of a tatami straw mat maker. He led an ordinary life until a journey to the Himalayas to study Buddhism and Hinduism left him a profoundly changed man, and he returned to Japan obsessed with the coming end of the world. More to the point, he had taken it as his God-given duty to see that end wrought by his own hand.

In pursuit of that goal, he founded his Aum Shinrikyo cult to engage in a final fight leading up to Armageddon. Toward that end, Aum Shinrikyo established a number of chemical factories and stockpiled various chemicals in preparation for at least nine biological attacks on different installations in Japan. Targets had included the legislature, the imperial palace, and the US base at Yokosuka. Cult members sprayed microbes and germ toxins from rooftops and convoys of trucks.

With one exception, though, all the attacks failed; and the one that succeeded led to what the world believed was the cult's ultimate demise, once Shoho Asahara was arrested and tried for spreading sarin nerve gas in a Tokyo subway station in 1995. The gas killed thirteen passengers and injured over five thousand. But if his technicians had not made errors in preparation and dispersal of the gas, thousands of innocent subway patrons would have been killed and tens of thousands injured instead.

Katie had thought the resulting trials and imprisonments of the cult members, including Shoho Asahara himself, had ended Aum Shinrikyo forever. But the fact that Asahara's son was standing before her now clearly indicated otherwise.

The end of the world, Katie thought again.

"I want the means to bring my father's vision to fruition," Shinzo Asahara told her, "the means that oil rig uncovered six miles beneath the surface of the sea. I want the very same thing you must have, and I want to know what you learned of it while on board."

"I can't help you. I don't know what *it* was that they uncovered, other than it wasn't oil."

Asahara tilted his head slightly to the side and regarded her closer. "Then you're going to die, Katie DeMarco, slowly and painfully unless you tell me what I need to know," he said as the man nearest her chair eased a knife from inside his jacket.

CHAPTER 35

New Orleans

The knife looked to Katie like a smaller version of the samurai sword one of her rescuers had wielded in the restaurant earlier that day. Clearly just as sharp and managing to shine even in the dingy basement's meager light.

"Not much of an incentive," Katie managed, still eyeing the blade.

Shinzo Asahara continued to regard her closely. "Who are you really, Katie DeMarco?"

"What's the difference?"

"Only that you should be much more frightened than you are. Pleading with me, begging for your life."

"Maybe you're just not as scary as you think you are."

"Who are you?"

"Why are you wearing that mitten on your hand?"

"Would you like to see?"

"Why don't you tell me if it has anything to do with your father and Aum Shinrikyo wanting to destroy the world? Is that your supreme truth?"

"The world is already destroying itself, Katie DeMarco. My father was driven by his core beliefs, the enlightenment he encountered and passed on to me. I share those beliefs along with a desire to finish his work to spite the world that has martyred him. What the *Venture* uncovered can give me the means I need to finish the job." Asahara held up his left hand, the one cloaked by the dark mitten. "You want to know why I wear this? To hide a souvenir left from the last time I encountered the very force you know full well that the *Venture* found."

"What force?"

"Ignorance renders you useless to me. If you have nothing to tell me, our business is done and so is your life."

"So you're a murderer just like your father, and you'll die just like he did. I believe he was hanged."

Asahara's expression flattened, his breathing steadied in resignation as he stepped closer into the thin spray of light, ignoring the pain it sent shooting through eyes he fought to keep open.

"We have all made sacrifices for our beliefs," he said, starting to tug at the tight mitten covering his left hand. "My father paid his price for his beliefs, just as I have paid mine. The difference is when I go, I will take the rest of the world with me. One final chance, Katie DeMarco, one final chance to aid me in that task."

Her mind cleared now, Katie used that final chance to lurch up out of her chair and close her hands on the basement's single dangling lightbulb. Steeling herself against the pain, she compressed the bulb between her hands, shattering it and driving some of the thin shards into her palms as the basement was plunged into darkness.

Men yelled, men shouted. Footsteps pounded the floor. Shinzo Asahara's voice shouted orders in Japanese, and Katie felt shapes converging on her as hands flailed out, brushing against her clothes.

But she'd already memorized the exact location of the stairs from her chair. Twenty-one steps by her estimation. Katie kept her pace steady and measured through the darkness, nothing to give away her position to men likely trained in the martial arts and thus accustomed to fighting in difficult conditions.

Sounds of pursuit had begun to close upon her when her hand grasped a wooden railing and she rushed up the steps, bursting through a door into what looked like some kind of storage room. Another door marked Exit was just to her right and she surged through it into a back alley and the stormy night beyond.

She felt the rain wash the blood from her hands, realizing only then how much they hurt. Katie burst into an all-out sprint to the nearest street. She sped across it and swung right immediately down another, safe from her pursuers for now and struck by a dread fear of the enormity of whatever the *Venture* had uncovered six miles below the surface.

". . . I will take the rest of the world with me . . ."

Katie heard Shinzo Asahara's words in her mind again, as she disappeared into the night.

CHAPTER 36

Northern Gulf Stream

"What do you mean it's gone?" Captain Merch said from the bridge of the Coast Guard cutter *Nero*, as they steamed toward the *Deepwater Venture*'s position.

"We've finally got the satellite feeds back up, sir," his exec told him. "I checked the positioning myself. Nothing. The *Venture*'s gone, lost to the sea."

Merch nonetheless raised the binoculars to his eyes, peering at the sun burning through the thick mist, the storm's residue still clinging to the surface. As a result, the sea gave up nothing, and they were still a mile out from the rig's coordinates.

"No sign of *anything*?" Merch groped, letting the binoculars dangle again.

The exec shook his head. "The Gulf got it all, sir, every last piece and bone."

"We'd best be sure. Keep us on course. Full power."

It was only last month that Merch had taken command of the *Nero*, part of a new generation of Sentinel class patrol boats that were easily the most advanced for their time of any the Coast Guard had enjoyed since being conceived by Alexander Hamilton around 1790.

"Captain," the exec barked suddenly, "sonar's got a hit!"

"Debris?"

"No, sir, it's moving. Straight, I say again, straight for our position."

"Sound the general alarm," Merch ordered, not about to take any chances. "Go to battle stations."

The *Nero* sliced through the mist, riding effortlessly over the choppy seas. Since the storm was clearing from the west, visibility was already increasing and Merch caught the first hint of the sun's dawn rays above. Then, just like that, the mist was gone and the chop with it, replaced by a frighteningly calm sea empty with the exception of an object coming straight for them from a thousand yards out now.

"Captain, is that a—"

"Yes," Merch said, before the exec could finish, "I believe it is."

CHAPTER 37

Northern Gulf Stream

Hours before, amid the storm-swept darkness, McCracken had just been about to drop below the surface to avoid whatever hunk of rig debris was sweeping straight for them.

"Wait, Blainey," Wareagle said, halting him. "It's the life pod."

He spoke just as the orb seemed to halt itself in the waves, a top hatch opening enough for Captain Seven to pop his upper body out.

"Somebody call for a taxi?"

They'd ridden out the rest of the storm within the life pod's ample confines, using its small engine and controls to avoid the harshest swells as best they could and then following the course they expected the Coast Guard to take to the *Venture*'s former position as soon as the seas allowed. Those seas had ravaged Captain Seven's computers, but all the most pertinent data had already been uploaded to the mainframe and he'd somehow managed to salvage the samples he'd taken from the *Venture*'s freshly reformed superstructure.

"You're something, Captain," a soaked McCracken said, shoulders sheathed in a blanket.

"You should see me when I'm stoned."

"I have, plenty of times. Remember?"

Captain Seven's eyes had gone down at that, his tone turning uncharacteristically somber. "Lots of people talk about that war now, but almost none of them have any idea what the fuck it was really like. Or about."

"Some days even I don't remember what it was about. But I guess all wars are like that in one way or another."

Captain Seven sucked in a hefty breath, as if he were smoking from an imaginary bowl, his twisted tangle of graying hair having dried into patches with the texture of steel wool. "I saw you at the Wall once," he said suddenly, referring to the black carved granite shape of the Vietnam Memorial in Washington. "Both of you."

"I know."

"You saw me, too?"

McCracken nodded.

"Should have come over. I was beyond stoned at the time. What was your excuse?"

"Respect for privacy, yours as well as mine. Besides, I already had plenty of company, even if their names weren't there," said McCracken, turning toward Johnny Wareagle, whose gaze was locked out a small window facing back toward the last remnants of the *Venture*. "What's eating you, Indian?"

"I haven't felt anything this powerful in a very long time, Blainey."

"With good reason, my friend," said Captain Seven. "Because there *isn't* anything more powerful than what took that rig down, not in this world anyway. It's what I was looking for in the Mediterranean five years ago and may have found here. It could mince up and scramble the entire world the same way it did the *Venture*. Mix up the contents of the planet in the spin cycle and pour out whatever's left. Forget a Level Six event, this is a genuine Level Six Thousand. Only one problem."

"What's that?" McCracken asked him.

"What's responsible doesn't exist."

CHAPTER 38

Pyrenees Mountains, Spain

"You've found it at last, Mr. Roy."

Pierce's report had gone on to detail as much as was currently known about the inexplicable fate of the *Deepwater Venture*, updated hours later to include the fact that the rig had been lost to the sea.

Disappointment over losing all chance to examine the rig and prove his theories conclusively had first stolen Sebastian Roy's sleep and then left it racked by nightmares. He tossed and turned, a cold sweat covering his skin even in the oxygen-rich, normally comfortable chill of his bedroom.

The nightmares had started with a trip through time, back to the day of the explosion and fire. His entire family together outside of Stuttgart, Germany, on the grounds of what had once been a nuclear power plant. In his career Roy had been blessed above all else with foresight, his gift of prescience fueling his meteoric rise to the stratosphere of business. Foretelling the future of energy was impossible for most in an industry riddled by misjudgments and cutthroat competition.

In the dream he saw himself addressing a crowd devoid of faces, mere shapeless forms before him, explaining that Germany and all industrialized countries would someday turn away from nuclear energy to less dangerous alternatives. This was because a catastrophic accident, a meltdown, was inevitable. So he explained how he had gone against the grain of energy investment by putting huge resources into plants specializing in fossil fuel development and enhancement. The dinosaurs of the energy industry. Huge, blackened anachronistic assemblages of steel beams and concrete smoke stacks belching poison into the air.

"Germany was ahead of the curve when it came to reducing its dependence on the seventeen nuclear plants helping to power the country," he told the faceless mass before him who, he realized in the dream, sat rigid and motionless like toy figures fit into the chairs. "So I elected to build my flagship, fully modernized fossil fuel plant on the grounds of the country's oldest nuclear facility that was shut down for good after coming only minutes from a potential meltdown in 2004."

Moments later the first explosion sounded, a blast furnace swallowing the world. His family was around him and then, once again in what felt like a recorded replay, there was only smoke and desperate people racing blindly about in search of escape. Roy heard horrible rasping coughs amid the screams, himself in motion now jostled by panicked shapes slamming into him on both sides, stealing his orientation in the smoke-ravaged darkness.

The moments that followed had given birth to Sebastian Roy in his new incarnation. The media branded him a tragic hero for what he and witnesses said happened next, when Roy managed to extricate himself from the throngs of the desperate and screaming and reach an exit where a security team pulled him the rest of the way out.

"My family, my family!" he screamed at them.

They shook their heads grimly, one of the news stories said, *and Roy rushed back into the fire in search of his son, daughter, and wife.*

He battled the surge of bodies before him, screaming their names until his throat was scorched and he realized he could no longer breathe. Saved only when other bodies piled atop his, sparing him from the flames and the worst of the heat.

Roy woke up in a hospital bed swathed in bandages and fighting off the first of the infections that seemed sure to kill him in days, if not hours.

"Punishment," he'd muttered to first a nurse and then a doctor in the hospital, his voice barely rising over a whisper. The pain he felt was intense, constant, resisting the attempts of painkillers to make any more than a dent in it. "I'm being punished for my sins."

He'd asked them for a priest to whom to confess those sins, certain he was going to die. When the priest came, Roy could sense his revulsion at what he heard, the man struggling to offer him final absolution. Sebastian Roy might not have been a religious man, but he nonetheless felt the need to share a truth he had shared with no other. Then, shortly after Roy made what was deemed a miraculous recovery, the priest disappeared. The doctor and the nurse followed soon afterward.

Meanwhile, Roy Industries had managed to retain its status as an industry stalwart. The stock dropped precipitously at first, but it recovered just as fast when the world learned Sebastian Roy was recovering and had every intention of returning to the helm of his company. Above all else, he could not let the tragedy deter his plans for the future, especially when sabotage was found to be the cause of the explosions and resulting fire. The authorities called it terrorism, likely on the part of radical environmentalists, which only strengthened Roy's personal resolve. Destroying them meant destroying their cause.

He would shove it in his enemies' faces. Use his newfound status as a truly tragic figure to help him build hundreds, even thousands, of fossil fuel plants all over the world, all of them belching black hydrocarbon smoke into the atmosphere to stain the air and dirty the clouds. Clean energy meant little to him; the future he saw was one where the world wanted heat, light, and convenient transportation above all else and wouldn't care about the environmental price paid as long as their switches worked and they got where they wanted to go.

Then came the tsunami-caused disaster at the Fukushima nuclear plant in Japan. Suddenly demand for fossil fuel replacement facilities, a market now cornered by Roy Industries, exploded. Rival energy companies imploded under the strain and poor planning to be sucked up and absorbed at Roy's whim for pennies on the dollar. Once a powerful force in the industry, Sebastian Roy became the prevailing one to whom former rivals were beholden if they wanted to share in his production of the gigawatts that were far more valuable than any single resource in controlling the world.

Still, that wasn't enough. He wanted more, some ultimate source of power that would render all others obsolete even as it brought meaning to the loss of his family. And now, because of what had happened a half world away in the Gulf of Mexico, he found himself on the verge of finding that source at long last.

Roy used his call button to summon Pierce as soon as the nightmares had relinquished their hold on him.

"You thought I was crazy when I told you what I was after, didn't you?" he said.

"I thought this was a fool's errand, yes, Mr. Roy."

"And what do you think now, Pierce?"

"Nothing. Because I'm too scared."

"All great achievements require sacrifice," Roy reminded him. "There is nothing to fear from that, no more anyway than that experienced by those involved in the Manhattan Project, the men who changed the world forever at Alamogordo."

"With all due respect, Mr. Roy, none of your theories accounted for whatever happened to the *Deepwater Venture*."

"Going back to the Manhattan Project," Roy told him, "there

was a letter circulated by some of the foremost scientists in the world claiming an atomic detonation could create a chain reaction that might destroy the entire planet. Had those behind the project heeded their warning, we never would've developed the bomb. Mutual deterrence would have gone out the window, the Cold War progressing down an entirely different route. Just imagine, Pierce."

"I have, I am."

"We must proceed, as the Manhattan Project did, in spite of the risks. Because, make no mistake about it, what we are working toward here has the potential to change the world in even more profound ways."

"It can't be harnessed, Mr. Roy. Even those who've been trumpeting its existence for decades have no idea how to contain it."

"Then we'll find a way and once we do, the world will never be the same again. Contact the scientists in Geneva," Roy continued. "Tell them a jet will be coming to pick them up first thing tomorrow."

"Should I tell them why?"

"Only that the time has finally come."

CHAPTER 39

New Orleans

Hank Folsom arranged for Captain Seven to set up shop at the New Orleans Homeland Security offices inside City Hall downtown on Perdido Street. Doubling as the region's headquarters for Emergency Management, the offices occupied the sprawling tan and glass slab of a building's top three floors. The lowermost floor was accessible only via a dedicated lobby elevator and restricted to authorized personnel.

"Here's the thing," Folsom explained, after meeting them outside. "Homeland has created these regional centers to be capable of overseeing operations on a national level in the event some kind of catastrophe or attack knocks out our main headquarters and command centers."

"Sounds wise," McCracken acknowledged.

"What you need to know is that this New Orleans center is a kind of prototype with enhanced security procedures."

"Meaning?"

"Better you see for yourself, McCracken."

~

McCracken saw exactly what Folsom had been referring to as soon as the elevator deposited them in a reception area outside the entrance to Homeland's self-contained floors inside City Hall. A waist-high robot on treads, looking like a minitank, stood vigil outside the glass entry doors.

"During the early days of the Iraq war," Folsom explained, "our technicians converted bomb-disposal robots to carry machine guns, grenade launchers, even rockets. Within a year, a bunch of these SWORDS, or **S**pecial **W**eapons **O**bservation **R**emote reconnaissance **D**irect action **S**ystem, robots were deployed in the arena."

"First I've heard of that," said McCracken.

"That's because there were problems, MacNuts," noted Captain Seven. "Isn't that right, B-rat?" His final remark was aimed at Folsom.

"Kinks we've now ironed out."

"Sure, whatever you say," the captain smirked, turning to McCracken. "Dude, I could build better machines out of Tinker Toys."

Through the glass, McCracken could see SWORDS bots patrolling the Homeland facility's halls. And perched on twin pedestals just inside the entrance were a pair of humanoid robots nearly as tall as Johnny Wareagle complete with arms, legs, feet, and torso but no head he could discern.

"That's the Atlas model," Folsom said, noting McCracken's interested gaze. "Built by Boston Dynamics as the next step in robotic evolution. The Atlas will move through difficult terrain using humanlike behavior: sometimes walking upright as a bipod, sometimes turning sideways to squeeze through narrow passages, and sometimes, when the terrain gets its nastiest, using its hands for extra support and balance. Unlike most other humanoid robots that use static techniques to control their motion, Atlas will move dynamically, leveraging the advanced control software and high-performance actuated hardware."

"Sounds like a sales pitch you've given before, Hank."

"Oh, once or twice."

"Why don't you tell him about the reason for the Atlas deployment delays?" Captain Seven prodded.

"They're off-line. For display purposes only."

Captain Seven looked toward McCracken. "That's because one of the prototypes played trash compactor with its programmer. Apparently it had temperament issues. Vision problems, too, since prototypes like these have continued to have trouble distinguishing between the good guys and the bad guys."

Folsom swung toward McCracken. "Who is this guy?"

"Specialist you authorized to help the cause."

"What's your security clearance?" Folsom demanded of Captain Seven.

"Higher than you've ever heard of, B-rat. I've been designing shit that actually works since you were crapping your diapers. In fact, I once made a bomb made out of crap."

"Can we just get started?" Folsom asked, flashing his ID card for the sentry SWORDS machine guarding the door.

"What's he doing now?" from Folsom once they were inside a high-tech conference room, as Captain Seven walked the perimeter of the walls, tracing a finger down the center.

"I don't know," said McCracken. "I'm not even sure he does. Must be something they do on the planet he comes from."

Captain Seven suddenly stopped and turned. "Building wiring wouldn't keep a seventh grader working on a science project from breaching the firewall." The captain's dull blue eyes fell on Folsom, shaking his head with a cocksure smile. "And you're trying to build robots, B-rat?"

"What does 'B-rat' mean?"

"Short for 'bureaucrat' in the captain's lexicon," McCracken elaborated as Wareagle stifled a smile and a wheeled SWORDS robot stopped in the doorway as if to register who was present inside.

"Synonym for asshole," Captain Seven continued, eyeing Folsom. "Hey, you smoke dope? I hear the government grows some badass shit for approved medical purposes only. In my mind, you should distribute it to Congress and watch legislation finally get passed along with the joints."

"I have no idea how to even respond to that."

Captain Seven's eyes twinkled. "Speaking of which, my supply got ruined in the storm. Caught a natural high for a time off being on that rig, but I feel a need coming on."

"No worries," McCracken told him. "The DEA has offices in this building too. Maybe I can rustle some up for you from their stash."

"Really?"

"No."

Captain Seven didn't bother to hide his disappointment. His long gray hair hung in twisted ringlets from the storm and sea's effects hours earlier. He plopped down into a rolling chair set before a computer and leaned back far enough to splay his leather vest over the arms.

"Think I'll get to work."

"How bad I say this was last night and this morning?" Captain Seven asked an hour later after running any number of computations and reviewing the data off the NSA site he'd hacked.

"Bad," McCracken told him.

"Well, it's worse."

"So what else is new?"

"The *Venture*, as in on the subatomic level. Another level beyond molecular, in case you were wondering. I've been chasing this off and on for five years now, ever since it nearly got me killed in the Mediterranean. Man oh man, I never thought I'd find it."

"Find what?"

Captain Seven hesitated ever so slightly before responding. "Dark matter."

PART THREE:
DARK MATTER

CHAPTER 40

New Orleans

Katie DeMarco had tried them all—every phone number, the contacts for WorldSafe she'd long committed to memory—to no avail. All of them had gone to ground in the wake of what happened in Greenland.

Or worse.

She'd spent the night walking the streets of downtown New Orleans, lingering in hotel bathroom stalls and in the darkest corners of fast-food restaurants out of view from the street as she dried out from the storm's deluge. She let instinct guide just how long to remain in each, her thinking finally clearing with the approach of a dawn that had found her huddled in the damp dewy mist rising off the ground of Saint Louis Cemetery Number One. The aboveground burial vaults offered plenty of cover, and the cemetery's location close to the Mississippi River just one block from the start of the French Quarter provided ample escape routes if it came to that.

She'd found a spot to hide herself amid the cold stone, granite, and marble vaults where she greeted the sun's first warming rays. Fear and fatigue had made it hard to collect her thoughts, but the sun revived Katie enough for her to consider her next move in clothes that felt stale, damp, and musty.

WorldSafe, its name now sadly ironic, offered no respite. Her contact Twist was dead. The Aum Shinrikyo cult was after her for one reason, the killers behind the massacre in Greenland for another reason entirely.

All because of whatever had happened to the *Deepwater Venture* in the hours following her hasty departure.

Katie rose and peered out from behind the crypt holding Etienne de Boré, scion of New Orleans's early sugar industry and first mayor of the city. Finding the cemetery still deserted save for her and whatever ghosts might be about, she slid out with the trees as cover and clung to side and back streets en route to the French Quarter, where she used a side entrance of the Hotel St. Marie. She ducked into a restroom toting a drugstore bag stuffed with fresh bandages and antiseptic to redress the cuts on her palms that still smarted from closing her hands around the basement lightbulb.

Her mind began to crystallize around a plan beyond that, as she wrapped her wounds with fresh dressings and chucked her original dressings in the trash. There were a few other contacts she could call upon, fervent supporters of WorldSafe who would be made understandably livid by what had transpired. Katie wouldn't tell them everything, not even close, just enough to make them understand she needed their help.

She emerged from the restroom, reconstructing phone numbers in her mind when a pair of police officers with guns drawn lurched out before her.

"Stay where you are! Show us your hands!"

Heavy footsteps pounded the floor behind her, more police closing from there as well.

“Down on the floor!” the first cop ordered, gun steadied straight on her. “Do it now!”

Katie complied, crying out in pain as her arms were yanked behind her back and cuffs slapped on her wrists.

CHAPTER 41

New Orleans

"What?" was Captain Seven's only response to the skeptical stares cast his way.

"I was hoping for a more rational explanation," McCracken told him.

"You want rational, you got the wrong guy. You knew that when you called me in."

"I still wasn't expecting something out of science fiction."

"You mean like milking jellyfish for their toxin? Wonder if that rig's crew would've felt any better if they knew it was only something out of science fiction that killed them."

"I get the point."

"You better," Captain Seven said, shaking his head. "So typical. I expected more from you, MacNuts, you of all people who hijacked a space shuttle, stopped a Russian death ray from destroying the country, fought genetically enhanced supermen, saved the country from a coup, saved Disney World, the Alamo . . . Oh, and did I forget to mention New York City?"

"Same man," McCracken told him. "Just younger and less jaded back in those days."

"Superweapons are nothing new, MacNuts; you've been fighting them for thirty years now. But this one's different from anything you've faced before. We're not talking here about a city or even a country. We're talking about dumping the whole freaking world into a Mixmaster and seeing what's left. You want somebody to blame for what happened in the Gulf and it pisses you off there was no hostile action involved."

"But somebody ordered them to drill in that spot, and that somebody got Paul Basmajian killed."

"You can't bring him back, Blainey," Wareagle said abruptly, breaking his own silence.

"I think I know that, Indian."

"I wasn't talking about Baz. I was talking about the hostage we lost. You never had a chance to save Baz, but you could have saved that boy. Don't let this be about that."

"Give me some credit here, Johnny."

"I just did," said Wareagle. "Saving the world's not a bad way to make up for losing one hostage."

"Hey," said Captain Seven, "I hate to interrupt you guys but . . ."

"Go on," McCracken urged.

"So what if it wasn't?"

"Wasn't what?"

"An accident. What happened to the *Deepwater Venture*."

"Keep talking, Captain."

"Somebody associated with Ocean Bore was looking for something, even though they must've had at least some idea of what might happen if they found it."

McCracken's black eyes narrowed. "Talk to me about dark matter. Science *fact*, not fiction."

"Goes back to the big bang theory. You think the universe just showed up or grew randomly?" Captain Seven shook his head. "No such luck, MacNuts. Close your eyes."

"Is this guy for real?" Folsom wondered aloud.

"He once devised a heat-sensitive explosive disguised as cough syrup that helped us take out a terrorist mastermind with a cold. That real enough for you?"

"You heard me," Captain Seven reiterated, "close your eyes."

All three of them finally did.

"All right," Captain Seven resumed. "Can you see me?"

"Is this some kind of joke?" Folsom snapped.

"Answer the question."

"How can I see you if my eyes are closed?"

"Exactly, B-rat. You can't see me, but you know I'm here. Same thing with dark matter. Nobody's ever seen or isolated it, but we know it's there. You can open your eyes now." Captain Seven waited to meet their gazes before continuing. "Dark matter makes up around a quarter of the universe while traditional matter composes only around five percent of it. We know that because of gravity and the study of other solar systems through telescopes like the Hubble. I'm giving you the CliffsNotes version here, so bear with me."

Captain Seven shifted about in the chair, suddenly looking antsy.

"Dark matter, or something like it, *has* to exist. There's simply no other explanation for the creation of the universe through mass and energy. The problem and the challenge is to quantify something no one has ever identified or even positively confirmed the existence of. All we've got are theories and one of them, I'm afraid, explains exactly what happened on the *Deepwater Venture*. You familiar with the work they're doing at CERN in that giant supercollider tunnel on the French-Swiss border?"

"Not very," McCracken told him.

"Well, it's pretty much been a circus with not an awful lot to show for the several billion spent across the board," Captain Seven explained. "Great fanfare, a doorway to the fucking future opening on day one in September of 2008. Lots of champagne bottles popped and then this multibillion-dollar piece of machinery gets shut down nine days later. Press and officials were told a badly soldered electrical splice overheated and set off a chain of damage to the magnets and other parts of the supercollider."

"A lie?" McCracken said.

"For sure. They found something all right—they found that they could indeed prove the existence of dark matter, even create it, but containing it proved the real wild card. And when a bunch of atoms got loose in the system, they ended up spending a couple years repairing the damage."

"How much is a bunch?"

"Maybe one one-thousandth the size of a pinhead." The captain shook his head. "You cannot make this shit up, I kid you not. So they're ready for the big dramatic restart with all the fanfare, champagne on ice again. This time, the geniuses at CERN are going to be cautious. Take things by the numbers and start up slow, building the energy beams of protons gradually toward reaching record-setting collisions."

"Collisions," McCracken repeated.

"That's what it's all about if you want to remake the big bang. You get these photons slamming into one another with enough force to create a boom. The faster they hit, the bigger the boom."

"Where's dark matter fit into all this?"

"Well, MacNuts, a bunch of their experimenting has been in the area of antimatter, which is something else entirely. See, prevailing theory says both matter and antimatter must have been created in equal amounts in the big bang, but antimatter went bye-bye. Half the universe, in other words, disappears and the nursery school students at CERN want to know what happened to it. Along the way they manage to actually isolate and trap some antihydrogen atoms for the first time. Lo and behold, parts of the prevailing theory go out the window because they realize what they've really got on their hands is dark matter. That antimatter didn't leave the building, it just went into hiding in another room, another form. Dormant like bees in the winter."

"Until somebody bangs their hive with a stick," McCracken picked up. "Just like the *Deepwater Venture* penetrating that pocket more than six miles below the surface of the sea."

"I always thought that was a billion to one shot, as much chance of it happening as the sun flaming out tomorrow. Now I'm thinking maybe I should get my thermals ready. Take notice, B-rat."

"I'd pay attention to him if I were you, Hank."

"Pay attention to what exactly?"

Captain Seven took it from there. "To me telling you to get on the horn and seal the area around the *Deepwater Venture*'s position, as in lock it down tight to a two-mile radius. Call your friends at Homeland, the Coast Guard, the Imperial Navy, the Barbary pirates, and the ghost of motherfucking Jean Lafitte if you have to, but just get it done."

"What's the point?" Folsom challenged. "The rig's gone, the crew's dead."

"But what killed them is still there, B-rat, in a very big way."

CHAPTER 42

New Orleans

"Under the sea," Captain Seven continued. "More of those thermal pockets originating at the earth's core where somebody else with a drill bit might get seriously unlucky. Once word gets out about dark matter, you're gonna have a scientific feeding frenzy that'll turn the Coast Guard into traffic cops. And everybody who shows up will be sure they won't make the same mistake as the *Venture*, that they can control a force we now understand went away for a very good reason. Man, I could use a joint right now. . . .

"The existence of the planet," he went on when none miraculously appeared, "of life, of everything is based on a constant push and pull of forces, energies, confronting each other. Picture a massive combustion engine, your car on a scale of a quadrillion, and you'll have some idea of the force holding the planet together."

"Gravity," said McCracken.

"But what is gravity, what creates it? One prevailing theory says dark matter and light matter struggling to exist together in the same plane. That explains everything, including life itself. Our very existence, in other words."

"What happened on the *Venture* is nothing about life," Wareagle said, his tone hushed. "Quite the opposite."

"Ah, but it is, kemosabe. It is indeed. Prevailing theory has it that dark matter is composed of neutrinos: tiny particles that have no electric charge and little or no mass. They interact with atoms of matter so rarely that the average neutrino can pass through Earth without hitting anything. Scientists assume that great numbers of neutrinos constantly stream through human beings and everything else on Earth, causing neither sensation nor discernible injury.

"Now comes the fun part." Captain Seven rose from his chair and began pacing up and back across the length of the room, careful to avoid the darkened window for some reason. "Part of the neutrino flow reaching the earth comes from the thermonuclear reactions that fuel the sun, but there are too few solar neutrinos with high enough energy to cause appreciable biological damage. On the other hand, the torrents of neutrinos produced by the quick collapse of massive stars are a more serious matter. In such a star's final stage of collapse when it has used up its nuclear fuel, the star's ordinary atoms are crushed by gravity into a kind of superdense neutron soup, and most of the binding energy that had held together the original atomic nuclei is released in the form of neutrino particles."

"Does he always talk like this?" Folsom asked McCracken.

"You get me some of that high-end government dope and I will change your world forever."

"Just tell what this has to do with dark matter."

"Weren't you listening to what I said before, B-rat? Neutrinos, according to theory, *are* dark matter; at least they compose it. And the collision of any one of these neutrinos with an atom anywhere in the universe is highly unlikely. But because stellar collapses produce such astronomical numbers of high-energy neutrinos, the chances that some would hit other atoms are greatly increased. Neutrino detectors built at laboratories in various parts of the world usually consist of enormous tanks of water, in which the rare impact of a neutrino produces a tiny flash of light.

"That's because when a high-energy neutrino hits an atom, it transfers most of its recoil energy to the atom, which then becomes a microscopic but potentially deadly projectile. A recoiling atom can rip deeply into biological tissue, releasing its damaging energy very rapidly along its track, destroying cells essential to life, causing mutations of DNA genetic material."

"I think he's getting to the point," McCracken told Folsom.

"I am indeed, MacNuts, I am indeed. Working this shit out is better than drugs. I'm flying on an incredible natural high on the express train to Pluto."

"Get to the point, please," Folsom said, rolling his eyes.

"Back to CERN for that. They built the world's largest Hadron collider under the Swiss-French border. We're talking a seventeen-mile tunnel where high-energy beams of protons are sent crashing into one another at virtually immeasurable speeds. In a nutshell, CERN scientists are trying to re-create the big bang that created the universe when light and dark matter collided in an incredible moment. Call it the ultimate cosmic fuck. The dark matter ended up concentrating from the center around, organized like an incredibly dense ball that kept sucking in billions upon billions of neutrinos like a vacuum. Forming a core. Have I enlightened you sufficiently yet?"

"You're talking about the *earth's* core."

Captain Seven stuck his hands in the pockets of his bathrobe. "If you were stoned, you would've figured that much out five minutes ago. That's where the energy, the heat, the weight that gives ballast to the planet originates. Gravity, B-rat; only even Einstein never envisioned the center of the planet as the actual source for every major theory he ever developed. Dark matter is the ultimate power in the universe, even though we can't see it. Harness that power and, well, fossil fuels will be as extinct as the dinosaurs. But dark matter doesn't like to be harnessed, and every time scientists from CERN and elsewhere have managed to isolate it for a single nanosecond, it disappears. Violently. Harmless enough with a single particle and resulting single flash of light. But consider multiplying it geometrically as more particles join the party. Same nanosecond, bigger boom. Way, way, way, way, way, way, way bigger."

"The missing six seconds," McCracken remembered.

"What happened on the *Deepwater Venture* didn't take even that long, MacNuts. More than six miles down, deepest any rig has ever gone, their drill cut straight into a thermal pocket and released a fractional amount of dark matter contained since the dawn of time under incredible pressure, which pushed it up the line at a speed too fast to calculate. Remember that single flash of light? Well, boys, multiply it on the order of a billion and you get the idea of what essentially melted everything on board the rig in the shadow of a second. And I do mean everything and I do mean shadow and I do mean we face the very real possibility of the same thing happening to the entire planet if enough dark matter gets released."

"You said *essentially* melted, Captain," noted McCracken.

"The qualification comes from the fact that melting is associated with heat. Heat had nothing to do with the cosmic convergence that took place on the *Venture*. In fact, there was no heat or even air—all that got sucked up by the vacuum effect in the same split second the rig's molecules were scrambled and re-formed."

"That's impossible," snapped Folsom.

"Only to small-minded bureaucrats who aren't convinced they've got an asshole since they can't see it in front of their faces."

"I think you're making this up as you go along."

"Am I?" Captain Seven shot back, enjoying the challenge Folsom presented. "Okay, drop an ice cube in a bowl, wait for it to melt, and refreeze it. Altogether different shape, right?"

Folsom nodded grudgingly.

"Even though it's otherwise the same, identical amount of water but in an entirely different configuration. Have I slowed the speed down enough for you to follow, B-rat?"

"I start my day reading the SIT reports from the best theoretical weapons minds in the world," started Folsom. "And I've never heard of anything like this being possible. Not even close."

"That's because it's not a weapon, B-rat, at least not until yesterday. And as for those minds of yours, they're functioning in a realm of reality that cannot conceive of harnessing the power of dark matter, even if you could contain it, 'cause therein lies the problem. Scientists who've been able to isolate dark matter for a nanosecond have no clue whatsoever as to how to contain it. Whoever figures that one out and . . . well, let's just say all bets are off. And I mean all. Nuclear power would become today's version of black-and-white televisions. You could wipe out an entire nation the size of Texas, scramble it like eggs, with a device no bigger than a Coke can. Sounds tempting, B-rat, doesn't it?"

Folsom remained silent.

"Bad idea," Captain Seven told him. "Perish the very thought. You send a team to go poking around down there around the same spot the *Venture* struck and they could end up releasing a bunch more dark matter than what it took to take out the *Venture*. Like sticking a pin in a balloon to the nth degree. Release too much and you could end up rupturing the earth's crust to the point where tsunamis the size of the Empire State Building roll toward every coast in the hemisphere. A genuine extinction event. Level Six million. Need I go on?"

"I think what the captain is saying," picked up McCracken, "is that you need to throw a blanket over this whole mess. Forget investigation, exploration, dissemination—all the usual suspects. You need to button this up and contain the damage, Folsom."

"Will do," said Folsom. "But I think I'll leave mention of dark matter out of the reports for now."

"No need," Captain Seven told him. "People a lot higher up the food chain than you have been after it for years."

"How could you know that?"

"Who do you think sent me to the Mediterranean five years ago? That almost got me killed, and I have no intention of repeating the experience."

CHAPTER 43

Pyrenees Mountains, Spain

"Thank you for coming, gentlemen."

The two scientists, Gunthar Bol and Peter Whitcomb, sat side by side on a couch in Sebastian Roy's hyperbaric home, facing a man they'd heard much about but were meeting for the first time.

"You didn't leave us much choice," said Whitcomb, his shoulders stiff and expression locked in a caustic sneer to show his annoyance. "Our experiments at CERN have reached a critical juncture. We've finally isolated a new subatomic particle we believe to be Higgs boson, and us being here serves no one's best interests."

"You mean the experiments that *I* am funding? And I'll decide what lies in our best interests, Doctor. That's why I had you brought here. There is exciting, if not earth-shattering, news to report. The theory of dark matter being contained at the earth's core since the planet's origins has been confirmed: a small pocket was uncovered six miles down in the northern Gulf Stream."

The two scientists sat in stunned silence, shocked and barely able to exchange even cursory glances with each other in the well-appointed chamber that made them feel they were in a commercial airliner, right down to the steady whir of constantly recirculated air.

"There was chatter about an incident in the Gulf yesterday," said Dr. Gunthar Bol.

Bol was tall, thin, and balding. He wore thin glasses in gunmetal frames that looked terribly out of fashion. Bol supervised the largest particle physics lab in the world, known by its French acronym CERN, or the European Organization for Nuclear Research. Bol's immensely qualified team there had been trying for years to recreate the big bang in an attempt to understand the true origins of the universe. That incredible explosion and release of energy had dominated much of Sebastian Roy's thinking for years. Harnessing such energy would render all other sources obsolete, and the man who controlled it would control the world.

"Chatter?"

Bol nodded, exchanging a brief glance with Whitcomb, a Harvard-educated Swiss American who'd written books aimed at explaining quantum mechanics and theory to laypersons. He was boyish in appearance with red, ruddy cheeks and a shock of blond hair he wore overly long and parted from left to right. "Something specifically pertaining to an oil rig."

"I have reports and transmissions on that subject for your review. That review will be crucial to the steps taken from this point. But for now, I'd prefer to—"

"It was destroyed, wasn't it?" Dr. Whitcomb interrupted.

"Suffice it to say we are dealing with something unprecedented here. The fate of this oil rig aside, I'd prefer to focus on the ramifications of what it means for your work, *our* work."

"This was not random, then," Bol started. "You made sure this rig was drilling in the area where you had determined dark matter mostly likely to be."

"A theory, gentlemen," Roy told them, "and nothing more. I started to suspect the possibility after reading the latest research on the earth's core, which, it turns out, is radiating far more heat and energy than previously believed. Existing models for its structure and true composition suddenly needed to be rethought and the only thing scientists could agree on was that something was going on with regard to the release of thermal energy that none of them could explain. I was especially struck by a quote from Dr. Dario Alfè from the University College London in the *New York Times* to the effect there might be something going on down there, and some force present, no one has ever considered before."

"Dark matter," said Whitcomb.

Roy nodded. "I've had other exploration crews searching the seas for a possible breakthrough ever since, for over a year now. The difference here was the depth achieved. As for the location, its choice was based on seismic readings that indicated the area beneath the seafloor to be soft and sediment based, thus far more likely to contain pockets that extended up from the very core of the planet. Theoretically, as you know, the weight of dark matter makes it most likely to settle at the lowest point."

"Actually," corrected Bol, rubbing the bridge of his nose with a single finger, "there is no proof that dark matter has any weight at all."

"An assumption, then," Roy conceded. He felt himself growing frustrated with the lack of deference these men paid him. He was used to dominating his foes in business and used to being treated as such. But these weren't businessmen and, as scientists, they held knowledge as power more than money. "And another reasonably accepted assumption is that dark matter is highly pressurized, meaning it will follow the flow to any venting."

"As in a high-powered drill piercing a pocket in the earth's crust," noted Bol.

"I am to understand, then," picked up Whitcomb as caustically as he could manage, "that your experiments continued, in spite of our warnings to the contrary about the potential unintended consequences."

"Specifically," elaborated Bol, "that finding and isolating dark matter is nothing compared to containing it. In point of fact, Mr. Roy, we have just recently managed to trap all of several hundred antihydrogen atoms, the first step to figuring out how to contain dark matter."

"Mr. Roy," Whitcomb started, but Bol wasn't finished yet, interrupting him.

"What happened to this oil rig exactly?"

"Why don't you tell me, Doctor?" followed Roy.

"I can't; nobody can. Because nobody knows what the release of anything more than a few molecules of dark matter coming into contact with normal matter would do. Nobody knows because it's never happened, at least not since the world was created."

"It has now," said Sebastian Roy, rising and moving to the back of his chair. He grasped it tightly, displaying his impatience. "And I summoned you here to discuss the next steps, not rehash the old ones."

Whitcomb could only shake his head. "I don't think you understand. The big bang released in a single moment more energy than the collective world has ever known. Each time particles of dark matter are released, that big bang is replicated in a minute form. The antihydrogen atoms Dr. Bol's team has managed to isolate and contain are to be the basis of replicating that event in the *controlled environment* we've created at CERN."

Bol was nodding along with Whitcomb's words. "Releasing dark matter without the necessary safety protocols in place would be . . ."

"Would be what, Doctor Bol?" Roy challenged.

"It goes back to containment," Bol explained. "Your oil rig witnessed firsthand the effects of releasing dark matter within an uncontrolled environment."

"Fine," said Roy, squeezing the back of his chair, "and what if such a controlled environment, a means of containment, existed?"

The scientists again gazed at each other.

"I don't believe I heard you correctly," said Bol.

"Yes, you did. The means to contain, to store dark matter already exists; we just have to find it."

"Find what?"

"Pandora's box."

"It was actually a jar," Roy continued after the collective shock of the two scientists before him had worn off. "Calling it Pandora's box was the result of a mistaken translation that has endured through the ages. Large, though, perhaps even as big as a man."

"You summoned us here because of a *myth*?" asked a visibly perturbed Whitcomb.

"I imagine many said the same thing about Nicolaus Otto and Karl Benz when they developed the internal combustion engine on different tracks a decade apart. The principles for a horse and buggy world were equally incredible in 1880, maybe even more so."

"Mr. Roy," said Bol, rising to his feet, "Pandora's box doesn't exist."

"If you're referring to a mythological artifact that contained all the evil in the world eventually to be released once opened, you are of course correct. I'm speaking of something else entirely."

Whitcomb joined Bol on his feet. "All the same, we're physicists, not archaeologists or historians. This isn't what we do."

"And I need physicists on-site once we find what we are looking for. Your expertise will be crucial in assuring that lesser minds don't make a potentially catastrophic mistake."

"Mr. Roy," said Bol, "with all due respect, our work at CERN is reaching a critical stage. You should let us get back there immediately."

"With all due respect," added Whitcomb, "I insist. This fantasy has gone on long enough."

Roy took no offense at the remark, showed no reaction at all. "With all due respect, when was the last time either of you spoke with your families?"

Bol stiffened. Whitcomb's knees nearly buckled.

"Not in the past twenty-four hours obviously," Roy continued when neither man responded, "since both your families have been in my custody since then. And if you ever want to see them again, you'll join my teams searching for Pandora's jar off Greece right now."

CHAPTER 44

New Orleans

"So who was it that sent you to the Mediterranean five years ago?" Folsom asked.

"Who do you think? They're all just names to me. I don't pay much attention to which uniform or three-letter department is paying my freight. They say jump, I say I like being high," Captain Seven said with a twinkle in his eye. "Started with me reading some recently uncovered lost works of the Greek historian Herodotus, containing the truth behind something that might not have been a myth or legend after all."

"Herodotus wrote about dark matter?"

"Not exactly, B-rat; more like the only place I'm pretty certain it can be found and what I was looking for in the Med: Pandora's Temple."

Greece, 1672 B.C.

"Your king has a job for you, Pathos Verdes."

Verdes knelt on the hard gravel floor before the king's messenger, his knees already aching from the strain he would never let show on his features. He squinted from the afternoon sun streaming in through the open door and wall slats, edges of the light casting the messenger's face in what looked like a halo.

Verdes had dismissed his wife, who was pregnant with their first child, from the modest hut in which they lived. Verdes saw no reason to live exorbitantly in spite of his reputation as the greatest builder of his time. Although humble, he'd built his own home in the lee of a hillside to provide ample shade in the warm summer months like these, leaving the king's messenger comfortable on the bench seat fashioned out of clay. Beyond that there were only straw mats on which to sleep and shelves formed of laced-together branches to store their meager possessions. Verdes had fashioned the plates, bowls, and cups out of wood, coating them in a fine resin of tree sap as his father had shown him. So, too, his home was the lone structure built to feature open slots carved into the walls, constructed to allow the breeze to pass through in the warm season and then be filled in with a combination of moss, clay, and stones when the weather turned cold.

"There is a weapon greater than any ever known to gods or mortal man," the messenger continued. The light sifting through the open slots caught his face in splotches, making it seem formless—more mask than flesh. But Verdes shook off the illusion. "This weapon has the power to control the world or destroy it, to kill even a god. As the greatest builder of our time, your king orders you to construct a temple capable of containing this weapon so it remains protected from mortal hands. You must be sure to build this temple so no mortal can ever reach it, apart from man where it will remain for all time."

Pathos Verdes felt the rough canvas stitching of the shapeless robe he wore over his undergarments digging into his legs. Those undergarments were made of a rolled combination of tree bark and dried fig leaves, stitched by his wife thanks to her own considerable talents. He was humbled by such a royal visit under escort to his home, but overwhelmed at the same time. He had met the king once before when both were younger men. Verdes had served as apprentice on the build of the royal palace until the king ordered the master builder executed when they fell behind schedule, and Verdes volunteered to take his place.

"Such an undertaking," he told the messenger, "would take vast reserves of funds, men, and materials, not to mention ages. Unlimited reserves, with all respect to my king, and I am not a man of such means."

"All your needs will be met. Understand, Pathos Verdes, that your king would never have commissioned such a project if not with the gods' blessing. And so that blessing will be yours. And know that you will be rewarded with the gratitude of the gods in the afterlife for your service."

The messenger rose from the wooden bench, Verdes rising with him and bowing reverently. "Tell my king his temple will be built. But your name, I seem to have forgotten it."

"Hermes."

Once the messenger had taken his leave, Verdes set his mind to consideration of building the largest structure ever known to mortal man. It commanded his days, bringing him to large tapestries of papyrus where he drew out his plans for each phase of the temple—every layer and level, including the vast materials needed to bring the grand vision to fruition, often drawn from dreams the previous night. The task was daunting, terrifying in scope even when tempered by the assurances of the king's messenger that all his needs would be provided for.

Any doubts Pathos Verdes may have harbored were erased when his wife summoned him weeks into his planning. Lying before the entrance to his home was a wooden chest. Verdes opened it under the rays of the sun and was blinded by the glow off the thousands of gold pieces contained inside—the very bounty required to retain the men and acquire the materials to build the temple to the king's grand specifications. He knew such an undertaking mandated a site reasonably close to water, in this case the shores near the meeting point of the Mediterranean and Aegean Seas, so the vast stores of wood, limestone, marble, bronze, and terra-cotta could be transported from ports the known world over. Similarly, though, the messenger had explicitly ordered Verdes to make sure the temple could be rendered safe from mortal intrusion. That made for a seemingly impossible contradiction to resolve.

Still, Verdes held fast to his faith, seeing it rewarded when a vast storm laid waste to the coastline, followed by a severe drought that reduced the lush countryside to a wasteland, a desert traveled only by lost souls where death awaited in the relentless heat. Legends quickly spread of those who strayed into this desert being set upon by inhuman creatures who served as centurions to deny approach to those not deemed worthy, their ravaged remains found by others with the good sense to turn back. This as shiploads of materials began to arrive, along with the men required to utilize them. Neither Verdes nor his workers ever encountered any of these monsters themselves, but they hardly ever left the area of the temple's ongoing construction. Verdes's wife gave birth to their first son the day the first stone was laid and his second three years later just as the initial column was raised into place.

The ensuing years passed with Verdes living on less and less sleep, descending into a madness he neither understood nor resisted. From that madness came the solutions to architectural problems never encountered or solved by mortal man before. As one month, and then year, drew into the next, the great gleaming temple rose from the desert toward the sky and Zeus himself.

The death of his first son barely registered with him, but the passing of his second plunged Pathos Verdes into an even deeper fit of madness that left him questioning his faith in the very gods he had relied upon. Even so, that did not diminish his resolve to complete his task, knowing as the end neared not how many years had fled until he caught a glance of his aged reflection in a shiny piece of bronze. He hardly recognized the face that looked back at him, but his eyes still worked well enough to follow his drawings and lay the buttressed roof into place, supported by the heaviest pilasters mortal man had ever known. He imagined this must be what Zeus's temple on Mount Olympus looked like, rejoicing in how his king would be pleased with the result of his efforts and labor.

Upon completion, the temple stood sixty feet at its highest point, the top of a marble dome inlaid with real gold that made it shine and shimmer beneath the sun. From even a modest distance, the temple appeared to be golden everywhere, an illusion Pathos Verdes fostered by constructing it to best seize the light of the day. The majestic entry doors stood twenty feet in height out of respect for the gods who alone would be invited to pass through them. Beyond these, jutting out to the sides and layered atop beveled columns, were twin, multileveled appendages that looked like wings attached seamlessly to the dome.

Pathos Verdes had begun the process by modeling the temple after palaces of legend, those he had never laid eyes upon himself but heard described by scribes and tellers of tales from ages past. But his vision of finely etched narrowing layers topped by a majestic dome was more than an amalgamation of his accumulated knowledge. He could not say exactly from where the design ideas had sprung, nor why exactly he had decided to build the grand façade to the scale of giants and the gods themselves, with doors fashioned from polished stone no man could open on his own.

No mortal man anyway.

Inside its vast octagonal walls, Verdes had laid floors of marble speckled with bronze dust and added pillars that connected the multitiered levels contained beneath the dome. The walls and grand stairs were fashioned of limestone pulled from quarries as far away as ships could sail. Verdes set crews of workers to polish the limestone to a bright hue under both sun and moon before it was set into place inside. His sculptors, meanwhile, were busy fashioning marble life-sized statues of the gods drawn from strange visions that had come to the builder on the few nights when he found sleep. This temple was as much homage to them as anything. It gave Pathos Verdes pause long enough to dapple his cheeks with tears, until the warmth of accomplishment was lost in the messenger's final instruction to him:

Any mortal with knowledge of the temple must take that secret to his grave.

Any rejoicing he might have done or pleasure he may have felt was lost to that. Verdes ordered his foremen to kill the final workmen who'd survived the ordeal of the build and then poisoned those same foremen during a feast to celebrate the project's completion. That night, he and his wife slept inside the temple walls upon its marble floor, awaking to the sight of a large jar centered beneath the nave. The jar was ivory colored and rose to heights nearly that of a man. Pathos Verdes had long been gifted with the ability to identify the composition of an object by sight, but this jar was smoother than any surface he had ever known while giving off no reflection whatsoever. Similarly, the jar appeared to be seamless, as if it had been poured out instead of fashioned or molded.

Just like the great temple Verdes had finally completed.

He approached the jar reverently and touched the surface, pulling his fingers back immediately. The jar had felt fiery hot and icy cold at the same time. Still his fingers bore no wound or mark. Some form of markings covered the jar's oblong center, symbols like none he'd ever seen before and could not decipher. Verdes stood there and recalled the messenger's instructions to him so many years ago:

"There is a weapon greater than any ever known to gods or mortal man. This weapon has the power to control the world. Or destroy it, to kill even a god. As the greatest builder of our time, your king orders

you, Pathos Verdes, to construct a temple capable of containing this weapon so it remains protected from mortal hands."

And now, with the temple complete, this jar must contain that very weapon.

Verdes felt his eyes mist with tears, too awestruck to wield a hand to wipe them. In that rare moment of sanity, he fully grasped the scope of his accomplishment and the rewards to be visited upon him for his labor.

Any mortal with knowledge of the temple must take that secret to his grave.

He drew his wife in close against him and plunged a knife deep into her back as he held her. He felt the last of her life ebb away and then eased her body into the crypt he had prepared in anticipation of that moment.

And in that moment, his final depths of madness yielded the name of the grand temple. The gods, whose bidding he had so faithfully done, wished the temple to be christened after the first woman known to man: Pandora.

Pandora's Temple.

CHAPTER 45

New Orleans

"Named for Pandora herself, dudes," Captain Seven continued, "a woman Zeus ordered Hephaestus to fashion out of clay, or some shit like that, to punish mankind for Prometheus stealing fire from the gods. According to the myth, she was entrusted with a jar and told never to open it. But curiosity got the better of the bitch, so off came the lid and out flew all the evils of mankind, unleashed on the world. Then she seals it again, leaving only hope inside, so the equation never got balanced. At some point the jar got mistranslated as a box, but you get the point."

"You're saying it wasn't a myth at all," McCracken concluded. "You're saying Pandora's jar really exists."

"You realize how crazy this all sounds," Folsom said, shaking his head.

"If you'd seen what we did on board the *Venture*, I believe you'd feel different, B-rat. A Level Six event, remember? And no more nuts than that alien invasion you've been prepping for."

Folsom blew out some breath.

"You weren't in the Mediterranean five years ago, B-rat. You didn't see what I saw there either."

"Which was?"

"I don't know."

"You don't know?"

"Could have been the temple. Tsunami got me before I could be sure."

"A tsunami," Folsom repeated. "And how long before you were rescued?"

"A day or so."

"A day or more at sea with no food or water after surviving a shipwreck? Doesn't lend much credibility to your recollection."

Folsom's comment was enough to bring Captain Seven up close to him, right in his face. "Let me tell you something, B-rat. I might be a burnout, but as these boys'll tell you, when it comes to the job, I got the clearest head known to man and I'm only telling you what the cameras showed. So kiss my ass."

"You try looking for the temple again?"

"You bet. Only whatever it was I caught a glimpse of before the tsunami hit was gone. Like it flat out disappeared again. Don't ask me how. Dudes who sent me there told me to pack it in, so I did. Didn't want to give me the time I needed to find what I knew was down there somewhere."

Folsom backed off, arms raised as McCracken moved in between them. "Assuming you're right," he said to the captain, "how exactly did the temple end up under the Mediterranean Sea?"

"Another part of the story, if you want to hear it."

"No," snapped Folsom. "I've heard enough."

"Then hear this, B-rat: How many atoms of dark matter you think it took to remake the *Venture* at the molecular level? Normal explosions generate incredible heat and percussion. The result is char, melting, debris, pretty much utter destruction at the physical level, which means the molecular level too. There was no heat associated with what happened on the *Venture*, no percussion, no searing, no residue—nothing. The dark matter atoms released by the drill encountered traditional matter atoms and, with apologies to the coneheads at CERN, you got your big bang, all right. For an immeasurable shadow of an instant, too brief to be recorded by any device in existence, the *Venture*, and everything on board it, ceased to exist in the sense that its atoms no longer coalesced to form recognizable matter. When they coalesced again, you ended up with what we found."

"You said as much on the rig," McCracken recalled, "like somebody dumped the *Venture* into a blender and poured its contents back out."

"Now go back to your question about how many atoms of dark matter were in the collision. I don't know that, but what I do know is that if you double whatever that amount was, you'd have a tsunami the size of a skyscraper destroying the entire Gulf coast. Double it again and you'd have a blast that would dump New Orleans and every city within a hundred miles of the southern coast into the same blender that turned the *Venture* into a molecular mess. Get up to ten, maybe twenty times and you'd create a cosmic blast capable of ripping a hole in the atmosphere, kind of like popping a balloon. Then it's sayonara to life on Earth." Captain Seven settled back with a deep breath, strangely at ease, his argument with Folsom seemingly forgotten. "Don't you just love this shit?"

McCracken had thought the captain's question was posed to him, then realized the captain had aimed it at Johnny Wareagle. "Looks like you've got something on your mind, Indian."

"Ancient tales from my people and other tribes dating back thousands of years tell of a race of 'star beings' who were marooned on Earth and sought a way to return to their planet. Versions of the tale differ on virtually anything, with the exception of the star beings finding the means they needed to leave." Wareagle hesitated as if to collect his thoughts. "There are drawings, Blainey, of something being drawn from the very core of the planet to fuel vast ships that have the look of spacecraft."

"You think these aliens used dark matter to get out of Dodge."

"I think history speaks to us of the inexplicable or impossible that we choose to brand as legends and wives' tales. But the fact is the ancient legends and myths I'm speaking of weren't limited to the Hopi in the American desert Southwest. Identical tales and drawings sprang from the Incas, the Aztecs, and the Mayans. Separate continents with the same stories occurring at the same time on each."

"Chariots of the Gods, dudes," chimed in Captain Seven. "I've heard they were not averse to toking up, either. In fact, I heard those Indian tribes introduced them to the original wild-grown, badass weed and peyote. Folks could've left anytime they wanted to but chose the natural high instead. Didn't fly the coop until supply ran low. Or maybe they packed that shit into their cargo holds and flew off to distribute it through the final frontier where no man had gone before. Original fucking drug cartels from that perspective."

"So these star beings used dark matter to . . ."

". . . power up their flying saucers, or whatever they were driving, and get the fuck off our then primitive planet. Come to think of it, this is still a primitive planet. Until they make weed legal, we are truly in a bad state."

"There a point here somewhere, Captain?"

"Plan B, MacNuts. Before the big fella's star beings could pump dark matter gas into their engines, they'd have to figure out a way to contain it, since therein lies the real problem that's stopped the kindergartners at CERN from getting any place in a hurry. How can you isolate and study something you can't even keep hold of for more than a nanosecond in any truly measurable quantity? You can see what I'm getting at here."

"Not really. I prefer to leave the tech stuff to the experts," McCracken told him.

"Then kneel before me and listen. We figure out how those ancient flyboys contained dark matter and we can keep what the *Venture* found from blowing up the planet. That means I'm headed out," he finished, rising and cracking his knuckles.

"Where to, Captain?"

"Greece, scene of the crime. Finish the work I started five years ago and find Pandora's Temple once and for all."

"I need you to finish something else for me before you leave," Blaine said. "A couple of things actually starting with all e-mails originating from the *Deepwater Venture* referencing supplies."

"Sounds pretty broad, MacNuts."

"Focus on ordnance."

"That I can do. What else?"

Before McCracken could respond, Folsom looked up from a text message he'd just received. "We've got her!"

"Who?" McCracken asked him.

"There was a woman, an assistant to the operations manager, who fled the *Venture* yesterday morning just a few hours before your expert's big bang struck. She's now in the custody of the New Orleans police." Folsom held the grainy picture displayed on his BlackBerry out for McCracken to see. "Don't suppose you recognize her?"

CHAPTER 46

New Orleans

"Come with me, ma'am," the police officer said, holding the cell door open.

He was a black man with a tight-fitting cap covering his bald dome and an accent that sounded lightly Cajun. The building's heat had brought a light sheen of sweat to the surface of his skin although it felt cold and dank to Katie down here in the basement.

Katie rose from the concrete slab seat of the holding cell in the bowels of the New Orleans Police Department headquarters on North Rampart Street.

"Where we going?" she asked the officer.

"Just come with me."

He took tight hold of Katie at the elbow and steered her on. One flight of stairs up and a single corridor length later, she found herself inside what looked like the same interrogation room where she was questioned hours before by a detective named Hurst. Her answers had been cryptic, not about to give anything away with no clear idea of how the police had found her or why they'd been looking. Katie hadn't asked for a lawyer because there seemed to be no point in involving yet another outside party in the muddle of the past day. She needed to collect her thoughts, buy time, and determine who out there might be able to help her.

Katie surmised from Detective Hurst's questions, along with his producing a grainy picture of her taken from a dock-mounted security camera, that her arrest had everything to do with her flight from the *Deepwater Venture* and nothing to do with all that had transpired since. No questions were posed about Japanese kidnappers, executed environmentalists in Greenland, the battle in K-Paul's yesterday afternoon, or Twist's murder in a movie theater the night before.

Everything had been about her infiltrating the rig using a false identity, thereby suggesting she was up to no good.

"I had nothing to do with what happened."

"Why don't you tell us what happened exactly?" Detective Hurst asked, making Katie realize he didn't even know as much as she did.

That had been several hours ago, and this time she'd been brought up to a different interrogation room with brighter walls, a newer table, and floor complete with heavy-duty industrial carpeting.

Hurst pushed his way through the door, looking ruffled and annoyed. "You really should talk to me," he said, standing across from her with palms planted on the table. "Might be my last chance to help you out here."

"Why's that, Detective?"

"Because you've drawn some pretty big attention from the kind of people you don't want noticing you."

Katie felt a flutter in her stomach. "I don't know what you're talking about."

"Homeland Security's on their way down now." Hurst spun a chair around from the table and sat down, straddling it. "This stays local, maybe I can keep them off you."

Katie remained silent.

Hurst shook his head and shoved the chair hard against the table as he rose. "Hey, lady, just don't blame me when they make you disappear." Heading for the door now. "Send me a postcard from Guantanamo," he added, before it closed behind him.

CHAPTER 47

New Orleans

Shinzo Asahara, son of the great martyr Shoho Asahara, practiced his martial arts kata in front of the full-length hotel mirror. He was naked save for his boxer shorts and ever-present mitten on his left hand.

The practice made him feel alive, joined his mind and body in ways that led to an enlightened sense of the world from which his greatest ideas had been birthed. For Shinzo, life itself meant nothing; he had effectively died the same day his father had been executed and his father's spirit, the great man's very essence, had become melded to his own. In that moment, Shinzo had inherited his cause, Aum Shinrikyo, along with the cult's overriding goal to destroy the world in all its ugliness.

He had long believed that his father's near blindness had imbued him with the ability to see what other men couldn't; specifically, in this case, a vision of a world that had betrayed itself. Shoho spoke and preached about doomsday often, but the truth was that Aum Shinrikyo under his leadership had never managed to strike a balance between that stated goal and resulting deeds. The subway attack was as close as they came, feeble and ultimately pointless, leading only to the arrest and ultimate death of a great man and thus serving no purpose at all.

Shinzo's goal, on the other hand, was nothing less than the complete realization of Aum Shinrikyo's true purpose that lay in the destruction of the world as it was known. Not individual attacks that branded the group as no different from any terrorist organization, but one single, final destructive action that would see the world burn.

Shinzo continued his movements, lithe and graceful before the mirror, his skin now glowing with perspiration. He had turned the room's heat up as high as it would go, thirsting for the discomfort he equated with pain and punishment for his failure so far to finish his great father's work.

He could not close his perpetually cold left hand into a fist; some days he could barely move the fingers at all. The accident had happened when Aum Shinrikyo had infiltrated a Japanese laboratory conducting experiments into re-creating the big bang theory even before CERN was up and running. Shinzo's sources had told him that the Japanese lab, actually housed in China, had managed to isolate a minuscule quantity of dark matter. If the lab had managed to uncover the means to contain it as well, Aum Shinrikyo might at last have the means they needed to achieve their desired ends. Never mind feebly releasing toxic gas into the Tokyo subway system. Let enough dark matter loose in the world and doomsday, the group's cherished goal and purpose, would finally dawn in the shadow of an instant.

Shinzo recalled the day of the Tokyo subway attack with painful clarity, the memories striking him hard and fast once more as he turned to study the precision of his moves in the mirror.

And his father looked back, eyes narrowed and squinting, disapproving as always.

"What are you doing, my son?"

Shinzo went cold, in spite of the sweat now soaking his body in the stifling heat of the hotel room, the blinds closed over the windows to shut out the light of the day. Was this an apparition, a product of his imagination, a ghost?

"I am practicing, refining, perfecting."

"I speak of your actions out of view of this mirror."

"As do I, Father. To finish your work, to realize the dream on which Aum Shinrikyo was founded."

"The end of the world . . ."

Shinzo bowed slightly, in affirmation as well as respect.

In the mirror his father shook his head disparagingly. *"You miss the point of all my teachings."*

"But, Father—"

"Do not speak; listen. My time with you is limited."

"I am listening, Father."

"I too once sought this same goal. It was my life's singular purpose, what I believed I had been born for. Why else would I have been born without sight if not to destroy a world I could never lay eyes upon? But I learned the world itself is without sin—it's man who has corrupted and soiled all of existence. It is man who must pay. The attack on the subway was meant to be a test, nothing more. To poison those who have corrupted and soiled while leaving the world itself intact to find its own second chance."

"There can be no second chance; you taught me that."

"As I learned it myself too late to make a difference, a task that now falls upon you."

"And so it will be done, Father."

His father's spectral visage seemed to regard his covered left hand. *"In spite of the terrible price you have already paid to fulfill my legacy."*

"That price fuels my desires even more."

"I only wish I was there to stand by your side on your great day of victory."

"You will, Father, in death instead of life."

"Prove it to me."

"How?"

"Tell me of that day, my son, the day you were changed forever."

Shinzo looked down at the mitten covering his left hand. "It was not long after your death."

"Clouding your judgment, perhaps."

"We were not expecting to encounter resistance."

"But you did."

"We were prepared."

"And many died, some from Aum Shinrikyo's own ranks."

"Martyrs to the cause," Shinzo said sadly. "*Your* cause."

The apparition ignored his final comment. *"All that death while you ventured to the main laboratory."*

"We'd come at the perfect time, right in the midst of their most advanced experiments into isolating dark matter. It was panic, everything I'd hoped for!"

"You got our wish."

"Yes, Father, yes! I managed to reach the main lab before lockdown was fully achieved." Shinzo realized his left hand felt even colder than normal, more numb. "The experiment involving dark matter was under way in a huge vacuum chamber. There was a feeling in the room—a heat, an energy—I could feel in the pit of my stomach. I thought something was trying to steal my breath. An inspiration gripped me. I thought if I broke the seal on that chamber, if I freed the dark matter, our goal would be achieved."

"Our legacy, my son."

"You died for it, Father," Shinzo told the cloudy shape in the mirror before him. The apparition had turned fluttery now, as if losing strength. "My thoughts were of joining you in the afterlife as I threw open the seals to the laboratory's supercollider."

"And the price you paid for this?"

"A terrible one, Father, yet one that will forever remind me of my duty and obligation to complete your work, to realize your dream. I won't let you down. I must be true to your legacy."

"It is your own legacy, Shinzo, that concerns me more, and accepting failure is no legacy at all."

"I have not accepted failure, Father! I will never accept failure!"

"And yet you stand before me now without purpose or plan."

"Tell me what I must do, tell me my next step."

"You already know it, my son. Even if I was still blind, I'd be able to see it."

"Then show me what escapes my own vision."

"Face your fear, Shinzo."

"I am not a coward."

"And yet you cannot see the answer that lies literally before you. Because going back confronts you with the day that changed you forever. But that is what you must do to finish the work I began. So speak of it to me. Tell of how it happened so you might purge your fear."

Shinzo's left hand was starting to itch now, but scratching never brought any relief or even feeling. "Inside the laboratory, I threw open the seals, and the heavy doors to the vacuum chamber blew outward. I felt something slam into me, thought it would blow me backward. But then I felt as if I had been lifted into the air, hovering above the floor when in reality my feet remained planted in place. I realized I'd thrown my hands up to protect myself against whatever force I suddenly felt passing straight through me as if I was made of water. I felt weightless. I remember looking at the hands still raised protectively before me. I remember feeling great joy that I had achieved the fate you yourself had long contemplated."

"Then what, my son?" the apparition challenged.

"I blacked out. When I woke up, I was being tended to in the van. That's the first time I realized . . ."

Again Shinzo glanced at his covered hand, his voice tailing off.

"We are close, my son, closer than we have ever been before. Find the woman again. Learn everything she knows about the oil rig to plan your next steps."

"The police have her now, Father. But she has been transferred to the custody of Homeland Security," Shinzo said, reporting what he'd learned from e-mailed reports from the agency's New Orleans office. His specialty had always been computers and hacking, chosen to complement his father's skills in the expectation they'd wage their battle side by side for years to come.

"Then you know where they'll be taking her."

"I suppose."

"Don't suppose—do! Use your men, your resources."

"A suicide mission. The headquarters is impregnable."

"So you're giving up."

Shinzo swallowed hard.

"Concede and all you've suffered will be for naught. Show me the source of your suffering. Show me what you show no other."

Shinzo tugged off the thin black mitten from his left hand with his right and held both up to the mirror for his father to see. But the ghostly specter was gone, revealing only his own form reflected in the murky light and steaming warmth of the room. Arms held upward, palms out, to reveal the price he had paid for the relentless pursuit of his father's goals:

Shinzo Asahara had two right hands.

CHAPTER 48

New Orleans

Folsom parked in a red zone in front of the police building on North Rampart.

"Perks of the trade," he announced to McCracken and Wareagle.

The five-story, clay-colored building looked bland but functional, with dozens of equidistant windows indicating a simple design of like if not identical and interchangeable office spaces. A parking garage rose parallel on the building's south side while its north overlooked a side street closed off to vehicular traffic.

Folsom's Homeland Security ID got them quickly through lobby security and into the reception area leading into the squad room where the real police business actually went on.

"More of you?" the clerk, a large-jowled man with thick glasses that still left him squinting, said to Folsom.

"What do you mean more of us?" Folsom asked him.

"I just checked another two agents from Homeland Security through a few minutes ago."

"Lock the building down, Folsom!" McCracken ordered.

"It's probably—"
"Just do it!"

"They had IDs exactly like yours," Detective Hurst said, handing Folsom back his identification.

They had reached the interrogation room the two imposters from Homeland Security had entered mere minutes before. Uniformed officers stood on either side of the door with guns drawn, three more standing slightly behind them while McCracken and Wareagle hung back ready to push their way forward as soon as it became necessary.

The officers, led by Hurst, burst through the interrogation room door in the next instant, guns raised and ready. Folsom followed, McCracken and Wareagle staying exactly where they were but still close enough to see inside.

The room was empty.

"You knew, didn't you?" Folsom asked McCracken. "You knew they'd be gone."

"Men like this don't stick around any longer than they have to."

"I've ordered the building and surrounding block closed off. Nobody in or out."

"Knock yourself out, Folsom."

"You have a better idea, *sir*?"

"We check out the building security station. Then, Hank, you get the chance to work some of your Homeland Security magic."

"That's them," McCracken noted, as the police tech froze a picture of two men escorting a woman between them across the third floor of the adjacent parking garage. "I recognize the woman too."

"She calls herself Katie DeMarco," said Folsom. "But that's not her real name."

The tech zoomed in and clicked his mouse, enlarging the shot so the grainy, underpixelated quality masked any identifying features.

"See the way the men are holding her?" McCracken asked, pointing at the screen.

"One on either elbow," Folsom answered. "So what?"

"So the man on the right's positioned behind her, the way I would be if I were holding a knife or gun against her back."

Folsom regarded the screen again. "The way you would," he repeated.

"Tough world out there, Hank. You should visit it some time."

According to the *Deepwater Venture* work logs and preliminary police report, Katie DeMarco was the rig's assistant to the operations manager, and as such was privy to pretty much all its inner workings. McCracken had already reviewed a picture of her exiting a boat upon its return to the Port of New Orleans from a resupply run to the *Venture*. Pulled off a security camera as well, it was similarly grainy but provided just enough resolution for him to be certain the women captured in both shots were one and the same, a match for the woman he and Johnny Wareagle had saved yesterday at K-Paul's from figures nearly identical to those impersonating Homeland Security agents here at the police station.

"Who are you really, Katie DeMarco?" McCracken asked out loud.

Folsom had arranged to run the young woman's likeness through the massive databases maintained by Homeland, but as of yet the software had yielded nothing. Apparently an e-mail had reached the *Venture* two nights before the incident asking Assistant Operations Manager Paul Basmajian to detain her, since her fabricated identity didn't pass the muster of a more detailed background check. Obviously Baz never saw the e-mail, because if he had, McCracken was sure the woman never would have gotten off the rig.

He watched as the tech started the tape again, another camera picking up the trio reaching a dark green SUV. One of the men eased Katie DeMarco ahead of him into the backseat while the other climbed into the front.

The tech froze the screen there. "This was thirteen minutes ago according to the time stamp," he reported. "She's long gone by now."

McCracken swung toward Folsom. "How far does Homeland's surveillance reach extend into New Orleans?"

"Far enough."

Wareagle jerked a second chair out from beneath the monitoring station.

"Prove it, Hank," said McCracken.

CHAPTER 49

New Orleans

Folsom sat down and wheeled the chair back into place. He copied a still shot of the dark green SUV, then logged into an ultrasecure Homeland Security site that required multiple access codes and passwords to enter.

"Can you move any faster?" McCracken prodded.

"You ever hear of procedure?" Folsom shot back at him.

"Sure and it's mostly good for getting people killed."

Folsom's fingers started typing quicker as he plugged in the police station street address in one box and pasted the picture of the SUV into another, then hit Enter.

"Talk to me, Hank, and talk fast."

"Every camera in a fifteen-mile radius is now looking for the vehicle," he explained. "That means every ATM, traffic cam, security camera, every drive-through window—all are sending visual data toward that purpose. Their feeds will all be compiled and extrapolated in real time by one of our supercomputers, and if we're halfway lucky we'll have a hit in minutes."

"Keep extrapolating," McCracken told him, already backing up for the door with Johnny Wareagle. "The Indian and I will get ready to hit the road."

"Wait," Folsom said, reaching into his pocket, "take this."

He handed McCracken what looked like a high-tech version of the standard Bluetooth earpiece.

"Long-range transmitter?"

Folsom looked as if he had to stop himself from shaking his head. "Not what we call it, but close enough. Operates on a dedicated bandwidth and frequency with direct satellite feed. So we can stay in touch."

McCracken fit the earpiece into place. "Aren't I lucky?"

He and Wareagle had just reached an unmarked sedan with a big block V-8 provided them courtesy of the NOPD when Folsom's voice chimed hollowly in his ear.

"Okay, McCracken, I've got our vehicle heading southeast on Martin Luther King Junior Boulevard and making a U-turn at Oretha C. Haley Boulevard and then taking a right onto South Claiborne Avenue eight minutes ago now."

McCracken climbed behind the wheel and gunned the car's powerful engine.

"Next shot I've got is two minutes later in traffic approaching the ramp to the I-10, west for Baton Rouge."

Wareagle fastened his shoulder harness as McCracken screeched off, following the SUV's identical path.

"I've got them on US-90 for a half mile before merging onto I-10 heading west."

McCracken picked up speed, weaving in and out of traffic and honking his horn instead of using the big car's siren. "How long ago?"

"Six minutes," Folsom reported. "Wait, I've got them taking the Causeway Boulevard North exit and proceeding onto North Causeway less than one minute ago. Christ . . ."

"What?"

"They must be headed across Lake Pontchartrain. Where are you?"

"Merging on I-10 now. How far does that put me behind them?"

No response.

"Folsom?"

"Yeah, sorry. I've got them passing onto the Lake Pontchartrain Causeway just now in real time. That puts you exactly five-point-one miles behind them."

"So you can see me too?"

"On a separate screen. Why?"

"Because I just gave you the finger, Hank."

"We don't have nearly the camera coverage on the other side of the causeway, McCracken. We stand to lose them if you can't intercept prior."

"Expecting a miracle?"

"Just like Mexico."

"I lost one in Mexico, Folsom. Don't intend for that to happen today."

"Then you better step on it," McCracken heard Folsom say in his ear loud enough to cause a flutter in his skull.

"Wait," McCracken said, realizing something. "Check the long view of the causeway. I believe you'll find the bascule drawbridge at about the center of the span."

"Holy shit, you're right."

"Then work your magic and order it opened."

The drawbridge was actually located at the sixteen-mile marker of the Causeway Bridge, activated under normal conditions with only substantial notice and never during peak daytime travel hours.

"You read me, McCracken?" Folsom's voice blared in his ear.

"Loud and clear, Hank."

"Traffic has been stopped and the drawbridge will be raised in three minutes' time."

McCracken realized the easy flow of cars on the causeway was slowing, a sea of brake lights flashing ahead. "Where's the SUV?"

"About a mile ahead of you and one mile in front of the drawbridge."

"How long does that give Johnny and me to reach it?"

"Six minutes to raise, six minutes to lower, and, say, another five to approximate a ship passing through. So figure twenty before traffic flow resumes. Is that enough?"

"Guess it'll have to be, won't it?"

"You don't sound thrilled by the prospects."

"A gunfight in the open with whoever nabbed Katie DeMarco's going to do lots of collateral damage. Not a lot of places for bystanders to go other than over the side."

"This coming from the legendary McCrackenballs?"

"The bad guys these days seem to operate with entirely new rules of engagement. Shoot fast and often and hit whatever you can."

"Then I guess you'll have to shoot better."

"First we'll have to get close enough. Any ideas, Folsom?"

"Well," the man from Homeland Security started, "you're about to hit the snarl so whatever you do, it'll have to be on foot."

"Thanks for the tip."

Ahead, McCracken could see a number of men holding hand-scrawled cardboard signs up for those now stalled in place to see. The signs were pretty much uniform in message, held in cracked, soiled hands by those claiming to be homeless, jobless, or both. And, judging by their appearance, McCracken disputed none of that. There was even an older man advertising himself as a Vietnam vet rolling about the snarl in a wheelchair.

"Indian?" he raised, aware Johnny Wareagle's gaze had tilted in the same direction.

"My thoughts exactly, Blainey."

"Then let's get to work."

CHAPTER 50

New Orleans

"If you'll come with us, Ms. DeMarco."

Katie had sensed something amiss as soon as Detective Hurst ushered the two men into the conference room and closed the door behind them. Something was wrong about their demeanor, their eyes too furtive and intense. She could try to pass it off as the paranoia expected under the circumstances, but there seemed to be no inquisitiveness in their gazes or their intentions, their mind-set entirely wrong for the task.

"I'd like to use the bathroom first, if that's okay," Katie had said, hoping to create the opportunity to separate herself from these men, while unsure about what exactly she'd do once she managed that.

"Certainly," one of the men said. "On our way out."

Instead, though, they'd made straight for the parking garage with her request to visit the bathroom ignored. The two men walked with her always in the middle, one or both of them with a firm grasp on her elbows or arms. And, as soon as they reached the garage, she felt the barrel of a gun pressed low against her back.

"Keep moving," the man holding it said. "Don't stop, don't cry out, don't look at anyone passing by."

Katie heard the static-riddled cackle of a soft voice providing instructions in the other man's nearly invisible earpiece.

"I think I'm going to be sick," she said amid the garage's dark confines smelling of oil, concrete, and lingering exhaust fumes.

The men kept leading her on, the gun pressing against her harder.

"Just keep walking," one of them said quite calmly, brushing off her lame attempt at escape with what looked like a smirk.

It was the last thing either of them had said, through the drive that took them across the Lake Pontchartrain Causeway where they suddenly became mired in traffic in view of a rising drawbridge. That respite gave Katie fresh opportunity to consider her options for flight. These men didn't care what she knew, any more than the men who'd followed her into K-Paul's yesterday did.

Or the men who'd killed Todd Lipton and his team in Greenland. And Twist last night.

Katie watched the driver touch his barely visible earpiece, the soft garble of static reaching her again.

"New orders," he said, his gaze cocked back toward the man on her right.

Katie felt his free hand take her by the hair and jerk her downward. She glimpsed the silenced pistol steadying on her skull, and was about to to close her eyes when someone rapped on the window.

CHAPTER 51

New Orleans

McCracken had approached the white-haired man in the wheelchair with Wareagle looming just behind him, dropping a ten-dollar bill into the cup held on the man's seat between his two legs.

"What unit were you with, soldier?"

"Twenty-Fifth Infantry Division. Tropic Lightning," he said proudly.

"Saw plenty of action in the Tet and more, then. First Brigade or Second?"

"First."

"Bet you were pleased as punch to get back home to Schofield in '71. May, wasn't it?"

"It was. Remember it like it was yesterday."

"Except," McCracken said, "you're remembering it wrong. First Brigade of Tropic Lightning was gone by the previous December. And those gloves you're wearing are plenty worn, but not in the spots from wheeling that chair around. Tell me I'm wrong and I'll throw you over the side."

The man looked up at McCracken, his expression that of someone who'd just swallowed something sour. "You want your ten dollars back?"

"Nope. Consider it a rental fee."

"For what?"

"Get up."

McCracken eased the wheelchair with Johnny Wareagle resting in the seat the final stretch to the green SUV parked in clear view of the raised drawbridge.

"Remind me next time it's your turn to do the pushing, Indian," he said between labored breaths. "Man, HALO drops from five miles were easy compared to this."

Of course, Johnny Wareagle's vast bulk made him stand out under any circumstances, but less so in a seated position that allowed him to hunch his shoulders and crane his body to hide his true size. McCracken eased the pistol Folsom had procured for him into easier drawing range when they drew to within three vehicles of the SUV.

"Just in case, Indian."

Wareagle grinned slightly. "Just in case," he repeated.

Her captor's hold slackened enough to allow Katie to peer upward. The man rapping his knuckles on the window had his hair clubbed back into a ponytail that was rimmed with gray strands where it pulled back from the temples. His eyes looked like liquid pools of darkness. Katie had just registered how big his chest and shoulders were, easily wider than the breadth of the wheelchair, when her captor in the backseat lowered the window to shoo the beggar away.

Go for his gun!

But the man's gaze was back on her too fast. Still, an open window, a distracted captor, the driver's attention divided between the stalled traffic and the opportune appearance by the panhandler.

Go for the other door now . . .

But Katie felt too heavy to move, her legs like lead weights. She was aware of her rapid breathing and nothing else.

Until a sudden blur of motion wiped out the rest of her thoughts, so fast as to seem impossible for anyone to manage, much less a man the size of the disabled beggar. In one blink he was seated and in the next he was out of the wheelchair and through the window, seemingly with no space or time in between.

Before the window had fully lowered, the giant's left hand had swallowed the throat of the man seated next to Katie and slammed his head against the car's roof, the pistol gone from his grasp and clamoring to the floor. Then, just as the glass sank all the way into the sill, the giant launched his entire torso up and forward, gliding smoothly and agilely into the car itself. Katie thought she smelled something like incense, as the giant's right hand clamped onto the throat of the driver whose attempt to draw his pistol was left suspended between intention and action.

Katie watched the giant bring the heads of her two captors together with a force that resulted in a mashing sound that reminded her of ice crunching under a boot in winter. They looked like rag dolls in the giant's huge hands, discarded to the sides with an effortlessness that appeared almost superhuman.

The door on the other side jerked open and Katie spotted her second rescuer for the first time, a stubble-faced man with gray-tinged thick hair and a gun palmed like an extension of his hand.

Wait, Katie thought, *I know these men. . . .*

Her rescuers from the K-Paul's in the French Quarter yesterday!

"The name's McCracken," the bearded man said behind fierce eyes that seemed to burn right through her. "Nice to see you again."

CHAPTER 52

New Orleans

Back at Homeland Security regional headquarters in New Orleans's City Hall, McCracken led Katie DeMarco into an office Folsom had emptied for him on the eighth floor, the middle of the three Homeland occupied in the building. He closed the door behind her and watched the young woman collapse into a high-backed leather chair behind the desk.

"I froze back there on the causeway," she said, seeming to melt into the leather. "They were going to kill me and there was nothing I could do."

McCracken sat down on the edge of the desk directly before her. "Ever had a gun pointed at you before?"

"No," she said, almost shyly.

"It tends to have that effect on people."

"Nothing new for you and that big friend of yours, I guess."

"You guess right."

Katie rocked her chair forward and leaned over the desk closer to McCracken. "So I guess I was lucky you showed up. Again."

"First time, in K-Paul's, we were already there. It was you who showed up."

"And I didn't even get to enjoy the food."

"Neither did we, as it turned out."

McCracken was captivated by the young woman's energy and vivaciousness, as well as the sense of vulnerability she was showing. Not bothering to pretend she was strong and fearless. He guessed she was in her late twenties, but the raven black hair tumbling past her shoulders cast her as even more, and perhaps perpetually, youthful. That hair had the dual effect of disguising her features, cloaking them in shadows as if she'd made friends with the sporadic lighting of an office that seemed to be missing bulbs somewhere. But she regarded McCracken with gray eyes filled with a distinct unease, something furtive and faux about her entire demeanor, as if she were posing for a picture. And there was something sad and empty about her as well that was hardly befitting a young woman of her energy and beauty.

In his world, trust came at a premium; it was a commodity to be brokered like any other and valued as much for its importance as the lack of it that more often than not prevailed. Thanks in large part to that, McCracken had learned long ago how to read people's intentions and see through the masks they wore as if every day was Halloween. He didn't know much about Katie DeMarco for sure right now, but he was as certain as he could be that she was hiding something she wasn't about to share no matter how much or hard he prodded. The key was to hear what she *didn't* say, conclusions to the truth gained by what he liked to call listening between the lines.

That skill had helped keep him alive for forty years through more battles than he could count.

Katie DeMarco seemed to stiffen a bit, or pretended to.

What are you hiding? McCracken thought to himself.

"Was it really only yesterday?" she said, trying to sound casual. "It seems like a month." She looked at him closer, running her gaze from his dark eyes to ridged chest, broad shoulders, and forearms that were knobby with muscle.

"Welcome to my world."

"Same world those guys in the car come from?"

"If it was, you'd be dead now."

Beyond the windows, the sky darkened with the first signs of night. After Johnny Wareagle had disabled the men pretending to be Homeland Security agents, they'd placed their unconscious forms on either side of him in the backseat. By the time McCracken climbed behind the wheel with Katie alongside him, the drawbridge had been lowered and the causeway reopened. At that point, he'd simply driven across to the other side of Lake Pontchartrain where he instructed Folsom to arrange pickup for the three of them and the two unconscious gunmen.

McCracken had no doubt they were independent operatives, just like the ones in K-Paul's yesterday. Men part of nothing bigger than the assignment they were brought in to complete, in this case to deliver Katie DeMarco to someone somewhere. Their involvement would end there. They had no idea for whom they worked or the purpose of their assignment beyond that. It was the way such things were done these days, and the explosion of private security companies, like the infamous Blackwater, left a glut of paramilitary pros on the market for jobs just like this. The pair would be interrogated appropriately, but McCracken was under no illusions that would yield anything; they knew what they needed to know and nothing more.

"So what is it you do exactly, when you're not saving kidnapped women?" Katie DeMarco asked him from behind the desk.

"Saving the world."

"I'm being serious here."

"So am I. We thought you might be able to help us this time."

"And why's that?"

"Because you were on the *Venture* and the *Venture*'s gone."

"I don't know anything about what destroyed the rig. I'd tell you if I did. All I know is that they were drilling for oil where there wasn't any oil." Katie rested her elbows on the naked desk with chin cupped in her hands. "Why don't you call Ocean Bore, the company that owns the *Venture*?"

"That's someone else's department."

"Someone else who doesn't carry a gun or save kidnapped women, Mr. McCracken?"

"Call me Blaine."

"Blaine. Are you like a spy, some kind of agent or something?" she asked him.

"Something, young lady. Goes all the way back to this war called Vietnam, fought before you were born, and you have no idea how old it makes me feel saying that."

"You don't look old."

"Thanks."

"I mean it. Not a day over fifty."

"Just don't say I remind you of your father."

"I won't, don't worry," Katie said stiffly, her sudden change in tone making McCracken take notice.

"Good. Bad enough I turned sixty yesterday. You interrupted my birthday lunch at K-Paul's."

"Sorry, Blaine. What about the other guy, the big man?"

"Johnny Wareagle. We were in the same special-ops team back in what Johnny likes to call the Hellfire. Stayed together pretty much ever since."

"Sounds tiring."

"Not for the last two years. Things cooled off."

"What changed?"

"They got hot again."

CHAPTER 53

New Orleans

"The cold period mostly started with 9/11 and the new mind-set it brought to the country. Suddenly the work Johnny and I had been doing without anyone noticing was replaced by the likes of SEAL Team Six and drone attacks. The rules of engagement changed, and old dogs like us fell out of fashion."

"You don't look like the retiring type."

"Figure of speech." McCracken folded his arms and leaned further forward over the desk. "What about you?"

"I wasn't finished yet."

"I get a turn too, young lady."

"I feel a lot older than I did yesterday." Katie DeMarco looked at him, those light gray eyes narrowing into focused beams of intensity. "I guess being kidnapped twice in twenty-four hours will do that to you."

"Twice?"

"Last night it was Aum Shinrikyo's turn."

"The Japanese doomsday cult?"

"I see you've heard of them."

"I thought they were history."

"Far from it."

"So where does their interest lie with you, young lady?"

"They thought I knew something I didn't too."

"So what's the source of their interest in the *Deepwater Venture*?"

"They didn't say exactly, other than it had to do with bringing on the end of the world."

"Is it my turn to ask the questions yet?"

"That's your second one already. And the answer to your third is twenty-eight."

"I didn't ask it yet."

"You didn't have to. You wanted to know how old I am, so I'm telling you. Not as far from fifty as you think."

"Too bad I'm sixty."

"What else would you like to know, Blaine?" Katie said, leaning forward too.

"Everything you can tell me about the *Deepwater Venture* for starters."

"I infiltrated the crew for an environmental organization called WorldSafe."

"Your purpose being . . ."

Katie didn't answer.

"You need to tell me the truth, young lady."

She rolled her eyes. "Don't call me that."

"This isn't the time to change the subject. We're on the same side here. Or would you have preferred if Johnny and I had just left you with those guys in the SUV?"

"I was on board the *Venture* to gather intelligence . . ."

"To use for propaganda purposes, no doubt."

"I didn't say that."

"You didn't have to. A few pictures here and there, maybe steal a video of oil leaking out of a well seal. You know the problem I've got?"

"What?"

"You could have managed that a lot quicker than the three weeks you were on that rig."

Katie looked away. "There was something else."

"You want to look at me when you're talking?"

This time she did. "I planned on sabotaging the rig's software to shut down its operations."

McCracken nodded, weighing what she'd told him. "They've got a word for that where I come from."

"What's that?"

McCracken met her focused gaze with his own black eyes. He felt warmth radiating through his cheeks and knew Katie DeMarco had noticed the scar that ran through his left eyebrow, courtesy of an errant bullet a million years ago. She had the look of someone who had just realized you can't eat Halloween candy through the mask that earned it.

"Terrorism," was all he said.

"WorldSafe wasn't a terrorist organization."

"Past tense?"

"Our leadership was wiped out yesterday. Murdered in Greenland, I suspect by the same group that sent those fake Homeland Security agents to kidnap me."

"And who would that be?"

"Your guess is as good as mine."

"I don't believe that. I think you know exactly who you're dealing with here, but something's stopping you from telling me."

"Like what?"

"Haven't figured that out yet."

Katie leaned closer to him still, her expression lightening. "I think you've got me wrong."

"You're not a terrorist?"

"Environmental activist," she corrected, shaking her head.

"So it was environmental activism, not terrorism, that was responsible for the Hastings Chemical plant bombing three years ago. Environmental activism, not terrorism, that was behind the sinking of a Royal Dutch Shell supertanker the year before that. Environmental activism, not terrorism, that was linked to the poisoning of two-dozen coal mining company officials in West Virginia. How am I doing so far?"

"You forgot to blame WorldSafe for destroying the *Deepwater Venture*, too."

"Well, someone less informed might be curious about the timing of your departure."

"Maybe we should be focusing on the execution of the WorldSafe team in Greenland instead."

"Okay, let's," McCracken agreed, seeing the sadness, even guilt, building in her dark eyes now. "Who was responsible?"

"I have no idea."

"You're lying, young lady. I think you've got a very good idea who was behind it. I think it was the same party that ordered the *Venture* to drill where there was no oil, and now you're going to tell me who they are so I can stop them before they kill millions. That clear enough for you?"

Katie propped her elbows on the desktop and rested her chin in her palms. "Maybe you were right before."

"About what?"

"You're too old for the tough guy act to work."

"And you're just young enough to figure you don't need me."

"For what?"

"To help you. You're not telling me who's behind this because you plan on going after them yourself."

"Really?"

"It's in your eyes. Everything else lies, but not the eyes, young lady, and yours aren't the eyes of an environmental activist."

"You've got me wrong, Blaine."

McCracken had started to respond when gunfire rang out in the hallway beyond.

CHAPTER 54

New Orleans

"Stay here!" McCracken ordered, shoving Katie back into her chair when she started to jerk out of it.

Then he burst into the hallway with the Glock Hank Folsom had provided him drawn. He expected to find Homeland headquarters under a full-scale assault by a commando team, likely residue of the group from which he'd just rescued Katie DeMarco. But he saw nothing.

At first.

Then an armed security guard lurched out at the far end of the hallway, opening fire down the adjacent corridor only to be pulverized by a quick barrage, thrown backward with his torso stitched by bullet wounds. McCracken heard a light mechanical whine and watched one of the SWORDS robots round the corner at the head of the hallway, angling its 7.62 mm center-mounted machine gun right on him.

Shinzo Asahara felt as if he were in some kind of trance as the fingers of his right hand danced across his laptop's keyboard. He had bypassed the firewall of Homeland Security's regional office altogether, choosing instead to tap into the control systems of the building's robotic security force.

The system had been manufactured in Japan, the required access codes having been provided months before by an Aum Shinrikyo supporter who worked for the company in question.

Ordering the SWORDS machines to open fire indiscriminately had been as simple as changing their programming to fire on all motion and heat signatures. Six of them operating on three floors creating the chaos needed for the six-man Aum Shinrikyo team he'd dispatched to storm the building and get the woman back. The front-mounted cameras of the robots showed him all he needed to see on a screen now divided into six separate grids.

Hopefully, Shinzo thought, the woman would not fall victim to their fire, as a bearded man lurched out into the center of a hallway, caught immediately by one of the SWORDS robot's targeting systems.

McCracken dove to the floor just in time, opening fire with his Glock on the robot at the other end of the hall. His bullets clanged off its steel frame, having no effect at all as it righted its gun barrel in line with him.

McCracken rolled, feeling the heat of the machine's bullets singe the air over him and then carve out chips from the tile floor that followed in line with his roll. The machine's treads squeaked slightly, as it churned on, and McCracken escaped its line of fire only by pinning himself behind the thin cover of a wall abutment fronting the offices within which Katie DeMarco was now hiding.

He stilled himself in the hope the machine keyed its actions off motion sensors. But when it kept right on coming he knew it must have been relying on thermal imaging as well, meaning there was no hiding from it even behind doors and walls.

McCracken's intention was to lie in wait for it here and pounce when he caught sight of the barrel that extended slightly ahead of its frame. With turret raised, the machine remained barely three feet high, hardly imposing if its weaponry was neutralized.

The churning and squeaking grew louder. McCracken readied himself.

Only when the SWORDS bot reached the abutment, he saw its gun turret already angled straight his way, the moment frozen until fresh gunfire flashed from the far side of the hall.

"Blainey!" Johnny Wareagle called.

He spoke as the robot spun its gun turret around and headed back in the opposite direction, firing anew. McCracken could visualize Johnny diving for cover, even as he rolled back into the center of the hall and opened up on the machine with his Glock. It actually seemed confused, caught between responses before ultimately twisting back toward McCracken.

He pressed himself tighter against the floor to use the robot's inability to steady its gun this low from such a narrowing distance, then slammed a fresh magazine home and resumed firing. It was as much for distraction as anything since his bullets achieved nothing more than harmless clangs and clacks against the thing's titanium frame.

But it cleared the path for Johnny Wareagle to surge down the hall with the grace of a gazelle and force of a bull. Before the SWORDS robot could swing its gun back on him, Wareagle had raised all two hundred and fifty pounds of it into the air and was slamming it into anything hard and heavy he could find. First the floor, then the wall, over and over again before dropping it onto its back with the turret still struggling to spin and its machine gun now clicking off nonexistent rounds with the feed chamber smashed.

"A new enemy, Blainey," he said, barely even breathing hard.

"Yeah, but controlled by who?"

Shinzo Asahara watched one of his six screens go dark just after the camera caught the face of what looked like a Native American taking the attacking SWORDS in his grasp. Strangely, the robot did not transmit any sound, missed now since it might help tell him how many in the opposition were as capable as this one and the bearded man were.

Whatever the case, Shinzo turned his attention to the other five screens where the remaining SWORDS machines continued to pour fire toward anything that moved or gave off heat. They seemed to have trouble at first negotiating the bodies crumpled in their path, then quickly acclimated, or reprogrammed their mobile treads to better account for the unexpected terrain.

Whatever the case, based on the presence of the two figures offering the most competent resistance, he believed the woman was somewhere on the middle of the three floors. So the fingers of Shinzo's right hand began flying across the keyboard, instructing the four robots on the floors above and below to converge on the target even as the second SWORDS on the middle floor rounded the corner.

Wareagle was poised over the disabled SWORDS, wrenching its machine gun free when McCracken heard the whine of a second robot approaching from the hall's opposite side.

"Johnny!" he yelled, eyes locking on the knife sheathed on Wareagle's hip.

McCracken unsnapped the clasp and yanked the blade free in the same motion, twisting just as the second robot came around the break in the hall directly in front of the emergency exit door with its machine gun angling upon them. It had just opened fire when McCracken and Wareagle pressed themselves against the wall, McCracken crouching to better his throwing angle with the knife. He sent it spinning through the air, aiming not for the robot's gun or armored engine compartment.

But for its right tread.

The blade lodged in the rubber and stuck, forcing the robot into a wild, uncontrolled whirl that spread its fire in a circle slicing the walls in perfectly symmetrical fashion. McCracken seized the moment to time a dash toward the SWORDS, dropping into a slide just as its turret spun his way. His feet crashed into it with muzzle flashes and bullets flaring over him anew, the impact forceful enough to shove it all the way through the emergency exit door where it rattled down the stairs, exhausting the remainder of its bullets.

McCracken lurched back to his feet and burst into the room occupied by Katie DeMarco just ahead of Wareagle.

"What's happening?" she asked, hands wrapped around her knees on the floor.

"Good question," McCracken said and jerked her upright.

With Wareagle leading, they charged back into the hall and headed for the exit door on the other side, halfway to it when that door jerked open. A third SWORDS robot barreled through just as a fourth emerged through the exit at the other end, bullets pouring at them from both directions.

CHAPTER 55

New Orleans

They rushed into the chaos of Homeland personnel charging about or barricading themselves in offices, downed bodies littering the floor everywhere. They reached the elevator bank among others frantically pushing buttons, as if that would make the compartments return faster.

"Go, go, go!" McCracken signaled the Homeland personnel, herding them inside when one set of doors finally slid open.

He and Wareagle followed, shoving Katie behind them.

"Come on, come on!" he willed, slamming the down button repeatedly.

He heard the grinding squeal of the robots converging, glimpsed their shadows coming just as the doors began to slide closed. Then came an ear-screeching rattle as the robots' 7.62 mm fire pummeled the compartment's doors just ahead of its descent.

He tried to breathe easier, but stopped as quickly as he started.

"Indian!"

Wareagle had come to the same realization, already pushing the elevator's occupants toward both sides of the compartment and making sure they were pressed tight there. He and McCracken joined them with Katie DeMarco shielded, safely out of the line of fire when the compartment doors opened on the lowermost floor occupied by Homeland's offices.

A SWORDS robot lying in wait opened up with a constant stream that pulverized the elevator's rear wall and filled the compartment with gun smoke. McCracken and Wareagle glanced at each other a moment before pitching themselves airborne, up and over the machine's line of fire on an angle that propelled them to either side of its frame. The robot tried to readjust its turret, but they had it in their grasp by then, their hands stung by heat as it opened fire, obliterating a huge plateglass window toward which McCracken and Wareagle continued to drive it, smashing the robot through the remaining shards and out into the night beyond. Both watched as it broke apart upon impact with the sidewalk seven stories down.

Shinzo couldn't believe what he was seeing. The same two men, the bearded one and the Indian, destroying a third of the SWORDS robots, the woman still safe in their protection.

Who were they?

He felt the muscles in the fingers of his right hand seizing up, no longer working the keyboard efficiently, while his left hand flopped uselessly in his lap. He felt his own indecision and lack of anticipation had let his father down again. But it wasn't over yet. He still had three SWORDS machines left and six of his best men ready to attack.

But he had no idea where his two prime adversaries were exactly, as the cramped fingers on his right hand sprang back to life atop the keyboard.

"Find them," he said out loud, ordering the remaining SWORDS robots to the first level of the Homeland Security offices.

Wareagle slammed the conference room door closed behind McCracken and Katie, the three of them finding Captain Seven at work frantically behind his computer with Folsom hovering over him.

"Not good, dudes," the captain reported, "not good at all."

"Someone's in our system!" rasped Folsom. "Someone's taken over the SWORDS machines!"

"Okay, tell me something I don't know, Hank."

"Jesus Christ," was all Folsom could muster.

"Yeah, real combat's not too much fun, is it?"

"Blainey!"

Wareagle's warning came just in time for McCracken to take Captain Seven and Folsom down with him to the floor, while Wareagle covered up Katie in the far corner. The next moment found the twin fire of two robots chewing through the walls and pulverizing everything inside the conference room. Flecks and chips of plaster showered the air, mixing with window glass to form shrapnel-like debris. Exposed wiring appeared behind ruptured walls, the next bursts of fire sending split heavy rubber cables dangling from the drop ceiling that shed chunks and tiles downward. Sparks flew when the severed cabling struck the floor.

The robots' fire, meanwhile, continued to weaken the front wall on both sides of the door, McCracken and Wareagle locking their grasps around spark-spewing cables together. The rubber felt like slithering snakes trying to break free of their grasps, but both were ready when the walls finally gave way and the two SWORDS robots broke through and churned forward into the conference room. They didn't get very far before McCracken and Wareagle jammed the severed cables against their frames.

Sparks quickly turned to flames and the machines shook violently enough to almost lift them off the floor before shutting down in twin clouds of noxious smoke. Their collapsed gun turrets gave them the look of overpriced, broken-down toys as they sizzled and popped.

"I really hate those fucking things," managed Captain Seven from the floor, pushing himself back to his feet just as what was left of the windows shattered ahead of black-garbed figures hurdling inside.

Shinzo had ordered his first wave into motion the moment the two SWORDS robots he'd sent into attack mode went dark. There was no longer a choice, no longer any more time to waste. He would not fail, *could* not fail, not with the potential means to achieve his greatest dream so close.

He only wished he could see the product of his planning, but the loss of the robots had rendered him blind, able only to envision the victory soon to be his, as he readied to send in the second wave of his men.

Ninjas!

Or, at least, members of Aum Shinrikyo, McCracken thought when the spectral, masked commando figures crashed into the room through what remained of the glass.

Wareagle was ready as soon as the first two hit the floor clustered too close, just ahead of the third. Their narrow spacing allowed him to grasp both men, rag dolls in his powerful grasp, by the scruffs of the neck and slam both of them face-first into the remnants of a wall. He held them there as they kicked and writhed, flailing futilely for the weapons that the impact had stripped from their grasps.

The third man had the sense to drop farther aside, far enough to make McCracken lunge, reaching him just as the man's finger found the trigger of a silenced submachine gun slung round his chest. McCracken wedged a finger into place to keep him from firing and they pirouetted across the floor. He felt more than saw the man's eyes dart back for the shattered window, the chill wind of an approaching storm pushing inward, everything a haze amid the emergency lighting that felt like spots shining down upon him.

McCracken had already gotten his own finger into place atop his adversary's when the next trio of attackers swooped into the room. They landed ready to fire, but the lack of focus on their targets cost them.

Badly.

Because McCracken found them in his sights before they could lock in on him, Wareagle, or anyone else. He opened up with a sound-suppressed fusillade. There was no thought to his action, only instinct, just as instinct led him to crack his captive in the face twice with an elbow, mashing bone with each blow after recording the downed frames of the three men his bullets had dropped.

The next moment found armed Homeland personnel flooding the room, guns sweeping about in search of targets.

"Hold your fire!" Folsom blared, lurching to his feet with arms raised. "Hold your fire!"

Wareagle let go of the two attackers he'd been holding and stepped back, leaving their faces stuck in the wall.

"Just in time," McCracken said, releasing the attacker he was holding and letting him crumple to the floor, as the final SWORDS robot rolled by in the hallway, its empty machine gun clacking hollowly.

CHAPTER 56

New Orleans

"We're getting out of here, Hank," McCracken said moments later, taking Katie DeMarco in tow.

"Couldn't agree more," Folsom acknowledged.

"So where does Homeland Security go when Homeland Security breaks down?"

"This way," said Folsom.

Shinzo Asahara could only assume the worst. With no contact from the members of his assault team, he knew the unexpected presence of the ponytailed Indian and bearded man had destroyed his plans to retrieve Katie DeMarco and learn what she knew. He could almost feel his father looming behind him, shaking his head in disapproving fashion.

Shinzo didn't blame him.

"We're not finished yet, Father," he said out loud, the fingers of his right hand returning to the keyboard. "There's still one card left to play."

The chaos in the halls had dissipated, the vast majority of on-duty Homeland personnel who'd survived the onslaught having managed to flee or find safe hiding spots they were reluctant to leave. The office's lowermost floor approaching the lobby and reception area was eerily quiet amid the debris strewn everywhere and the smell of blood, sulfur, and burned wires. A storm wind pushed its way through the shattered windows, and the walls were marred with bullet holes carved neatly in place as if by an artist's brush.

McCracken took lead with Johnny Wareagle at the rear, both wielding submachine guns now. Folsom, Captain Seven, and Katie DeMarco were clustered tightly between them, all breathing a collective sigh of relief when they reached the lobby's glass doors leading out into the reception area. McCracken yanked back on the handles to open them.

Nothing.

"Your security system do this, Hank?"

Folsom moved forward and tried the doors just as Blaine had. "Something's wrong."

"Something's missing, too," Captain Seven noted, gesturing toward the two pedestals on which the prototypes for the Atlas humanoid robots had been perched.

And that's when the metallic ring of crunching footsteps sounded, the Atlas machines moving in menacingly on them from corners untouched by the emergency lighting.

McCracken realized the robots had no real heads or faces he could see, just boxlike extensions at the base of what would have been their necks. Two red static antennae rose from the prototypes' shoulders, curving inward toward each other at the top.

He and Wareagle spun out toward opposite sides, opening fire with their submachine guns. The bullets clamored off both robots, unable to pierce the armor protecting the machines' inner workings but drawing sparks upon severing tight bands of coil extending out their legs and arms. The coils had the look of an external circulatory system, carrying lubricant and diode-generated power instead of blood.

The prototypes kept right on coming, seeming to home in on Katie DeMarco with a straight line of red LED lights built into their boxlike heads going from flashing to static. McCracken aimed more of his fire for what he thought were the antennae to no avail, the group backing up as far as it could against the lobby's glass entry wall.

He and Wareagle spun toward the glass doors, submachine guns leveling toward them until Folsom jerked McCracken's barrel down.

"It's bulletproof—don't bother!"

"Blainey!"

Wareagle tossed him a fire axe he'd yanked out of a nearby wall-mounted glass firebox, keeping what looked like a four-foot steel bar, curved at the end like a fireman's wedge tool, for himself. The Atlas on his side was nearer the group and he stepped out to confront it, lashing his wedge around like a baseball bat. It impacted against the thing's shoulder extremity, steel meeting steel leaving barely a ding. The prototype blocked Wareagle's next strike as he went for a spearlike jab into the thing's rectangular head extension, the attack resulting again in no more than a small dent.

By that point, across the floor McCracken had brought his fire axe around low, going for an articulated visible ball joint where the prototype's knee and ankle extremities converged. His intent was to sever the lowermost portion of a leg to rob the thing of balance and thus motion. But, again, his effort drew only a resounding clang, the titanium steel too strong to sever.

Next, he brought the axe up and around, feeling his whole body shudder from the impact of the axe blade against the Atlas's arm, raised in blinding fashion for a block. The prototypes continued advancing for Katie again, forcing McCracken and Wareagle to lose precious ground between them and her.

In the reception area beyond, meanwhile, all three elevator doors opened to allow a slew of New Orleans police personnel to flood out, helpless to do anything else but watch the ongoing battle through the glass wall and doors.

McCracken let the axe rebound off the prototype's arm and rerouted it for a blow akin to chopping firewood, a looping overhead blow that sank deep into the space between the thing's shoulders. Sparks showered outward, the prototype going shuddery in what looked like pain. McCracken tried to jerk the blade free for a follow-up strike, but the axe had wedged in too tight to pull out.

The thing started on again with the axe stuck in place, McCracken backpedaling to keep himself between it and Katie, noticing the red lights flashing again as the Atlas sought to retrain its sensors on her.

"Find me a way to blind this thing, Captain!"

"Already on it!" Captain Seven screamed back at him, ducking under a wild blow from the prototype that had broken off its battle with Wareagle to try to cut him off.

Wareagle worked the heavy wedge tool nimbly about, lashing it one way and then the other, searching for some weakness in the prototype's defenses. It countered with a series of blinding, powerful strikes with its overly long extremities, each drawing only air as Wareagle managed to duck under or arch back from each one.

For his part, McCracken lurched in toward the prototype on his side, grabbing a cluster of strung together cables and twisting, hoping to disable the thing that way. But the cables wouldn't give in the slightest, his fingers trapped within the cluster long enough for the thing to hammer a powerful blow downward. McCracken evaded that one, but not the next that came in from the side, crashing into his shoulder and sending him sprawling to the floor. The prototype continued on past him, brushing Hank Folsom aside effortlessly and measuring off the final distance toward Katie DeMarco who was pinned in the corner.

"Johnny!"

Wareagle continued to battle the other Atlas to a stalemate, and could do nothing about the oncoming one without freeing up this one to attack as well. McCracken struggled back to his feet, his shoulder exploding in pain and his arm on that side hanging limply. He pushed himself into motion in the same moment Captain Seven tore the fire extinguisher from its bracket and rushed toward him, yanking out the safety pin and righting the nozzle straight for the Atlas that had downed McCracken.

His first thought was that the captain was going to use the extinguisher as a ram. Instead, though, McCracken watched as he angled the nozzle straight on with the thing surging straight for him, steadying his aim.

"Take this, *motherfucker*!"

And Captain Seven opened up on the thing with a shower of white, foamy spray. Absurd at first glance until McCracken realized the captain had focused all the spray toward the bank of red LED lights and lenses that held the prototype's sensory and visual capabilities along its boxlike head extension.

"Heeeee-yahhhhhh!" he wailed as the thing suddenly veered right, then left, then right again.

It seemed to refocus its attention on Wareagle this time and swung blindly toward his shape, looking almost drunk with its motions turned clumsy and awkward and leaving Johnny to battle both prototypes now.

Beyond the glass entry in the reception area, meanwhile, a pair of helmeted SWAT police frantically worked explosives into place along the doors, wedging a transistorized detonator into place. The rest of the police scurried for cover, obeying orders unheard within the Homeland office's lobby.

McCracken rushed across the floor toward Wareagle, forgetting the pain long enough to knock him aside and sparing him a wild blow from the now blind prototype. Instead, the strike slammed into the other Atlas, which retaliated by hammering its twin with a pair of strikes that left them tied up like wrestlers, whirling across the floor together and obliterating anything they struck.

BOOM!

The glass entry doors blew open in a spray of glass behind a white-hot flash. SWAT personnel poured into the Homeland lobby and opened fire on the prototypes in a nonstop stream, continuing until they keeled over to the floor as a single, twisted assemblage of smoking steel.

Wareagle helped McCracken back to his feet, Blaine careful not to test his injured shoulder, which that ached badly but felt structurally sound. Folsom was still down and dazed, while Captain Seven clung to his fire extinguisher the way a gunfighter would his pistol after shooting down someone intending to do the same to him.

McCracken started for the corner where Katie had pinned herself, freezing just as fast.

"Shit," he muttered.

Because Katie DeMarco was gone.

PART FOUR:
THE TEMPLE

CHAPTER 57

New Orleans

Leander Levy watched Shinzo Asahara enter his shop and approach the counter with hands clasped behind him. Four other Japanese men followed him inside, their motions so precise as to appear robotic right up to their eyes that didn't seem to blink.

"It's been a long time, Shinzo-san."

Asahara bowed slightly. "Too long, Levy-sensei. But I understand a samurai sword fashioned by a disciple of the great Masamune has come into your possession."

"It did," Levy nodded, feeling himself stiffen, and he leaned forward casually to appear more at ease. "But I'm afraid I've already placed it with another party."

"How disappointing," Asahara told him. "I thought we had an agreement on such items, that I would always be informed of their procurement first."

"These were extenuating circumstances. It won't happen again, I assure you."

"I trust that it won't, Levy-sensei." With that Asahara pulled his hands forward and swept the one encased by a black mitten sideways, sending an elegant crystal vase tumbling to the floor where it smashed into unrecognizable fragments. "You must forgive my clumsiness," he apologized, holding up his covered left hand as explanation. "An unfortunate malady, I'm afraid." His gaze moved to the shattered vase. "I trust it wasn't too valuable a piece."

"Waterford dating back two centuries. Priceless," Levy managed, through the thick clog forming in his throat.

"Another pity then," Asahara said, reaching into his jacket pocket with his uncovered hand. "But if you help me with something else, I can assure you I will be more careful."

He unfolded the simple sheet of copy paper and laid it on the counter. Levy lifted the reading glasses dangling at this chest to his nose to better regard a series of unrecognizable symbols. Based on the discolorization and degradation of those symbols, Levy guessed the copies had been made from photographs taken of whatever had originally contained them.

"I've never seen anything like these before," Levy told Asahara.

"Any idea what they mean, Levy-sensei?"

Levy lifted a magnifying glass from the counter, trying to still the trembling in his hand.

"They aren't figures or drawings," he said, running the magnifying glass up and down, and then side to side. "Nor are they from any symbol language I've ever seen before. There's no pattern, no discernible repetition that would indicate any language at all, at least none I or anyone else is familiar with. Except . . ."

"Proceed, Levy-sensei."

"Well, these do somewhat resemble portions of ancient cave drawings found in the Andes Mountains and elsewhere. While those drawings and symbols have never been successfully translated either, I see some similarities, particularly in the use of lines, dots, and circles, that would indicate they may have originated with the same source."

"Those Andes drawings have sometimes been linked to extraterrestrial beings legend says once visited earth, yes?"

Levy nodded and lowered his magnifying glass.

"And can you draw any conclusions based upon that?"

"I've read some linguistic analysis that speaks of those symbols forming a warning, Shinzo-san. Perhaps as simple as Do Not Enter or No Trespassing."

"And if not as simple?"

Levy found his mouth too dry to swallow, the unblinking stares of Asahara's four henchmen now locked upon him. "A warning about the end of the world."

"You've piqued my interest, Levy-sensei," Asahara said, leaning forward over the counter closer to Levy. "What about a location? Do the symbols say anything about a location?"

Levy pretended to regard the symbols again. "There's not enough here to—"

"Mention of a weapon," Asahara interrupted. "Is there any mention of a weapon?"

This time Levy didn't bother checking the symbols again. "If you could bring me more, perhaps . . ."

Asahara moved his gaze to a lush landscape hanging directly behind the counter, centered over Levy's head. "I'm told some of the most valuable paintings ever have been found behind other canvases."

"That's correct, Shinzo-san."

"Then perhaps the message of these symbols is hidden in plain sight as well. Could that be?"

"It could."

Asahara backed away from the counter, leaving the page containing the symbols atop the glass. "Then find that message for me. Tell me where I can find the means to end the world, Levy-sensei," Asahara said, staring him right in the eye. "Or next time I come I'll break more than just crystal."

CHAPTER 58

New Orleans

"There," McCracken said, pointing at Captain Seven's computer inside an office they'd appropriated still lit eerily only by the emergency lighting, which made the screen seem unnaturally bright.

Standing next to him, Folsom leaned in closer to better see. Outside, the wail of sirens continued to split the night, and they'd closed the office door to at least temporarily shut out the sounds of law enforcement and rescue personnel frantically at work beyond. "What am I looking at?"

"SF-5-16ARM," the captain explained, reading the screen before McCracken had a chance to. "It's the short code for a form of underwater explosives. Been around forever, and nobody's come up with anything better since the very dawn of . . . well, something."

"Who authorized the req order?"

"The e-mail notation belongs to the *Deepwater Venture*'s operations manager," McCracken answered this time. The first paramedics on the scene had confirmed his shoulder was strained but not damaged, then offered him painkillers he refused. "But if you check the logs, I'll bet you your pension that his assistant was actually the one who filed it."

"Katie DeMarco? But why would—"

"Smart girl," Captain Seven interrupted, words aimed at McCracken. "Doubt anybody would question a requisition for underwater ordnance on a deepwater oil rig."

"And," McCracken followed, "SF-5 works just as well above water as under it."

Folsom backed away from the screen, hands planted on his hips. "Where the hell are you going with this?"

"We had it wrong, Hank," McCracken told him. "Katie DeMarco, or whoever she really is, was on that rig to sabotage it the whole time."

"There's more, MacNuts," said Captain Seven. "Just like you thought."

"What I did was this," he continued. "Took a still picture of our girl lifted off this building's security camera and ran it through facial recognition technology in areas around the attacks at the Hastings Chemical plant bombing, the Royal Dutch Shell supertanker sinking, and the Valley Coal poisoning. I shit you not, managing that all straight was no easy task. If you don't score me some primo weed like yesterday, I am going on strike and I mean that sincerely."

"What'd you find?" McCracken asked.

"When was the last time you were wrong?"

"When I decided to come to New Orleans to celebrate my birthday. Now talk to me."

Captain Seven hit the Enter button on his keyboard and rolled his chair backward to make room for McCracken and Folsom. "Voilà, boys!"

Four shots of Katie DeMarco, looking different enough in each one, appeared in equal sizes, each occupying a quarter of the screen. Her hair color and style altered, eyes changed by tinted contact lenses, but it was unquestionably her in each instance.

"Going clockwise, boys, that's her at Hastings, the pier where the Royal Dutch Shell supertanker was docked, and Valley Coal headquarters."

"So WorldSafe's taking environmental terrorism to a whole new level," picked up McCracken, "with her as their chief operative."

"And she was going to make the *Deepwater Venture* her fourth target," added Folsom, "before something else intervened."

"You mean fifth," said McCracken.

"What?"

"Fifth. Check out the screen. Looks like Captain Seven has earned himself a promotion to Eight."

The captain wheeled his chair back in front of the monitor, working the mouse so the final, unidentified shot of Katie DeMarco filled the screen. "Software uncovered this, MacNuts, not me. This is the oldest of the four, which probably makes it her first job. Almost seven years ago at a fossil fuel plant outside Stuttgart, Germany. This chick really knows how to make things go bang."

"And we let her get away," Folsom bemoaned, shaking his head. "*I* let her get away."

McCracken laid a calm hand on Folsom's shoulder. "Time for me to return the favor, Hank."

"Favor?"

"You brought me back into the game, and now I'm going to make sure you stay in it." McCracken waited for Folsom to turn from the computer screen toward him before continuing. "I think I know what Katie DeMarco's next target is."

CHAPTER 59

Houston

Two nights after surviving the attack at Homeland Security headquarters in New Orleans, Katie DeMarco found herself crouched on the roof of a building neighboring the corporate headquarters of Ocean Bore Technologies. Located at the northwest corner of Interstate 45 and Beltway 8 in the Greenspoint area of Houston, Ocean Bore occupied an eight-story, 108,000-square-foot steel and glass building. Security was relatively heavy, but nothing she wasn't expecting. And her plan did not even involve entering the building.

Her research and previous recon of the site indicated that Ocean Bore used Overnight Express as a delivery service, a leaner version of FedEx, chosen in large part for the twenty-four pickup and delivery services the company offered. Ocean Bore maintained interests all over the world, so deliveries came in at all times and shipments went out that way too.

Overnight Express maintained a fleet of navy-blue trucks, one less in number as of this afternoon, the same one she'd parked ten minutes ago in the circular drive just out of sight from the security desk before positioning herself on the roof. If anyone grew suspicious of the truck, an inspection of the rear would reveal only properly wrapped, addressed, and invoiced packages of various sizes and shapes; WorldSafe was nothing if not thorough, and forming a storehouse of intelligence on the group's potential targets had been one of the group's hallmarks.

In this case, all the packages stored in the rear of the Overnight Express truck parked before the building entrance contained a hybrid mixture of layers of cotton soaked in diesel fuel, ammonium nitrate, and mechanical-grade ball bearings. Katie watched from the rooftop and pictured the effects of the blast force turning the building's multitude of glass panes into deadly projectiles propelled in all directions at virtually immeasurable energy and speed. The initial blast and accompanying shock wave would be enough to lay waste to the building's front section, turning it into a jagged, charred shell. Had this been daytime, hundreds of people would die. At night it would be considerably fewer, but her point would nonetheless be made.

How do you feel about that?

Her one visit to a psychiatrist had featured that question being posed to her at least a dozen times and now Katie posed it to herself.

Something, I feel something . . .

And Katie would rather feel guilt, remorse, *anything*, because it was better than feeling nothing; and nothing was all she had felt for a very long time. She did not enjoy killing and had never observed any of her victims close up, with the exception of the fire in Stuttgart that was never supposed to happen. But acting on her aggression, fighting to relieve the demons that had haunted her for so long, was the only thing that made her feel anything at all. She knew it was wrong, but her entire life had been based on wrong, casting both her judgment and viewpoint through a jaundiced eye. Initially, she'd hoped the process would end with Stuttgart; instead, it had only begun there and showed no signs of abating now. Like a drug. She needed her fix. Like an addict.

This was supposed to have been her sixth attack coming in the wake of her intended bombing of the *Deepwater Venture*. But fate had intervened in the strangest and most ironic of ways; her identity being thrown into question had ended up saving her life still days away from using explosives to disable the rig's entire drilling mechanism.

Before he was murdered, Twist had formulated the explosives and packed them appropriately into the packages now in the truck's rear. All Katie had to do was steal an Overnight Express vehicle from the poorly guarded depot, drive it to the storage unit containing the boxes, and then park it with the product of Twist's labor. Beyond that there was only a number to dial on her cell phone to reach an identical phone serving as detonator in the truck's rear.

Ring, ring, ring, ring . . .

All it would take.

CHAPTER 60

Guangdong, China

"We go on my signal," Shinzo Asahara said into the small wrist-mounted microphone.

His Aum Shinrikyo troops, composed of his most devoted followers with military or police backgrounds, were stationed at critical points of access to the Nagasaki Yangjiang High Tech Center. The building was the showpiece of the Shenzhen Techno Center, an industrial park in Guangdong, China, that housed small and medium-sized Japanese enterprises specializing in joint research between the two nations involving industry, academia, and government. As far as Shinzo knew, though, only Japanese were employed inside the Nagasaki Yangjiang building.

Asahara was under no illusions that Leander Levy's study of the symbols akin to those supposedly etched upon Pandora's jar would yield the jar's true location. So he had opted for an all-out breach of this building, the most daring operation Aum Shinrikyo had ever attempted. He felt his left hand begin to tingle with numbness and a strange sensation that felt like it was being pricked by icicles. The deformity had happened here in this very building in what felt like another life, just days after Japan's Supreme Court upheld the order for his father's execution in September of 2006. Shinzo had believed then that if the rumors were true of the Nagasaki Center's research into particle acceleration and dark matter, the potential to find the very means he had long sought would at last be in the hands of Aum Shinrikyo. That would have served as his father's final legacy with the group, one that would have lent meaning to his pending execution.

So Shinzo had assaulted the building with his most trusted followers that night too, raiding the main laboratory to see his life changed radically forever as a result. His hand might have been the most dramatic but was far from the only wound he'd suffered. His vision was cloudy at times, sensitive to light, and often switched from color to black and white like a broken television. He suffered from pounding headaches distinctly different from migraines in that they seemed to radiate outward from the center of his skull. And on top of all that, there were the visions of his father captured in fleeting glimpses in window glass or longer ones in mirrors that had now grown into full-fledged conversations.

Was his father really appearing to him? Had his first fateful experience with the Nagasaki Center's particle accelerator opened a door between dimensions, between worlds?

Shinzo did not know and chose not to consider the ramifications of what such a truth might mean to human existence: proof of an afterlife, of the ability to coexist with departed souls who in death, apparently, differed little from life.

The possibilities were staggering, and Shinzo found himself wondering if all this was the true plan, if his fate was to use dark matter to destroy the material world so it could join with the spirit world now inhabited by his father. The mere thought, the very possibility, set Shinzo trembling as he again lifted the wrist-mounted microphone toward his lips.

"Take the building. Kill anyone who gets in your way."

CHAPTER 61

Houston

Katie DeMarco had entered the triggering phone number but had yet to hit Call. She was conjuring up the memories, until they crystallized enough in clarity to make her head pound.

The ghosts of her past reared themselves up again, refusing to be forgotten or ignored.

Haven't I done enough? Haven't I suffered enough?

Who was she challenging in her mind? Moments like this gave form to her pain, her anguish, how all the violence and destruction had begun. From that first day in Stuttgart, with the attack on the fossil fuel plant, they had been the only things that made her feel alive, vital. Katie recalled a visit she'd made to a psychiatrist a few years before Stuttgart, hoping to find the relief that had eluded her everywhere else. The psychiatrist was a woman, kind and compassionate enough, who had at least tried to understand.

"I want you to close your eyes for me."

Katie, who was still going by her real name back then, did.

"You're on a beach. What's the first thing you think of?"

"I'm in the water, caught in a riptide. I'm fighting it, even though I know you're supposed to go with it, parallel to shore. I'm getting weaker."

"What time of day is it?"

"It's night."

"Look around. Is there anyone to help you on the beach, hear your screams if you cry out?"

"I'm alone. I'm looking for someone. I think there was someone else with me, someone the riptide's already taken."

"But you don't know who."

"No."

"Can you guess?"

Katie remembered feeling as if she were in a trance, almost hypnotized. It was like a dream unfolding before her conscious mind.

"I don't want to," she told the psychiatrist.

"Why?"

"Because I'm afraid he might be dead."

"He?"

Katie remained silent.

"Tell me more about him," the psychiatrist persisted.

"I want him to be dead."

"I thought you were afraid for him, worried."

"This is someone else."

"Who?"

"My father."

"Is he the one in the water with you?"

"No, but he's the one I wish was drowning."

In that moment, the trance broke and the memories returned, bringing the pain with them. Katie opened her eyes to find the psychiatrist staring right at her.

"Tell me your happiest memory."

"There are so many . . ."

"Tell me one that involves your mother."

"Why?"

"Because she wasn't in the water with you."

"Shopping in Paris when I was a little girl. Just the two of us. A beautiful day on the Champs-Elysées."

"Where was your father?"

"Business. Like always."

"You're leaving someone out."

"How can you tell?"

"Because I think it was the other person caught in the riptide with you."

"My . . . brother."

"Was he the one in the water?"

"I don't know."

"Where was he the day you went shopping with your mother in Paris, on the Champs-Elysées?"

"At prep school."

"You missed him."

"Yes, but glad he was away. I hated when he was home, when the family was together."

The psychiatrist leaned forward, aware they were coming to a crucial moment. "Can you tell me why?"

"No."

"Do you know why?"

Katie opened her eyes and nodded, her throat suddenly feeling clogged.

"Close your eyes. Picture yourself in the water again."

Katie closed her eyes, feeling her lungs tighten in anticipation of the riptide.

"Where is your brother?"

"I . . . can't see him."

"But he's there."

"He went under. The tide's got him."

"Someone's holding him under, aren't they?"

Katie gnashed her teeth.

"Someone's drowning him."

"I want to help . . ."

"But you can't."

"I want to dive under the waves. I want to save him."

"Why don't you?"

"I'm not strong enough. I'm too scared. I'm too weak."

"Who's holding him under the water?"

"I'm too scared!"

"Are they coming for you next?"

"I'm too weak."

"Katie—"

"No!"

"Open your eyes, Katie, open your eyes."

She'd opened her eyes, left the psychiatrist's office without another word, and never returned. How much she wanted to save her brother, how much she wanted to be strong enough . . .

Katie hadn't told the psychiatrist about the sounds she heard while he was drowning. Not cries for help, not desperate screams. Just murmurs, sobs, and muffled pleas. How could she hear them if he was trapped underwater?

But she heard them again now, finally hitting Call and counting the rings. One . . . two . . . three . . .

Katie tensed in anticipation of the fourth, the brief lag between the third ring and the one that would set off the explosives and ravage the Ocean Bore building proving interminable. Then it finally sounded and she tensed; even her breathing halted, flinching in anticipation of the Overnight Express truck exploding violently.

Until the fifth ring sounded, then the sixth, seventh, and eighth that were followed by the clatter of footsteps behind her on the rooftop.

CHAPTER 62

Guangdong, China

The Nagasaki Center's security was no match for the forces of Aum Shinrikyo. Men fully prepared to die, who accepted if not embraced death, had been the hardest to kill from the time of the samurai. They wanted to see the end of the world, yes, but more importantly they wanted to help bring it about, and that was what tonight was all about.

Shinzo Asahara's second right hand began to tingle when he moved for the building, once his men had taken it. Strangely, the building bore little resemblance to the one he recalled from six years ago, looking as if it had been totally remodeled. Engulfed by his soldiers, Shinzo entered the elevator and descended toward the center's laboratory level a dozen levels belowground. His heart was thudding, breathing starting to pick up. A layer of cool sweat brought a sheen to his face, and he suddenly found it difficult to swallow. This was where he had been remade; this was where the rest of his life's course was determined for him. He thought he might pass out when the elevator doors finally opened and he emerged from the compartment onto the laboratory level.

And froze.

Because this, too, was unrecognizable, having been renovated and reconstructed since his fateful visit seven years before. Shinzo held a hand over his heart, as if to hold it inside his chest. The walk down the long, dully lit hallway passed with thoughts and memories clashing in his head, on the verge of surrendering to what felt like a panic attack when he finally reached the main laboratory and control room.

Because of the inherent danger involved in its experiments into dark matter, the Nagasaki Center's main lab had been forged out of heavy rock, shale, and a triple-thick layer of concrete for good measure covering the five immediate stories above. Once inside, Shinzo realized it bore no resemblance to what he recalled either, the lab having been utterly rebuilt from scratch.

Something had happened, something had changed, and Shinzo saw a quartet of his Aum Shinrikyo commandos hovering over four scientists in lab coats. They were Yoshihiro Shibata, Kana Hosokawa, Hisanori Ito, and a younger man he didn't recognize. Shibata had been the man in charge of the dark matter experiments on Shinzo's last visit and, by the look of things, that much anyway hadn't changed. But he had no recollection of the two-feet-thick glass walls that now ran the length of a much-expanded accelerator tunnel that stretched as far as the eye could see on the other side of the glass.

Shibata saw him approaching and his eyes filled first with shock, then fear, and finally resignation. Asahara thought he may have even smiled ever so tightly.

"I thought you'd be dead by now, Shinzo-san."

"As the Americans say, those reports have been greatly exaggerated."

"Let me see your hands."

Shinzo Asahara tugged off his mitten and showed both of them to him.

Shibata's smile widened almost smugly, his gaze focusing on

what had once been Shinzo's left hand. "I would imagine there's no feeling, no sensation at all, even when you touch something."

"None."

"You have use of your fingers?"

"Somewhat," Shinzo said, clenching his second right hand as best he could, "although I can't tell when I'm gripping something or not. It feels like someone else's hand."

"Because it is, Shinzo-san, it is indeed. Not another man's, but not yours either."

"Looks like you've enjoyed a very thorough upgrade in the time since. More funding from the Japanese and Chinese governments?"

Shibata remained silent, spine tightening just enough to tell Asahara he'd struck a nerve.

"From who then?"

Shibata found the strength to meet Shinzo's gaze. "You're too late."

"For what?"

"The experts you seek, the men who have worked virtually nonstop since our last visit, aren't here. They were called away."

"To where?"

"The airport to board a private plane. That's all I know. I've had no contact with them since they were summoned weeks ago."

"Summoned?"

"This a private facility now," Shibata explained. "We are just glorified employees with walls full of diplomas and awards."

Asahara looked unconvinced.

"I'm telling you the truth," Shibata insisted. "I have no reason to lie."

"You have every reason to lie when the man who should have killed you seven years ago is prepared to rectify that mistake."

"Then consider the price you paid for that visit."

Shinzo stepped back, spine straightening as he gazed about again before refocusing his attention on Shibata. His numb, tingly hand held before him. "What would exposure to dark matter do to an entire human body?"

"I prefer not to think about that."

"Then perhaps we should experiment with you inside the particle accelerator."

"Go ahead."

"So calm in the face of death, Shibata?"

"I've had plenty of practice. I'm dying, Shinzo-san. Inoperable brain cancer. Kill me now and all you accomplish is stealing six painful months from me."

Asahara looked to the younger men flanking Shibata, the one he didn't know looking somehow vaguely familiar. "Then perhaps you'd like to join me in witnessing your younger associate here exposed to your accelerator."

Shibata's face tightened in fear, and in that moment Asahara realized the source of the familiarity between the two men. He moved behind that younger man and clamped his good hand on his right shoulder.

"Your son looks much like you, Shibata."

"Please, there's nothing I can say that can help you!"

"I'll be the judge of that," Asahara said, signaling his commandos to take the younger Shibata in tow.

"What do you want?" his father pleaded.

"Who called your scientists away? Who is this man you take your orders from now?"

Shibata remained silent, looking down at the floor. Asahara nodded to his two commandos who instantly began dragging the man's son toward the heavy steel doors that accessed the Nagasaki Center's totally remodeled and expanded particle accelerator.

"No, *stop*!" Shibata cried out.

"Not until you tell me who you are beholden to now, Shibata."

"I-I-I am not to speak his name."

Asahara flashed his numb, second right hand before the man. "What do you think will happen when your son is exposed to the accelerator?"

His commandos were almost to the heavy steel doors with the younger Shibata in their grasp.

"Sebastian Roy!" his father screamed, and Shinzo Asahara looked back at him. "We all work for Sebastian Roy! The Nagasaki Center is his now!"

"The energy tycoon?"

Shibata nodded. "He took it over when the economy destroyed our other sources of funding!"

"And he was the one who ordered your scientists away?"

"Not my scientists anymore, Shinzo-san. *His* scientists."

"Tell me where they were sent!"

"I don't know, I swear it! I only fielded the call, relayed the instructions from Roy himself. The men were taken to a private airstrip. But I have no idea where their plane was headed. That's all I know!"

But Asahara wasn't listening to him anymore. Someone else, the energy tycoon Sebastian Roy, must be after the dark matter as well. And, in point of fact, had located a potential source of it strong enough to call for an army of scientists to be dispatched *somewhere.*

"You must believe me!" Shibata was pleading.

"Oh, I do, Shibata, I do."

Shibata seemed to breathe easier. "Then my son, you will release him. . . ."

Asahara glanced at his commandos holding the younger Shibata, flaccid and weak-kneed, between them before the steel door. "No, Shibata, I don't think I will. I want to see what the accelerator will do to an entire body."

He nodded to his men, then turned back to Shibata, starting to tug his mitten off.

"You see, I already know what it can do to a single limb."

CHAPTER 63

Houston

Katie lunged to her feet and twisted to flee, managing to scamper only a few strides before McCracken tackled her to the gravel-laden rooftop. She looked down at the cell phone that felt warm in her hand.

"Looks a lot like this one," McCracken told her, lifting the matching one she'd wired as a detonator from his pocket, still holding fast to her with his good arm. "And you've already done enough running for one lifetime, young lady."

She struggled futilely in his grasp. "You don't know anything about my life!"

"I know you're a murderer and a terrorist. What I don't know is why. Because some monsters are born and some are made." McCracken released his hold on her. "You were made."

Katie back-crawled, putting more distance between them. "You're letting me go?"

"Depends how much you tell me about why you're doing this. It's not for you and has nothing to do with the environment. That much I know, which means there's something lots more important I don't."

"Take a guess, Superman."

"How about revenge? That usually works."

Katie didn't bother denying it. "Am I supposed to be impressed?"

McCracken shrugged. "It's written in your eyes."

"So what now, you arrest me, something like that?"

"Something," was all McCracken said.

Katie tried to look away from him, but failed. Enough of the light shed from the complex's exterior lighting reached them to frame McCracken's face with the same intensity Katie recalled from the car when he'd rescued her and then in New Orleans in the battle against the robots before she'd escaped. He never seemed to lose that intensity, that focus, his switch perpetually in the on position. His thick hair looked too long for his age, yet the way the light touched his face made him seem younger.

"How did you know I'd be here?"

"Revenge, remember? That made your next target pretty obvious under the circumstances."

"And what circumstances might those be?"

"One: you had every reason to believe Ocean Bore was behind the men who were after you and the kill team that wiped out your friends in Greenland."

McCracken watched Katie stiffen, a pallor falling over her expression. "You finally checked out Greenland."

"You were right—a massacre in all respects. We're talking professional all the way, meaning men who'd done this kind of thing before. Lots of times. And you think Ocean Bore sent them, young lady."

"I *know* Ocean Bore sent them. And don't call me that."

"Then tell me your real name."

"I'd rather you just stick with 'Katie'; I like to be on a first-name basis with all the superheroes I get to know."

McCracken bristled slightly. "All the heroes I know are dead."

"That's because they weren't as super as you and that Indian friend of yours." Katie looked around. "Speaking of whom, where is he?"

"Out and about, making sure you came alone."

"All my friends are dead too, remember?"

McCracken responded by rising and starting to walk off, gesturing for her to follow. "Come on."

"Where we going?"

"I haven't decided yet. I'm still waiting for you to explain the connection to me."

"What connection?"

"Between all the targets you've hit. What makes this personal for you."

Katie fought to remain calm. For a moment, just that moment, she felt as if she was back in the psychiatrist's office being confronted with truths she didn't want to see.

"There's no need to tell you something you've already figured out on your own," she said finally.

"Point taken," McCracken conceded. "Roy Industries owns all the companies you've hit."

"Very good."

"Not really. That's only part of the story. I haven't figured out the why yet, where the personal part comes in."

Katie shifted enough for another sliver of light to catch her eyes starting to tear up. "Sebastian Roy is my father."

CHAPTER 64

Pyrenees Mountains, Spain

Sebastian Roy would never forget the first blast. He was standing on the podium inside the final unfinished section of his fossil fuel plant in Stuttgart. The cavernous space had been sectioned off by curtains and risers, the walls plastered with final renderings of what the facility would look like once all seven phases were complete. It would be up and running with only two online and capable of powering an entire city with four up.

His wife was alongside him, his son and daughter just behind them but spaced so any pictures or broadcast would include them in the shot as well. He was especially gratified to have Alexandra here since they'd been estranged, off and on but mostly on, ever since she'd gone off to college. From the e-mails Roy had read, she'd even tried to convince his son, Christian, to join her in that estrangement, robbing him of his heir, the young man destined to lead Roy Industries someday.

Before beginning his remarks, with the applause thundering before him, he'd turned to look at the boy—always a boy to him—

but found Alexandra's glare instead, as hateful and intense as ever. He owed neither her nor anyone else any explanation for his actions; that was a gift of power. Sebastian Roy understood that making others beholden and dependent was the swiftest route to domination and control. There was no middle ground between success and failure, no compromise. Strength was everything.

His father had not hugged him a single time Roy could remember; he could not recall any touch other than a handshake, and even that proved cold and fleeting. His father had such dry skin that it felt like shaking hands with a lizard. He promised himself he would treat his own son differently, promised that the boy would be his to mold and fashion. He would not be cold and aloof as his father had been. He would be . . .

Stop it!

The memories, long banished from thought, came flooding back, even though Roy had fought long and hard to vanquish them from his psyche.

I'm being punished. . . .

He fought the thought down, dismissed for its utter absurdity. Roy knew that men who wielded power must not be held to the same standards as others, that they must be judged through a different prism entirely since the spectrum of light they radiated bore no resemblance to that of ordinary men. Men of great power understood the value of their most base nature, that strength came from first succumbing to temptation and then becoming the master of it.

He was not being punished, because he had done nothing for which to be punished. The license to act was his, every move undertaken shrewdly as a means to a greater end, all aimed at using his power to gain control of a world he could never walk within again. His life extended to the walls of this chamber and no farther, and in that life he found even greater purpose in seizing that control he so desperately sought.

Fuel was the world's life force. Without fuel, man would be

reduced to the primitive, so dependent was he on flipping a switch for light, heat, coolness, transportation, communications, entertainment, food. Without fuel, there would be nothing. No dreams, no progress. It made something out of nothing. Control energy and you controlled everything. And in dark matter Sebastian Roy saw the means to accomplish just that.

Just a few more days and it would be his, Roy thought as he waited for the call from Greece.

Another distraction from yet another terrible truth from the day of the fire that had imprisoned him within these walls forever. A truth no one else would ever know as even Roy himself had come to accept the lie.

Mostly, but not always.

Not today.

The phone rang.

CHAPTER 65

Houston

"What do you mean there's been a change of plans?" Folsom said, loud enough for Katie DeMarco and Johnny Wareagle to hear inside the car without benefit of speaker.

McCracken could picture him shaking his head on the other end of the line, cursing himself for bringing in the subject of his thesis in the first place. "Just what I said. We're headed to Greece to meet up with Captain Seven. We have a bad connection or something?"

Folsom cleared his throat. "Let me try this. Do you have the woman or not?"

"Yup, got her."

"I'm waiting for the but."

"I've got another lead she's going to help the Indian and me follow up, so it might be a while before I bring her in."

"This the same domestic terrorist we've been talking about? Four bombings, twenty-six deaths total if you include Stuttgart?"

"That's right. She's sitting right next to me now, if you want to call that custody. Want me to put her on?"

McCracken could hear Folsom sigh so deeply it sounded like a growl. "It's really true, isn't it?"

"I don't know. What?"

"Everything I've heard about you, how you earned that nickname of yours: McCrackenballs . . ."

"Just get the plane refueled and ready, Hank."

"How much do you charge?" Katie asked him, after several long moments of silence once Johnny Wareagle had driven off back into the night for the private airport they'd flown into from New Orleans.

"For what?"

"Killing."

"I'm not a hit man."

She rolled her eyes. "Could have fooled me."

"And if I was, you'd want me to kill your father, is that it?"

"Why not? It's what you do best, isn't it? Just like those men in Greenland."

"Difference is I only kill bad guys."

"Me too," Katie said, shaking her head. "Forty years you've been doing this, right? I could never keep doing this kind of shit for that long."

"That's because you're on the wrong side."

"Not from where I'm standing."

"If Johnny and I hadn't stopped you, you would've killed another couple dozen people tonight."

Katie stiffened, visible even through the darkness. "They deserved it."

"They never hurt you."

"They were part of Ocean Bore, Roy Industries, extensions of my father."

"So you hate them as much as you hate him."

"That's right."

"Hmmmmmmm . . . How many people does Roy Industries employ?"

"I've never bothered to count."

"You can't expect to kill all of them. Or is that what it's going to take to stop your crusade?"

"No, I only need to kill one person to manage that: Sebastian Roy."

CHAPTER 66

The Mediterranean Sea

Sebastian Roy's computer was already on in anticipation of the Skype call, filled now with a quivery picture of Doctors Gunthar Bol and Peter Whitcomb on the deck of the ship that had become their de facto base for the past three days. The equipment the mission required had been installed on board weeks before, having been on the verge of a breakthrough when Roy had dispatched the scientists to the site.

"I want to talk to my family," Whitcomb said. "I need to be sure they're safe."

"They're safe, Doctor Whitcomb. Your family, too, Doctor Bol. How long they remain that way depends entirely on you from this point."

"We can't do the impossible!"

"I'm not asking you to, gentlemen. Bring me Pandora's jar and you'll be with them the next day. And I understand there's significant progress to report."

Bol and Whitcomb exchanged a quick glance, as if to decide which of them would respond.

"Your hydrographic survey team, aboard this and the additional five ships, has now completed a detailed review of the seafloor in a fifty-mile grid centered with Athens," Whitcomb reported stiffly. "And you're right, they found something."

"With oil," Bol picked up, "you would look for sandy layers of sediment under domelike caps of shale, which normally signify the location of a potential reservoir, since oil rises through permeable sediment to the highest point it can go, collecting under unyielding shale mounds. Since your ships weren't looking for oil here, they used the salt to study disruptions in the seafloor at the subsurface level, figuring if the temple remnants were, in fact, present, they'd be buried under the same shale and sediment that might otherwise reveal oil reserves."

Now it was Bol's turn again. "Two quirks of fate in the form of major geological events proved to be the keys here. Had your team conducted this study prior to them having a profound effect on the seafloor, in all probability we'd have nothing to report. The first event was a strong earthquake centered along the southern Greek island of Crete in 2008, in itself not unusual since this is a very seismically active area believed to be riddled by literally thousands of quakes every year that normally cause little damage and often go unnoticed."

"Except this one," picked up Gunthar Bol, "caused a deep sea tsunami and seismically reoriented the sub-seafloor. Pandora's Temple, if it ever did exist, would be buried under so much sand and sediment that it would be effectively unreachable by man, which also explains why no geological or archaeological survey team ever uncovered it before. It would take a seismic event of much greater proportions to make the temple accessible again."

"Not necessarily greater proportions," noted Whitcomb, "so much as an event of properly focused intensity, something approximating the original quake that triggered the tsunamis responsible for destroying the temple along with the entire southern coastline of Greece in 1650 B.C. And that's exactly what happened in January of 2012, once again accompanied by an eruption of the Santorini volcano."

Bol's turn now. "Up until then, Santorini hadn't been active since 1956 when a large earthquake and subsequent eruption resulted in the destruction of the buildings and evacuation of the entire coastline. The 2012 quake, registering 5.2, occurred in almost the identical spot as the one in 1650 B.C. on what is now known as the Santorini Fault."

"Two earthquakes nearly four thousand years apart," said Sebastian Roy. "The first plunging Pandora's Temple into the sea to be buried forever and the second exposing its final resting place."

"Even then," elaborated Whitcomb, "standard geothermal tests never would've revealed the find. It took Ocean Bore's geomapping technology to uncover the shadow outline of something big down there. The problem is that none of the unmanned submersibles have caught anything with their cameras in the general area. Nothing at all."

"We know something's down there, Mr. Roy," Bol picked up. "But either it's invisible or there's something else we somehow haven't considered. That means we need the best underwater salvage equipment Roy Industries can get their hands on to find what's down there."

"It will be en route today, Doctor."

"What about our families?" asked Whitcomb.

But Sebastian Roy ended the transmission before responding.

CHAPTER 67

Athens, Greece

Captain Seven angled the small digital camera, linked wirelessly to his laptop, further upward.

"Yo, boys, can you see what I'm seeing?"

Squeezed behind the laptop screen on the plane streaking across the Atlantic, McCracken, Wareagle, and Sal Belamo did their best, squinting to better view the lush scene dominated by what looked like an endless array of villas nestled into sloped hills outside of Athens. McCracken thought he recognized Mount Hymettus, if memory of his own travels through the region served him correctly.

"Looks like a resort community," he said. "All that's missing is the golf course."

"This used to be the location of a wasteland known as the Desert of Lost Souls. The site of Pandora's Temple."

Captain Seven moved so close to the screen his face grew absurdly large in the oblong view of the webcam.

"What have you been smoking, Captain?"

"Some badass bud, MacNuts, I shit you not. Got it from this old hippie dude named Pat I ran into. I might just hang out here for a while when all this is done."

"You too stoned to explain what the hell happened to the desert that used to be there?"

"Not at all, MacNuts, not at all. See, according to that good old Greek historian Herodotus, there's more to the story of Pathos Verdes. . . ."

CHAPTER 68

Athens, Greece: Near 1650 B.C.

The elders wrote that the man wandered out of the vast desert wasteland where few ever dared venture. The Desert of Lost Souls, as this wasteland was called, had been named that for a reason. Many residents of Athens believed it was populated by monsters. Others claimed to have had relatives or friends who years before had trekked there in search of work on the construction of a vast palace or temple at the behest of the gods, only to never return. They spoke of a builder being visited by a messenger dispatched by Zeus, a builder who they say was bequeathed with the visions of a design in scope and complexity like none the world had ever known to be constructed amid the arid wasteland seldom traveled by man. And that tale had drawn more out from the city in search of the structure, almost all of whom never returned. The ones who did professed to have no memory of what they had seen.

But this ragged shell of a man, his bare feet cracked and filthy from the mud-strewn street, claimed to have emerged from this very wasteland. He was emaciated with wild white hair sprouting in all directions, the pupils of his eyes so big they seemed to have swallowed the whites.

"I am Pathos Verdes, and I come bearing a warning," the raggedy man announced from atop an earth berm fashioned by the endless storms that had recently racked Athens in the center of the square. Residents from the mud and wood huts layered into hillsides on either side of the city center gathered around him, attracted there by something they could not explain. "You, all of you, must avoid the Desert of Lost Souls. The gods grow angry at your trespass, your intrusion. That you would dare become interlopers in a world where entry is denied to mortal man. Desecrate their temple and risk destruction of your world. There are no second chances, no additional warnings beyond the storms the gods have seen fit to bestow upon you so you may know their wrath. Know that a much worse fate awaits your city if you do not heed their warnings now."

"And who you are to know of this, to be so bold as to threaten us this way?" challenged a city elder.

"Builder of the temple, and the only man alive to know of its existence and purpose. I cannot speak of that purpose other than to say your people have exhausted the patience of the gods."

"And what do you truly know of this holy place?"

"That it is not holy at all, but cursed—as is any man who dares climb the steps it took me years to fashion. More years have passed since its completion, how many I know not. But those years have seen me try repeatedly to join my family in the afterlife, failing on each occasion no matter how great my resolve or how sharp the blade."

"So why do you come here now, after all these years?" another from the crowd yelled out.

"Because your city's population swells. And with the travelers who enter your walls come more and more mention of the temple's existence spoken by those without knowledge of its purpose, a purpose forged by the gods themselves who all trespassers spit upon in their intrusion."

"There is no law against exploration, Pathos Verdes, or growth," said one elder.

"No, but there is a terrible price to be paid when either threatens to forfeit or betray the temple's ultimate purpose. Know, as I have known, that the gods do not bluff or issue second warnings. If the Desert of Lost Souls is not closed to your people, the gods will visit upon your city a great and terrible cataclysm, unleashing a wrath not seen in a century."

"Yet," another dweller cried out accusingly, "you live."

"For this purpose—I see that now. The gods preserved my life so I could save yours. To deliver their message unto you. This will be your only chance to heed the gods' warning. There will be no other."

The next morning, Pathos Verdes was gone, having vanished as quickly as he had appeared. Some say he was spotted walking back to the east and the Desert of Lost Souls. Others insisted that he seemed to be steering himself toward the rising sun when he simply vanished, the way a god might. For a brief time anyway, his warnings were heeded, but then men grew bold with ambition and greed. And before long the words of the strange disheveled man were first questioned and then ignored. If there was truly a golden temple out there, it would be found, threats of the gods or not.

Days after the expedition of explorers and warriors set out in search of the great bounty, the earth rumbled, shook, and began to split in places. Structures collapsed, throwing the city into a terrible panic. The residents ventured out into the streets in fear but also in hope that the worst was over.

It wasn't.

The quakes set off the long quiet volcano Santorini, its terrible force churning the seas into massive waves stretching toward the skies and blackening the sun as they rolled toward shore, growing with each foot. It is said that all Athens was destroyed, and the Desert of Lost Souls, along with the golden temple it contained, was lost to the seas forever. And the final part of the story, to this day and forever unproven, was that accounts of the survivors tell of a "man ghost" with mad eyes and wild tangles of white hair trudging amid the refuse of the city, muttering and sobbing to himself.

CHAPTER 69

Athens, Greece

"Stoned or not, do you really believe all this?" McCracken asked when Captain Seven had finished his own recapitulation of the historian's words.

"Stoned for sure, let me put it this way, MacNuts. The Aegean volcanic chain and numerous deepwater fault lines didn't just show up yesterday. A study in 1959 concluded that the tsunami inundation caused by the 1650 B.C. earthquake did indeed reach a height of fifty meters above sea level and that its effects were felt as far away as what is now Tel Aviv."

"A hundred and fifty feet plus?" Sal Belamo could only shake his head. "You gotta be fucking kidding me."

"Hey, don't shoot the messenger here, old man. This is four thousand years ago we're talking about, practically prehistoric when you think about it and that means a different world with different geophysical rules entirely where destructive waves like this were as common as car accidents. Best way I can prove that fact is to hook you up with some badass Hawaiian lava bed ganja. That shit will rock your world and show you the magic of times long gone by. Couple tokes and you'll believe in the Easter Bunny, old man."

Belamo swung toward McCracken. "He calls me that again, I'm gonna knock his teeth out, boss."

"Well, in the meantime, chill your uptight ass and listen up. Bottom line is, near as I can tell, Pandora's Temple was washed out to sea by this massive tsunami in 1650 B.C., along with the entire wasteland known in the legend as the Desert of Lost Souls. Essentially, a new coastline was forged as much as thirty miles inland, not far from where I'm standing right now. You want beachfront property, this is how you do it."

"So the remains of the temple might still be somewhere underwater off the Greek coastline," McCracken concluded.

"Remember that old hippie dude Pat I told you about who scored me the kick-ass dope? Turns out he's heard all about Pandora's Temple being lost somewhere under the sea. And you'll be interested to hear that your girl's daddy has a flotilla of survey ships scouring the area for some hint of its existence. Pat gave me the word they may have found something."

"Now that's interesting."

"It gets better, MacNuts. He told me the local fishermen have another explanation for why the temple has never been found before."

"What's that, Captain?"

"They say it's guarded by a sea monster."

CHAPTER 70

Hiroshima, Japan

Shinzo Asahara stood outside the fence in the shadow of the A-Bomb Dome, the shell of the last remaining structure in Hiroshima to be hit by the atomic bomb. He held an iPad in hand, currently loaded with reams of intelligence, everything he could find, on Sebastian Roy, which, unfortunately, included nothing of substance on his current residence in a Pyrenees mountain fortress. A phone conversation with Leander Levy had yielded a few tidbits, but Asahara needed much more than that. So he paid a fortune to a contact in the Japanese government to have a satellite illegally retasked and was now waiting to receive the resulting reconnaissance photos.

Meanwhile, his mind could not let go of what had happened to Yoshihiro Shibata's son once inside the particle accelerator. Asahara had forced one of the other scientists to switch the machine on and then watched as nothing at all happened.

Until everything did.

The son of Yoshihiro Shibata . . . disappeared in a white flash swallowed almost immediately by a cloud of what looked like black specks.

Those black specks had turned red as the younger Shibata's body ruptured into what looked like a million tiny pieces of matter mixed between bone, flesh, and blood. The pieces sprayed against the glass as if shot out of some cosmic hose, plastering it in an even, unbroken coat of what had been a man, no trace of which remained beyond.

Asahara felt strangely at peace, at ease with his place in a history of his own making, a history that had its origins with the bomb that struck the city on August 6, 1945, destroying everything in its path. Almost no one within eight hundred meters of the bomb's epicenter survived. The decimated land was such a horrifying site that authorities, fearing retaliation from the Japanese even after formal surrender, seized all photographs showcasing the unprecedented devastation and destruction.

Even then, there was no way to accurately capture the despair of the survivors, many of whom were unknowingly doomed themselves. Already traumatized by the bomb's effects, they had to confront the collection and disposition of the bodies of the eighty thousand dead where there was still something left to bury. Beyond that, there was debris to be cleared and wreckage to remove over a twelve-square-mile radius, and Asahara knew this arduous process took all of four years to complete.

One of these orphaned by the blast and its immediate aftermath was his father, Shoho Asahara. Though his birth date was later given as 1955 to spare him the constant scrutiny arising from his status as a Hiroshima survivor, it was actually thirteen years earlier. He was already mostly blind by the time of Hiroshima and often told his son not being able to see the carnage was what had saved him. Indeed, when the mood struck him, Shoho would ruminate on the possibility that his lack of sight allowed him to "see" what must be wrought from the ashes of the devastated city. He was a true child of the bomb, and Aum Shinrikyo had effectively been birthed in the dark days he spent wandering through the city's ash-ridden and chalky air.

Because Hiroshima had taught him that there was no such thing as an innocent life. The actions he was long committed to undertaking need come with no guilt or be morally justified.

And now all that fell to his son, Shinzo. A memorial plaque, forged out of smooth, mirrorlike granite stood nearby, and Shinzo Asahara turned toward it as if answering a voice.

The visage of his father gazed back at him, not nearly as clear as back in the hotel mirror and looking more like Marley's ghost appearing to Scrooge in a doorknocker.

"This man Roy is the key."

"I know, Father."

"His work has brought you to where you stand today and now you must confront your greatest challenge yet."

"I am prepared."

"You miss my point. I know you are prepared. But now you must ask yourself if you would visit upon the world a millionfold what was visited upon this city."

"You doubt me, Father?"

"Not at all," the spectral visage answered. *"The truth is I'm not sure I would have taken advantage of the opportunity you have been given had it been presented to me instead."*

"I don't believe that for a minute."

"You should, because it is the truth, Shinzo. Doomsday was never the real goal for me. It was more a state of mind. A frightening possibility forged out of the necessity to give meaning to my words and make the world listen. But you are stronger than I was. You have a greater gift of conviction, which, in this case, can also be a curse because the actions you contemplate, once put into motion, cannot be undone. A man destroying the work of God."

"You were a god to me too, Father. You taught me that the world must be punished, that it cannot be saved."

Shinzo could see the visage of his father's gaze turn sad. *"True enough. But also true is the fact that I never stopped being that young boy wandering the wasteland after the bomb went off. I have no memory of what happened to my parents or of my parents at all. But I do remember the terror, the despair all around me. Perhaps doomsday was about wanting others to know what I knew. And if you find the dark matter, they will."*

"Father?"

"Follow your fate, my son," the visage of his father said before fading out.

And then Shinzo Asahara's iPad beeped with the arrival of the satellite imagery of Sebastian Roy's mountain compound he'd been waiting for. He was studying the images when he received a call from Leander Levy in New Orleans.

"I was beginning to think you'd forgotten me, old friend," he greeted Levy. "Have you news about those symbols I asked you to translate?

"I'm afraid not. But I have uncovered something else I think you'll find equally interesting."

"My thoughts have moved on to another means of gaining what I seek," Asahara told him.

"So you informed me," said Levy. "That's why I'm calling."

CHAPTER 71

Over the Atlantic Ocean

"You ever think, MacNuts," Captain Seven had said, *"that some things just don't want to be found?"*

The conversation had ended there with McCracken pondering the words further as he sat across the aisle from Katie DeMarco in the back of the cabin.

"You haven't said anything since I told you I was going to kill Sebastian Roy," she said suddenly, breaking his brief trance.

"I'm still waiting for you to tell me why."

"I thought I had."

McCracken shook his head. "Plenty of daughters have daddy issues. This is something more."

Katie looked away, staring out the window on her side. "No one was supposed to die at the plant in Stuttgart, no one was even supposed to get hurt. I fucked everything up. Is that what you want to hear?" she asked, choking back tears.

"Only if that's what you want to tell me."

"I"—Katie swallowed hard here—"misjudged the strength of the explosives."

"Misplaced them more likely, judging by the fire and how fast it spread. The charge you set must have ruptured a gas line, turning a small boom into a big one."

"The reports said there were multiple bombs, but I only planted one."

"The other explosions likely originated from the gas lines themselves. It happens. Next time, try explosives one-oh-one."

"Don't mock me, McCracken."

He grabbed an architectural magazine from the seat next to him, obtained by Sal Belamo before the jet had picked him up in New York. "So you know nothing about the logistics of this place Sebastian Roy had built in the Pyrenees after the fire."

"It's not written up in there?"

"No, just quotes and a write-up from a few years ago," McCracken said, flipping to a page that displayed a series of pictures of Grecian urns and jars.

Katie regarded the page too. "He always did like old things," she said, looking right at McCracken. "Maybe it runs in the family."

"I'm glad to see you respect my advancing age."

"Like you said, I have daddy issues."

Their gazes met and held until McCracken broke it off to return to the twin facing pages again, studying the artifacts. "Plenty of people think I'm a relic, just like these things."

Katie posed her next question thoughtfully. "Do people blame you for the things you did that went wrong?"

"I've been blamed when things go right, too. It comes with the job description. The Indian and I have been dealing with that ever since the Hellfire. Hard to explain the feeling and even harder to find someone who understands what I'm talking about. It's a pretty small fraternity that I'm a member of."

That seemed to resonate with her. "There are things I've never told anyone. I've tried, I've . . ." Her voice tailed off and for just that moment McCracken saw her as the young woman she was, lost and scared.

"It doesn't suit you," he said suddenly.

"What?"

"The avenger's mask. The crusader who doesn't need to justify her actions."

"You think that describes me?"

"Not at all, young lady. But I believe that's how you'd like people to think of you. Problem comes when the job description ends up as an epitaph on a gravestone. That's one of the reasons why I've stayed at this for so long. We try to keep the personal shit aside."

"Oh, so you mean your friend's death on that rig means nothing to you."

"I didn't say that."

"So this *is* personal?"

"I didn't say that, either, because I know the Indian and I would be flying across the Atlantic now anyway."

Katie DeMarco looked down, then up again. "Why do you call him that?"

"What?"

"Indian."

"It's what I've always called him."

"It's racist."

"Not to us."

"What about the rest of the world?" she challenged.

"You're real good at changing the subject. . . ."

"Is that what I was doing?"

". . . and asking questions so you don't have to face answers you'd rather avoid."

Katie leaned across the aisle closer to him. "Try me."

"What's your real name?"

"Alexandra. But don't call me that because she died in that fire in Stuttgart."

"I think that, for all intents and purposes, she died well before then. You didn't destroy your father's fossil fuel plant in Stuttgart because you were an environmental terrorist; you became one after the fact to justify your attacks on other Roy Industries facilities."

Katie DeMarco, born Alexandra Roy, and whose obituary listed her listed her as being dead for seven years now, met McCracken's gaze and saw something in his eyes she had seen only once before, in those of the psychiatrist who seemed to sense where she was going until Katie had stopped in midstream. She'd fled that office but had the very real sense there was no fleeing from the dark eyes boring into her now.

"You think you've got everything figured out, don't you?"

"That's not for me to say, young lady."

"Then what is?"

"I've dealt with a lot of monsters in my time, many whose deeds would make any normal person's skin crawl. But you're not a normal person, because you've been hurt, badly hurt. That kind of pain makes you look at the world differently. But that doesn't give you a pass to do what you've done."

"So I don't get to kill and maim as much as I want to like you? What makes you any different, McCracken? Where's your moral justification?"

"We weren't talking about me."

"We are now."

McCracken's gaze turned reflective. "Maybe twenty, twenty-five years ago, I found out I had a son. Happened while I was chasing down something called the Gamma Option. Turned out he wasn't my kid at all—somebody was just using him to force me to figure out a mystery dating back to World War II. So they kidnap the boy I'd been led to believe was my son and all of a sudden, for the first time really, it was personal for me." He continued to hold her gaze. "Like it's always been for you."

"You make it sound so simple."

He reached out and touched her shoulder. "I don't mean to, believe me."

Katie swallowed hard. "What happened to the kid?"

"I told you, he wasn't mine."

"But you stayed in touch, didn't you? I'll bet you're still in contact even today."

McCracken nodded, conceding her point. "He's serving in the SAS, British Special Air Service."

"Because you managed to save him."

"I suppose."

"But he wasn't yours," Katie said, spine straightening. "You've got no one, just like me, no one you can save who really matters. Only thing you can do to compensate is save the world instead."

"As opposed to destroying it, one piece at a time."

"Still makes us the same, McCracken, or at least damn close."

"Really? I don't think so. I've always been who, what, I am. But Katie DeMarco didn't exist until Stuttgart, did she?"

Katie swallowed hard.

"Your hands are calloused. You move like an athlete. You know poison, demolitions, weaponry—things you knew nothing about until things went wrong in Stuttgart. My guess is you went back to school, probably several of them. Learned the skills you needed to reinvent yourself into an avenger to better live with what happened in Germany. Creating a rationale after the fact." He stopped and held her gaze, not about to let go. "You may be right about me trying to save myself by saving the world. Explains why these past two years have been such hell. You, on the other hand, chose to save yourself by trying to destroy as much as you could. Get the distinction?"

McCracken thought he caught tears welling in Katie's eyes as she tried to swallow again, but stopped. "That the kind of life you want for your almost son, to follow in the footsteps of his almost father?"

"Which brings us to your real one, Katie. When I said I knew monsters, there are some of them even I can't reconcile. I know how I felt when a boy I thought was my son was in danger. Hurting a child takes depravity to a whole other level."

Katie started to look away, then stopped. "So maybe I really am as much a monster as my father. I have to live with the fact that my mother and brother died that day. And if I don't keep doing what I'm doing, if I don't get it right, it'll all be for nothing."

McCracken shook his head, slowly and sadly. "It won't get rid of the pain. It can't change what he did to you."

"He didn't do anything to *me*!"

Katie didn't realize she'd nearly shouted the words until Sal Belamo and Johnny Wareagle turned around in the front of the cabin. But she kept her focus on McCracken, continuing.

"It was Christian, my brother."

CHAPTER 72

Port of Piraeus, Greece

"Here's what I found out, boss," Sal Belamo said to McCracken who sat next to him in a rental car outside the sprawling Port of Piraeus with Johnny Wareagle squeezed into the backseat. "That nutjob techie of yours nailed things dead-solid perfect. Roy Industries has had a bunch of survey ships at sea for weeks now. This has been serving as their home base."

The port was the primary one operating in Greek waters as the largest passenger port on the European continent and the third largest in the world. Its lusciously scenic locale belied a hectic, if not frantic balance of cargo and passenger ships, not to mention ferry boats and the geological survey vessels forever scouring the nearby seas for pieces of Greece's long storied history. Practically every cruise liner venturing into the Mediterranean and Aegean Seas stopped here as well, in large part due to the port's convenient location close to Athens and all its richness.

"Central port's right there," Belamo continued, gesturing out the open window. "You can see the private water hangars dead ahead.

Roy Industries leases four of them, but only one is currently under watch by armed guards: four guards, two inside and two out."

"What exactly are they guarding?"

Belamo turned back toward McCracken and winked. "Just what the doctor ordered."

Late that night McCracken and Sal Belamo stumbled down the pier, pretending to be drunken cruisegoers having lost their way thanks to the bottles each held in his grasp. The armed guards posted before the hangar Belamo had earlier identified cut them off at the head of the pier where it broke both left and right.

"Hey, we can't find our ship," McCracken mumbled drunkenly. "Any idea where the *Titanic*'s docked?"

The two guards looked at each other.

"How about the *Lusitania*?"

The nearer guard reached out to grab him.

"The *Andrea Doria*?"

McCracken and Belamo felt the grasps tighten, just as Johnny Wareagle appeared behind the two guards.

McCracken knocked on the hangar door that was locked from the inside, kept his pounding hard and constant until the side entrance was jerked open. The guard standing there noticed the pistol in Sal Belamo's hand first and the unconscious frames of his two associates, held up by Johnny Wareagle as if they were rag dolls, next. Behind the guard, resting on the water's surface between the floating piers was a manned underwater submersible with a pod-shaped frame attached to a pair of pincer-like extremities made for grasping and tugging objects from the seafloor.

"We need to borrow your submarine," McCracken told the guard.

"Hey, boss," Sal Belamo said, after they'd finished tying all four men up, "you know how they say hope for the world got stuck in Pandora's jar forever?"

"I do."

"Well," Belamo grinned, looking straight at McCracken, "you ask me, it finally got out."

CHAPTER 73

The Mediterranean Sea

Doctors Bol and Whitcomb made the trek down the pier to the covered water hangar an hour past dawn. The sun burned exceedingly bright for so early an hour, courtesy of the direct angle this time of year. The crystal blue water was flat and calm, the sun's blinding reflection making it seem brighter still.

The *Crab*, a six-passenger submarine designed for deepwater research and salvage, had arrived the day before and been checked thoroughly in anticipation of setting out in search of Pandora's Temple first thing in the morning.

"Can you hear me, Mr. Roy?" Whitcomb asked.

"Loud and clear, Doctor."

Both Whitcomb and Bol were wearing helmets affixed with both a microphone and camera, so Sebastian Roy could both see and hear everything that went on once they boarded the *Crab*. Neither of the CERN scientists had ever been aboard a submarine before and each had prepped heavily for the rigors the night before, though they fully expected the excitement of the journey to temper any ill effects.

The *Crab* came with a complete crew specifically chosen for their areas of expertise in underwater exploration, archaeology and salvage. The salvage part seemed especially important, given that manipulation of the robotic, fully articulated, pincerlike arms would be the order of the day once they reached the area where the mapping process had identified the presence of something large and sprawling. The previous night had been spent prepping the crew for exactly what they were in search of, the coordinates and all available reconnaissance data already programmed into the *Crab*'s computers.

At first glance the ship looked like something from a *Terminator* movie: dark gray in color with thick tinted glass for front windows that could have passed as rectangular eyes. The dual arms, which pinioned and rotated like something out of a high-tech automotive assembly line, were foreboding in both size and power. An able controller could wield them with the dexterity and strength required to either pick up a walnut off the seafloor or crush it into dust.

"Should you find anything that even remotely resembles Pandora's jar . . ." Sebastian Roy started.

". . . we will break off and await further instructions," completed Whitcomb. "We know how to obey orders, Mr. Roy. We both want to see our families again."

"Then for your sakes, I hope you complete your mission successfully."

Bol reached the water hangar first, surprised the guard he expected to find there was nowhere to be seen. The double doors were open and he started to walk through.

"We're entering the hangar now, Mr. Roy," Whitcomb said. "Right on schedule."

The two men entered. And froze.

Because seated on the floor before them were the security guards, bound and gagged.

And the *Crab* was gone.

CHAPTER 74

The Mediterranean Sea

Sal Belamo effortlessly piloted the *Crab* to within a hundred yards of the seafloor, relying on the course preprogrammed into its onboard computer.

"Told you I can drive anything, boss," he said to McCracken. "Of course, it helps I drove steel buckets like this back in the day. I ever tell you about that?"

"Indian and I would love to hear about it someday, Sal," McCracken said, seated next to Johnny Wareagle. "Always thought you were army back in the day, though."

"I was, but the kind of missions we handled, it paid to be versatile, you know what I mean."

"All too well."

"I ever tell you about the Puerto Rican boxer I knocked out in the sixth to win my first title shot?"

"Don't tell me . . . Against none other than the great Carlos Monzon who you took to a decision even though he busted your nose in the third round."

"Nineteen seventy, not long before he stopped Emile Griffith in the fourteenth. Second time we fought he knocked me out in the fifth. But I was an old man by then."

"So what does that make you now?"

Belamo grinned. "You'd think we'd finally be too old for this shit, boss. Be far away on a beach in Cancun instead. A real vacation."

"What do you call this?" McCracken asked, as they continued to slice nimbly through the sea.

Katie DeMarco leaned forward in the next seat back. The *Crab* could accommodate six, four plus a pilot and a technician to work the sub's remote-operated arm assembly. The confines felt cramped and claustrophobic even with only five of the seats taken. Katie imagined she could actually hear the rapid heartbeats of the others, along with their slightly labored breathing. And a single glance at McCracken told her he was just as anxious, or nervous, or both.

"You really believe we're going to find this temple?" she asked him.

"Let's ask the expert. Captain?" McCracken prompted.

Captain Seven responded without ever taking his eyes from the thick twin glass panes that formed the *Crab*'s face. "I am in desperate need of a joint, MacNuts. My supply from that old hippie is long gone. And in case you've forgotten, last time I tried this I almost ended up as fish food."

"You better be wrong this time, Captain."

"About what?"

"Some things not wanting to be found."

"When did I say that?"

"Then let's try this. What exactly does the computer on this thing say about where we're headed?"

"That there's something down there for sure, just like Pat said. It's big in scope and mass, and relatively intact since there's no debris field or scatter." Captain Seven continued to gaze out into the sea beyond, brought to life in thick ribbons of light from the six million candlepower beams focused outward from the *Crab*'s bow. "Just like five years ago . . ."

"One big difference between then and now, Captain."

"What's that, MacNuts?"

"The Indian, Sal, and I weren't there."

"Doesn't change the waters."

In that moment the *Crab* hit what felt like a headwind, its nose pitching upward as it started to roll to the side until Belamo worked the controls to desperately right it.

"Like I was saying," from Captain Seven.

CHAPTER 75

The Mediterranean Sea

Sal Belamo continued to steer the *Crab* deeper into the depths of the sea, the exterior lighting providing an incredible view of the changing marine life the deeper they descended. Schools of fish thinned in favor of smaller packs or lone swimmers, scavengers mostly at this depth notable for their oversized-looking eyes. That feature made them seem almost thoughtful when investigating the *Crab*, but it was strictly a natural feature of species operating at these depths. But McCracken found himself looking at Katie DeMarco instead, replaying the remainder of her words about her brother in splotches.

"He was younger than me, two years. I was older. I was supposed to protect him."

"You were a child."

"So was he. I'd hear his door just down from mine creaking open in the night sometimes and I'd know, I'd know . . . But I didn't do anything. I did . . . nothing."

"You could blow up every company your father owns and the

pain would still be there. And until you realize that, it will eat you alive."

"Spoken like a man who knows."

"Because it came close to eating me alive a bunch of times. But I always stayed a step ahead."

"How?"

"By never enjoying it. Once you begin to enjoy it, you're lost forever. That's what makes me, and you, different from your father. He gave in, he surrendered." McCracken hesitated, unsure whether he was getting through to her or not. "Your father killed Christian a long time before Stuttgart, Katie."

"Don't bullshit me, McCracken."

"I'm not. Maybe Johnny's spirits are finally speaking to me, I don't know. But I do know your father's actions set the wheels in motion that kept spinning right up until that day. He might as well have set the fire himself."

"You honestly believe that. . . ."

"I've seen men try justifying their actions a host of different ways, all to avoid the consequences they deserve. Your brother's and mother's deaths are on your father's conscience, not yours—that's the price he's got to pay."

"And me?"

"The pain is yours to bear. That's the honest truth. No bullshit."

She looked across the aisle, seeming to size McCracken up for the first time. "How do you do it, how have you done it so long?"

"To me saving one life's as important as saving a thousand. Keeps things in perspective, because I'm not doing it for me."

"Then what happens when you finally meet the man who got your friend killed on that rig?"

"There's something big down here all right, boss," Sal Belamo said from behind the *Crab*'s controls. "Sonar readings are off the fucking chart."

The seas beyond the *Crab*'s windows continued to darken, the exterior lights revealing schools of fish darting aside en masse to avoid it. The depths weren't excessive, but the drop-off was extreme for waters close to the Greek shoreline. Just over fifteen hundred feet, according to the onboard computer, deep enough for a find even as big as the temple to remain elusive. Still, plenty of others had explored these depths, likely in search of something else. That left McCracken wondering how it could be possible that no one had stumbled upon the temple in passing; even a buried structure would give off some indication of its presence.

He could feel the pressure in his ears growing. Diving had never been his specialty, nor had water-born missions. Special-operations training back in his time had been a bit thin in that regard, though he might have preferred it to HALO drops from upwards of five miles up sucking air from a tank on the plunge downward.

McCracken felt Belamo slow the *Crab* and let it settle into a hover twenty feet from the seafloor. Belamo then switched on all the underwater cameras to portray the scene on the jagged seafloor now directly beneath them.

"We've arrived, boss. Showtime."

CHAPTER 76

The Mediterranean Sea

"There's nothing here," McCracken said, running his eyes across the greenish-black world portrayed on the television monitors.

"Geophysical indicators say what Roy's survey teams found is somewhere right around here."

"Right around *where*?"

"Directly below us, boss."

Belamo eased the *Crab* forward, rotating the cameras as he moved in search of some indication of the temple's presence, anything to tell them it was, in fact, here. But all that lay before and beneath them was the empty seafloor awash in clouds of sand and sediment.

"Only it's not," Belamo resumed.

"Wait a minute," McCracken said, "tell me what you see, Captain."

Captain Seven interrupted his smoking of an imaginary joint to study the scene pictured on the television monitors. "Absolutely fucking nothing, MacNuts."

"Sal, anything moving out there?"

"Nothing, boss, and the seismic sensors on this thing could pick up a goldfish."

"So where are the blobfish?"

"Huh?" from Captain Seven.

"He's right," said Katie DeMarco. "The ocean floor is populated by bottom feeders that look somewhat like blobs. Because of the extreme pressure out there right now, these fish have this gelatinous texture of flesh with a density slightly less than seawater. They should be visible on camera right now. At this depth, there should be plenty of them in plain sight."

"Sal," began McCracken, "can you scan temperature readings in the waters ahead?"

"You bet, boss. Another toy for me to play with," Belamo said, working the touch screen before him in search of the proper menu. "What am I looking for?"

"Variations. Look for a temperature spike."

"Ding-ding, ding-ding!" Captain Seven chimed. "Man's looking for a hydrothermal vent."

"A what?" from Katie.

"A fissure in a planet's surface from which geothermally heated water gets blown upward like the ocean's farting," the captain explained. "Most commonly found near volcanically active places, areas where tectonic plates are moving apart. And I believe that describes the Greek coastline perfectly. Anybody got a joint?"

"I got something," Belamo said. "Temperature spike a couple hundred feet to our port side."

"Steer toward it, Sal."

"You know something I don't, boss?"

"Just playing a hunch. What I'm thinking is if Pandora's Temple is really down here, why hasn't a single shred of evidence of its existence ever turned up before? Even if it's been buried all this time, there should be an artifact, a relic, *something*."

"Makes no sense I can see, Blainey," Wareagle echoed.

"Exactly. And I think I know why."

Belamo sliced the *Crab* through the currents, steering for the coordinates locked in on his nav screen. "Man, this baby handles like a dream. Cadillac of goddamn submarines. Here we go, boss. Coordinates are dead ahead. Check out the main screen."

The largest monitor, located directly over the pilot's seat and offering an enhanced look at the view directly ahead, filled with a huge black cloud churning outward in from beneath the seafloor.

"What now, boss?"

McCracken held his thought and then his breath briefly. "Steer into it, Sal," he said less surely than he'd intended.

"Into *that*?"

"Into and through the vent. We make it through and we end up just where we need to be."

"Fine, boss, but what if we don't? Or what if it leads nowhere? Or narrows like a funnel and we end up getting our asses stuck?"

"You trust me, Sal?"

"You trust yourself on this one, boss?"

McCracken again regarded the plume on the monitors. "Close enough."

Belamo steadied himself with a deep breath and drew the *Crab* closer to the vent, slowing when they were just outside the reaches of its plume. The pressure rattled the craft's interior, feeling a bit like airplane turbulence.

"Last chance to change your mind, boss."

"This is the only explanation for what the captain found five years ago and Roy's survey teams found days ago," he said, trying to convince himself as much as Belamo. "Only way survey equipment could home in on something that isn't there."

"In that case, fasten your seat belts, people," said Belamo, angling the *Crab* downward into the vent.

It felt like an amusement park ride when they entered, a combination of a roller coaster and flume attraction. The *Crab* first seemed to stall as it battled the plume pouring outward from the vent. The world turned pitch-black save for the *Crab*'s interior lighting, which faded out only to return a moment later, the process repeating itself as the craft dipped and darted in sudden fits and starts.

Sal Belamo felt the craft's controls bucking in protest as it shuddered and shook in the vent's concentration of geothermal energy. Then, all at once, the plume was gone and Belamo leveled the *Crab* off, a new subsurface world around them—a world that was utterly black beyond the limited reach of the *Crab*'s lighting. McCracken had the sense of being trapped in a jar, the vent above them now serving as the lid. He was struck suddenly by the fear there was no air to breathe, feeling his lungs thirsting for it while feeling they were all floating outside the *Crab* like astronauts helpless into space after their spacewalk lifelines had been cut.

"Did I just do a hit of acid or what?" Captain Seven wondered, as if to echo McCracken's thoughts, his face pressed against the nearest view window in search of something, anything. "Maybe that was a wormhole; maybe we are back in the time when dinosaurs roamed the earth and pot plants the size of oak trees grew wild."

"Try an underwater cavern," said McCracken, as a thick school of the blobfish he noted were missing from the seafloor above swam by the front view windows, "likely the largest in the world, even bigger than Sac Actun in the Yucatán."

"That one's mostly just long. This baby's deep too," Captain Seven noted. "Plenty deep enough to hide what we come looking for, dudes. Man, that explains it," he added, as if realizing something.

"Explains what?"

"Last time I was in these parts, before I got swallowed by the tsunami, instruments got a hit on the temple everybody else discounted because the depth gauge read five hundred feet *below* the seafloor. I should've figured this cavern shit out back then. See what not being under the influence does to me?"

The *Crab* continued to churn through the blackness broken only by the spill of its underwater floodlights pouring forward, scattering more blobfish from its path.

"Boss," Sal Belamo said suddenly, "something big, really big, dead ahead."

Spoken as he slowed the *Crab* to a crawl, Sal worked his touch screen to make the cameras go to ultraviolet to provide a clearer sense of what lay ahead of them. Silence took over the cabin, the recirculated air that had grown stale and rank only adding to the anxiety that showed itself in the uniformly tight expressions and quick, shallow breathing of the *Crab*'s occupants. Being on the verge of finding something lost to myth and unseen by man for four thousand years was dramatic in its own right; the fact that discovery had the potential to change, or destroy, the world ratcheted the apprehension up all the more.

"Maybe some things don't want to be found."

Captain Seven's warning gained new resonance this deep and this close. In that respect the mythology of Pandora's "box" and temple had made sure the possibility of its actual existence was never taken seriously. And perhaps that was the point, not coincidence at all.

McCracken realized he had been holding his breath, when the shape of a large structure, blurred and indistinct, appeared on the main view screen, not yet visible through the front view windows.

"Make that two hits of acid," Captain Seven said, sucking on a fake joint.

"Holy shit," echoed Sal Belamo, as the structure finally began to take shape before the naked eye as well.

CHAPTER 77

The Mediterranean Sea

"Pandora's Temple," McCracken muttered, not believing it himself.

"You wanna tell me gods designed this place, boss," Sal Belamo managed, "right now I'm inclined to believe you."

"Frigging amazing," said Captain Seven, pressing out his imaginary joint. "Almost four thousand years and still standing. Well," he added, as they drew closer and the picture on screen sharpened further, "mostly anyway."

The temple's façade had broken away, its majestic stairs and massive entry lost to the centuries, storms, and pressure of the deep sea. Otherwise, though, the structure looked incredibly intact, even untouched. It sat, buried to varying levels by sand and silt, on the cavern floor, looking to be angled sharply to the right with that side suffering from a significantly lower drop as if the left-most portion had settled on firmer ground.

At its highest point, the temple stood between fifty and sixty feet. Its marble frieze and majestic dome, myths like everything else about it until now, looked pristine and untouched, the *Crab*'s powerful floods reflecting off the patches of gold inlay. Even in the dark bleakness of this underwater world, true to its legend the temple appeared to be golden everywhere, a testament to the work of its builder, Pathos Verdes, and his efforts to make optimum use of the light of the day forty centuries before.

Based on the jagged chasm at the front, the missing entry doors must have indeed been at least twenty feet in height, which, of course, begged the question, Who exactly had they been designed to accommodate? While they'd been too heavy to be opened by any single man, they hadn't proven strong enough to withstand the tumult of wind, storm, quake, and seawater. Beyond where they had once been, jutting out to the sides and layered atop beveled columns, were twin, multilevel appendages that looked like wings attached seamlessly to the dome.

"How many years later did the Romans build structures like this?" Katie DeMarco asked, realizing her mouth and lips were bone dry.

"Maybe fourteen hundred," McCracken answered, "and they never built anything like this."

"Wait," Johnny Wareagle said, rising out of his seat slightly when something on the *Crab*'s view screens caught his attention. "Can you pan the cameras back?"

Belamo slowed the craft and worked the controls, spotting the shapes on the cavern floor that had drawn Wareagle's attention. "Holy shit, tell me those aren't—"

"Shipwrecks," McCracken completed for him.

The submarine's underside cameras caught the remains of any number of underwater crafts comparable to the *Crab*, both remote and manually operated, twisted and crushed on the cavern floor. Drawing closer, the cameras caught stray bones and skeletal remains as well, broken apart and splintered as if picked clean.

Wareagle was studying the screens so hard his forehead wrinkled. "Strategic points of their frames were crushed. And those ruptures look more like tears made from the outside in." He looked toward McCracken. "They were attacked, Blainey. Something destroyed them."

"Sea monster," said Captain Seven. "Just like I told you."

CHAPTER 78

The Mediterranean Sea

"Guess we know one of the reasons why nobody ever found the temple before," McCracken managed, as the structure took shape before them.

Despite the damage wrought by the centuries, it remained a portrait in flawless construction. Save for the missing doors and façade and angle on which it listed, the structure likely exposed once more by the 2012 earthquake and Santorini volcano eruption looked as if it had been assembled right here, perhaps two thousand feet below the surface of the sea. Species of fish McCracken couldn't identify swam in and out of the open front, giving the temple the appearance of a decorative object placed at the bottom of a massive aquarium.

"What now, boss?"

"We all bought our tickets, Sal. Let's go get our money's worth."

The sub was moving at a crawl when Belamo eased it through the breech in the temple where the façade had stood. The darkness seemed even thicker here inside, an illusion fostered by the sense of claustrophobia within its vast walls and so far underwater to boot. Those walls were octagonal in design, and the lights shining down from the bottom of the *Crab* radiated off floors of marble flecked with bronze. A number of the pillars connecting the multitiered levels of the temple to the dome were splintered, likely lying somewhere on the temple floor yet reached by the *Crab*'s floods.

The interior walls and stairs, unlike the façade, looked remarkably intact, save for algae grown so thick in patches that it took on the shape of vast beings ready to be roused from their sleep. If legend was correct, the temple had spent the bulk of its existence in the wake of being pushed into the sea by the earthquake and massive tsunami that followed. In all likelihood, the chill of the waters this deep had acted as the ultimate preservative even for limestone, its finish only slightly dulled by the centuries.

Most impressive, and perhaps intimidating, to McCracken were the life-sized statues of what could only be renderings of the gods themselves fashioned from marble. The statues stood almost as high as the entry doors would have had they been intact. Pandora's Temple, the largest structure ever built by mortal man at the time of its construction, had clearly been sized to accommodate occupants of far greater dimensions than mortal man.

Suddenly a rumble sounded around them, causing a ripple in the currents trapped inside Pandora's Temple and forcing the *Crab* to buck. The temple seemed to quake slightly, the way a skyscraper might in the midst of an earthquake.

"What the hell was that?" from Sal Belamo.

"Don't say it, Captain," said McCracken.

But Captain Seven couldn't help himself. "What do you expect from something that doesn't want to be found, MacNuts?"

"Anybody notices a jar lying around, give me a shout," said Sal Belamo, sweating up a storm now from tension over maneuvering the *Crab* about without striking anything that might bring the structure down.

"It's supposed to be the size of a dude, right?" raised Captain Seven. "Big enough to hold the mother lode of sacred weed."

"Opinions and visual renditions of the jar differ," said McCracken. "But as far as size goes that's the prevailing thought."

"Sorry to disappoint you then, but so far we got no trace of anything even resembling a relic, never mind one that big. 'Course with the right drug, a man can see anything he wants."

"Still early in the ride, Captain."

The *Crab* continued to cruise about the temple's cavernous confines. Here, so far underwater and in darkness, the feeling was that of being contained in a massive tomb, a fact not lost on any of the craft's occupants, whose heart rates quickened and breathing turned shallow and thin, as if the air was fighting them. There was still nothing given up by the sub's powerful exterior lighting that even resembled a jar or anything else that might have once filled the structure's many shelves and built-in storage cases, all of which were empty.

Then one of the *Crab*'s lights, and cameras, passed over something ivory colored and rectangular that looked like an extension of the floor itself.

"Go back, Sal."

"Already am, boss. I saw it too."

Belamo switched the craft to a hover directly before what from this angle looked like a husk of marble rising from the temple floor, utterly untouched by algae, unlike all other parts of the temple.

"It looks like a . . . pedestal," realized Katie DeMarco.

"That was my thought too," said McCracken. "Only one on the entire level. Tells me something very important once rested upon it."

"It was traditional for the ancient Greeks to display their most valued items on mounts or bases like this," Katie added.

Something seemed to catch McCracken's eye. "Get us closer, Sal."

Once he did, nothing further about the pedestal was given up to the naked eye, but under ultraviolet light, the main view screen showed a series of unrecognizable symbols, not unlike hieroglyphics but considerably more detailed and sophisticated at the same time, adorning the pedestal on three sides.

McCracken leaned forward to better study the symbols, then leaned back slowly with eyes wide and not seeming to blink.

"Blainey?" Wareagle raised, sending his unease.

"Any read on that, Captain?" McCracken asked, instead of responding.

"Why you asking me?"

"I thought ancient languages were one of your specialties. Basis for those codes you developed in Vietnam."

"Stoned maybe. Straight, forget about it. But I don't have to be stoned to tell you I've never come across anything like those symbols before."

McCracken nodded. "That's what I thought. I believe we've shown up after the show's over. Get us out of here, Sal. The jar's gone. Somebody beat us to it."

"What am I missing here, boss?" wondered Sal Belamo. "What's so important about those symbols on that pedestal?"

Before McCracken could respond, the rumbling and quaking resumed, only more powerfully. He could feel it along his spine like a feather brushing up against his skin, unsettling him. This time the feeling persisted, as the waters around the *Crab* bubbled up into a lightly churned froth.

"Believe it's time we made our exit, Sal."

"Couldn't agree more, boss."

Katie jerked herself forward, straining the bonds of her safety harness. "No, we've got to keep looking!"

"The jar's not here, young lady," McCracken told her.

"You can't be sure of that."

"Yes, I can."

"How?"

"Because I think I know where it is."

~

"Get us out of here, Sal," McCracken continued.

Belamo had already brought the *Crab* around and was easing toward the temple's façade. "You don't have to tell me twice."

"There's something approaching from outside the temple, Blainey," Wareagle said suddenly, half out of his seat.

At which point, the sonar screen on Belamo's main control panel began to flash a warning too. "The big fella's right, boss."

CHAPTER 79

The Mediterranean Sea

"Anything?" McCracken asked, after the *Crab* had emerged through the temple's open façade.

Belamo rotated the exterior floodlights that struggled to make a dent in the blackness beyond. "Your guess is as good as mine, boss. Steering back for that vent now. Trip back up should be loads easier than the one down."

With the coordinates programmed into the craft's computer, Belamo worked the controls to cant the submarine on a slight upward climb toward the hydrothermal vent through which they'd originally entered the cavern. Then something big crossed the spill of the lights, a shape that looked more like a pale blotch amid the darkness, and proceeded to slam into the *Crab* before backing off again.

"Is that a—"

"Giant squid," McCracken completed for Katie DeMarco.

"And people say drugs make you see things," managed a wide-eyed Captain Seven. "Guess we don't need any of them to see this."

The monster first seemed to be retreating before laying itself sideways in the water with its caudal fin angled farthest from the *Crab*, positioned so it could reach out to test its prey with its two extralong tentacles. Its body alone looked to be even longer than the craft and almost as wide. Its eight arms, meanwhile, flailed and thrashed about as if seeking purchase with the attached suction cups.

"Man, that thing looks mean," Captain Seven added.

"At least we know what made that graveyard of wrecks on the cavern floor," said Sal Belamo.

The squid's massive eyes seemed to be peering straight through the view window until it lashed three of its arms against the glass in search of grip. The squid pulled its arms back, the feel of the glass and lack of suction it provided forcing the thing to continue pawing about the craft's frame.

"Let's see if we can give this thing a fight," McCracken said, taking the chair before the controls of the robotic pincers beyond.

Belamo twisted the *Crab* to pull away from the squid and, when that failed, tried to tow it along for the ride. When that strategy failed too, he was left with nothing more to do than use the craft's engines to hold its ground and fight against the squid's determined efforts to drag them downward to join the rest of the wrecks in the watery graveyard.

If McCracken didn't know better, he'd say the squid was trying to swallow them. But he knew just enough about the creature to figure it saw them as potential prey, having likely feasted on occupants of the other crafts entombed on the cavern floor. And with no whales, the giant squid's only true predator, in the area, that left nothing above it in the food chain.

McCracken familiarized himself with the controls for the articulated arms as best and as quickly as he could.

"I don't want to push the engine any more than I already am, boss."

"Just give me a sec here."

He drew the left pincer inside and down, slamming the squid in the side of the mantle, or torso, with a force sufficient to at least stun it. It was like hitting jelly, though. So McCracken opened the left pincers and drove them forward in the same moment he brought the pincer apparatus on the right around to reach the base of the mantle from which the squid's arms extended and where the gaping black eyes peered out.

The squid had small fins at the rear of the mantle it used for locomotion. Like other cephalopods, it propelled itself by pulling water into the mantle cavity and pushing the water through the siphon, in gentle rhythmic pulses. The monster could adjust its speed by expanding the cavity to fill it with water, then contracting muscles to jet water through the siphon. McCracken also knew the creature breathed using two large gills inside the same cavity, as difficult to target as the thing's closed circulatory system.

These monsters hadn't existed for tens of thousands of years by being vulnerable.

The squid found the *Crab* in its reaches, clamping its arms all along the steel, while its longer tentacles tried to wrap themselves around the entire circumference of the craft. They looked ready to squeeze, perhaps strong enough to pierce the sub's hull, when McCracken latched one of the pincers onto the far and thinner end portion of the mantle that looked like a tail and closed them tight.

Outside the view window, something changed in the squid's eyes. Maybe it was panic, inbred from so many years of avoiding contact with predators and rarely encountering resistance. Based on the creaking sounds that filled the *Crab*, though, it was actually tightening its hold on the craft more than enough to get McCracken working the second robotic pincer apparatus into place on the tip of the mantle as well. He closed it on the squid's spongy skin and then worked both pincers into a lifting action.

The apparatus strained to lift the near eight-hundred-pound weight of the squid, coupled with eight arms' worth of suction cups fastening into place on the craft's steel to hold itself in place.

"Take us down, Sal. Fast."

"What?"

"You heard me."

Belamo dropped the *Crab* into a dive at the same time McCracken drew both pincers upward. Both gravity and inertia worked in their favor, the combined force just enough to pull the squid's arms free of the craft and leave it struggling to escape, or at least right itself for another attack.

"Believe we made our point, boss."

Belamo had barely finished his comment, when the squid pulled free of the pincers and lashed at the *Crab* with its arms, again seeking deadly purchase with its longer tentacles. The creature's body alone looked to be at least twenty-five feet long, that size nearly doubled when the length of the arms and tentacles was added in; in other words, it was easily bigger than the *Crab*, which explained why the monster had attacked in the first place. Now, angered and threatened, it wasn't going anywhere.

To prevent the *Crab* from joining the other rotting wrecks, McCracken closed the pincers and crashed one into the squid where he thought it might be most vulnerable, nearest the eyes. Impact rattled the creature, but it lurched toward the sub again, this time from the other side. McCracken fended off this attack with a blow from the other pincer while poking at the squid with the free pincer as if it were a spear.

The monster responded by turning its attention to the pincers themselves, seeing them as the protector of its potential meal. It went for the one on the right first, dipping and then sweeping about to try and catch it in the grasp of its tentacles. McCracken used the left pincer to fight it off and the thing pivoted to that side next.

After McCracken countered with the right pincer this time, incredibly, the squid altered its strategy to focus on both pincers at the same time. The result was a twisted sea-based pirouette as

McCracken used the pincers to parry with the monster in the hope it would ultimately tire of the effort and just swim off.

And that's exactly what happened.

Or at least started to when one of the giant squid's tentacles got snared on the now-closed pincer on the right side of the *Crab*. The creature responded instinctively by squeezing harder still with the tentacle, which succeeded only in snaring it even tighter.

"Not good, boss."

"I'm working on it, Sal."

He tried to use the second pincer to help free the squid, but the creature was in panic mode now, focusing all its strength, and arms, on its escape. That pincer bent under the intense escape effort, the controls for it seizing up in McCracken's hands as the joints that allowed for articulation were ravaged by the squid's desperate attempts to pull free.

"Any ideas, Indian?" McCracken asked as the submarine bucked and rocked precariously.

"Just one, Blainey," Wareagle said, moving toward the craft's single hatch in the rear of the cabin with the sheath holding his Gerber MK-2 knife in hand.

CHAPTER 80

The Mediterranean Sea

Wareagle swam out through the pressurized hatch wearing a high-tech, much lighter version of the traditional atmospheric diving suit, or ADS, stretched to the limit to accommodate his proportions. Entering the water without such a suit at this depth would have meant instant death due to the pressure. But this particular ADS model had been tested up to depths of thirty-five hundred feet, giving Johnny as much as another thousand to play with even within the cavern.

The suit might have been pliable, especially when compared to earlier less technologically advanced models, but it still wasn't constructed with battling a giant squid in mind. The more the thing struggled to free its tentacle from the pincer, the more tightly it seemed to fasten itself to the *Crab*.

"Don't know how much more this thing can take, boss," Sal Belamo reported, his entire console shaking from the squid's thrashing about outside. "Few more minutes and our structural integrity might be for shit."

"Then it's up to Johnny."

Wareagle had just reappeared within camera and naked eye view swimming toward the monster that continued to thrash about. But at the last moment he veered away, seeming to think of something else, an alternate strategy.

"That's it, Indian," McCracken urged quietly, realizing his thought as if of the same mind.

Wareagle moved to the pincer assembly itself, swimming around the squid to avoid detection as long as possible. It continued twisting and yanking while he settled into place at the insertion point where the pincers joined the articulated arm itself. Johnny went to work instantly with his knife on the fasteners, couplings, and wiring that connected one to the other.

Wareagle's initial efforts succeeded in shedding pieces of the connection with each turn or thrust of his blade. Until one stubborn task forced him to use the knife's hilt like a hammer to dislodge a stubborn clamp. All at once at that point, the squid's eyes fastened upon him, reorienting itself to attack with its massive swirling arms.

Wareagle pushed off at the last possible moment, narrowly escaping its deadly grasp. The squid, seeming to forget it was snared, pushed itself after him only to be reined in by its captured tentacle, leaving it eye to eye with Wareagle from twenty feet apart and jostling the occupants of the *Crab*.

Instead of retreating farther, or at least holding at the safe position, Wareagle began propelling himself closer to the creature at a snail's pace. The squid first lashed at him again with its arms, and Johnny brushed the blows aside with incredibly nimble dexterity given the confines and restrictions of his suit. As he continued his slow approach, never varying from the creature's line of sight, he began to softly stroke its captured tentacle.

The squid first seemed to panic but then simply stiffened, its arms lashing about in far less threatening fashion, as if it somehow recognized Wareagle's intentions. Giant squids were known to possess large brains likely capable of some complex thought. Since not a single one had ever been studied and so little was known about them, though, it was impossible to judge them capable of any level of actual decision making. Yet the creature, to the fascination of everyone inside the *Crab*, had broken off its attack and taken to following Wareagle's movements, as if somehow grasping the fact he was trying to help it.

Its arms continued to brush against him, some of the blows hard and harsh but not enough to impede Wareagle's efforts. He no longer even regarded the creature, as if pretending it wasn't even there; if McCracken didn't know better, he'd say the squid appeared confused, even somehow intimidated by its first real direct encounter with a worthy opponent, and now ally, as well.

Wareagle continued his labor, working the knife into the assembly connecting the pincer to the articulated arm this way and that until it finally loosened. When his attempts to dislodge it the rest of the way with only his arms failed, he backed off enough to try the task with his legs.

The pincer came somewhat free, but not enough.

"Come on, Johnny," McCracken urged. "Come on. What about using the other pincer, Sal?"

"I can try, boss, but if I spook that thing again, it just might—"

"Wait!" Katie said abruptly.

"Holy fucking shit!" from Captain Seven. "I'm definitely either stoned or dreaming here!"

Outside the creature had wrapped a pair of its massive arms around the pincer apparatus, suction cups digging into place. Then, as Wareagle backed off, seeming to urge the creature on, it twisted and pulled until the pincer came free in its grasp.

Captain Seven couldn't stop shaking his head. "You gotta be fucking kidding me."

The squid darted off with its tentacle still snared in the now severed pincer, though not for long given the force of the current and power of the sea to ultimately dislodge it.

McCracken unbuckled his safety harness and moved to open the hatch for Johnny. "Get ready to get us out of here, Sal."

"Easier said than done, boss."

McCracken stopped halfway to the rear of the *Crab* and swung back toward Belamo to the sight of emergency lights flashing everywhere on his console.

CHAPTER 81

The Mediterranean Sea

The *Crab* began to buck and thrash as soon as Belamo angled it upward back toward the vent, a feeling akin to being rocked by midair turbulence aboard a plane. A regular beeping sounded shrilly in rhythm with the flashing red lights, and McCracken watched Belamo working the controls frantically to keep the craft stable.

"Hold on, everybody!" he warned, when the sub edged toward the vent and finally entered the plume, riding it upward with the grain this time.

The *Crab* burst out from the cavern with the pincers leading on a near ninety-degree-angle pitch. Belamo struggled to level the craft off, the controls fighting him every step of the way, the craft's stability clearly compromised by the damage done by the giant squid. There were no leaks anywhere McCracken could detect, but the cabin was growing steadily warmer, evidence that the air processors and climate control had been damaged as well.

"How long to the surface, Sal?"

"At this rate, between fifteen minutes and never, boss. Power drain's starting to scare me. I think we lost our generator."

"I can handle it," said Captain Seven.

"It's accessible only from the outside."

"I can't fix it. But I've got another idea."

Moments later, the captain was at Belamo's side working various controls with a keyboard.

"Used to be all you had to know was how to hold a flashlight in your mouth and splice wires together. Now, you gotta know how to talk to machines instead and get them to do what you want." He hit Enter a final time. "There."

The exterior lighting died, and the screens all went dark. Inside the cabin, power switched to the auxiliary back-up batteries.

"Yeah, nice work," Belamo said with a frown.

"You bet, since now all the battery power lost to lighting, view screens, and cameras is yours to do with what you please."

"Enough to get us to the surface?" asked McCracken.

"You ask me, it better be," Sal Belamo told him.

"What's our ETA?"

"Twelve minutes, forty-seven seconds."

"Pretty specific."

"That's because it's all the air we have left."

McCracken found himself counting down the seconds when the seas around them brightened and then the surface drew within view. With three minutes to go, the *Crab* sputtered and nearly stalled; with two, it started to roll into a drop Belamo just managed to correct in time.

"Come on, baby, come on," Belamo willed. "You can do this. Don't let me down."

As if in answer to his plea, the craft crested over the surface of the Mediterranean, straining at the seams, with thirty-five seconds to spare.

"Whoa," Sal Belamo said, retracting the *Crab*'s glass panes to open it to the fresh sea air with the craft dead in the water, "that was a close one."

The craft was fully able to operate on the surface in the form of a speedboat with speeds ranging up to thirty miles per hour, enough hopefully to keep Sebastian Roy's forces, certain to be scouring the seas for the *Crab*, from finding them.

"We're not done yet, Sal," said a hardly celebratory McCracken.

"Boss?"

"How's the communication gear on this thing, Sal?"

"Good enough to connect to Mars, boss."

"Just need to reach New Orleans for starters."

"I'm opening the e-mail now," Leander Levy said from his shop in the French Quarter.

"You're going to see video stills of some symbols I can't identify. Need you to put on your historian's cap."

"I never take it off, old friend. Ah, here they are, taking shape now. Most interest—"

"What's wrong, Leander? Why'd you stop?"

"Because I've seen symbols like these before. Last week, just after our meeting. Another client paid me a visit, a man I wish I'd never met in the first place: Shinzo Asahara."

McCracken swung toward Katie, locking stares with her as he continued.

"What'd you tell him?"

"The same thing I'm telling you. That I've never seen anything like these symbols before. That they're part of no language ever created by man and no civilization on any record."

"That's all?"

"Not quite," Levy said. "I was able to finally link the symbols to a man Asahara asked me about more recently."

"Don't tell me," said McCracken. "Sebastian Roy."

"I need to contact Folsom to arrange for pickup and then transport to Spain."

"Spain?" Katie asked, as if needing confirmation she'd heard him correctly.

"We need to get to Sebastian Roy, and we need to do it now, before Asahara and Aum Shinrikyo get there."

"What makes you think Roy'll see us, boss?" Belamo wondered.

McCracken angled his gaze over to Katie DeMarco. "Because we've got something he wants. And I don't intend on taking no for an answer."

"Blainey?"

McCracken turned toward Wareagle. "He's got Pandora's jar, Indian. He's had it all along."

PART FIVE:
PANDORA'S JAR

CHAPTER 82

Tokyo

Shinzo Asahara stood in the elegant walled flower garden, facing the assemblage of his most loyal soldiers. There were thirty in all, modern-day samurai warriors carefully culled from members of the Japanese military whose personal beliefs had drawn them to Aum Shinrikyo's extreme politics and goals.

The night before, Shinzo had lingered long over the still waters of the garden's pond in the hope his father's visage might appear. But there was nothing, no sign at all. Or, perhaps, he was too preoccupied to open his mind sufficiently since the attack on Sebastian Roy's compound would come tomorrow.

Soft raindrops began to fall, accompanied by a light breeze that ruffled the pond's calm surface and led Shinzo to return his attention to his men, warriors chosen not only for their prowess and the rigidity of their beliefs, but also for their own histories. Shinzo had made sure to select those with backgrounds of loss dating back to the fateful day atomic bombs had been dropped for the first and only time in human history. It was their fate, their karma, to join him in this quest and finish the job the bombs had started. The wastelands that were Hiroshima and Nagasaki from that day would soon be visited upon all the world.

This was all fated; it had to be, since no other explanation sufficed for the fact that he now felt certain that Sebastian Roy was actually in possession of Pandora's jar.

But not for long.

"Prepare yourselves," he said to his warriors, "because tomorrow we end the world."

CHAPTER 83

Pyrenees Mountains, Spain

"My name is Henry Folsom, Mr. Roy. Also on this call is Ben Yaretz and Cassidy Sing, assistant directors of Homeland Security."

Sebastian Roy kept his eyes glued to the screen in anticipation of the helicopter's arrival, replaying the conversation with the official from Homeland Security in his mind.

"First, I need you to understand this phone call is totally off the record. It's not being recorded and as soon as our conversation is over, any trace of it ever being placed or logged will disappear. Am I making myself clear?"

"I'm a busy man, Mr. Folsom, please state your business."

"We have your daughter, Alexandra, in custody, sir. She was captured in the midst of attempting to blow up one your subsidiaries, Ocean Bore Technologies."

Roy felt a chill ride up his spine and a flutter in his stomach. "I'm still listening."

"Just checking my notes, sir. This is a fluid situation. But we have her, and it has been strongly suggested that she be returned to your custody to avoid any embarrassment or, er, future entanglements."

Sebastian Roy's eyes remained riveted on the scene pictured on the helipad, a phalanx of his security personnel awaiting Alexandra's arrival under escort by agents of Homeland Security. It had been the third attack on a Roy Industries facility, four including Stuttgart, before his security forces had managed to isolate a photograph of the perpetrator. He looked at Alexandra's picture with first denial, then shock, and finally recognition of the ultimate denunciation of his power. What was it all worth if his daughter had seen fit to do this, starting the day her actions led to the deaths of her brother and mother? He had moved heaven and earth to find her, but she always eluded him to continue waging her own personal war, backed by an environmental group Roy had traced to a camp in Greenland before eliminating the nuisance they posed for good.

"The White House," the man named Folsom had continued, "believes this is a matter best kept quiet, that remains in the family. *Your* family, sir. I'm sure you agree."

Roy said that he did.

"The men who captured your daughter work outside the system. They're prepared to transport Alexandra to you. Once they hand her over to your custody, their part in this ends and there will be no record whatsoever of their involvement. You understand what that means."

I do indeed, Sebastian Roy thought, as the helicopter appeared on the screen before him.

CHAPTER 84

Pyrenees Mountains, Spain

McCracken felt the helicopter slow to a hover over the helipad and then descend toward the white circle emblazoned on the concrete landing deck below.

"You up for this, Katie?" he asked the woman seated between him and Johnny Wareagle, their headsets dangling now.

"Thank you."

"For what?"

"Not calling me Alexandra. She really did die in that fire. At least, she might as well have."

"You're welcome. Now answer my question."

Katie DeMarco nodded. "I'm ready. I just hope you're right."

Wareagle turned from the window, the rotor wash spraying dust and stray bits of foliage everywhere beyond now. "Eight security guards, Blainey," he said. "Six we can see and two that we can't. Four more watching from windows inside."

"Roy's got no reason not to trust us."

"He doesn't trust anyone," Katie snapped. "And he'll never let you inside."

With that, McCracken slapped a pair of chain handcuffs formed of both stainless steel and ordnance-grade polymer onto her wrist and then his own. "We'll see about that, young lady."

CHAPTER 85

Pyrenees Mountains, Spain

Sebastian Roy's security forces, dressed in black commando gear and armed with both Heckler and Koch submachine guns and Beretta pistols, noted the high-tech handcuffs binding McCracken to Katie DeMarco, unsure of how to respond until a slight, well-dressed man slid forward through the grouping of well-armed men.

"The name's Pierce, sir. I'm Mr. Roy's executive assistant. He wishes me to pass on the message that he is most grateful for your and Homeland Security's efforts in returning his daughter. You have his undying gratitude and he hopes someday to be able to return the favor to Homeland as well." Pierce stepped a bit more forward, his eyes lingering on Katie in recognition. "Your job is done now," he told McCracken. "We'll take things from here."

McCracken raised both his and Katie's cuffed arms, as Belamo and Wareagle tensed slightly on either side of them. Wareagle's gaze moved from one security man to the next and then back, ready to move if it came to that. "I'm afraid I can't do that. Our orders are to deliver the woman to Mr. Roy directly."

"We both have our orders, apparently."

"And unless mine are followed, we'll be getting back onto that helicopter. All of us."

A few of Roy's black-garbed security men moved to block the path between their positions and the still idling chopper. McCracken quickly sized them as ex-military selected from the ranks of private security forces. Solid operatives who'd likely seen combat in Iraq or Afghanistan.

"Bad idea, Mr. Pierce," McCracken said. "We're on the same side here, and both of us have our orders."

Pierce weighed his options, picking the only realistic one he had. "Then if you'll follow me, I'll escort you to Mr. Roy."

McCracken fell into step behind him with Katie in tow, followed by Wareagle and Belamo.

"You are aware of the condition Mr. Roy suffers from and his living situation as a result," said Pierce.

"We've been briefed, yes."

"Then I'll rely on your professionalism to not gawk or stare. Mr. Roy receives extraordinarily few visitors and is not comfortable among strangers."

"Like his daughter, you mean."

The corridor was long and seemed to slope slightly downward before angling up again, perhaps to accommodate the grade of the mountain. The shiny tile flooring along a brief entry stretch gave way to a polished light hardwood, as the fortress took on more the look of an elegant home and less that of a bunker. McCracken imagined it was a combination of both and found the irony striking that Roy would never be able to safely spend time amid the lavish layout and furnishings that surrounded the hyperbaric chamber in which he lived.

"Everything you're looking at," Pierce told all of them, sounding like a tour guide, "right down to the wood floors, were lifted from homes Mr. Roy will never return to again in all probability. The original plan was to convert a much larger portion of the structure to accommodate the hyperbaric conditions Mr. Roy requires, but the logistics involved proved impossible."

"Is the prognosis that bad?" Katie asked.

"Ms. *Roy*," Pierce said, exaggerating her real last name, "your father's condition makes any ordinary infection potentially life-threatening. Beyond that, there is the very real possibility that his wounds will fester into gangrene and perhaps lead to the need to amputate limbs. An inevitability even. It's just a matter of time."

The last of the first hallway felt more like an art gallery, with paintings hanging on both walls beautifully illuminated by invisible, focused lighting. Pierce steered them into an elevator and up three flights to the complex's top floor where Roy's chamber was held and where a number of his company's top executives maintained offices in order to have regular contact with him. Folsom had mentioned that quite a power struggle was under way to determine his successor now that Christian Roy's death had created both a crisis and an opportunity.

Before passing through the vaultlike entrance into Roy's private inner sanctum, Pierce instructed them to don surgical gowns and masks to further preclude any chance of leaving germs behind that could prove deadly for Sebastian Roy. Then he moved to a nearby wall-mounted intercom.

"They're here, Mr. Roy."

"Show them in, please," a crackling, slightly raspy voice instructed.

Pierce punched a code into a nearby keypad and the heavy vault-like door began to ease open. McCracken felt Katie stiffen, her legs suddenly too heavy to move. He slid a key from his pocket and removed the handcuffs, easing an arm around her shoulders.

"I need you to help me finish this," he said softly to make sure only she could hear, maneuvering her toward the door. "Are you with me?"

She nodded and felt him slide a pistol into her jacket pocket, whispering, "Just in case."

Together they followed Pierce into the hyperbaric chamber to find Sebastian Roy standing there with hands clasped behind his back, a single thick, Permaseal window uncovered to the black night beyond.

CHAPTER 86

Pyrenees Mountains, Spain

The Blackhawk helicopters carrying Shinzo Asahara and his two-dozen warriors sliced through the night sky. The helicopters were American issue, the very same model the SEALs had used in their famed raid on the Bin Laden compound in Pakistan. The Japanese government had purchased several for use exclusively by its anti-terrorist forces, from which a number of his warriors had come to Aum Shinrikyo. One of these, a former colonel named Kuroda, had arranged for the appropriation of two of the Blackhawks along with a transport plane to take them to the staging area forty miles from Roy's mountain compound.

Asahara knew his men were ready, just as he was himself. He felt exceedingly calm in spite of the excitement over the fact he was mere minutes away from their target, which was impregnable to attack from anything but above, a full-fledged commando strike of a kind his warriors were exceedingly well versed in. Yes, mere minutes from the compound and just a few more after that from snatching the means to bring on doomsday from Sebastian Roy.

Pandora's jar.

Asahara longed for a mirror, anything that could yield his father's reflection. Not for advice or counsel, but praise. He wanted the ghost of his father to look him in the eye and say how proud he was. In death Shoho Asahara had been able to lay eyes on his son for the first time, and Shinzo so desperately wanted those same eyes to regard him fulfilling their mutual destiny.

In contrast to him, his thirty warriors evenly split between this chopper and the trailing one were stiff and tense to a man. The logistics and timing of this nighttime raid had precluded any opportunity to stage a rehearsal in a mock-up setting, a procedure to which they were more accustomed. He had assured them that fate was on their side, that their role was predestined and meant to be. They need only trust in their own skills and the schematics of the compound they'd all committed to memory. The placement of Roy's protective forces was predictable; they were professionals for sure but no match for these samurai-like warriors, who were even more lethal because of the singular purpose that drove them to this moment, united in their goal.

Shinzo closed his eyes and visualized his father sitting before him smiling. He felt himself slipping into a serene trance, heard himself speaking to his father, and felt the great man lay a hand on his shoulder.

"Shinzo-san?"

The voice of Colonel Kuroda, formerly of the Tokushu Sakusen Gun unit, Japan's Delta-Force-like commando force established by the Japanese Defense Agency to counter terrorist activities on Japanese soil, jarred him from his trance. The unit was based in the Narashino, Chiba garrison in Funabashi with the First Airborne Brigade from which the colonel had procured the Blackhawks and transport plane. In ironic counterpoint, the unit was established in the wake of Aum Shinrikyo's attack on the Tokyo subway.

Kuroda had selected Aum Shinrikyo's commandos personally,

culled from the best Tokushu Sakusen Gun had to offer whose politics proved the right fit. All had backgrounds that included the tragedies of Hiroshima and Nagasaki. Though obviously none had been alive at the time, they understood pain and loss and believed to a man the world would be better off gone. Perhaps in their hearts they really didn't think that would come to pass, but they reveled nonetheless in the purpose the process provided them.

"Shinzo-san?" Louder this time.

Shinzo opened his eyes.

"I didn't hear you. Could you repeat your words?"

"Just thinking out loud, Kuroda-sensei. Our time grows near."

"It does indeed," Kuroda said, casting his gaze out the window where the shape of Sebastian Roy's Pyrenees fortress had come into view.

It was lit up enough for Asahara to formulate its shape and sprawl in his mind, the growing picture before him remarkably akin to the satellite photos taken from miles up in the atmosphere. The compound had been built to take full advantage of the natural defenses of the Pyrenees, and he could hardly imagine how even a man of limitless wealth like Sebastian Roy could possibly have managed a construction task so difficult.

To begin with, no road led to the compound or even close to it. So, too, any climber attempting to reach it would have to negotiate sheer rock face on all sides, except for the rear that was layered to almost appear part of the mountain that rose jaggedly over it. The compound looked modern and modular in design and Asahara could picture massive freight helicopters toting individual sections, hovering overhead while workmen below readied to fit the sections into place one at a time. The connections had been managed so seamlessly as to make the structure look as if it had been crafted by hand out of a single slab of stone. It was four levels in the front and three where it sloped upward to conform to the pinnacle's shape and shaded the very same grayish brown as the mountain itself. Smaller one-story subsections jutted out the side featuring a trio of helipads, two of which were currently occupied.

Asahara had familiarized himself as much as possible with the compound's internal structure as well. According to the plans, the design featured a maze of smaller rooms, offices, bedrooms, laundry and storage facilities, and a self-contained power station for generating its own heat and electricity. None of this told him how many security forces to expect, although he figured the number to be less than that of his warriors. Roy's forces would never anticipate a full-scale attack under cover of darkness, and by the time they realized one was under way, his warriors would have won the day.

From within these walls, Sebastian Roy had continued to run an empire based on control of the world's energy supply, a quest that had brought him to the dark matter Asahara now desperately sought. He turned to the window and just for a moment, in a brief flicker of light, thought he caught his father's reflection smiling at him.

Shinzo glanced down at his second right hand garbed in a mitten, willing at least some feeling into it.

I won't let you down, Father, he thought.

CHAPTER 87

Pyrenees Mountains, Spain

"It's been a long time, Alexandra."

McCracken watched Sebastian Roy shaking his head, scalding the woman who'd become Katie DeMarco with his eyes.

"What am I to do with you?" Sebastian Roy resumed finally. "Perhaps I should let these men keep you in custody so you can be treated as the murderer that you are, all the lives you've taken including your own mother and brother."

McCracken could see Katie was shaking ever so slightly, her face a mask struggling to reconcile fear with hatred. "My brother was dead a long time before the fire. You saw to that . . . *Father*." That final word was spoken venomously with her upper lip curled in the semblance of a snarl.

"You can leave us now," Roy addressed the others without bothering to regard them. "Show them out, Pierce. Their job is finished."

"No, Mr. Roy," said McCracken, "we can't leave, and it's not finished."

Sebastian Roy seemed to regard McCracken for the first time. He let his gaze linger on him as if first studying what he saw and then nodding as if recognizing it. "It was you, wasn't it? You're the one who stole my submarine in Greece, you and your friends here."

"It was nothing, believe me," McCracken said to Roy. "I stole a space shuttle once."

Something changed in Roy's expression, the tepid and then scowling reaction that had greeted the view of his long-lost daughter replaced by wonder and realization. McCracken caught the scent of something vaguely antiseptic wafting off him, as if alcohol was seeping from Roy's pores instead of perspiration. It mixed with something stale and unsavory, and McCracken was struck by the same feeling he got when viewing a body on a pathologist's slab, the man's skin looking wan and gray-toned under the thin lighting.

"You found it," Roy managed, stumbling over the words, "you found Pandora's Temple. . . ."

"Indeed we did. In pretty good shape, too, for a structure that's been at the bottom of the sea for almost four thousand years. I'm more interested in what we didn't find: Pandora's jar. The problem is I'm not the only one interested; someone else is after it, a Japanese doomsday cult likely on their way here now."

"Here?"

McCracken nodded. "Because you've got the jar, Mr. Roy. You sent your teams scouring the Mediterranean for something that was here all along."

"That's ridiculous!"

"I haven't got time to argue with you, and neither does the world. This doomsday cult arrives before we can get the jar out of here and that disease you've got will be the least of your problems."

"I think you're lying," Roy told him. "I think you've concocted this whole story in league with my daughter. I think she put you up to this. You're not really from Homeland Security, are you?"

"Nope."

"As I was saying. In the future, I'd advise you not to heed the word of a killer," Roy said to Katie.

"There are worse crimes, Mr. Roy," McCracken said, letting his gaze linger on him before moving it to Katie. "Like what you did in your son's room those nights while your daughter was listening. If she's a killer, it's because you made her one. You're lucky she didn't kill you instead years ago." McCracken hesitated to take a closer look at Roy framed in his self-imposed prison. "Or maybe you're not."

Roy stiffened, eyes darting between his daughter and McCracken. "You think I should be sorry for what I did? I was once, but not anymore. If I'm still sorry at all, it's because what I did to Christian failed to achieve its desired effects."

"Oh, I'm sure it produced some effects in at least one of you," McCracken said, not bothering to disguise his meaning. "By the way, I owe you a debt of gratitude."

"For *what*?"

He glanced quickly again at Katie to find her gaze locked upon him, then back at Sebastian Roy. "For reminding me why I'm still doing this when I'm almost ready to start collecting Social Security."

Roy smiled tightly, smugly. "I've seen your kind before."

"My *kind*?"

"I know your type, men with nothing in the world, no stake at all, who find purpose in convincing themselves they must save it because otherwise you have to face the fact that you're nothing more than a mercenary, an assassin." Roy paused long enough to study McCracken again. "Why, you're as much a prisoner as I am."

"But I'm not a liar, Mr. Roy. You should fess up to the truth."

"And what truth would that be?" Roy shot back, unruffled.

"About Stuttgart." McCracken took a step closer to him. "The story about you rushing back into the fire to save your family—how brave and heroic. Be even more brave and heroic if it were true."

Roy stiffened. "I don't know what you're talking about."

"Yes, you do. See, this friend of mine pulled all the video footage, both from security cameras and television feeds, and managed to string it all together chronologically. Know what he found?"

Roy swallowed hard, made no response.

"You ran at the first sign of trouble. You ran and left your family to die. Trouble was, you ran the wrong way and ended up getting caught in the flames yourself. Only thing true about your story was that getting pinned beneath other bodies *is* what saved your life. And your whole life, if you want to call it that," McCracken added, looking around him, "goes back to that lie. All this power, all this money, and this is what you're left with. I may be little more than a killer, but I know true weakness when I've got it centered in my crosshairs. And you—"

Before McCracken could finish, a crack and a slight ping sounded almost simultaneously. McCracken saw a spiderweb-shaped fissure form around a neat hole in the window; in the same moment, Pierce pitched over forward, the back of his head reduced to a pool of bone and gore as he fell to the floor.

CHAPTER 88

Pyrenees Mountains, Spain

The Tokushu Sakusen Gun snipers opened fire on their targets from perches half extended into the night air in the same moment the commandos in the lead chopper fast-roped down onto the fortress. With the chance of resistance now substantially diminished, these initial dozen would deliberately and systematically eliminate Sebastian Roy's guards at their normal posts, revealed by the satellite reconnaissance photos thanks to their thermal heat signatures.

Of course, Asahara's numb hand ruled out fast roping and he lacked such specialized training anyway. So the plan was for the second chopper with the other half of his Tokushu Sakusen Gun warriors inside to land on the helipad and prepare to enter once the compound had been secured.

In the night ahead, his warriors were mere specks of motion, which was nonetheless enough to show them reaching the fortress roof and fanning out to their assigned grids to execute Roy's remaining guards. Asahara felt no remorse or regret, only excitement over his anticipated entry into the compound to seize Pandora's jar.

~

"Down!" McCracken shouted. "Everybody down!"

And he barreled into Katie, taking her beneath him to the floor, as more gunshots blew out the rest of the glass and peppered the room.

"I've got security!" Sebastian Roy managed, having pinned himself against the wall over Pierce's corpse still leaking fluid and brain matter from his ruptured skull. "Whoever's out there, they'll stop them!"

"A doomsday cult's out there, and I saw your men. They're no match for Aum Shinrikyo, trust me on that. But you do have one ace up your sleeve to stop the cult from getting their hands on the jar."

"What's that?"

"Us."

The second helicopter touched down only long enough to allow its passengers to exit quickly. Asahara did so in the middle of a group of Tokushu Sakusen Gun commandos, following their motions as best he could and hoping not to slow their efforts. He had fit the earpiece Kuroda had given him into his ear and the chatter was coming fast now.

"Six down!"

"Seven!"

"Eight and nine!"

"Ten!"

Sebastian Roy's unprepared guards were being felled in just the effortless fashion Kuroda had promised. This was, after all, a holy mission, and Asahara wondered if his father was watching as he moved to enter the compound with his warriors.

"How many, Indian?" McCracken asked, back on his feet in Roy's chamber now.

"Two choppers, Blainey," Wareagle replied without needing to check the window. "One's already dropped its passengers; the other should be landing soon."

"Thirty men, maybe a couple more, boss," said Sal Belamo, his tone like he'd swallowed stomach acid. "Pros for sure."

"Stay down," McCracken warned Roy, as the three of them started for the door. "We'll be back."

Almost there just behind Wareagle and Belamo, McCracken saw Katie DeMarco following in tow.

"Uh-uh, you're staying here too."

She looked revolted by the prospects, stealing a glance back at her father who had slumped against a wall in the corner. Amazing, thought McCracken, to note how even the most powerful wilt when faced with the terror of combat. For the untrained and inexperienced, there was simply no way to describe what it felt like to be under fire by men determined to kill and trained to do so.

"Looks like you were right, after all, old man."

"How's that, young lady?"

She smiled sadly. "Nothing much changes."

"Not today, anyway," McCracken said with a wink.

Despite Kuroda's assurances, Shinzo had had trouble believing it would be this easy. The resistance his warriors encountered was feeble at best and wouldn't have even reached that high if they'd had the opportunity to first practice this assault in a controlled environment.

The group of commandos of which he was now a part entered the complex through the south, the others through the east and west, with the north side being accessible only via a sheer face of rocks. The rendezvous point was fluid, based on the ability of the warriors who'd fast-roped down under Kuroda's command to eliminate as much resistance as possible and then funnel the rest here to the south. For his part, Asahara was to remain with the second wave of Tokushu Sakusen Gun warriors outside the heavy bulkheadlike doors just inside the compound.

He'd wait here in accordance with Colonel Kuroda's instructions. Time seemed to crawl, nothing but garbled splotches of exchanges going off in his ear, as the first wave of his commandos continued to encounter little additional resistance. Some sporadic exchanges of gunfire were swiftly quelled, with his warriors triumphing. Any stragglers would be forced this way to be concentrated in a cross fire from Kuroda's force in pursuit and Asahara's lying in wait. And, once all the security forces were neutralized, they would move on to a defenseless Sebastian Roy who would be utterly at their mercy—an asset until Pandora's jar belonged to Asahara.

He closed his eyes, settled himself with a few deep breaths, and instantly began to breathe easier when he opened them again.

Until the sounds and cries of panic began to resound in his ear. They seemed to come from the whole first team of his warriors at once, followed by gunshots, wails of pain, calls for help, or warnings to others.

What was happening?

Time crawled again in agonizing fashion now, Asahara left to ponder his next move when the heavy door burst open and Colonel Kuroda stumbled through, heaving for breath and bleeding from a shoulder wound.

"Sensei!" Shinzo managed.

Kuroda staggered to the wall and laid his shoulders against it. "It's them!"

"Who?"

"The same men . . ."

"The same men who *what*?"

Kuroda looked at him for what seemed like a very long time before responding.

CHAPTER 89

Pyrenees Mountains, Spain

Times changed. Places changed.

But not the battle.

And Wareagle and McCracken took to this one, just as they'd taken to all the others dating back to times long past but never forgotten. Nothing was forgotten, each piece of every war they'd ever fought leaving an indelible mark. In these moments, age was rendered meaningless in the face of purpose. There was no age, there was no time. There were only moments between kills both had long trained themselves to remain as indifferent to as possible.

Something happened in the moments they slid about the corridors moving downward and out from the fortress's top floor, the world slowing down, becoming surreal. Starting when McCracken lay in wait after glimpsing a Japanese man on a stealthy patrol.

Aum Shinrikyo's forces had penetrated the compound now.

Additional footsteps pounded up the stairs from the level below, and McCracken dropped the nearest man with a single shot to the head from his pistol, then stripped off the silenced submachine gun slung from his shoulder. It took a pair of three-shot bursts to kill a second and third man in the stairwell, both plummeting down the stairs, dead.

McCracken kept a mental count in his head, hearing the echo of gunshots indicating both Johnny and Sal were encountering similar resistance, and using the same element of surprise, in their sweeps. He'd seen it all before, more times than he could count: a superior invading force having too much confidence in their intelligence and reconnaissance to be prepared to face an opposition they'd never expected to encounter.

Doomsday was going to have to wait for the members of Aum Shinrikyo.

McCracken padded down the stairs as softly as he could manage, emerging on the second floor and propping himself in the dark cover of an adjacent alcove. Sometimes victory was about patience, which meant waiting for the next man to show himself instead of going on the hunt. Sure enough, the next pair of men converged from either end of the hall, hoping to catch him in a cross fire. But their initial barrage, the only one that mattered, singed the air above him when McCracken dropped to the floor, firing the Heckler and Koch submachine gun as he rolled to cut down both enemy gunmen in a single spray. At this range, the high-velocity bullets pulverized them even through their Kevlar vests, the lighter variety worn by high-end commando teams just like this.

He bore no illusions it was going to be this easy from start to finish; it never was. No, McCracken had the very real sense the actual battle was still to come, and it would have to be fought with the element of surprise gone.

Katie crouched on the floor, glad for the almost incessant drone of gunfire because it distracted her from the fact that her father was just ten feet away from her. She was ten feet away from the monster who'd made her into one too.

"Alexandra," Sebastian Roy, his shoulders slumped, said suddenly from a seated position against the wall across from her.

"Don't call me that."

"It's your name. Your mother chose it, the mother you killed, along with your brother." Roy rose slowly, a portrait in utter calm. "I have a tape of what happened in Greenland," he told her. "Would you like to see your friends all murdered, cut down as they slept? Would you like to see your leader running for his life, dying in the mud? That's what happens to those who oppose me. You think this ends tonight? You think you're up to killing me? You think that assassin who brought you here will do it for you?" Roy shook his head, slowly and surely. "I'm not finished yet, and now I see you'd never be fit to succeed me. Because you're too weak, a prisoner of emotions that have destroyed you because you never learned to control them." Roy's indifferent demeanor slid from his expression, replaced by a tight mask of condescending evil and power. "You want to know why Christian never stopped me, Alexandra? Because he was too scared, just like you are in the end without your assassin to back you up."

Katie sank to her knees, Roy breaking out into a wide grin when he saw the pistol in his daughter's hand.

"That's better, Alexandra. Go ahead, prove me wrong. Show me how strong you really are."

"Are you sure, Kuroda-sensei?" Shinzo Asahara asked when Kuroda's breathing steadied and his eyes returned to normal. "The same men from the building in New Orleans?"

Kuroda grimaced in pain while nodding. "The very same. Ghosts, phantoms, spirits—I've never seen anything like this."

"So what can we do to defeat them?"

"They're going to circle back to the rooms Roy occupies. We use that knowledge against them."

"What if they continue to advance toward us instead?"

Kuroda shook his head, calm in his consideration of the enemy's strategy. "They know we still hold the advantage, and their trick of surprise is gone. They'll believe they can wait us out, so we will move to a plan of attack that makes that impossible."

"Attack ghosts, spirits?"

Kuroda moved off the wall, shoulder straightening and arm extending as if he was never wounded at all. "Even the dead can be killed, Shinzo-san. A wise lesson for you to remember. Now, prepare yourself to move."

"Now?"

Kuroda nodded. "I'm going to take you to Sebastian Roy."

CHAPTER 90

Pyrenees Mountains, Spain

McCracken and Wareagle met up in the center of the first floor together, the last of the first wave of attackers dispatched on the floors above.

"What do you say we slow the rest of them down, Indian?"

"I was just thinking the same thing myself, Blainey."

That meant moving as far down the hallway as they dared, south toward the helipads, since that's where the next wave of Japanese commandos would be concentrated. They closed and snapped off the locks on four different decoratively heavy wooden doors with steel cores to maximize their resistance to fire. The strategy had the dual effect of negating the enemy force's still superior numbers, while making them vulnerable every time they had to blow or shoot their way through a barrier. Normally such a slowing ploy would be employed when reinforcements were expected. Even though that wasn't the case here, it would serve a similar purpose by making the three of them, including Sal Belamo, much more effective fighters in comparison with an enemy thrown onto the defensive.

Starting at a hallway junction two-thirds of the way to the exit leading out onto the helipad, they sealed that door, another, and then set to wait behind the cover of the next junction.

"Nothing ever changes, Blainey," Wareagle said, as they lay in wait behind the cover of a junction in the first-floor hallway.

"If it did, they wouldn't need us anymore."

Katie's hand trembled, the pistol McCracken had slipped her wobbling in her grasp.

"Go ahead," her father said, a cold bitterness ringing in his voice. "Shoot me. It's what you've been doing since Stuttgart anyway. Killing strangers in my stead. Well, here I am right before you. The real me, no more surrogates."

The gun continued to shake.

"You can't, Alexandra, can you? Because you're weak, just like your brother was weak. I thought I could toughen him up, could make him hate me. Because if he hated me, he'd find the strength and resolve he needed to run Roy Industries when I was gone."

"Which only proves how little you knew your own son. Christian could never be made to hate anyone, and he never would have come into the company; he wanted to get as far away from you as possible."

Roy tried not to let his daughter see how much her remark stung him. "We'll never know that for sure, though, will we, because you killed him. He died in that fire you set and now you can take his place."

"You killed Christian long before Stuttgart."

"Maybe you were jealous of him, Alexandra."

Katie's eyes bulged in disbelief. "Jealous? Of what you did to him?"

"Of my plans *for* him. That's what I wanted you to feel so you'd want it even more. I always knew you were better fit to be my successor. That was always the plan. Was I wrong, Alexandra? Tell me, was I wrong?"

The pistol quivered in Katie's hand. She felt like a frightened little girl again, hearing the soft patter of footsteps in the halls beyond her bedroom, stopping at the door to her brother's room.

"I won't shoot you," she heard herself say.

"Then I was wrong."

And with that Katie eased the pistol upward until the cold steel was squeezed against her own temple. "No, you weren't."

An out-of-breath Sal Belamo joined McCracken and Wareagle just as the Japanese commandos neared the door behind which they lay in wait.

"Where you been, Sal?"

"Guess I'm not as young as I used to be, boss. Wait until you hit seventy."

"You said the same thing about me turning sixty."

"Good thing I'm a better shot than prophet."

The strategy they were about to employ had been a classic since the dawn of war: make a stand, fire until the enemy advances, and then retreat to repeat the process at the next strategic point—in this case using the compound's winding, multilayered structure to their best advantage. It was a strategy well founded in all respects, except one.

"You ask me," said Belamo, "all they have to do is advance up a level and double back to take you from behind."

McCracken swung toward Wareagle, feigning shock. "How could we not have thought of that?"

Just then the booby traps they'd set on the second floor were tripped, a series of ear-wrenching blasts sounding followed immediately by shrieks and screams. Wareagle had strung a trio of grenades together with simple twine he carried in his belt pouch. Loop the twine through the door frame and it would yank the pins from the grenades once the door was open. Three seconds later the boom had sounded, the effects of the blast magnified all the more by the closed confines of the hallway.

Japanese commandos reached the first blocked junction mere seconds after the blast above. McCracken waited until three men were all the way through and their targets clear before he, Belamo, and Wareagle opened up with a barrage that dropped the trio before they could get off a single shot.

Too easy.

McCracken had barely formed that thought when a cascade of fire opened up on them from the other end of the hall. He cursed himself for never considering approach from *below*, a subbasement or crawl space layered beneath the compound's structure. The first three Japanese commandos had been nothing more than decoys, sacrifices in the true nature of the samurai code; and McCracken, Wareagle, and Belamo now found themselves trapped in a cross fire as another group stormed through the original breech pouring bullets their way.

Maybe he was too old, maybe a decade ago he would have considered such another route of potential access, and his whole plan wouldn't have gone to shit. Now all McCracken could do was train his fire on the far end of the hall, while Johnny and Sal concentrated theirs toward the near. The submachine gun danced in his grasp, heat radiating off its barrel and fanning up into his face with smoke as he switched to three-shot bursts from automatic fire. He was vaguely conscious of the spent shells clanging to the hardwood floor, stubbornly remaining exposed long enough for his shots to find the three gunmen who'd expected to find easy targets upon their ascent from the basement. McCracken exhaled and took a deep breath, as he jammed yet another fresh magazine home.

Downing this wave of attackers succeeded only in opening the route for yet more surging out from both sides of the hallway again. With Wareagle taking point, they managed to beat back the assault from the original point long enough to get another heavy door sealed, enabling them to focus all their attention on the forces pouring up from the basement crawl space.

Whoooosssshhhhhhh . . .

McCracken registered the sound an instant before an RPG obliterated the entire door and blew the splintery remnants and jagged chunks of wood into them. Another group of commandos charged in from that side of the hall, restoring the cross fire McCracken knew full well they couldn't outlast forever. But for now the firing continued, the murky darkness broken by orange muzzle flashes that looked like campfires flashing in the night. Husks of the ceiling and chunks of the floor exploded in all directions amid the hail of bullets that puckered McCracken's eardrums and left the air smelling of gun oil, bitter with smoke and a light bluish haze that lifted toward the ceiling like a vapor cloud.

"Change in strategy, Indian!"

"With you, Blainey!"

With what seemed like endless twin waves of Japanese commandos coming, McCracken, Wareagle, and Belamo backed through the next door, managing to seal it and continue toward a set of stairs, lurching up them just as a second RPG blasted debris up the steps after them.

At sixty, McCracken's ears seemed to have borne the worst brunt of his years of blasts, bombs, and gunplay. They'd lost their tolerance for loud noises and stretches like this when sound was stolen from them grew longer each time. Not being able to hear cast the battle in a strange, surreal light, in the course of their pulling back toward Sebastian Roy's hyperbaric chamber on the top floor of the complex built against the rock face of the mountain.

Halfway up the final flight of stairs, Wareagle ejected both magazines from the twin submachine guns he was wielding and snapped two more home in blinding fashion, missing barely a beat. Belamo was more selective with his shots as they reached the top floor, pursued by the last half-dozen Japanese commandos.

"We're running out of room, boss!"

"Least of our problems, Sal!" McCracken shouted back, his hearing fading in and out.

"You won't do it," Sebastian Roy said, not sounding sure or confident at all with his daughter pressing the pistol so tight against her temple that her hand was quivering. They could hear the nonstop gunfire pounding beyond, but at that point it seemed inconsequential to both of them.

"Why not? I won't feel anything; I haven't felt anything in a long, long time."

Roy raised a hand as if to make a point, then lowered it, his expression fighting for calm. "Think, Alexandra, think what you could do!"

"That's exactly what I'm thinking," she said, starting to squeeze the trigger, welcoming what was to come.

"NOOOOOOOOOO!"

How much pleasure she took in her father's desperate plea, the fact that he was seeing his own inevitable demise magnified by witnessing hers. It was so wonderful to *feel* something, *anything* . . .

Until a heavy pounding on the chamber door lifted her from the trance she'd slipped into.

Katie jammed the pistol McCracken provided into her belt and moved to the heavy steel door, working the latch. But it wouldn't budge, the locking mechanism having been tripped. Requiring a code to open now from either the inside or the out.

"The code!" she screamed to her father.

He remained against the wall, still flinching from the sounds of fire from outside.

"*The code!*" she yelled again, coming toward him with McCracken's pistol raised.

Roy remained motionless. "It's just us now, Alexandra. You had your chance. Now you're not going anywhere."

"The code," she said, meeting her father's gaze. "Give me the—"

She stopped when she saw his eyes, because she knew. Somehow she *knew*!

Back at the heavy door she entered three two-digit numbers into the keypad.

Click.

"Christian's birth date," Katie told him, her eyes bulging in fear as the door opened all the way.

~

They ran out of space at the same time they came down to the last of their ammo. McCracken's hearing was almost all the way back, his ears burned anew by the constant din of gunfire blazing from the end of the hall that accessed Sebastian Roy's hyperbaric chamber. The bullets seemed to own the air, almost visible in his imagination as sizzling specks fired from an endless array of barrels. The narrow spacing of the remaining Japanese commandos created the effect of a wind tunnel, increasing the sensory overload to an unfathomable degree, even for McCracken.

Still firing toward the onslaught raining on them from the other end of the hall, McCracken, Wareagle, and Belamo continued their retreat, just one flight to go before reaching Roy's chamber.

With the last of their bullets draining fast, McCracken entered the same key code he'd watched Pierce press out. The only thing saving him, Wareagle, and Belamo from an all-out rush from the final grouping of commandos was the narrowness of the hall, reducing any attack the enemy force might launch to single file. That negated their advantage in number, firepower, and even positioning. But once McCracken and friends' ammo was exhausted, all that would be rendered moot.

Still, Roy's chamber would offer them protection and defensive positioning Aum Shinrikyo could never breach without sacrificing the remainder of their dwindling numbers.

It was over, Pandora's jar certain to be kept from the doomsday cult's hands now.

McCracken watched as the door eased open before him, revealing a grinning Shinzo Asahara standing next to another Japanese man holding a gun to Katie DeMarco's head.

CHAPTER 91

Pyrenees Mountains, Spain

"Drop your weapons," Asahara ordered.

McCracken, Wareagle, and Belamo all shed their guns to the floor, noting the presence of two more armed Japanese commandos holding their guns on Sebastian Roy.

"Now I want the jar," Asahara demanded between heavy breaths. "Give me Pandora's jar!"

"No," said McCracken.

"Then the woman dies."

"The jar's not here."

"I don't believe you."

"I don't care."

"Otherwise, *you* wouldn't be here," Asahara said surely, the other Japanese man maintaining his hold on Katie and positioned in such a way there was no chance McCracken could reach him before he killed her.

"Why should I give you the jar if it means we *all* die?"

Asahara grinned, McCracken noticing the black mitten covering his left hand for the first time. "Because men like you always believe you can conquer all. Because given the opportunity, you're convinced you won't fail whatever the odds. And maybe you're right. And even if you're not, you'll always take that chance."

"What can I say? Something works for me, I stick with it."

"Then perhaps we should change the equation."

With that Asahara signaled his other two commandos to move away from Roy. McCracken watched them train their submachine guns on Johnny Wareagle and Sal Belamo instead.

"Your two associates will die first. Then the woman, then you. Your sacrifice will have accomplished nothing."

McCracken met Katie's eyes. "Guess we'll see about that, won't we?"

And in that instant she jerked her face downward and bit hard and deep into her captor's hand. Kuroda flinched in pain long enough for her to twist his pistol away from her, as Johnny Wareagle seized the very same moment to barrel into the two commandos, jerking their weapons upward where they stitched two jagged patches of fire through the drop ceiling. A hissing sound erupted, the oxygen feed lines for the chamber ruptured, as Wareagle drove the men backward, one clutched in either hand, into the nearest wall and slammed their skulls against it over and over again.

By that time, McCracken had already engaged the Japanese man who'd been holding Katie. The man surprised him initially by totally abandoning her to focus on him. His gun coming around was just a decoy for the blow from his other hand McCracken proved ready for. Kuroda's eyes told McCracken the rest he needed to know about him, a worthy opponent as well as a deadly one.

He was vaguely conscious of Belamo struggling with Shinzo Asahara, who seemed able to use only his right hand in the fight. McCracken's next move was to use Kuroda's possession of the gun against him, wrenching it up against his frame to make the man focus his efforts on freeing it. McCracken thought this would open up his face and neck for a strike. But Kuroda managed to deflect it and tie him up with a hand looped around his arm at the bicep, driving McCracken sideways.

The result of the stalemate was an ugly pirouette that twirled them across the room, past Katie DeMarco who was standing stiffly over the form of her father slumped against the wall in terror. McCracken lashed out with a blow that Kuroda effortlessly blocked, just as McCracken deflected his counter in similar fashion. The men continued to parry, McCracken feeling himself gain control of the pistol when . . .

BOOM!

The chamber door burst open ahead of Asahara's remaining commandos charging inside, leveled guns searching for targets when Johnny Wareagle spun around with the floppy frames of the two men still in his grasp.

Along with their submachine guns.

Wareagle found both triggers at once, opening up twin streams of fire at the final commandos and downing them as their shots flew wildly through the chamber sparking flame bursts against the ceiling where the oxygen supply had been freed.

One of the errant shots grazed McCracken in the shoulder, turning his arm numb and useless. The advantage all his now, Kuroda hammered him hard in the jaw and wrenched the pistol from his grasp. McCracken met the Japanese man's eyes, saw his own end in them.

Until Katie DeMarco sprang from the wall, catching Kuroda by surprise as she brought her gun in close. The advantage was hers until Kuroda lashed a hand upward and knocked it aside.

But not far enough.

The bullet she'd managed to fire entered under his chin, obliterating his face en route to exiting his skull and rupturing the already damaged oxygen tank directly above.

McCracken, meanwhile, reeled backward, shocked by what he'd just watched Katie do. Their eyes met through what looked like a ripple in the air in the moment before the blast. The flames cascaded downward from the ceiling, swallowing Katie in their grasp and just brushing against McCracken before the airburst slammed him against the wall.

That final moment found Katie feeling warm, cushiony, her last conscious thought one of comfort because she could *feel.* Sad, terrified, and elated all at the same time, reminding her what it felt like to be alive even as the flames claimed her.

McCracken watched her vanish, disappear into the fire-wrought oblivion, as Wareagle hoisted him to his feet and dragged him for the door. Sal Belamo had Sebastian Roy in his grasp by then, and McCracken realized Shinzo Asahara was unaccounted for. At the door, as the ceiling and roof began to collapse inside the chamber, he glimpsed Asahara amid the spreading flames reaching for an object displayed in the alcove housing Sebastian Roy's priceless collection.

"It's true," he said, sounding crazed, even militant. "It's all true!"

Suddenly he was a boy again, running toward his father in a beautiful garden. But before he reached him, Shoho Asahara melted like a wax figure, the pristine setting disappearing as if it were a tapestry embroidered on the world. Shinzo looked down to see both his hands, the boy's hands, normal again before he felt himself melting too.

CHAPTER 92

Pyrenees Mountains, Spain

Only charred and skeletal remains burned to the bone could be found amid the steaming, smoldering pile of debris when McCracken and Wareagle returned to the chamber after sprinklers doused the flames with water. All the chamber's furnishings had been reduced to molten char as well.

But McCracken knew there'd be one item left whole amid the rubble. He found it in what had been a display of Sebastian Roy's greatest treasures, not only whole but utterly and remarkably unscathed by the flames. Pandora's jar was still standing where it had been before the blast had struck. It was dry as well amid the puddles around it, the sprinklers' spray appearing to have somehow missed it altogether.

McCracken lifted the jar, expecting it to be heavy, only to find it light and even comfortable to hold.

"I've seen the symbols on the jar before, Blainey," Wareagle noted from just behind him, regarding what Sebastian Roy had thought to be no more than an ancient Grecian artifact in the sporadic spill of the emergency lighting.

"On the temple pedestal this jar had originally rested upon," McCracken acknowledged.

A picture of the jar, the largest and simplest in Roy's esteemed collection, and its symbols had been included among those in the magazine article Blaine had flashed to Katie DeMarco on the plane ride, recognizing the very same symbols on that pedestal inside Pandora's Temple. And now he was leaving with the jar it had been built to safeguard in his grasp.

"Not a bad souvenir, eh, Indian?"

EPILOGUE:

LAID TO REST

Washington, D.C.: One week later

McCracken and Wareagle stood in the shadow of the Vietnam Memorial, eyeing the latest, and perhaps final, names that would ever be added. Present now were the fellow soldiers they'd served with in Operation Phoenix and other covert ops during the same era. Names that had been missing until now.

Paul Basmajian was the last name added, a final gesture on the part of Hank Folsom as a token of Homeland Security's appreciation for their efforts.

"Not bad for a bureaucrat," McCracken noted. "At least he's a man of his word."

"A rare find these days, Blainey. Truly."

"He wanted to know if we wanted to come back on a more official basis."

"What did you tell him?"

"That he knows where to find us."

"And does he?"

"Unless we don't want to be found." McCracken turned from the wall to regard Wareagle closer. "I don't know about you, Indian, but I can't see myself retiring to a gated community and playing golf all day. Hell, I don't even know how to hold a club."

"You grip it like a gun someone once told me."

"Yeah, gives a whole new meaning to the term even par. What we call survival."

Wareagle looked at him briefly before responding. "You didn't tell Folsom about the jar, did you?"

"Nope, and I don't intend to. Man's not ready for that kind of power, the good guys or the bad guys."

Wareagle stiffened. First McCracken thought he was atypically ill at ease; then he realized bitterness and angst had claimed Johnny's expression. "It killed Baz, Blainey. It will kill far, far more unless something is done."

"And it will be, starting with the immediate suspension of all drilling below twenty thousand feet, if Hank Folsom is to be believed."

"Even if he is, is that enough?"

"It's a start."

"And Sebastian Roy?"

"Our next stop, Indian."

Wareagle turned his attention back to the Wall, drifting to other places full of rotor wash, the stench of spoiled mud, exfoliated jungles, rice paddies, and endless death. For a moment, just a moment, McCracken thought he heard Hueys coming in for extraction, the worst time always being the very instant of climbing on board for the vulnerability it carried with it.

"I'm sorry about the young woman, Blainey."

"I am too. Maybe that's the only way it could have ended for her. Maybe it's what she's been trying to do all along."

"Such words could just as easily be applied to yourself or me."

"Good thing they're not, I guess, Indian."

"You couldn't have saved her even if she had lived," Wareagle told him.

"I figured that much out for myself, Johnny. But I look at her and what do you think I see?"

"Younger versions of the two of us."

"More reckless, making all the mistakes we always steered clear of, making things personal being foremost on the list. That can carry you for a while but it always leads to the same place: nowhere."

"She could have been your daughter. Or mine, Blainey."

"In more ways than one."

Wareagle moved his gaze from the Wall back to McCracken. "When do we head back to Greece?"

"I never said we were, Indian."

"You didn't have to," Wareagle told him.

"After we deal with Sebastian Roy."

Sebastian Roy faded in and out of consciousness, lost to the fog of sedatives as doctors in Madrid struggled to reduce his fever, stave off further infections, and stabilize his vital signs. He had no choice but to surrender to his dreams that came in fits and starts, often with what felt like interminable lags and other times following each other in rapid-fire fashion. There were snippets of Alexandra, both as a girl and as the vengeful, bitter woman who formed his final memory of her. There were memories of his family before the fire and nightmares about the burned form of his son rising from the ashes of the fossil fuel plant. There were brief glimpses of the bearded man, his black eyes like liquid pools trying to suck Roy in. And once, when he opened his eyes in the dream, the bearded man was standing by his bedside, looming over him like a ghost.

"Time to go home, Mr. Roy," he said, and Sebastian Roy realized with a terrible fear that this visit wasn't the product of a dream at all.

McCracken and Wareagle waited for Roy to come fully conscious, having set him in a lush chair in an even lusher library inside his compound atop the Pyrenees Mountains. The burnt odor hung in the air the same way smoke stains claimed the walls in patches. Few areas were untouched by the explosions and gunfire and water pooled in irregular splotches from ruptured pipes and portions of the sprinkler system that had been activated by the smoke alarms. The stench of must and mold permeated the air in stark contrast to rooms like this that remained pristine and elegant. The emergency generators maintained a measure of the compound's lighting, though in flickering fashion.

Roy awakened to the sight of both of them, instinctively trying to pull free even though he wasn't bound. "What is this? Why have you brought me here?"

"So you can be alone with your thoughts," McCracken told him, the bitter scent he recalled from their last meeting seeming harsher and less antiseptic, like food in the first throes of spoilage. "Literally, once we leave. Everyone else is gone, and the Indian and I have made sure to disable all communications in and out. Should give you plenty of time to reflect on all your accomplishments and success, your hits . . ."

McCracken stopped to gaze about melodramatically, running his eyes over the most expensive furnishings money could buy before returning his eyes to Roy.

" . . . and misses."

"The jar," Roy realized.

"It was right here among all your other pieces, likely salvaged from the bottom of the Mediterranean God knows how long ago."

Roy's skin felt dank and clammy. The fever that had racked him in the hospital seemed to be worsening, light-headedness starting to plague him.

"No, that's not true! It *can't* be true!"

"I recognized the symbols on a pedestal inside the temple from a picture of the jar in that architectural magazine," McCracken told him. "Biggest jar in your collection and also the simplest. Ivory colored, except for those dark symbols."

Roy's eyes bulged. He knew that particular jar all too well, so large he'd had to change the spacing of the shelves in his display to accommodate it. The very jar he'd offered to the green energy magnate Landsdale before he'd taken over the man's companies.

Roy's lips quivered, his whole body shuddering. He leaned backward, the chair seeming to swallow him.

He'd had Pandora's jar all along!

McCracken started to back off, drawing even with Johnny Wareagle. "I don't know how long you'll be able to survive outside your chamber before the infections worsen. The power's on and the computers still work, if you want to try putting the whole story down. Just remember you killed your family, your whole family now. It might have been your daughter who set the bomb in Stuttgart, but you lit the fuse long before that." McCracken stopped, then resumed just as quickly. "Oh, and one more thing about your story, sir."

Roy looked at McCracken blankly.

"Now it has a happy ending."

They returned to Pandora's Temple with a professional crew on board a craft almost identical to their original *Crab*. Wareagle kept his eye peeled out the windows the whole stretch after they slipped through the same vent into the cavern below, as if expecting the giant squid to make an appearance again.

For his part, McCracken held Pandora's jar in a carefully padded case. The simple ivory-colored jar itself weighed extraordinarily little. Prior to making the trip back to Greece with Pandora's jar in their possession, McCracken had watched as Captain Seven put the jar through every conceivable test, determining ultimately it was composed of materials clearly not of this world. X-rays, thermal scans, and all manner of high-tech diagnostics and analysis had further revealed nothing contained within the jar—at least nothing bearing any weight, mass, or shape. In those moments, McCracken was never gladder for the fact that the seamless, lidless nature of Pandora's jar made it impossible to open.

And now it never would be.

"The tsunami that sank the temple in 1650 B.C. must have dislodged Pandora's jar and sent it drifting in the ocean," McCracken said, even though he knew Wareagle was barely listening. "It settles on the bottom and, at some point, gets recovered by an archaeological or geophysical survey team. Ends up in Sebastian Roy's private collection."

Wareagle finally turned his way, shaking his head. "To have what he most wanted all along and not realize it . . ."

"Maybe that's the whole point of the jar."

"What?"

"Pathos Verdes built Pandora's Temple to hide a weapon not fit for mortal man, capable of killing a god . . . and a planet. Could be the temple wasn't needed at all. Could be the jar was capable of taking care of itself just fine."

"Maybe the jar found us, Blainey."

"Then let's go treat it right."

They used the craft's single robotic arm and pincers to return Pandora's jar to its pedestal, retracing their route out and climbing fast without encountering the giant squid again. After rising up through the vent, the underwater explosives experts McCracken had brought with him used those same pincers to lay powerful, shaped charges across the seafloor above the cavern housing Pandora's Temple, concentrated in the areas around the vent.

McCracken personally triggered the blasts from closer to the surface to shield the craft from the shock wave and percussion. He felt only a rumble and watched as the underwater cameras they left behind revealed the sea itself seeming to cave inward in a rolling cloud of sand, silt, and sediment.

Then nothing at all.

When the cloud cleared on the screens before them, nothing

remained but the darkness of an abyss that would keep the secrets of the sea safe.

And seal Pandora's Temple forever.

Captain Seven stood onshore, unable to see anything so far at sea while still being struck by the odd feeling the deed was done at last. Something shifted to his right, and he turned to find the old wild-haired hippie he remembered from his last visit to Athens standing beside him. He was smiling serenely, his eyes looking larger now that they seemed to be showing more of the whites.

"Yo, Pat dude, what brings you out here?"

"Same thing that brought you."

"You come bearing more of that primo weed?"

"No, my friend, but I have another gift for you."

With that he produced an iron mason's square, or "angle" to the Greeks from which it had descended, formed of two legs of unequal length set at an angle of ninety degrees. A crucial tool for builders from ancient times.

"A token of my appreciation," the man continued.

Captain Seven took it, turning from the sun so he could see the square better; he was surprised by its heft and pristine condition. "But what did I do to—"

The captain stopped when he saw Pat walking away from him into the sun.

"Deserve it?" the man finished for him, turning. "You helped finally end this. And now it's over, over at long last so I can finally rest."

"Fucking A!" Captain Seven shook his head in disbelief. "You're not . . ."

"Yes, I am," the man said, continuing on. "And my mission is finished at last."

"Pathos Verdes," Captain Seven muttered, looking down at the mason's square that had helped construct the now entombed Pandora's Temple.

He turned back toward the wild-haired man's dwindling shape, holding a hand to shield the sun from his eyes as the builder vanished, disappeared, lost to the present just as he had been lost long ago to the past.

A Biography of Jon Land

Since his first book was published in 1983, Jon Land has written more than thirty novels, many of which were national bestsellers. He began writing technothrillers before Tom Clancy put them in vogue, and his strong prose, easy characterization, and commitment to technical accuracy have made him a pillar of the genre.

Land spent his college years at Brown University, where he convinced the faculty to let him attempt writing a thriller as his senior honors thesis. Four years later, his first novel, *The Doomsday Spiral*, appeared in print. In the last years of the Cold War, he found a place writing chilling portrayals of threats to the United States, and of the men and women who operated undercover and outside the law to maintain U.S. security. His most successful of those novels star Blaine McCracken, a rogue CIA agent and former Green Beret with the skills of James Bond but none of the Englishman's tact.

In 1998 Land published the first novel in his Ben and Danielle series, comprised of fast-paced thrillers whose heroes, a Detroit cop and an Israeli detective, work together to protect the Holy Land, falling in love in the process. He has written seven of these so far. The most recent, *The Last Prophecy*, was released in 2004.

Recently, *RT Book Reviews* gave Jon a special prize for pioneering genre fiction, and his short story "Killing Time" was shortlisted for the 2010 Dagger Award for best short fiction and included in 2010's *The Best American Mystery Stories*. Land is currently writing *Blood Strong*, his fourth novel to feature Texas Ranger Caitlin Strong—a female hero in a genre which, Land has said, has too few of them. The second book in the series, *Strong Justice* (2010), was named a Top Thriller of the Year by *Library Journal* and runner-up for Best Novel of the Year by the New England Book Festival. The third, *Strong at the Break*, was released in 2011, and the fourth, *Blood Strong*, followed in 2012. His first nonfiction book, *Betrayal*, written with Robert Fitzpatrick, tells the behind-the-scenes story of a deputy FBI chief attempting to bring down Boston crime lord Whitey Bulger, and was also released in 2011.

Land's most recent work is *Pandora's Temple* (2012), the latest in the Blaine McCracken series. He currently lives in Providence, not far from his alma mater.

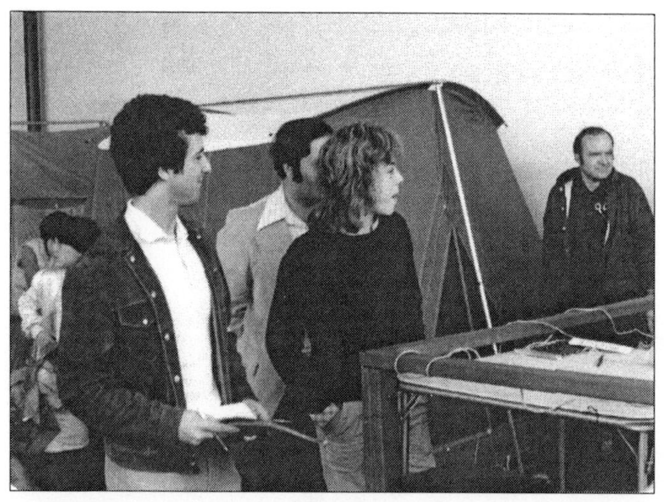

Land (left) interviewing then–teen idol Leif Garrett (center) in April of 1978 at the dawn of Land's writing career.

Land (second from left) at Maine's Ogunquit Beach during the summer of 1984, while he was a counselor at Camp Samoset II. He spent a total of twenty-six summers at the camp.

Land with street kids in Rio de Janeiro, Brazil, which he visited in 1987 as part of his research for *The Omicron Legion* (1991).

Land on the beach in Matunuck, Rhode Island, in 2003.

Land pictured in 2007 with Fabrizio Boccardi, the Italian investor and entrepreneur who was the inspiration for his book *The Seven Sins*, which was published in 2008.

Land emceeing the Brunch and Bullets Luncheon to benefit Reading Is Fundamental at the Renaissance Hollywood Hotel in the spring of 2007.

In the fall of 2010, Land attended the first ever Brown University night football game, which he coordinated in his position as Vice President of the Brown Football Association. Brown beat rival Harvard 29-14.

Cover design by Mumtaz Mustafa

978-1-4532-2465-6

Published in 2012 by Open Road Integrated Media
180 Varick Street
New York, NY 10014
www.openroadmedia.com